FAMILY

OWEN MULLEN

Boldwood

First published in Great Britain in 2021 by Boldwood Books Ltd.

Cover Design: www.judgebymycovers.com

Cover Photography: Shutterstock and Yannes Kiefer / Unsplash

A CIP catalogue record for this book is available from the British Library.

Paperback ISBN 978-1-80048-418-4

Large Print ISBN 978-1-80048-414-6

Hardback ISBN 978-1-80162-559-3

Ebook ISBN 978-1-80048-412-2

Kindle ISBN 978-1-80048-413-9

Audio CD ISBN 978-1-80048-419-1

MP3 CD ISBN 978-1-80048-416-0

Digital audio download ISBN 978-1-80048-258-6

Boldwood Books Ltd
23 Bowerdean Street
London SW6 3TN
www.boldwoodbooks.com

For Hugh McKenna
a wonderful musician and my oldest friend

PROLOGUE

The Metropolitan Police corruption scandal has deepened after The Independent uncovered the existence of a previously secret investigation into criminal officers that went much further than the files destroyed by Scotland Yard.

Operation Zloty, a wide-ranging inquiry spanning at least nine years, found dozens of rogue detectives in the employ of organised crime and operating with 'virtual immunity'.

The long-term intelligence development operation included information on police corruption originally gathered by 17 other investigations – including Operation Othona, the contents of which were inexplicably shredded sometime around 2003.

Crucially, Zloty included bombshell evidence from Othona about a 'persistent network' of corrupt officers that could have been beneficial to a landmark review commissioned by the Home Secretary into how the Stephen Lawrence murder was handled by the Metropolitan Police.

Mark Ellison QC was forced to inform Theresa May earlier this month that he could not finalise conclusions on whether police corruption tainted the Lawrence case because a 'lorry-load' of Othona material was mysteriously shredded by the Met more than 10 years ago.

— The Independent, 26 March 2014

* * *

The car was back in the drive, parked behind the Merc. Twenty minutes earlier, Cheryl Glass had waved it away with her daughter seated in the rear. A big guy, thickset, in shades and shirt sleeves, sat behind the wheel. Marcus was a monosyllabic troll her husband had put in charge of the school run. She'd objected to a stranger being given responsibility for her daughter.

Their daughter, Danny had reminded her.

They'd had a right royal row about it but of course he hadn't listened. 'With the way things are,' he'd said, 'Rebecca needs to be protected.'

Hard to argue against, except if they were in danger it was him who'd put them there. Albert Anderson was a man better left alone. Instead, Danny had been edging him out of South London, street by street, until it became an affront that couldn't be allowed to go on. Wiser to agree the boundaries and live in peace, but Danny Glass didn't see it that way; as with everything, it was all or nothing.

So, the war began. And Marcus did the school run.

Cheryl leaned in the window, no pretence at friendliness. 'What're you doing here? Where's Rebecca?'

The minder returned the hostility; he'd seen how her husband treated her, clocked the disrespect and aped it. 'Inside. Forgot Sam.'

Once upon a time Danny would have wiped the floor with anybody who even looked the wrong way at her.

Ancient history.

'She's going to be late.'

He shrugged. 'She wanted the bear, what was I supposed to do? I'm just the taxi driver.'

'How about get her there before the bell stops ringing?'

Rebecca came running out of the house, bright with excitement, and threw herself against her mother.

Cheryl scolded her. 'You're supposed to be on your way to school.'

The six-year-old replied with logic that defied anyone to be annoyed with her.

'Sam wouldn't have anybody to talk to. He would've been sad.'

Cheryl smiled. Rebecca was absolutely the best thing – the only good thing – to come from the marriage; a small miracle she still struggled to believe she was responsible for bringing into the world.

'Well, we can't have that. But you must hurry.'

Rebecca clung to her. 'You take me.'

'I can't, darling. Mummy's late.'

The child was too young to hide her disappointment. Her mother tried to sound upbeat. 'For the hairdresser.'

The lie came so easily it shocked her.

'You want a beautiful mummy, don't you?' She knelt to coax her daughter. 'I'll see you later. You can tell me what you did today. Go with Marcus.'

'Want to go with you.'

Marcus listened to the mini-drama – family business, not his. He was paid to do what he was told. If the kid went with him, fine, if not, that was fine too. Babysitting wasn't what he'd had in mind when he signed on to work for Danny Glass. Rebecca stared with her father's dark eyes, so cute, and so like him. No wasn't a concept either recognised.

'You take me.' She pleaded as if her mother hadn't spoken.

'Honey, I don't have time and I don't have my car.'

'Why not?'

'Because it's in the garage.'

'We can go in another car.'

Cheryl glanced at her watch and sighed. 'All right. Come on.'

She snapped at Marcus. 'You're not needed.'

He started to object but she cut him off and walked to the house and a man standing at the door with his hands folded behind his back. Cheryl didn't know his name. So many people worked for Danny these days it was impossible to keep up.

'You're driving and we have to go now, school's started.'

Rebecca ran to the Mercedes, scrambled across the back seat and sat Sam in the middle.

Marcus made a last attempt to reason with her. 'Your husband isn't gonna like this. It isn't safe. You know the score.'

She brushed past him – he'd had his chance. 'I couldn't care less what my husband won't like. Move!'

The new guy got behind the wheel, took Cheryl's instructions and pulled out of the shadow of the house into the London sunshine.

Rebecca said, 'Where's Daddy?'

Her mother was tempted to reply that she had no idea where Daddy was because he hadn't come home again last night. Instead she lied. 'He's busy, baby. He said to give you a kiss from him.'

Albert Anderson was causing trouble, that much Cheryl knew, yet the previous day she'd called her husband's mobile and whined like a stereotypical suburban housewife unable to function without her man.

'It won't start, it just won't.'

Danny's response had been curt. 'Use the Merc.'

That was the last time they'd spoken.

The child pointed her finger at the driver, then at her mother, herself and the teddy. She counted. 'One, two, three, four.'

Cheryl checked her watch, her manicured fingers strumming the leather upholstery. She hated being late for anything, especially where she was going. Rebecca held the teddy bear to the window and began a game without rules. She turned to her mother. 'I like when you take me to school.'

'I'm going to take you every day from now on.'

'I love you, Mummy.'

The child drifted into a story, telling Sam about her friend, Amanda. Cheryl stroked her daughter's hair, blonde like her own. 'I love you too, darling.'

* * *

There was no warning. The car left the road, lifted by the force of the blast. Pieces of metal and glass ripped through a bus queue waiting for the 185 to Victoria. In that moment lives were irrevocably changed: people fell to the ground, blood pouring from wounds they hadn't had a second ago; the windscreen of a Vectra coming in the opposite direction shattered, blinding the driver, who lost control and ploughed into a West Indian fruit and veg shop, crushing a teenage assistant at the beginning of only her second day in the job; on the pavement, a man in his thirties hurrying to the beat from his iPod suddenly collapsed, his leg severed at the knee.

In the immediate aftermath of the explosion, silence hung in the smoke, then the full horror hit, people with blood on their faces screamed and ran and burst into tears. Sam lay in the gutter, undamaged apart from a patch of singed fur. The device had been hidden under the driver's seat so the new guy didn't exist any more.

Cheryl and Rebecca Glass died without knowing it.

* * *

His voice might have been coming from outer space – cracked and tinny and far away.

they're dead, Luke

that bastard Anderson

It was the first contact I'd had from my brother in days. Lately, I felt less and less like I was his good right hand as he waged the war against his enemy without consulting me.

The name was almost the only detail I was able to process; everything else was noise in my head. Realising I'd never see them again was unbearable. I smashed the mobile off the floor and overturned a coffee table, roaring against what Anderson had done. When something closer to sanity returned, I grabbed my jacket and ran to my car, determined to put him in the ground where he belonged.

Albert Anderson was a creature of habit. Every morning he had breakfast at the Marlborough Cafe, a greasy spoon in Bishopsgate that reminded him of the London he'd known as a boy. In his time, he'd done all right. Better than all right. He didn't need the rough and tumble any more, he'd made his money. Which begged the question: why fight Danny when he could've retired, quietly, no fuss no bother? Maybe Albert had been king of the castle for so long he couldn't give it up.

Driving across the city, I set aside every thought except the thought of killing him.

He was sitting with two of his heavies under a blue and white awning, out of the sun, all eighteen stone of him, reading a copy of the *Daily Mail* and forking scrambled eggs into the ugly hole in his face – a white-haired pensioner with a favourite-uncle smile, kindly and obese. Except, he wasn't kind. Anderson was ruthless, a thug who didn't let murdering innocent civilians affect his appetite.

When my car mounted the kerb and squealed to a stop a yard from his table, he dropped his fork and ran.

The bodyguards jumped to their feet. Hard geezers. But with a madman charging towards them they responded like the amateur tough guys they were. I crashed a chair over the first one's head and kicked his gorilla mate in the groin. Big and slow, he went down in instalments.

If you pay peanuts...

Running had never been Albert's game. He lumbered, half staggered, across the street fifty yards ahead, dragging his fat arse. For a big man, his pace was deceptive; he was slower than he looked.

I smiled. I could afford to. I had him.

Until he disappeared from sight.

I raced to where he'd been, certain he must have ducked into a shop and was posing as a customer. No sign. Panic started in me. I'd been enjoying myself, savouring what I had intended to do instead of nailing the bastard. Out of the corner of my eye, a cage registered, rising against the side of a building under construction, a taller-than-tall mother no doubt destined to be the new home of some Far East banking corporation, the sort of eyesore that dominated the city skyline. Anderson was inside, staring at me through the mesh grill. Our eyes locked and we both understood how it would end. Going up against Danny had been a mistake. Climbing into the sky was another one.

Dumb, Albert! Dumb!

The tension in me melted. He was trapped.

* * *

I came around a corner into grey space, cool air, plaster walls and a black water tank sitting like a Buddha in the middle of the floor. Far below, London whispered. In the morning light the Thames was a silver ribbon carelessly cast on the ground, and south of the river firemen would have finished hosing water on the car's charred shell.

they're dead, Luke

Anderson was standing on the other side of the room, sweat glistening on his bulldog jowls, the corner of his mouth twitching. Behind him, through the opening where a window would go, a plane streaked towards Heathrow. Over his shoulder I read the logo on the tail, and brought my eyes back to the bastard, expecting him to produce a weapon, come at me, do something. It didn't happen. He'd assumed his men would be enough.

Another mistake.

Albert was having a bad day.

Fear rolled off him in waves. He stepped away, protesting his innocence. 'It wasn't me. Nothing to do with it.'

He was remarkably well informed considering the bomb had gone off less than thirty minutes ago. I hadn't told him, so how did he know?

I shook my head. For all his success he was thick.

'Don't believe you, Albert.'

He seemed disappointed, as if he'd expected me to take him at his word, then remembered I was Danny Glass's brother and, of course, couldn't be trusted to see it his way.

He'd got that right.

His fingers left sweat marks on the pale concrete. Underneath his coat he was trembling. I moved closer, close enough to smell him. A baby step backwards took his heel over the lip; the wind ruffled what was left of his hair while gravity tugged at his shoes. Workmen in another futuristic high-rise stopped what they were doing and pointed at us.

Anderson swayed; the layers of his bloated jaw quivered. 'What would I have to gain?'

Forty-three stories up, on the edge of nowhere, it was a good question. I assumed it was rhetorical and let it pass.

'It wasn't me.'

'Yeah, it was you all right.'

Somewhere behind me I heard the lift start the descent to the ground. Albert heard it too and knew his men were coming. Hope washed through him, his massive shoulders relaxed, the familiar cunning returned to his eyes, and he sighed, imagining he was about to be saved. Spoiling it for him was a pleasure.

'Forget it. They won't make it in time.'

He realised I was telling the truth, dragged a sleeve over his brow and played his last card. 'Four hundred thousand. In cash. And a truce.'

I joined in his fantasy. 'Shake hands and start again? Clean slate? Everybody on their own side of the fence?'

Desperate enthusiasm bubbled in his voice. 'Why not? Why not, Luke?'

Yesterday Albert would've pissed on the idea, that was why not. And yesterday he hadn't murdered Cheryl and Rebecca.

'Should've spent that money hiring better people when you had the chance, but then you always were a cheapskate, Albert.'

A police siren wailed in the distance. When I came down, they'd be waiting. That didn't matter. In the end, as Albert was about to discover, life came down to balance. And duty.

England expects and all that bollocks.

I placed my palm on his beating heart and took a last look at his puffy face. His life was about to end; he was in tears. He whimpered. 'They'll throw away the key. Please! Five! Five hundred!'

I wasn't listening.

'Goodbye, Albert.'

He fell into space, mouth open, starting on his back and rolling with the grace of a gymnast, slowly getting smaller and smaller. Following his progress was like watching a movie with the sound turned off. His ankles clipped the side of some scaffolding and flipped him in an arc. He landed on his smile on the bonnet of a green Mondeo parked across the street.

If plunging to your death was an Olympic event, he'd have been in the medals for sure.

PART I

1

SEVEN YEARS LATER

This is what I know: they let you leave by the front door when they release you from Wandsworth. A nice touch. No goodbye or good luck, none of that. They expect to see you again, and a lot of the time, they'll be right. But they wouldn't be right with me. I wasn't going back. Not ever.

No chance.

My trial and the verdict the jury returned that afternoon seemed like a dream. But it wasn't. The Crown hadn't been able to make a murder charge stick. Although witnesses testified to seeing me forty-three stories up standing close to Albert Anderson, none of them could swear I pushed him. I guessed my brother had something to do with that. But the history of Anderson's family and mine was well known. In the end, the prosecution settled for manslaughter and asked the judge to sentence to the full extent of the law. Lord Justice Peyton Richardson obliged and nobody shed any tears.

I stepped through the gate into rain falling from an overcast sky and a world that hadn't missed me. The air was as sweet as the clichés promised it would be and an overwhelming sense of relief washed through me: I'd survived. From here on in, what I did with my life was my decision.

Maybe it was because I wasn't used to the space but the hairs on the back of my neck stood up, my fingers tingled and I had the feeling somebody was watching me. Weird. Between the warders and my fellow cons, I'd had eyes on me night and day for the last seven years. It hadn't bothered me. After a while you got used to it. I put it down to first-day nerves and shook it off.

Across the road, a slim female in sunglasses leaned against the bonnet of a Lexus with blacked-out windows, waving like we hadn't seen each other in decades instead of just a week: my sister, Nina. I wasn't surprised to see her. I knew she would be. Nina was loyal – she'd visited me every week in Wandsworth, keeping me up to date with events beyond the walls. She'd been a difficult teenager – not having a mother or father hadn't helped – who'd grown into a troubled young woman. As time passed, during our conversations across a table in a crowded room, surrounded by whispering inmates and their visitors, I'd watched her shuck off whatever weight she'd been carrying, step out from the shadow of her brothers, and morph into an assured lady in no doubt about who she was.

Seven years was a long time; a lot could change. Nobody understood that better than me.

I hugged her, she hugged me back, tugged the arm of my suit and made a noise in her throat. 'Might want to rethink this.'

'Give me a chance. Only worn it once – for the trial.'

She laughed. 'No wonder they found you guilty.'

My first question wasn't intended to set her off, but it did. 'How's Danny?'

She pushed the shades up into her dark hair, checked the rear mirror and looked at me across the car, the whites of her eyes milky and clear against her smooth skin. Being her brother didn't stop me noticing she was a beautiful woman.

'If you're asking if he's still an arsehole, then the answer's yes.'

Her reaction made me smile. Nina and Danny had never got on. When she was in her teens, she'd driven him mad, defying him at every turn, sometimes just because she could. Not untypical behaviour at that age except, even then, there was an edge that didn't have to be there. Danny's reputation in South London as a hardman hadn't impressed her. Anybody else who'd spoken to him the way she did, including me, would've landed in the nearest A & E.

'You two still at it?'

'You wouldn't believe it. Didn't think he could get any worse.'

'And has he?'

Nina made a face and pulled out into the traffic. 'The guy's off his fucking rocker, honest he is. One of the reasons I'm glad you're back. He's losing it, Luke. Maybe you can calm him down.'

Except I wasn't going to be back. Nina couldn't count on me to referee the feud she and Danny had had going for as long as I could remember.

'He's your brother. He loves you and you love him.'

'Wrong. Can't stand him. Never could. Only now I know why.'

'Why?'

'When you've got another seven years of your life to waste, I'll tell you.'

Reasoning with her wouldn't get me anywhere but I gave it a shot.

'You should try more than you do to like him. Don't forget, he was there for us.'

Nina scoffed at the idea. 'And he reminds me of it every time he wants me to do something I don't want to do. Bringing up the past is how he keeps us just where he wants us. Whenever I disagree with him, he goes into his martyr routine and brings up how close we were to ending up in care. If it hadn't been for him...' She shook her head and overtook a red Vauxhall dawdling in the centre of the road. 'He's a control freak and you can't see it.'

'What's he done now?'

'It isn't what he's done, it's who he is. He wanted me to manage the property portfolio. Insisted I work out of his office.'

'Above the pub.'

Her mouth twisted in a smile that failed. 'I couldn't take it. He talks to himself, did you know that? Mumbles away under his breath. And the music on that fucking jukebox... it's the twenty-first century, for Christ's sake.'

'Some of it's all right.'

Nina agreed. 'Some of it, yeah. In small doses. Not all day every day. Drive anybody round the bend, that would. Which reminds me. Be warned, he's booked a band. I saw them bringing in their gear as I was leaving. The youngest had to be seventy-five. Can't blame me for giving it a miss.'

'You're not going?'

'I'll be in later. If I'm lucky, after the band stops playing.'

Nina wasn't joking and I didn't blame her. Guessing the rest of the script wasn't difficult: outside the pub a sign would say Private Function. Inside, they'd all be there, new guys most of them, press-ganged into raising a glass to their boss's younger brother, somebody they'd heard a lot about but hadn't met. Danny would bang on the bar, call for silence and propose a toast.

'To Luke!'

Cheers for the returning hero. By now, the story of Albert Anderson's swan dive was urban mythology and me with it. A couple of hookers – part of the tradition – would be laid on. No pun intended.

At some point he'd put an arm round my shoulder and guide me upstairs away from the noise into his vision of the future. He'd light a cigar and sit behind his desk under the framed photograph of the Queen. He was a staunch supporter of the royal family – God knows where that came from, or how it squared with a life of selling girls and drugs. The booze would make him sentimental; he'd tell me he loved me and trot out the spiel I'd been hearing since I was a kid, the Team Glass speech. Then I'd be a bad sport and spoil it with what I intended to say.

'Will you tell him today?'

'Maybe. I'll see how it goes.'

She squeezed my fingers with her free hand and I said, 'Drop me in Tooting Broadway. Say I'm sorry, I'll catch up with him. And that the car worked, I'm impressed.'

'Do your own dirty work. I'm meeting somebody.'

'Somebody as in...?'

'As in none of your business.'

'He won't be happy at the two of us ducking out.'

Nina turned her face away, the disdain in her voice undisguised, the same cheeky kid she'd always been. 'He'll live. It's good for him not to get his own way all the time. Reminds him he isn't the big shot he thinks he is. Besides I told you, I'll probably drop in later.'

Five minutes back and already it was as if I'd never been gone.

'You're supposed to take me to the King Pot... if neither of us shows up...'

'I would've taken you if you'd wanted to go. I'll return the car but I'm not staying. No offence, brother, got better things to do.'

'He won't be pleased, Nina.'

She went into her pocket and handed me her business card.

'Yeah,' she said, 'I think you're right. Shame.'

* * *

In Wandsworth the guard had stabbed a finger where he'd wanted me to sign. I'd given a signature in exchange for stuff I'd barely recognised. Apart from the watch it might have belonged to somebody else. The Rolex had been an early birthday present from Danny for my twenty-first, eight years before I was sent down. On the back was an inscription: *To L from D. Team Glass.* Seeing it again was like unearthing a relic from an ancient civilisation, an ironic reminder of lost time taking me back to when he'd given it to me on a warm summer's evening. We had been in Ye Grapes in Shepherd Market off Curzon Street in Mayfair, standing near the door drinking Spitfire, surrounded by great-looking women and men old enough to be their fathers. Danny had caught me checking out the ladies. 'Prostitutes. The most expensive in London. Perks of having a wife who doesn't understand you and more money than you know what to do with.'

Danny had pointed to a stunning blonde laughing at something a beefy, florid-faced guy who must have been in his late-fifties was whispering in her ear. His elbow had dug into my ribs. 'Just two professional people enjoying each other's company. The end of a hard day for one, the beginning of a hard night for the other. That where you'd like to be? Because that's where we're headed.'

He'd then pushed a square box into my hand, deep green with a logo in gold on the top.

'Happy birthday, little brother.'

I'd shaken my head. 'This is too much.'

'You're welcome and no, it bloody isn't. There's more where that came from.'

We had moved aside to let the blonde and the man with her pass; close up she'd been gorgeous.

Danny had said, 'You can't afford her. Not unless you sell the watch.' He'd placed a comforting hand on my arm. 'One day that won't be true, trust me.'

And I had trusted him. Danny had always been ambitious. Not just for him, for all of us.

* * *

Roland Anderson rested his elbows on the desk, steepled his fingers and focussed on the voice coming from the speaker phone – he'd waited a long time to hear what he was about to be told.

'I see him. I see our boy.'

'How does he look?'

'Fit. Really fit.'

Anderson tried to imagine it and failed. Rollie had been nineteen years old when Luke Glass had sent Albert to his death. He hadn't seen him since the final day of the trial but the look on Glass's face when the judge passed sentence had stayed with him; unblinking, standing straight, shoulders back. No sign of remorse. No flicker of regret. Only an expression that said seven years or seventeen years, it had been worth it. When they'd taken him down, he'd glanced at the gallery where his brother was seated, turned his back on the court and disappeared to the cells to start his time. Anderson had hated him then, and every day since he'd thought about what he was going to do to him. Except he hadn't reckoned with how far Danny Glass was able to reach.

In theory, cons should have been lining up to nail Luke. Instead, thanks to his brother, he was untouchable. Nobody was prepared to take the job on if it meant crossing Danny. Now, finally, the man who'd murdered his father was free and the vengeance Rollie demanded was closer than it had ever been.

The voice echoed in the room. 'He's getting into a Lexus with his sister.'

'Any sign of the other one?'

'Can't be sure, the windows are smoked. Could be in the back. You want me to follow him?'

'No, go ahead to the pub. Tell me when they get there.'

Twenty-five minutes later the information arrived. 'They're here. Car's pulling off the road. Going in the back. What should we do?'

'Nothing.'

'Everybody's in position. Everybody's ready.'

Anderson wasn't in a hurry. He said, 'No rush. It's a surprise party. Let them get a few down their necks. Then we'll give them a surprise they won't forget.'

2

Ahead of the lunchtime crowd, the pub on The Broadway was empty apart from the staff who were busy setting up. A good-looking guy dressed in a blazer and a white shirt open at the neck followed me in and took a stool at the end of the bar. He had style: his long hair was swept behind his ears like an artiste or an Italian chef with a name like Carlo or Luca, who'd made it big on daytime television, the kind older women with nothing better to do drooled over. He drew a *Daily Express* somebody had left towards him and leafed casually through the pages until he got to the racing section. Then he picked up one of those stubby pens you get in bookies and scribbled in the margin. While I studied him, his dark eyes never left the page.

I ordered a pint and a large whisky and took a seat at a table in the corner. Some nights I'd dreamed of Courage Directors, but now, with the frosted measure cold against my skin and the smell of hops and barley malt thick in the air, it didn't seem real.

The first sip is always the best, my father used to say. Who would know better than a man who'd dedicated his life to trying to find the same pleasure in the rest of the glass? And the ten after that. He died when Nina was fourteen and I was fifteen. Danny was twenty-two. Though my memories of him weren't good, at least I had some. I didn't recall anything about my mother. She ran out on us before I was old enough to understand – one day there, the next day gone. Any time I'd asked, Danny had told me to shut it and gone into a mood.

After a while I stopped asking.

Nothing about my father said he missed her, yet I never saw him with another woman. Maybe that told the story.

I suppose he did his best. Unfortunately, his best wasn't very good.

His best was shit, actually.

Our old man had been a boozer. With no wife to nark him he took to it in earnest and drank himself to death, leaving two sons, a daughter, a wad of unpaid bills and a pile of empty whisky bottles stinking under his bed.

Nobody would have blamed Danny for finally letting Social Services take the weight of the load he'd been carrying for years. My brother had other ideas. His cooking was crap and he couldn't iron a shirt worth a damn, but he needed no lessons in loyalty.

No surprise then that growing up I'd idolised him and wanted to be like him. Somewhere along the line that stopped being true. Wandsworth did the rest. Sending the Lexus was typical. Flash. In your face. Out to prove how well he was doing. Over-compensating for how hard it had been for him bringing us up on his own.

I went to the bar, ordered another round and saw my reflection in the mirror behind the optics. Most of what was looking back was all right. Nothing a bit of sunshine wouldn't sort. Letting my hair grow and wearing clothes that didn't make me look as if I'd stepped through a portal to the last century would help. Nina's blunt assessment when she picked me up came back to me. A smile would help, too, if I could find one. Cheryl used to wind me up because I didn't walk around grinning like an idiot.

Cheryl had been a nice lady. Her and Nina had been close – more like sisters really. During her visits to Wandsworth we sometimes talked about Cheryl and Nina would tear up and change the subject before it got too emotional.

By now, my sister would've reported my disappearing act and got a bollocking for her trouble. I expected the same. Danny wouldn't appreciate being stood up. Nor would he like the promise I'd made myself – Team Glass had been playing a man short and was going to stay that way: I was done.

In the middle of the day the pub was packed with office types in suits and ties, managing to make half-pints last forever. I was on my second by then, and feeling the effects, when a brunette I hadn't noticed started doing the rounds, wiping tables with a damp cloth. She kept her head down and didn't speak to anybody. The alcohol inspired me to lighten her load, my good deed for the day. I picked up my glasses so she could clean the surface.

'Cheer up, it might never happen.'

She made a sound in her throat that meant she didn't believe me. 'You sure?'

Her accent was thick, the kind that went with fur hats and vodka.

'Want to tell me about it?'

She shrugged and moved on, not interested. And no wonder. 'Cheer up, it might never happen.' Jesus Christ. Was that really the best I could do? Rusty was one thing, corny was something else. I needed to sharpen up.

The sense of freedom was almost overwhelming – I spent the next hour enjoying it until the spell was broken by a familiar voice, loud and aggressive, joking with me as he'd done since I was a kid. 'Who do I have to fuck to get a drink around here? Hope it isn't you.'

Danny studied me through tired eyes. My first impression was how much older he seemed: his face was lined, tinged an unhealthy grey. Success in his business came at a price. Dark hair – a lot darker than mine – brushed the collar of a white shirt straining the buttons at his belly; he'd put on weight. The workouts in the gym in Wandsworth had toned my body and I was fitter than I'd ever been. The thing we had in common was our height – we were both five feet ten. But, for as long as I could remember, despite the physical differences, anyone meeting us had immediately known we were brothers.

He dropped into the chair across the table. 'Didn't fancy it, then?

Don't blame you. Star fuckers the lot of them. Eat the food, drink the booze and piss off out of it. Only reason they turn up, that and being able to say they've rubbed shoulders with a famous face.'

'Needed a bit of space. Sorry, Danny.'

'Yeah, Nina said when she returned the car and pissed off. No problem. Who'd want a bunch of strangers gawping at them?'

Strangers invited by him, that bit was forgotten. My brother had a selective memory and a talent for rewriting the past. I hadn't seen him in long enough, although Wandsworth wasn't exactly on the other side of the moon. No surprise. The visits had never been a success. We couldn't bring ourselves to talk about the bomb or Cheryl and Rebecca. That hadn't left much and for most of the hour we'd stared across the table at each other, wishing it would end. In the beginning, he had endured the hassle of the security checks every couple of weeks. Then it was six weeks. Then a year. After a while I'd lost track. I didn't blame him for giving it a miss – he gave up pretending before me, that was the difference.

My brother stopped coming but Nina didn't, bringing gossip – a currency most inmates traded in – to distract me from my situation. Danny featured in a lot of stories inside. One rumour would have him ruling the South Side with an iron hand, in the next, he was dying of cancer and only had weeks to live.

My sister confirmed most of it was crap and anyway, if she was wrong, it would be waiting for me when I got out.

'Nina's told me she's working for you.'

Danny grunted. 'Not true, she's working for herself. She's...' laughter from the direction of the bar interrupted him and he scowled angrily at the intrusion '... part of the family. That means she's due a third – of everything. Only right she pulls her weight.'

'And does she?'

He thought about his reply. 'Her work isn't the problem. Matter of fact, she's done well. Added more than a few tasty properties to the portfolio. Got in at the right price, too.' He allowed himself a half-smile. 'Didn't know we had a portfolio, did you, little brother?'

'So, what's the issue?'

'Her attitude. Your sister isn't a team player. As soon as I say something, she's down my throat.'

Just like him.

'Why not let her just get on with it?'

A vein pulsed in Danny's temple; the suggestion didn't sit well. 'I have. I bloody have. Along with the property she deals with the accountant. But, at the end of the day, *I'm* the head of the family. When I ask a question, I expect an answer. And you'll remember her taste in men's never been great.'

'What's that got to do with it?'

He didn't reply and changed the subject. 'How're you doing?'

'Okay.'

'Pleased to hear it because I need you.' He saw my expression and backed off. 'Not right now. After you've had a holiday, somewhere with palm trees. Take a month.' From inside his coat he pulled a wad of notes tied with an elastic band. 'Scatter cash. Fun money.'

I guessed three thousand pounds.

'I'm all right. Got enough.'

He pushed it towards me. 'No such thing. Besides, your share comes to a helluva lot more than this. Check your bank account.'

'I didn't earn it.'

He snorted. 'What're you on about? 'Course you did.'

I left the money where it was.

Danny looked me over again. 'Great to have you where I can keep an eye on you. Last time I wasn't around it all went a bit Pete Tong. No offence, little brother. Made some moves while you've been away. You've got new people to meet, new opportunities to get your head round. Take a while to come up to speed. Like I told you, we're into property now.'

'Sounds good.'

'Yeah, it is and we're doing okay, all things considered.' He waved an arm in the air. 'Why this place?'

'They sell beer.'

'Not so you'd notice.'

A click of his fingers brought the waitress.

'What's that?' He pointed to my pint and answered his own question. 'Directors?'

I nodded.

'One of them and two Black Label. Doubles.' He brought his attention back to me.

'Been in half a dozen pubs before this one. Wish you'd told Nina where you were going.'

'I didn't know. Sorry.'

Danny swatted the apology away. 'Forget it. You go where you want to go, do what you want to do.' He handed me a mobile phone. 'Next time you feel like ducking out, give me a call. My birthday's coming up. See if you can manage to drag yourself along to that.'

I let the sarcasm fly over my head.

The waitress bent to lift a crisp packet off the floor, her ample arse stretching the material of her faded jeans.

Danny said, 'Crack a few walnuts with that, eh?'

An old line but it made me laugh; when I was a kid, he'd made me laugh a lot.

''Course, after seven years you'd probably take it on.'

'When I'm stronger, maybe.'

The drinks came. He casually tossed a fifty on the tray as if it was nothing.

'The flat's ready. Had it cleaned – new towels, new sheets and all that. Be good to sleep in your own bed. Might want to think about selling though, the neighbourhood's down the plughole.'

'Yeah?'

'Yeah. Everybody round there talks Polish or some fucking thing. Can't understand a word. The Chinese restaurant on the corner? Nice people, remember? You liked them, lived on their sweet and sour pork – 'least, they said it was pork. Don't know how you could eat that foreign muck. It's a dry-cleaner now. Lithuanians run it.'

Suddenly the Chinese were all right; my brother's selective memory in action. Before I'd gone inside, he'd called them yellow bastards and constantly complained about them buying up London.

'And the women...' He threw the whisky over in one go and screwed up his face. 'Jesus Christ... if ugly was contagious they'd be in quarantine. I'd move if I were you. To somewhere they speak English.'

'Like where?'

'In London? No idea. Let me know if you come across it. Up west the Arabs are buying everything they can lay their greasy hands on. Thirty million. Fifty million. For houses they don't even live in. Honest to God, this country's finished.'

I'd been listening to my brother's views all my life. No matter the problem, 'Bloody foreigners' were to blame.

'You know where I'm coming from. Don't pretend you don't.'

Yes, I did – he was being who he'd always been: a xenophobe and a racist. He ended his rant and eyed me up and down.

'Seriously, you don't look great.'

'Thanks, bro. I need that.'

The pub was returning to how I'd found it, empty apart from a few diehards, the poser in the blazer one of them. Danny pointed to my glass.

'Fancy another?'

'Think I've had enough. I'm not used to it.'

He overruled me. 'Go on. Just a splash. Have a break then get back in the game. And stay alert, some people have long memories.'

Rich coming from him. When he was fourteen, an older boy stuck a knife in the ball he was playing with. On a dark night five years later, somebody dragged the boy into an alley and beat the shit out of him. He'd ended up in hospital with concussion and a mouthful of broken teeth. Danny hadn't hurried to take his revenge. But he hadn't forgotten. The account got squared. The account always got squared. Nobody had a longer memory than my brother.

'That a warning?'

'No, an observation. Do it anyway.'

He leaned over and patted my cheek.

'The Glass brothers ride again, eh?'

I toyed with the dregs in my glass. There was never going to be a good time.

'Danny. There's something I need to say.'

He looked concerned. 'What? What is it? You ill?'

'Nothing like that.'

'Then... what?'

At the end of the day I owed him and we both knew it. This was hard.

'Ever since I was a kid you've looked out for me and Nina. I'm grateful but...'

He held up a hand to stop me from carrying on. 'Luke. Whatever's on your mind will keep. This is your day. Enjoy it.'

I realised he knew what I was going to say – he just didn't want to hear it. I said it anyway, blurted it out, shucking off a weight I'd carried around too long.

'I'm not coming back. I'm finished.'

Over the years I'd had plenty of opportunities to recognise the signs. He shot his don't-fuck-with-me look, the lines on his face deepened and the casual acceptance of me doing a runner from the homecoming party fell away. It had been an act. He edged forward and balled his fist. Danny had a temper – I'd seen him lose it many times. For a moment, I thought he was going to hit me. With an effort he pulled himself together and put a hand on my shoulder.

'Take whatever time you need. See how you feel about it then.'

3

Nina hadn't lied to Luke – she *had* better things to do than waste an afternoon talking: Eugene Vale was one of them.

She was naked, her clothes cast on the floor in her haste to be free of them, stretched across the desk, long legs curled behind her lover, binding him to her. The only sounds in the room were the shallow urgency of their breathing and the slap of flesh against flesh. Without words, they changed position; he bent her over the desk and took her from behind. Nina's manicured fingernails dug into the varnished wood as she climaxed. Vale lifted her up and lowered her to the floor, sucking her rigid nipples while his fingers worked between her thighs, bringing her to the edge before he mounted her a third time.

When it was over, they rolled away from each other and lay staring at the ceiling.

Vale said, 'Where does he think you are right now?'

'I've no idea and I couldn't care less. He's my brother, not my keeper.'

'Luke's coming out today.'

'I've seen him.'

'But shouldn't you be at the pub?'

Nina noticed the concern behind the question, the same unease she'd heard so often whenever Danny Glass was spoken about. She fired back. 'Shouldn't you?'

'Danny told me about the party a couple of weeks ago. He isn't expecting me.'

'Really?'

'I said I wouldn't be able to make it.'

'And he was fine with that?'

'Social events aren't my thing. Danny understands that.'

'Not even to welcome Luke back into the fold?'

'Not even for that. Why aren't you there?'

'Because I'd rather be here. Danny's got more than enough arse-lickers jumping when he says jump. In case you haven't noticed, I'm not one of them.'

Nina's face shone in the afternoon light, the unblemished skin glowing, defiance a dark star in her eyes. Stealing from her brother had been her idea and she'd made it seem so easy, it hadn't taken much to persuade him. Nina Glass was a handful, no doubt about that, driven by something Vale didn't try to understand. He didn't love her – with two marriages and two divorces behind him, the chances of him falling for another woman were nil – but being with her was exciting. Too exciting at times. The kind of exciting that got people killed.

'Damn right, you're not. Nobody sane would be doing what we're doing.'

She turned to face him. 'Then why're we doing it?'

He reached over and kissed her. 'Because we can. And because you suggested it.'

She smiled. 'I've bewitched you, is that what you're saying?'

He drew her to him. 'Correct. Now, stop talking before the spell breaks.'

* * *

They dressed in silence, each lost in their own thoughts. Vale hunkered down in front of a wall safe and spun the tumblers forward and back, until the door sprang open. From inside, he took two thick bundles of fifty-pound notes and tossed them onto the desk.

Nina weighed the notes in the palm of her hand. 'It feels like a lot.'

'It is a lot, and it's all yours. Put it with the rest and forget you have it.'

Concern furrowed Nina's brow. 'We aren't getting greedy, are we, Eugene? Greedy people get found out. Greedy people get caught.'

'Relax, there's so much cash coming in, Danny can't keep track. Only thing that bothers me is Luke coming out of prison. Now, we've got both your brothers to worry about.'

'Luke wants nothing to do with Danny's operation. He isn't hanging around.'

'That's not how Danny understands it. He talks like he has plans for him.'

Nina pulled on her coat and searched her bag for her car keys. 'It won't be happening.'

'Sure about that?'

'Absolutely sure.'

4

Rollie Anderson gave the driver his instructions. 'Slow down and park further along. Not too far, I want to be able to see.'

The driver did as he was told and pulled in front of a yellow Vauxhall.

Rollie said, 'Keep the engine running,' and unzipped a pocket of his black leather jacket with one hand, nervously drawing slender fingers through his ponytail with the other. He took out a packet of Gitanes and tapped one into his palm, his fifteenth so far today. Albert Anderson's son was on edge, chain-smoking to give himself something to do while he waited: he was twenty-six years old, overtly gay, automatically drawn to anything that brought oblivion. This was a big day for him, the biggest of his life and he didn't intend to miss a second of it. He wished his latest lover were here to share in it; desire made him hard.

But George Ritchie had taught him to keep business and pleasure separate – apart from the dope and the booze. Rollie lied to himself about those, considering them fuck-you-George rebellions rather than the addictions they so obviously were.

Outside the King of Mesopotamia, a tall, heavy-set man in a suit paced right and left, grey smoke from an E-cigarette drifting from his lips. Above his head, in contrast to the maroon facade edged in gold, a blue plaque claimed a public house had stood on this spot since 1645, and that Oliver Cromwell once spent the night under its roof.

Rollie intended to make some history of his own.

They were going to need a bigger plaque.

A wall of noise escaped from behind the door into the street caused by a band trying to be The Who making the mistake of thinking it was about how hard you pounded the guitar. Albert hadn't been a fan of loud music. A yammer, he would've called it.

Rollie pictured the scene inside the King Pot: the place would be heaving; animated faces, rosy-cheeked thanks to the free bar. All pals together so long as the booze kept coming. Glass would have made his speech praising his young brother. Preaching to the choir. Most of the people there depended on Danny Glass for their livelihood: soldiers and pimps and hard-faced women, even the odd hanger-on anxious to break into the circle. Anderson had a similar collection of arse-lickers around him, keen to do whatever he wanted done so long as he stayed a force south of the Thames. The few fortunate enough to be invited expected to be telling each other tomorrow how well Luke Glass looked after seven years, and didn't Danny know how to throw a party, eh? Except that wasn't what they'd be saying.

Some of them wouldn't be saying anything ever again.

Though why only one guard? Anderson had anticipated three or four at least. Glass was an arrogant bastard. He knew this was as good a time as any to even the score but perhaps assumed nobody would try it on his home turf. No doubt he had plans for his brother, plans that included using him to help put Rollie out of business.

Not happening. Definitely not happening.

Rollie flipped open his phone, pressed speed dial and spoke. 'Let's do this thing. And don't be shy in there. Put it about.'

A grey-haired old man walking with a cane, dressed in a dark overcoat and a green scarf, came around the corner. He stopped to read the Private Function sign, mouthing the words, then moved towards the door. The guard stepped between him and the entrance.

'On your way.'

'I just want to look.'

'Forget it. There's nothing for you here.' He shoved the old geezer. 'What part of "private function" don't you understand? Fuck off, Grandad.'

The pensioner dropped the cane, drew a gun from underneath his coat and shot the minder in the chest. He collapsed on the pavement, a cherry-red stain spreading across his white shirt. The shooter tore off the grey wig, threw it away and stood over the dying man.

'Ought to have more respect for your elders,' he said, and fired again.

Four figures in balaclavas appeared from nowhere and burst into the pub, unnoticed by the partygoers until a bullet shattered the mirror behind the bar and got their attention. The music petered out mid-song; conversation stopped mid-sentence. The leader swept glasses and drinks off the counter and walked to the centre of the room scanning the terrified faces, while his men herded people against the walls. He poked the man nearest him in the ear with the barrel of his gun. 'Where are they?'

No answer.

He opened the question up to the rest of the crowd. 'Where are they?'

Silence.

The nearest person was a redhead in her late forties, nervously gripping her drink. Gracie was one of the pub regulars who sometimes broke into song after she'd had a few. He shot her in the temple and turned away before she hit the floor. The stunned crowd tried to take in what had just happened.

'I'll ask again,' he said. 'Where are Danny, Luke and Nina?'

A voice from the back shouted, 'They're not here.'

'So, where are they?'

'Luke and Nina didn't show. Danny went to find Luke.'

Two of the gang raced upstairs.

The barman shouted after them. 'Danny'll do you for this.'

The bullet hit him in the leg and they left him at the bottom of the stairs screaming, blood pouring from the wound.

The office was empty. No sign of them. Frustrated and angry, the hooded men toppled the jukebox on its side and pumped three rounds into the image of the Queen. The picture flew into space and landed on the carpet. Down in the bar, the other raiders kept their weapons on the guests crowded together at the end of the room. One of Danny Glass's men made a dive at the guy nearest him and took a bullet in the heart at close range for his trouble. He died instantly, the third fatality in less than five minutes.

Felix Corrigan should've been at the door. Instead he was ordering a drink when the raiders burst in. Since the attack began, he'd been looking for an opportunity to redeem himself and he'd been given it. Felix drew a gun from underneath his jacket, fired two rounds into the man who'd murdered Gracie and ducked behind an overturned table. In the car, Anderson heard the shots and saw his men burst onto the street and scatter. With surprise on their side Rollie had imagined it would be fast and smooth, and when it ended the Glass family would be dead.

Nobody needed to tell him he'd failed.

5

I tried to make Danny understand.

'It's not about a holiday. I just don't want to do it any more.'

His response was everything I'd expected it would be.

'Don't talk daft. What else would you do?'

'Go abroad, maybe.'

His expression twisted in disbelief.

'Abroad? You mean away from England?' The idea appalled him. 'And then what?'

'That's as far as I've got.'

'Doesn't sound like you've thought this through. More like a reaction to coming out.'

His ringtone broke into our argument. Reluctantly he took the call. I watched his expression tighten and his mood change from bad to worse. The mobile snapped shut.

'Rollie Anderson just hit the King Pot. Let's go.'

We sat in the back of the Lexus, as far from each other as it was possible to be, him facing away, staring through the car's tinted glass so he wouldn't have to look at me. I'd gone from long-lost brother to the invisible man. When I was able to set aside my gratitude for what he'd done for us growing up, this was how I remembered my brother:

Danny got what Danny wanted or there were consequences. Experience had taught me it was better to leave him alone, so I did.

The car came to a halt thirty yards from the pub close to a line of blue-and-white tape already stretched across the road. Beyond it, two police cars, an ambulance and a body on the ground clearly showed that ducking out of the party had been one of my better decisions. An outside table had been knocked over and people stood in groups, strangers mostly, under wrought-iron hanging baskets filled with flowers, reminders that the King of Mesopotamia had been a decent local boozer, a typical South London watering hole, before my brother took it over – VE Day, the World Cup victory in 1966 and, for close on seventy years, the Queen's birthday had been celebrated here.

Danny got out and marched through the cordon. I followed. A young policeman who must have been new tried to stop him. He brushed the constable aside and didn't bother to glance down at the body on the pavement as we went through the door.

The first face I saw was the guy who should have been behind the wheel the awful morning Albert Anderson murdered Cheryl and Rebecca: Marcus. Still around. And he'd clearly come up in the world.

Acrid smoke and the sweet smell of burnt caramel caught in my throat. On the floor, surrounded by shards of glass, a redhead was having her picture taken from different angles by a police photographer who'd clearly seen it all before and wasn't impressed; he looked up at us and went on doing what he was doing. The victim's auburn hair was matted and dark with blood, her open eyes staring at the ceiling, seeing nothing, the surprise in them impossible to miss. When she was putting the finishing touches to her make-up the prospect of seeing Danny Glass's famous brother probably seemed exciting. She died because of me and we'd never even met.

Near her, a man stared at the ceiling waiting his turn to have his picture taken. His suit jacket had been oatmeal. Once. Now it was dirty red. It was no coincidence Rollie Anderson had chosen today to make his move. Walking away wasn't going to be as simple as I'd imagined.

The officer in charge broke from talking to his men and came towards us.

'Sorry, Mr Glass, we had no idea. DCI Stanford said—'

Danny grabbed his lapels and threw him against the bar. A banner with WELCOME HOME LUKE hanging at an angle from a solitary tack dangled above his head; the bullet had gone through the female's skull and obliterated the pin holding up one end.

'Shove the excuses. Tell Stanford I want to see him.'

The policeman stuttered. 'He's... in Hendon. At... at the college.'

'You tell him Danny Glass says to get his arse down here. Pronto.'

'I'll... I'll call him... call him now.'

'Yeah, you do that.'

Danny's eyes were wild and he was breathing hard, a heartbeat away from losing it completely. Marcus got it next. Cheryl hadn't liked Marcus and had complained to me more than once about his attitude. There was no attitude today. The guy was six feet two or three, towering above everybody in the room, but that didn't stop Danny.

'What happened?'

Marcus kept his answer short, no doubt wishing he wasn't the one who had to tell it.

'They burst in and shot Gracie. Didn't have to, just did. Our guy made a move and got the same.'

'How many?'

'Four, maybe five.'

'What did they say?'

'They wanted to know where the three of you were. Put a bullet in Harry on their way up the stairs. They didn't find you so they trashed the place. Felix killed one of them.' He pointed to a body.

'Is it anybody we know?'

'No.'

Danny nodded. 'So not local. Brought in for the job. His mates will be getting on a train in Euston to Liverpool or Bolton or some other hellhole as we speak. Who was outside?'

'Bruno and Felix. Bruno's dead.'

'And Felix?'

'Felix is okay. Told you, he killed one of them.'

Marcus hesitated and Danny said, 'If Bruno's dead, how come Felix is okay?'

The big man shifted uneasily. 'Because… he wasn't at the door when they hit.'

A full half-minute went by. Nobody moved. Danny stared at Marcus. Marcus looked at the floor. Eventually, my brother broke the silence; he went mental.

'Fu-u-u-uck! Morons! I'm surrounded by morons! Where was Felix?'

Marcus reluctantly replied. 'Having a drink.'

Danny cupped a hand behind his ear, pretending he hadn't understood.

'Say again.'

'At the bar. Felix was having a drink.'

'And you knew about this?'

'No, I was—'

'Shut up! Just shut up! Get Felix. Take him to Fulton Street and do him.'

'But, Danny…'

'Doooittt!'

Surrounded by witnesses and coppers, Marcus was being ordered to commit murder.

Danny said, 'Is he outside? Is he? Well, what're you waiting for? Go! We could all be dead. You're paid to make sure that doesn't happen. Felix gets what's coming to him. Think yourself lucky it isn't you going in the ground.'

So far, I'd been a bystander. This was my brother's kingdom, he made the rules, although a blind man could see he was beyond reason. Publicly ordering an execution in front of a room full of coppers was crazy.

I pointed at Marcus.

'Stay there. Just stay there.'

Danny was ashen, drained by the fury he'd let loose. I dragged him to the other end of the bar and tried to reach him.

'Listen to me. Go through with this and nobody can save you. It'll all be over. The end of Team Glass. Anderson will have won.'

I held onto him until he started to come back to me. His eyes lost the glaze and regained their focus.

I kept talking.

'We can't let that piece of shit beat us.'

He nodded and put an arm on my shoulder like he always did. When he spoke, his voice was hoarse from screaming.

'You're a good boy, Luke. A good boy.'

'I'll deal with Felix. In my own way and in my own time. Don't forget he took one of them out.'

'Yeah, you see to it,' he said, and let me lead him upstairs.

My brother kept a safe in the wall behind a drinks cabinet in the office above the pub. It hadn't been touched; the raiders weren't interested in money. Neither was Danny. He knelt, gently brushing glass off what was left of the photograph of Her Majesty, smoothing it out, close to tears, then picked up one of the records spilled from the toppled jukebox and cradled it like a bird with a broken wing.

For some guys it was cars or racehorses or houses. Even women were collectable if you looked at it that way. With him, it was British pop music; he was obsessed with it – nothing later than the early seventies. To him, the Swinging Sixties was about more than just music. It represented a time, a national identity, something to be proud of. His biggest regret was that he'd missed it. Every few weeks he'd put his current favourite songs on the jukebox. I couldn't say how many records he had, but it was a lot.

His voice was ragged with emotion.

'They've scratched "Waterloo Sunset". A fucking classic. One of the best songs Ray Davies ever wrote. Bastards!'

It didn't feel right to be there, so I left him alone and went back down. Marcus was at the other end of the bar talking to a couple of guys – one of them would be Felix – no doubt filling them in on

Danny's meltdown and discussing me, the unknown quantity. They stopped when I appeared.

'Who's Felix?'

A man nearer thirty than twenty, wearing a brown leather jacket and jeans, nodded. Instead of guarding the door he'd been at the bar ordering a drink. He looked like he could use one now. His tongue moved over lips dry with anxiety and his voice faltered.

He was afraid and he should be.

'I am,' he said.

'Make yourself scarce.'

He didn't need telling twice. When he'd gone Marcus sidled up.

'What're you going to do to him? He almost got you killed.'

He was forgetting his part in the security debacle, prepared to see somebody else take the fall. Cheryl hadn't liked him. Neither did I.

Footsteps on the stairs helped him decide it would be better to be somewhere else and he drifted away. Danny came towards me, glass crunching under his feet like fresh snow. His eyes were red and his voice was a monotone but the madness was gone. He stroked his chin.

'Your unexpected detour saved our lives. If we'd been here it would've been our brains on the wall. Two for the price of one. A result for Anderson. He'll be disappointed. But I wasn't the target. Neither was Nina. You were. It was you he was after.'

'I know.'

'The long memories I was talking about.'

'Yeah.'

'Don't blame yourself. It may look like a war started today – it didn't. It never stopped and it never will, until we kill Rollie Anderson or he kills us. Forget the crap you were spouting earlier, not coming back isn't an option. The Glass family stand together.'

* * *

Nina spent the drive to the pub thinking about Eugene Vale, the best lover she'd ever had – an unexpected plus she was more than happy about. In other circumstances, she wouldn't have given the twice-married twice-divorced accountant a second glance. For a start, he was in his late forties, too old for her. Seducing him had been a means to an end, the initial step in a plan made possible when Danny had put them together. After that, convincing him to do what she wanted had been easy because, like most men, he thought with his dick.

Vale ran his small firm from an unimpressive office above a florist down a side street in Lewisham – just him and a secretary called Yvonne, a tarty piece who came in three days a week. Nina disliked the woman on sight – over-confident for someone with nothing to brag about. Her lipstick was too red, her skirts were too short, and whenever she interrupted their meeting to get him to sign something, as she made sure she always did, she leaned across so her boss got a good look at her breasts. None of it escaped Nina. Nor did the barely suppressed I-know-something-you-don't-know smirk on Yvonne's lips.

She sensed a rival.

Much of Danny's business was done on the street and in cash. No paper trail, invoices or receipts; keeping track of the daily flow of money was almost impossible. Glass was Vale's only client. Danny trusted him – as far as he trusted anybody – although 'trust' in the true sense of the word didn't come into it.

Whoever was foolish enough to steal from him was too stupid to live, and wouldn't for long if he found out.

If, Nina emphasised. *If* he found out.

The trick was to make sure he never did.

Eugene had done all right out of the arrangement with her brother.

He was doing better than all right now.

The affair wouldn't last, in Nina's experience they rarely did, but it wouldn't peter out until she was financially independent and didn't need the accountant any more.

* * *

Nina turned the corner into the street and froze. Two police cars and an ambulance were parked outside the King Pot; through the crowd she saw a body on the pavement covered in a blanket. Nina braked hard, got out of the car and started running. As she pushed her way to the front, hands tugged at her coat trying to hold her back. She shrugged them off and ducked under the blue-and-white tape holding the onlookers at bay. A baby-faced constable barely old enough to shave made a futile attempt to stop her going inside. Nina brushed past and charged through the door screaming, 'Luke! Luke!'

Danny's temper was on an even shorter fuse than usual. He turned angrily towards the shouting. 'What's that fucking racket?'

Nina burst into tears and ran breathless into Luke's arms. 'You're all right. You're all right. Thank God.'

He held her, gently stroking her hair to reassure her.

'I'm fine. Absolutely fine.'

Danny watched his brother and sister, the edges of his mouth curled in a humourless grin. 'As it happens, I'm all right, too, Nina. Thanks for asking.'

She ignored him and spoke to Luke. 'Who did this?'

'Anderson.'

'Bastard.'

'If we'd been here, we'd be dead.'

Danny said, 'Rollie reckons he's waited long enough to settle the score.' He eyed Nina up and down. 'Where the hell were you, anyway?'

I was exhausted, so tired I could have lain down on the floor and slept forever. Booze and adrenaline had done me in. My first day of freedom and it felt like shit. The last thing I remember from that crazy afternoon was the smell of cigar smoke on Danny's breath as I fell into a taxi and him whispering the mantra I'd been hearing since I was a child in my ear.

'Team Glass. Team Glass, Luke.'

* * *

There were no dreams, only a block of nothing and a noise that wouldn't go away. My eyes opened. I was in the flat, on the couch, still dressed; my head hurt. It took a minute to realise there was someone at the door.

She was tall and slim in high heels and a mink coat, red hair falling in curls to what I knew would be flawless white shoulders underneath, and legs that went all the way to Australia. Two glasses twirled between the fingers of one hand; condensation trickled down the champagne bottle in the other. A silver ankle bracelet with a tiny replica of the Eiffel Tower caught my eye.

She smiled and spoke in a Lancashire drawl.

'Looking for a Luke, that you?'

I'd assumed Eiffel. I should have been thinking Blackpool.

'Yeah.'

'I'm Mandy. Danny sent me. Can I come in?'

* * *

The first time is never the best time. Strangers meeting in the dark. Too many unknowns for the earth to move. It didn't move for us. But it was good. I knew it would be. When it was over, she lay with her head on the pillow, tracing my face with her eyes, her voice husky with something she was reluctant to admit. Eventually she said, 'I lied to you. I promised myself whatever happened I wouldn't and I have.'

'About what?'

'About Danny.'

'What about him?'

'Danny didn't send me.'

6

Sunlight streaming in the window and a ringing in my head brought me round. My bones ached, even my eyes ached. I rolled off the bed and staggered towards the lounge, the room rolling with me – the noise in my brain got louder. Mandy's perfume drifted from the bedroom to the sofa next door, sweeter than I remembered. Just as I reached it the phone stopped. No prizes for guessing who it had been. He'd call again.

Half a dozen cans of Stella Artois in the fridge and an unopened jar of Carte Noire in the cupboard reminded me what a considerate guy Danny could be: three thousand pounds, a hooker, a phone, coffee and lager; this was my lucky day. Except it wasn't free. None of it. His generosity was calculated. Team Glass was an obsession he wasn't about to let go and he was reeling me in. I expected to open a drawer and come across keys for a car with my name on it.

While I waited for the water to boil, I opened a beer and thought about the previous day. Drinking takes practice and I hadn't had any. The lager had a metallic taste. Most of it got poured down the sink. My first twenty-four hours on the outside had been eventful, although somebody trying to kill me wasn't the kind of highlight I was looking for. I made coffee and carried it through to the lounge with a shaky hand. I'd been too out of it to notice anything different about the place; the delightful distraction of Mandy had made sure it stayed that way. Now it was like being in someone else's home. The only thing I recognised was the cricket bat Danny had bought me when I was twelve, sitting where it had always been, behind the door.

Because you just never know.

New wallpaper framed unfamiliar furniture: a sofa, an angular lamp, above the fireplace an ornate clock I wouldn't have taken if they'd been giving it away and a bookcase heavy with paperbacks purchased by the yard and unread. Then there was the carpet, an orange, yellow and green monstrosity nobody in their right mind would have in their house. My brother's taste was in his arse. Taken together, the décor and furniture made a powerful case for moving on.

The phone rang a second time. Danny, all business.

'Ten o'clock. Somebody I want you to meet. Get yourself round here pronto. Important you're in on this.'

'Round where?'

'The King Pot, where else?'

'Thought the pub would be closed.'

'Nobody shuts us down.'

He hung up.

I ran the shower and tried to ignore the empty champagne bottle in the bath and the black panties hanging from the tap. Must have been a great night. Shame I didn't remember it. Mandy had written her mobile number on the mirror in red lipstick; she deserved a call and she'd be getting one. The hot water helped bring me into the day, that and the realisation I wasn't in prison gave me the strength to face an unwelcome fact: Danny was winning.

The keys were where I couldn't miss them, by the bed, with a note written in his familiar scrawl.

Welcome back little brother.

A better man would've left them there. This morning, I wasn't that man.

On the bottom he'd scratched the registration so I'd know what to look for. The car was parked in the next street: a top-of-the-range A6, Mauritius Blue, bright and shiny with just two hundred miles on the clock. I pressed the start button, slid the clutch into gear and pulled away from the kerb with the smell of new leather around me.

My brother knew how the game was played. He'd even slipped '(What's the Story) Morning Glory?' in the CD player. Well remembered, bro. Oasis was my favourite group.

The Audi drove itself, all I had to do was steer. For a couple of miles, I was able to convince myself it was going to be okay. Then reality kicked in along with that feeling again, of unseen eyes on me. I checked the mirrors – nothing obvious. But that didn't mean nothing. Anderson had waited seven years and wasn't likely to let one bungled attempt stop him.

Outside the pub, a dark mark on the pavement and an already fading chalk outline were stark reminders of the day before. With our history, standing up to my brother didn't come easily to me, but I'd do it. And if Anderson was determined to fight until only one of us was left, I could do that, too. Taking on both of them at the same time was a different story.

The day was warm. Suddenly I felt cold and caught myself anxiously looking up and down the street. What was I expecting to see? Danny wagging a finger at me, putting me in my place, like he'd done ever since I was a kid? A couple of Anderson's men walking towards me blasting away?

Christ Almighty! Get a grip!

I knocked on the door. Keys rattled in the lock, before it edged open and a face peered at me: she was about forty, ash blonde with hazel eyes, still attractive in spite of the quirk of fate that had rocked her world. Her husband had been behind the wheel the morning of the explosion. Marcus should have been driving and would have been if Cheryl hadn't lost her temper with him. The stand-in driver had only worked a couple of months for the firm. That made no difference to Danny. Always big on loyalty, he'd given the driver's widow a lump sum and a job as cleaner at the King of Mesopotamia. Seven years on, she was still here.

She wiped her hands on her overall and stood aside to let me through. I introduced myself.

'Hi, I'm Luke Glass.'

Of course, she already knew. 'He's waiting for you.'

In the room upstairs, order had been restored: no sign of the damage done by Rollie Anderson's hired assassins. The jukebox was playing the Small Faces 'Tin Soldier' and a different photograph of the monarch was on the wall in a new frame. Danny sat like the chairman of the board, his fingers drumming impatiently inches from an open laptop. My brother was the biggest Luddite I'd ever come across. This would be one of the 'moves' he'd mentioned.

Nina was in a chair against the wall, shoulders back, unsmiling, her dark hair scraped back – a far cry from the weeping woman I'd held in my arms.

Without lifting his eyes from the desk, Danny said, 'You're late.'

I didn't answer. He should consider himself fortunate I'd bothered to turn up at all. He spoke again, more mellow this time, maybe realising I wasn't in the mood.

'Found the car, then?'

'Yeah, thanks.'

'Nice colour. Ladies will love it. Not that I'm suggesting you'll need any help. Got you off to a flying start, though, didn't I? From now on, get your own women, little brother.' He flicked a speck of dust off the desk. 'Knew Mandy would be your type, red-haired and slutty.' Danny laughed. 'Or is that my type I'm thinking of?' He laughed again.

'I liked her.'

''Course you did. She's in the business of getting men to like her. Mandy's a pro.'

He was having a dig at me, trying to get under my skin and

succeeding. 'Good news is: the Mandys of this world are ten a penny. Thank Christ.'

It was forced and fake and made me uncomfortable. A lot of people had reason to fear my brother. I hadn't ever been one of them. Until now. It was as if he'd suddenly become a different person, scoring points. His face was flushed and fleshy like Albert Anderson just before he fell, something sly and knowing watching from behind his eyes.

He laughed hard at a joke I didn't understand. 'You tell me, little brother, does it get any better?'

Then the mood passed as quickly as it had arrived and he was Danny again, brusque and direct like he always was, barking out orders and expecting them to be obeyed.

'Nina, come over here. Sit down, both of you, we need to talk.'

In that moment, I was back in the grubby council flat with our father passed out in the room next door, at one of the many family meetings Danny had called to reassure two scared kids that everything was going to be all right.

Nina didn't argue and drew her chair closer. Danny leaned forward, grinning like a gargoyle. 'Rollie certainly knows how to spoil a party, doesn't he?'

I said, 'We're here, that's what counts.'

'Yeah, but he almost killed you, I'm not having that. Told you, yesterday wasn't the beginning. It isn't just about you. He's been biding his time.'

'And my first day out was it?'

'Yeah. Finish it early. Minimum casualties maximum result.'

'Cheeky.'

'Got to give him that. Smart too. With us out of the picture he'd be top dog south of the river.'

'Fait accompli.'

'You what?'

'Fait accompli. French for done deal.'

The edge of Danny's mouth twisted. He brushed something that wasn't there off his jacket with a flick of his finger.

'Is it really? So, what's the French for jumped-up poncey fucker? Talk English, will you?'

Where Danny's patriotism came from, I'd no idea. God knows England hadn't given him much. As kids we'd learned to look after ourselves. I was young, maybe eight or nine, the first time my brother used me to distract the Indian guy in the corner shop while he reached behind the counter and stole fags. On the dodge, he'd called it – Nina's introduction came later. And Team Glass was born.

'You said there was somebody you wanted me to meet.'

'There is.'

'Who?'

'Hold on, you'll see.'

He closed down the PC and took a stroll through the past.

'Those two geezers who bullied you at school, yeah? Every other day you'd come home crying because they'd stolen your dinner money or put your head down the toilet and pulled the plug?'

The memory made him laugh.

'You were just a kid, Nina, but your brother remembers, don't you?'

'How could I forget?

'I caught them in the playground and warned them to leave you alone. Banged their stupid heads together to make the point.' He laughed. 'Then the older ones got involved. Seventeen or eighteen, I was. They'd be twenty-five or more. Thought that gave them an advantage.'

His eyes locked on mine. 'Straightened them out, didn't I? Sorted it. And I'm going to sort this. Rollie needs a good slap for what he did, and he's going to get one.'

It was a nice story the way he told it, but not exactly the truth. He had banged heads together, that much was true, and the kids did bring in the heavy squad, who turned out not to be very heavy; got the shit kicked out of them. End of, as far as Danny was concerned, though not for me. On the last day before the summer holidays they caught me on my way home and paid me back. The bullying went on for the best part of a year after that and only stopped when I cracked one of their skulls with a milk bottle. As they stretchered the unconscious boy into an ambulance, I was in the crowd, wondering if I'd killed him, knowing that, either way, my ordeal was over.

Danny hadn't sorted anything, he just thought he had. I'd let him go on believing; it was easier.

The sound of footsteps on the stairs told me whoever I was there to meet had arrived.

* * *

He was tall – six three, maybe more – and even with the suntan I knew he was police. He moved like a copper, deliberate and unhurried, while his eyes darted from Danny to me and back again. There was no fear in those eyes, only a detached superiority. Something about the scene amused him; his thin lips paused on the edge of a smile. I'd met him for less than thirty seconds and already would've liked to put his face up against a brick and throw a wall at it.

Danny walked round the desk and they shook hands in the middle of the room. His behaviour today was hard to understand: ratty over nothing, then wistfully recalling a fairy tale with him as the hero. Now, all smiles giving this visitor from the other side of the tracks a big hello. I didn't get it. He placed a hand on my shoulder and introduced me.

'Luke, this is Detective Chief Inspector, Oliver Stanford.'

The smooth skin round the detective's eyes creased as he studied me.

'The famous brother. Heard you were out.'

It wasn't a question so I didn't reply.

He saw Nina and grinned. 'And the sister, too. Well, well, the gang's all here, I'm honoured.'

Danny steered him to a chair next to mine and sat back down behind the desk.

'So, Ollie, how's your luck?'

7

Stanford shifted in his seat – this wasn't the reception he'd expected. Danny said, 'How's the house working out? Wife enjoying it, is she?'

'Elise loves it.'

'Yeah. Yeah.' Danny lifted a ballpoint and played with it. 'Good location that, Hendon. No riff-raff. Nobody like me living next door, eh? Handy for your cop school, too.'

He meant Hendon Police College.

'And the kids, settling into their new class?'

The DCI's features might have been dipped in concrete.

My brother had missed his vocation – he should've been an actor. I almost believed him. Stanford didn't. His reply was cautious.

'They're doing very well, Danny.'

'Good. Glad to hear it.'

He rubbed his palms together, got to his feet and leaned across until his face was close to the policeman's. Then, he roared. 'Because I'm fucking paying for it!'

Flecks of spittle showered the detective. Some of it landed on me. Stanford closed his eyes against the assault and turned his suntanned face away. Danny patted him gently on the cheek. 'Your nice life comes out of my pocket. Maybe you've forgotten.'

Stanford defended himself.

'Yesterday took everybody by surprise.'

Danny agreed. 'You're not wrong there, Oliver, not wrong there. Problem is, I hate surprises, even good surprises. Always have. You're supposed to make sure I don't get any. And you bloody didn't. I'd like you to explain that to me.'

'We're still waiting for confirmation on the identity of the dead guy. At this stage our best guess is he was part of an out-of-town crew.'

'Tell me something I don't know.'

The door opened. Marcus and a man I hadn't seen before came in. Stanford sensed them behind him and some of his poise ebbed. He loosened his tie and worked it free of his throat. Sweat beaded his forehead. But fair play to him, he didn't buckle.

'The attack was the best-kept secret in London. Nobody knew it was a goer. There was nothing I could do.'

Danny yawned and stretched, pretending he was bored. 'When you and I had our very first powwow, I told you what I needed. You told me what it was going to cost and it wasn't pennies, d'you remember?'

The policeman hesitated. His hand drifted to his brow.

'Yes.'

'Your career was going okay. You weren't short of a few bob. Two bright kids and the lovely Elise spreading her legs for you a couple of times a week. But it wasn't enough. There was more and you wanted more. I showed you how you could get it.'

He interrupted himself.

'Feel free to correct me if I'm not telling this right. I got you in. The house, the holidays, are just window dressing.' He paused to allow the bounty in Stanford's life to sink in. 'Nice tan, by the way. St Lucia, wasn't it? That one of ours or have we given it away like everything else in this fucking country nowadays? Doesn't matter. More important, you've made a couple of big scores, thanks to me. People in high places will have noticed. Keep on going and you'll be Ollie the Giant Killer, the man of the hour, drinking Earl Grey with the commissioner and Elise pally with his wife.'

The prospect amused him.

'Love that, won't she? Her husband on the road to being a fully paid-up member of the Lucky Bastards Club. Who knows how high a bent bastard like you can climb? Right to the top, why not? Wouldn't be the first.' He pointed at the detective. 'Am I right, Ollie, or am I right? But there are...' Danny paused '... other options.'

On cue, Marcus and the heavy came forward and stood on either side of the detective. Underneath the suntan he had to have been wondering if he was about to get a bullet in the head and decided it wasn't going to happen. At least not today. He brassed it out.

'If you'd intended to cripple me you would've done it already, so what do you want, Danny?'

The question seemed to surprise my brother.

'You're the professional, Oliver. The Man with the Plan. Thought you'd have some ideas.'

'I can take Anderson off the street for a while. Arrest him on suspicion.'

'Oh, better than that, surely, Detective Chief Inspector? That's what the taxpayer's paying for. What about me, what do I get?'

Stanford made a stab at asserting himself.

'I can only stick my head up so far before people start asking questions.'

It didn't go down well. Danny reacted.

'Don't get arsey with me, copper.'

The policeman's expression was stone; he wasn't used to taking shit, especially from somebody like my brother, and clearly hated it.

Too fucking bad. When you sell your soul, you belong to the devil.

Danny said, 'Rollie's interest in Luke is understandable, given old Albert's nosedive.' He jabbed the ballpoint at the detective. 'I'm holding you responsible for the safety of these two. Anything happens to either of them, we have a big problem. I'll sort Anderson myself, don't worry about it.'

Stanford had plenty of balls.

'What you're asking is impossible.'

'Make it possible.'

Stanford laughed a brittle laugh. 'How? Fucking tell me how. I haven't the resources to protect one of you round the clock, let alone two. Kill me and be done with it if that's where this is going.'

Danny smiled. 'Oh, I will, I will, Ollie. I'm saving you 'til last.'

The DCI's confidence returned with the confirmation he wasn't going to die today.

'I'd advise against a war. Wars attract attention. Who benefits from that?'

'You're starting to sound like a consultant, Oliver. That how you see yourself? Want to borrow my watch to tell me the time and charge an arm and a leg for the privilege?' Danny laid his palms face down on the desk and sat back. 'In case you haven't noticed, we've been at it with these fuckers, one way or another, for the last ten years.'

'I'm advising caution. For both our sakes. If it goes above me, I'm no use to you. All I'm saying is: think before you act. Anderson will be expecting a response. Don't give him one. Not yet. Let things settle down.'

So far, I'd been a spectator. Danny turned in his chair and faced me. 'What's your opinion, Luke? How should we handle this?'

Apart from the introductions, Nina and I had been ignored by the policeman. My brother was the boss, which made us invisible as far as he was concerned.

'He makes a good point. Anderson's expecting us to retaliate and he'll be ready. I'd disappoint him, keep him guessing. Anything else is too predictable.'

Not what my brother wanted to hear. His fingers went back to drumming the desk.

'So, we do what?'

'Wait.'

'Wait? For how long?'

'Until it suits us.'

Danny wasn't impressed.

'It suits us now. Every sleazebag in the city's watching. Doing nothing sends a message. Says we're weak. Any bastard who fancies his chances can try it on with Danny Glass and get away with it.'

I held up my hands.

'You asked. I'm telling you. Box clever.'

Blue eyes appraised me. I'd agreed with him and the detective was seeing me in a new light. The look on Danny's face was very different. 'Yeah? Box clever? And let Anderson think he can take a pop whenever he likes? Yesterday can't go unanswered. Let it go and pretty soon we'll be out of business.' He dismissed Stanford. 'You can fuck off out of it and start earning your money for a change.'

Stanford stood. 'I'll be in touch.'

'You'd better be.'

Marcus showed the policeman out. Danny called after him.

'Don't forget, I can cancel that membership—' he clicked his fingers '—whenever I want. Just whenever I want, Oliver. Love to Elise and the kids, eh?'

8

The door closed and Danny glared at me.

'Box clever? Joking, aren't you? Ever heard anything like it, Nina? Rollie Anderson tried to kill all of us yesterday and your brother wants us to box clever.'

Nina started to speak but Danny closed her down. 'Anderson's going to get what he deserves.'

I said, 'I agree.'

'Then, what was that about?'

'For Stanford's benefit. You don't believe he was in the dark about the raid, do you? My disappearing act spoiled the surprise. Otherwise he'd be discussing his new arrangement with Anderson this morning.'

'Thank Christ. Thought you'd gone soft.'

We spent the next hour discussing what to do, Danny as animated as I'd ever seen him, throwing out suggestions, each more violent than the last. Finally, I said, 'Forget the 'Gunfight at the O.K. Corral' stuff, he'll be prepared for that. Don't play his game.'

'So we do what exactly? Let him get away with it? Not a chance.'

'That's not what I'm saying. Hit him where it hurts, his earners.'

Danny needed action; he needed revenge. 'No. If people think Anderson's got us on the run, they'll start taking liberties.'

Nina interrupted him. 'Give Luke a chance. At least listen to what he has to say.'

Danny ignored her. 'George Ritchie's the key. Without him, Rollie's just a silly boy out of his depth. Ritchie's had a good innings, time he was retired.'

I struggled to believe what I was hearing. 'Are you serious? Word on the inside says Rollie's a ticking bomb. He's already crazy-mad at me. Ritchie's old-school and shrewd. I'm surprised he didn't take over after Albert. He'll put the brakes on anything too outrageous. We don't want him out of the picture at this stage. Later maybe, but not now.'

'Yeah? You think?'

'I do think.'

'Then tell me, where was this great influence yesterday when Anderson damn near ended you and me?'

I didn't have an answer for him. 'I'd bet the move on the King Pot didn't come from George. By himself, Rollie's unpredictable. You can't second-guess a lunatic. Ritchie's the wrong target. You wanted me involved, okay, I'm involved. Listen to what I'm saying or let me go.'

Danny didn't blink for half a minute, finally he said, 'So you're for holding off?'

'Only until we can do some real damage. Get Stanford to come back with information we can use to cripple Anderson. About his shipments and when he shifts his money. Everything. Cut him off at the knees.'

'All right, we'll do it your way, see where it gets us.'

Nina clapped her hands derisively. 'Finally, the fucking dinosaur sees sense.'

I carried on. 'We let him sweat. When we don't come at him, he'll get nervous.'

My brother agreed. 'Waiting's hard. Not everybody's built for it. Takes nerve. Let's find out how much he has.'

I turned the conversation back to the DCI. 'How long has Stanford been on the books?'

'Three years.'

'Value for money?'

'Over the course, yeah.'

'How much are we paying him?'

'Enough. It won't save him though because he's living beyond his means. Up to his arse in debt. Should see the house.'

'I don't trust him.'

Danny gave me a strange look. 'Do I seem thick to you?'

'No.'

His face coloured, the anger was back. 'Well, don't treat me like I am. Stanford's dodgy as a three-pound note. He doesn't trust us. We don't trust him. The perfect relationship.'

'All I'm saying is, he needs watching.'

''Course he does, he's police.' He spoke to Nina without looking at her. 'You can go, just stay alive to anything unusual. You might not be Number One on Anderson's list but he'd settle for you if he has to. And leave your mobile switched on. I want to be able to contact you at all times. Our family's under attack. We need to pull together.'

Nina threw her head back and confronted him full on. 'So that's it. I'm dismissed. No place for a silly woman at the Big Boys' table. Well, fuck you, Danny Glass. I'm here and I'm staying. This affects me as much as anybody, and here's a newsflash – I've got a vote, too.'

Before he could react, I jumped in. 'Of course, you've got a vote. What're you thinking?'

The intervention worked but it showed how brittle their relationship was.

Nina said, 'Anderson will do any of us, all of us if he can, but it's you he's really after.'

'Agreed.'

'Then take the heat out of the situation.'

'Yeah, how?'

'Get out of London – for a while at least? Leave tonight.' She glanced at Danny. 'He intends to go anyway.'

His right hand closed in a fist. 'Until this thing's over, nobody's going anywhere, get that through your skull. I need Luke here.

Running away – and that's what he'd be doing – isn't an option. Don't mention it again.'

Nina faced him down and said: 'If you're depending on that smarmy copper to protect us, you're kidding yourself.'

Danny rose out of his chair. 'Shut your mouth or I'll shut it for you. 'Course I'm not depending on Stanford, what do you take me for? Oliver Stanford's a snake. In some ways, worse than Anderson. I'll have people on both of you, so you can forget the little disappearing acts you're so fond of doing in the middle of the afternoon.'

Nina blanched, her jaw dropped and Danny smiled.

'Think I didn't know about it? You must be joking. And by the way, in case you've forgotten, my birthday's coming up. There's a party in the pub. I expect you to be there and that isn't an invitation – it's an order.'

When Nina left, Danny got up and paced the room. I waited a long time for him to speak; eventually, he did, and surprised me. 'I blame myself. Should've wiped the bastard off the map. Finished what you started. This is the result.'

'Why didn't you?'

He faced me. 'I'll tell you the truth but it never leaves this room. I bottled it. Danny Glass didn't have the stones.'

Admitting failure wasn't something my brother was famous for. He rubbed his eyes like a tired child. 'Rebecca and Cheryl were gone... you were gone... Nina didn't say anything but I knew everyone thought it was my fault for not being there. I don't know... Was as much as I could do to get out of bed in the morning.'

Hearing him open up about the bomb that killed Cheryl and Rebecca was odd, like listening to a stranger's story. I wasn't sure what to say. 'You were in shock.'

'Yeah, that's what I told myself.'

'How long did it last?'

'Months and months. Best part of a year. I tried to keep it from you.'

'By stopping coming to see me?'

'Got it in one.'

'Did you speak to anybody about how you felt?'

He let out a dismissive grunt. 'What? Do a Tony Soprano? Bawling my eyes out on a psychiatrist's couch? 'Course not.'

'Might have helped.'

'Yeah? And pay for some quack's villa in Marbella. Not likely. My childhood was shit. My father and mother fucked me up. So what? Nothing changes the fact I should have ended it there and then.'

Danny rubbed his eyes. 'Rollie was a kid and didn't look like a threat. Shows how out of it I must have been. I froze and gave him a second chance.'

'So, what's his strength?'

'Compared to us, he's nobody.'

'Nobody almost blew us away.'

'There's always that. He's been a pain in the arse for years but nothing serious. Until yesterday.'

'What's he into these days?'

'The usual. A couple of security firms, one in Peckham, one in Lambeth. Taxis. Two or three boozers. Part of his operation is the girls he runs. Sluts from Moldavia and the like – English tarts aren't good enough. Brings them in for half the gangs in London. Wouldn't mind taking that over. And a club: the Picasso. Rollie's the best customer, and he's as queer as a bottle of chips. Old Albert will be turning in his grave.'

'No drugs?'

'Nothing that affects us.'

'He's done all right, considering.'

'Because of George Ritchie.'

'Albert's Brain?'

'Except now, he's Rollie's Brain. Seven years ago, Rollie would've started something he couldn't finish. Ritchie talked him down. The idea of using outside shooters would have come from him.'

I glanced at the Rolex he'd given me. Danny saw me and wasn't pleased. 'Sorry. Am I keeping you from something? You do know we've got decisions to make?'

I made one last stab at changing his mind.

'Look. You hit Anderson, he hits back and, okay, you beat him. Maybe Nina's got a point. Wouldn't it be easier if I wasn't around? I mean, he hasn't been a real problem 'til I showed up. Inside I did plenty of thinking and...'

Danny interrupted, irritation in his voice. 'Thought this was settled. Forget Anderson, we'll deal with him, I need you here.'

'You keep saying that. Why?'

He stood, close to shouting. 'Because I do, that's why. Any idea how much we turned last year?'

'No.'

'Neither do I, that's how much. Things are a lot different these days. Rollie's getting a slap, no question, but it's time you started pulling your weight. Christ knows I've carried you long enough.'

The veins in his neck stuck out. 'I was a good sport about you giving the party a miss. You did us a favour, as it happens. Now it's time to make a contribution. Stop talking and start acting like a Glass.'

He calmed down as quickly as he'd blown up. 'It's about trust, Luke. Who can I trust if I can't trust my own brother, eh?'

England expects and all that bollocks.

Danny wasn't done. 'Putting Anderson back in his box is just part of it. It's the team that's important. The Glass kids play a team game.'

His understanding of a team game was everybody, including me, doing what he said. Buying into his bullshit had taken me where I'd never wanted to go. Prison was a great teacher and I'd had all the time in the world to learn and think what had gone wrong with my life: who I owed and who owed me. None of it was a defence against my brother. He felt my resolve weaken and pressed home his advantage.

'Nothing trumps family. Nothing.'

I shook his hand and said goodbye to everything I'd planned during the long dark nights in Wandsworth. He'd won.

* * *

I'd told Danny about not being able to shake the feeling of being watched, down-playing it because I didn't want him to think I'd gone soft. He'd studied me the way a boy studies a bee in a jar, his dark eyes a mix of curiosity and pity. 'Could be a reaction to almost getting killed the first day you're out. Or, because somebody *is* watching you.'

'You mean Anderson.'

'I mean anybody with a grudge, and yeah, he fits the bill. Told you yesterday – not everybody's pleased to see you back. It's a mistake to assume Anderson's planning to leave it a while before he tries again.'

Danny went into guardian angel mode.

'That's why we need you covered. What're you up to today?'

'Thought I'd have a look around.'

'Who with?'

'By myself?'

He snorted his disapproval. 'After what you've just told me? Forget it.'

'I'm a big boy, Danny.'

My independence exasperated him. 'Anderson almost did for you. From now on you don't go anywhere alone.'

I didn't fight it.

'Okay, where's Felix?'

'I meant somebody reliable.'

'Get me Felix.'

* * *

Marcus gave me a look that left me in no doubt he felt the same about me as I did about him. We hadn't had much to do with each other when Cheryl and Rebecca were still alive and there was no real reason for the animosity that hung between us. Maybe our paths had crossed in another life.

My brother said, 'Luke's going walkabout.'

'Sure, Danny.'

'He wants Felix with him, Christ knows why.'

In the car, I straightened out the confusion Felix might be feeling about what working with me meant. 'Any repeat of the King Pot fiasco and it's over for you. Get it?'

'Yeah, I fucked up. No excuses. Everybody was having a good time, everything was cool. I mean, who gatecrashes a Danny Glass party? I thought...'

I wasn't interested in his version.

'There's your trouble right there: you thought. In future do your job. Leave the thinking to other people.'

'Thanks, anyway.'

'You're welcome. It won't happen a second time.'

9

The Picasso Club was in darkness. In the basement, Rollie Anderson cradled a whisky, unaware that a few miles away Oliver Stanford was climbing the stairs to the office above the King of Mesopotamia and his meeting with Danny Glass. Rollie finished his drink, refilled the tumbler then emptied half of it in one go. Straight Scotch caught the back of his throat, its harshness pleasing him, about the only thing that did.

George Ritchie, his nephew, Jonjo Hart and Charlie Thompson watched their young boss drown his sorrows. Thompson, a heavy-set Liverpudlian more effective with his fists than most thugs were with a knife, shot a glance at twenty-three-year-old Jonjo Hart. Getting drunk wasn't a good idea right now. Hart had followed his uncle, George from the north-east to the capital and hooked-up with him in South London. Thompson and Hart didn't rate Anderson but would follow Ritchie anywhere.

Ritchie spoke to Rollie. 'Go easy on that stuff. We need clear heads.'

Rollie's petulant reply revealed his state of mind. 'Do we?'

'Yes. Today and every day from now on.'

Anderson glared at his father's old lieutenant for admonishing him and kept his hands out of sight so the others in the room wouldn't see his slender fingers shaking. He was gutted, unable to believe they'd failed. Yesterday, surprise was on their side. Now, regaining the territory Albert had controlled would be ten times harder. Even holding onto what they had might not be possible. The Glass family should've been stone cold on mortuary slabs, while he settled to the task of running the biggest criminal organisation either side of the Thames.

But the brothers survived the attack and the celebration he'd planned had become a wake.

Rollie Anderson was nineteen when his father was murdered, too immature and headstrong to be in charge of his operation. Fortunately for him, wise counsel was close by. George Ritchie, Albert's right-hand man for fourteen years, kept the young hothead in check and slowly helped him rebuild the family business. In the early days, Rollie had trusted Ritchie – he'd known him most of his life – and listened to him even when the advice wasn't easy to accept. But with time, that changed. Albert Anderson's boy grew tired of being told that sooner or later the solution or the opportunity would arrive.

Well, it had, and they'd botched it.

Rollie's face was pale; he didn't feel well. 'The chance was there and we blew it.'

Ritchie had been in the dark about the raid and only found out after it had happened. There would be a time for anger. This wasn't it. He kept his in check.

'It was bad luck. Nobody's fault. The brothers should've been in the bar. Who could've known they'd have other ideas?'

'"Nobody's fault."' Anderson repeated the phrase in a monotone, his eyes boring into his lieutenant. 'Is that supposed to help, George? Because it doesn't. It doesn't fucking help anything.'

'Rollie, it was—'

'Bad luck, yeah, you told me. We showed our hand. They've been warned. Our advantage is gone. And fucking Luke Glass is still breathing.' Anderson choked back his disappointment. 'That bastard murdered my father.'

Ritchie knew luck had nothing to do with it. The attack had gone wrong. Apart from the fact it obviously hadn't been properly planned – for Christ's sake, they didn't know the brothers weren't there – it was a crazy idea to begin with, a high-risk strategy he would never have sanctioned – the reason he'd been left out of the loop. History repeating itself. With Albert it had been a car bomb he'd put under Glass's car. Now, like a spoiled child, Anderson was lashing out. Weak and pathetic. Though it raised another issue: George Ritchie had stepped in and salvaged a leaderless organisation on the understanding that Rollie – still not yet twenty – would eventually take over. He'd assumed a gradual transition with him fading into the background. That time had come, except the son wasn't ready. And he might never be ready because he didn't have what it took.

Ritchie tried to reassure his young boss. 'We keep our heads down and tighten security. Glass will get his. In the long run, we'll nail him.'

'Will we? You sure? Because it didn't go off when it was supposed to, did it? We haven't enough men on the ground for an all-out fight.'

A pity the stupid bastard hadn't thought of that before. There was nobody to blame but himself. Ritchie was ahead of him, as ever smoothing the ground. 'Not a problem. I've already been on to Liverpool and Birmingham. We can turn this thing around. Six months down the line, it'll all look different.'

'That a promise, George?'

'That's a promise, Rollie. But first things first. They're bound to come back at us. We need to be ready.'

* * *

Luke had been gone less than a minute before Danny Glass pressed the buzzer on his desk. Marcus reappeared. 'Got a job for you. Find out everything you can about George Ritchie.'

'Everything meaning what?'

'Start with what he had for breakfast this morning and take it from there.'

'Thought it was his boss we'd be going after.'

'Don't think. Thinking isn't your strong suit, Marcus. Just do it.'

* * *

At the door of the King Pot, two men, hands in pockets, cigarettes wedged in the corners of their mouths, lowered their heads as Nina walked across the fading chalk outline on the pavement into the morning light. One of them let his fag fall from nicotine-stained fingers and crushed the butt under his heel, his crooked teeth locked in a lewd grin. He whispered something she couldn't make out to his mate and dropped into step behind her. A bodyguard, for fuck's sake. It seemed ridiculous.

Twenty-four hours earlier she'd been washing her hair, looking forward to picking Luke up outside Wandsworth. Having him around again, even for a while, would be good. Danny credited himself with bringing them up, and it was true; but it was Luke she'd been closest to. Then and now. Her favourite brother hadn't brought this down on them. That dubious honour was reserved for Albert Anderson. Danny felt having a sister put him and Luke at a disadvantage. In this case, he was right. It gave Anderson an option: kidnap her and use her as leverage, maybe even offer to give her up in exchange for Luke.

Not happening. Definitely not happening. Putting up with the creep her brother had ordered to follow her was one thing – she'd rely on herself to stay safe.

Nina fumbled for her car keys, fingers trembling, visualising the explosion that had ended the lives of Cheryl and Rebecca when the bomb had gone off.

Danny had always been a mad-arse but that was when his grip on reality had really started to slip. Yet, underestimating him would be a mistake – as his enemies had discovered over the years. The throwaway comment about her 'little disappearing acts' was almost as disturbing as the threat from Rollie Anderson. He was telling her he knew about her affair with Vale and they'd be smart to cool their jets before he sussed the true extent of her relationship with the accountant. That hadn't happened. Not yet, thank God, otherwise he wouldn't have allowed her to leave the office. Danny prized loyalty above everything. Team Glass and all that crap. After what he'd done for them growing up, her betrayal would anger him more than losing the money. Money could be replaced. Retribution would be swift and merciless.

The idea of stealing from him had come one day when she'd been remembering the past. Nina's version was very different from her brother's. Danny had strange notions about women, even his sister. According to him, they were only good for one thing. In their dysfunctional household, unlike Luke, she'd been tolerated rather than loved. Never rated, and she probably never would be – a realisation that had become her inspiration. He talked about a three-way split. Long ago Nina had decided not to depend on it. Making sure she got qualifications – even if it meant going to night school – was part of the plan. Danny had his finger in a lot of pies, including real estate, but how he earned most of his money was shifty. What she had in mind took cash. A lot of cash. Buying and selling property, heading a team of smart people, not the kind of moron tailing her.

She waited until she was in the car before calling Vale. They'd had a telephone conversation the previous night; Eugene had offered to come to her flat. A gesture she'd instinctively turned away; she didn't need a man to protect her.

The number rang out; she let it. Finally, he answered, breathless and surprised. 'Nina?'

Nina blurted out what she'd called to tell him.

'He knows.'

Vale couldn't keep his voice steady. 'What? Who knows?'

The name fell from Nina's lips.

'Danny.'

'Fucking hell! Hold on.'

The line went quiet. At the other end, Vale put his hand over the receiver and hissed impatiently to the woman kneeling between his naked thighs. 'Stop. Stop. Not now.'

Yvonne wiped her mouth with her hand and got to her feet, glaring at him. Vale pulled his trousers up and waved her out of the room. When she'd gone, he brought his attention back to his mobile, struggling to get the words out.

'Exactly what does Danny know, Nina?'

'About you and me.'

'About you and me and...'

'And nothing.'

Vale fell back in his chair. 'Thank God. What did he say?'

'We had a family meeting. As I was leaving, he called me out on my "little disappearing acts".'

'This is bad, this is very bad.'

The rush of fear in his voice almost had Nina feeling sorry for him; she'd had him down as weak from the beginning. And here he was, cracking at the first sign of pressure.

Her reply was cool, contempt lapping at the edges. 'It isn't a crime, Eugene.'

He tried to backtrack. 'No, no, of course not. That isn't what I meant.'

'Then what did you mean?'

'Danny isn't stupid. If he's made the connection it's only a matter of time before he puts two and two together and comes up with the right answer.' In the office, sweat filmed on the accountant's forehead. 'We're fucked, Nina. We're fucked. Oh, Christ—'

'Only if we panic.'

Vale spoke to the room. 'We haven't been greedy. Not really. But stopping now won't save us. He'll suss what we've been doing. The cash keeps coming in, the numbers will spike. He'll see the figures, ask himself what's different, and bingo!'

Listening to him go to pieces down the line, Nina recognised Eugene Vale was a bigger threat to her than her brother. She interrupted his meltdown and took charge. 'Get a grip. Be a man. First up, we don't lose our heads. Danny knows about me and you. So what? I'm a big girl. That's all he knows. If he'd had even a suspicion of something more, I wouldn't be here and you'd be in the back of a van on your way to Fulton Street. We'll be okay so long as we keep it together.'

Vale was a long way from keeping it together. The reference to Danny's retribution made him want to be sick; he covered his mouth to stop himself from vomiting over the carpet where Yvonne had been kneeling. At the end of the day, Nina was Danny's sister and blood was thicker than water. Chances were, he'd go easy on her and bury him – literally.

'Eugene? Eugene, are you still there?'

'Yeah...yes.'

'We act normal.'

'And keep seeing each other?'

'Of course. Anything else would attract attention.'

'Are you sure that's the right thing?'

Stupid question: of course, she wasn't sure.

Nina brushed a strand of hair off her forehead and forced confidence into her reply.

'Absolutely, Danny doesn't have to approve of my personal life. Whether he realises it or not, those days are gone.'

'What about the skim – should we cool our jets?'

'No, we continue, step it up, even.'

'Up? You can't be serious.'

Before making a move on him, Nina had done her homework. There was a reason he'd never taken her to his flat. Two divorces had cleaned the accountant out, he'd lost the nice houses he'd owned – one in Brixton, a cool place to live these days, the other in a leafy avenue in Clapham – and now he was living in a bedsit in Stockwell. Even in desperate times though, without Nina pushing him, he'd have been too terrified to touch a penny of Danny's cash.

'We agreed not to quit until each of us had what we needed. I don't know about you but I'm a long way short. Let's not kid ourselves: Danny will find out. Eventually. By then, we'll be gone.'

Silence on the other end of the line told her she had him. When he spoke, it was in a whisper. 'You're saying... you're saying...'

'I've no intention of stopping or scaling down. We have to go on.'

Nina took reassurance from the fact that Vale hadn't broken completely. That gave her something to work with, though not much. The new conflict with Anderson wasn't the worst news. The longer it went on, the better. It would distract Danny.

In Lewisham, Vale slumped behind his desk, his head in his hands; he needed the conversation to end. Nina sensed he couldn't take on any more and ended it. 'I'll contact you in a couple of days. Don't worry, it'll be fine.'

The accountant had a final question. 'You said if he'd found out I'd be on my way to Fulton Street. What did you mean? What's at Fulton Street?'

'Believe me, Eugene, you never want to find out.'

10

The sky above New Scotland Yard in the Curtis Green building on the Victoria Embankment was overcast and heavy. In the room, the atmosphere matched it. DI Trevor Mills and DS Bob Wallace were quietly discussing the events south of the river when the senior man came in and took his seat. DCI Stanford didn't acknowledge them.

Stanford dropped a manila folder on the table and pushed it away, his eyes travelling over their faces – men he trusted; people with more in common than anyone could ever know.

He let the silence do its work before he spoke. 'As you can imagine, it hasn't been a great morning so far. I've just come from a meeting with the commissioner, among others. Without going into details let me say... it wasn't pleasant.'

Stanford drew a deep breath and blew it out. 'Before that, I had a chat with Danny Glass. Another experience I didn't enjoy very much. Mr Glass wanted to tell me in person how disappointed he is with our performance and, despicable fucking low life that he is, I agree with him. So, a simple question. What happened?'

Trevor Mills shot an anxious look at Bob Wallace. The detectives had risen through the ranks and prided themselves on having their fingers on the pulse of the city's underworld. On the evidence, those fingers had been somewhere else.

Stanford said, 'I'll put it another way. What the fuck happened yesterday and why were we the last to hear about it?'

Blank expressions.

He drew the folder towards him and held it in the air. 'This initial report is crap. Absolute bollocks. Statements, eyewitness accounts, all of it. A gigantic exercise in time-wasting. Why? Because we know – the whole of South London knows – Anderson is responsible. I could've written it up without getting out of this chair and made it more believable.'

He glared at his fellow officers; his features taut with loathing. No humiliating third degree for them. They avoided making eye contact. Their record was as solid as anybody's in the Met and it was rare for the boss to lose his temper. When he did, the smartest thing was to keep your head down until the hurricane blew itself out.

Stanford got himself under control. Losing it wouldn't get them anywhere.

'Glass is angry. I don't blame him, don't blame him at all. In his shoes, I'd feel exactly the same. He's alive, no thanks to us.'

DS Wallace raised his hand. 'Why not just let them get on with it?'

A look passed between Stanford and DI Mills. Mills was a sallow, intelligent man with sharp eyes and a quick mind; quietly efficient and still ambitious, even after twenty years on the force. The two senior officers had worked closely together for ten of those years and were friends who knew everything about each other. Mills answered his colleague.

'Am I hearing right? If you really think that's an option, you're in the wrong room.'

'I'm serious. Let them kill each other – it's what they want. Save ourselves a lot of trouble.'

Stanford stepped between them. He didn't mind friction; it showed passion, and passion was a necessity in successful police work. Now wasn't the time – they were under pressure, which was only going to get heavier. The DCI saw his career stalling and that wasn't in the plan.

'We have a triple murder on our patch and already the media are jumping up and down calling it the first shots in a turf war. The home secretary and the prime minister are concerned, naturally. Likewise, Sir Ian. Cowboy shoot-outs on the streets of the capital aren't what the commissioner likes to read about over his eggs Benedict. He'll be making a statement later and stressed how important it is to prevent any escalation of violence. On top of that, the mayor's in on the act. Banging his drum about the capital's murder rate. It's up this year, as if we didn't know. He's expecting us, not unreasonably, to bring it down to something that doesn't make his well-known position on law and order look silly. Not hard to see where he's coming from, is it?'

He paused. 'And that brings us to our own little dilemma. We've cocked up and I want somebody to tell me why. Anderson's a vicious bastard, same as his old man, but you couldn't accuse him of being bright, so it isn't possible nobody knew what was going to go off. Yet the word didn't get through. Why is that?'

Wallace came in again. 'At the risk of getting shot down in balls of shit, how certain are we it was Anderson? I mean, Glass isn't short of enemies.'

'True, except yesterday his brother, Luke – the guy who sent Albert Anderson over the edge of a high-rise – came out of Wandsworth. There was a party in their pub. The three of them should've been there – Danny, Luke and their sister, Nina. They weren't, that's why they're still breathing. Rollie's waited seven years. Seems he thought that was long enough.'

'The brother was the target?'

Stanford said, 'Glass certainly thinks so. He wants us to protect Luke. Round the clock.'

Wallace wouldn't let it go. 'Isn't he capable of looking after his own?'

'He's getting his money's worth, Bob. Wouldn't you?'

Stanford anticipated the next question. 'And before you ask about overtime, the commissioner approved it an hour ago in the interests of containing the situation. He realises there's no love lost. Albert Anderson murdered Glass's wife and daughter in a car bomb. Luke sorted old Albert's hash for good. It's a tinderbox that's been smouldering away for years. Could go off at any minute and seems like it's going to. These people are locked together by family and history: Rollie adored his old man – Christ alone knows why – and Danny brought Luke and his sister up after their mother abandoned them and their father died of drink. Anything happens to his brother... remember who we're dealing with. Glass is a psychopath. But he's *our* psychopath. And don't forget it. Nobody benefits from a bloodbath. Too much publicity. The last thing we need is Channel Four doing an in-depth profile on gangland London and, inevitably, asking what the hell we're doing about it. Your informants must think you're pushovers. Let them know that isn't the case. As for the investigation—' he flung the folder into the middle of the table '—go over this junk. And get it right this time. I want proof. Anderson has to go down for this.'

He stood. 'Oh, one more thing. Glass doesn't intend to sit quietly while Albert's boy tries to do him in. He plans to hit him where it'll hurt, in his pocket. That takes information. Get anything and everything you can dig up about Rollie's operation. Lean on whoever you need to get it. Keep Glass believing we're on his side.'

Mills offered some black humour. 'And aren't we?'

It didn't get a laugh. Stanford took the question seriously. 'Actually, no, we aren't. There's only one side and that's our side.'

The officers headed for the door. Trevor Mills held back. 'What's up with Wallace? His attitude seems... strange.'

The same thought had crossed Stanford's mind. 'I agree. Keep an eye on him, Trevor. We can't afford any more cock-ups.'

Mills let his anxiety show. 'How bad is it really, boss?'

'Bad. Glass is almost out of control. If Anderson is stupid enough to attack him again, it'll be a battlefield down there and, whatever the commissioner chooses to tell the PM, there won't be anything we can do to stop it.'

'What if Anderson wins?'

'Then we'd better pray he leaves Danny Glass dead. I'll tell you, Trevor, there would be a reckoning. He'd take us down with him. All it would need is a word in the right ear.'

He allowed the consequences to sink in.

'Everything would come out. We'd be finished.'

* * *

We drove in silence through streets I should have recognised but didn't. This time yesterday I was stepping into the world, determined to make a fresh start. A day later I'd had a hangover, a hooker, a face-to-face with a bent detective chief inspector and somebody had tried to kill me. A busy beginning. Thanks to Rollie Anderson it looked like the old band was getting back together after all. I parked behind a building on a concrete space of open ground strewn with broken glass and unfastened my seat belt. Felix did the same.

'Don't bother, you're not coming.'

'Thought I was supposed to go everywhere with you?'

'Not everywhere.'

Felix wasn't having it. 'Sorry, Luke. Danny wants me glued to you. I'm coming.'

In the bank, he browsed through leaflets on savings accounts and mortgages while a girl with Rasta curls and dark brown eyes gave me a printout of my balance and went into her routine. I could see her mentally going through her lines. When she was ready, she cleared her throat, fluttered her eyelashes and said, 'You have a substantial sum in your account, Mr Glass. Would you like some advice about what investments offer the best return?'

'No, thanks.'

'Are you sure? I could check if one of our advisors is available to speak to you.'

'No, I'm fine.'

Without missing a beat, she moved to the next page from the training manual.

'Have you decided what you intend to do with your capital?'

'I've got a vivid imagination. I'll think of something.'

She smiled a wooden smile. 'Is there anything else I can help with? Anything at all?'

'Really, I'm fine. Thanks for your help.'

I put the statement in my pocket and resisted the urge to discover how much a 'substantial sum' was until I had a drink in front of me. Felix followed me out the door.

And there it was again, that feeling.

Felix picked up on the change in me – his hand went to the gun under his jacket in a reflex reaction. 'What is it?'

I looked up and down the street. 'No, it's nothing.'

But the sensation didn't shift.

* * *

The Admiral Collingwood rose like a ghost ship in full sail, stately and majestic on the corner. The Admiral was the kind of place my father had drunk in, a no-frills boozer that smelled the way pubs used to smell at opening time – a mix of hops and disinfectant. Danny bought me my first pint in the snug when I was fifteen, him doing the talking while I stayed in the background trying to look older.

In the old days, the barman was an ex-boxer with a million stories about what went on behind the scenes in the fight game. Fantastic tales you couldn't invent because he already had. If you believed him, he'd rubbed shoulders with the best of them. He was a character, a teller of tall tales, and he drew a following that stood at the bar egging him on. He was a likeable blowhard with the quality great barmen had; on a rainy Tuesday night when you were the only one in the place, he'd drop the act and become a guy you could have a conversation with. Good listener, too. Being deaf in one cauliflower ear probably didn't help.

One thing about him: he always looked pleased to see you. Not so the dour-faced weedy bloke in a grey cardigan pulling pints now, who turned a passive-hostile expression on me and drained the double whisky I'd asked for from an optic without so much as a word. The Admiral had gone the way of everything I'd come across. Felix stood with his back against the bar, taking in everything and everyone in the room. I couldn't complain; the guy was keen, anxious to make amends for his mistake during the raid.

'Orange juice okay for you?'

His face brightened when the barman put the pint I'd ordered in front of him.

I wiped crisps off a table at the back, sat down and opened the statement. The girl at the bank had been anxious to help. Now I understood why. Business had been good while I was away. Albert Anderson might've been an evil old fucker but he'd known how to turn a coin. With him out of the picture it had been easy for Danny to take over some of his territory. This was my share. Seven years' worth. And it was a lot.

I was struggling to get a hold on my new financial status when a blast from the past walked in the door: Vincent Finnegan.

Finnegan and Sean Poland, another Irishman, worked for my brother doing jobs where finesse wasn't a requirement. They were an odd couple and they stuck together. You bumped into one, you could bet the other wasn't far away. I hadn't met either of them since before the trial and remembered Poland as stocky and quiet. More than quiet, deep; the type you'd stay on nodding terms with for a lifetime. Finnegan was the opposite, a swaggering bastard with plenty to say for himself: streetwise, handsome and, like his pal, tough as buggery. In those days he'd been a sharp dresser, spending most of his money on clothes. The snappy image added menace, though he wasn't short in that department whatever he was wearing. Danny hadn't employed the paddys for their good looks or social skills. If you were unfortunate enough to have them appear on your doorstep you were in the shit. Today there was no sign of Poland. Finnegan was by himself.

A morning of surprises didn't prepare me. Vincent Finnegan's swagger was replaced by a limp, his coat had seen better days and he leaned on a stick. He squeezed in at the end of the bar, ordered a drink and counted change to pay for it into his hand with the deliberation of a backward child. It didn't take a genius to figure that, physically as well as financially, Vincent had gone down in the world.

We were never friends – his kind didn't do friends – but he was a familiar face in an alien landscape and once upon a time he'd been a force to be reckoned with. Except, that was then. Today he was a disabled man in middle age, watching the pennies. I'd no idea who Danny had on the payroll these days. Finnegan couldn't be one of them. Not in this state.

He took a sip of his beer and looked round the bar, but I was beside him before he realised I was there. Up close, the skin on his forehead was dry; dandruff gathered like confetti on his collar. It took him a moment to recognise me. When he did, he tried to shuffle away. I put a hand on his shoulder and stopped him.

'Hi, Vincent. Long time no see.'

He shrank from me, fear in his eyes. A nervous smile appeared and disappeared, then returned as he pretended to be pleased to see me. We shook hands and I said, 'This your local?'

He was reluctant to commit himself. 'I come in most days, yeah. When did they let you out?'

'Yesterday.'

He nodded. 'Hung over?'

'Nothing a hair of the dog won't fix.'

'Party, was there?'

'Didn't fancy it. Gave it a miss.'

Vincent made a face. 'Then you're a brave man.'

'What makes you say that?'

He didn't reply and changed the subject. 'Any plans?'

'Too soon.'

'Yeah.' He shuffled his feet. 'It takes the time it takes.'

'What about you?'

'Retired.'

'You're kidding, you're too young. Nobody told me you'd packed it in. Thought you were still working for Danny.'

The mention of my brother's name brought a change in his expression.

'Not for a while.'

'What're you doing?'

'Bit of this, bit of that. Getting by.'

He didn't look like a man who was getting by. I realised it was kinder not to ask too many questions. 'Listen, I'll put a word in. Tell him you could do with a tickle.'

He scratched the stubble on his jaw. 'Rather you stayed out of it, Luke. Danny and me didn't end well.'

'How do you mean?'

'There was a... a misunderstanding.'

'A misunderstanding? What you on about?'

I'd touched a nerve.

'Leave it, will you?'

Vincent was part of the original team. He and my brother went way back. Being told something had come between them was difficult to believe. Yet something had because Finnegan couldn't get away from me fast enough. He gulped down his pint and put a hand on my shoulder. 'Good seeing you. Always liked you. I'm fine. Honest. Take care of yourself. And, Luke, watch your back, eh?'

He limped to the door and tried some of his old bravado on for size, gave me a thumbs-up and winked. Jack the Lad to the end.

'Don't do anything I wouldn't do, kid.'

From what I remembered of Vincent, that gave me plenty of scope.

11

Yvonne smiled a tight, humourless smile and closed the door, her cheeks burning from the humiliation she'd suffered at the hands of Vale. He was a bastard; then again, she'd known that from the beginning. The affair with Danny Glass's sister wasn't a shock: a womaniser like Eugene couldn't keep his cock in his trousers. Yvonne had no problem with that. For both of them it was about uncomplicated sex, pure and simple. Eugene Vale wasn't husband material, his two divorces spoke eloquently to that. Betrayal didn't come into it; they'd promised each other nothing. But treating her like something stuck on the bottom of his shoe wasn't on.

Yvonne realised the conversation meant trouble. Trouble big enough to make Eugene's prick die in her hand.

His raised voice drifted to the outer office, almost daring her to eavesdrop. Who could resist? She pressed her ear to the space between the frame and the panel. On the other side of the door, Vale was clearly still agitated.

'This is bad, this is very bad.'

His words set her mind racing, trying to figure out what was going on. 'Danny isn't stupid. If he's made the connection it's only a matter of time before he puts two and two together and comes up with the right answer. We're fucked, Nina. We're fucked. Oh, Christ—'

If Danny had made the connection. What connection?

The old floorboards creaked as he paced the room. 'We haven't been greedy. Not really. But stopping now won't save us. He'll suss what we've been doing. The cash keeps coming in, the numbers will spike. He'll see the figures, ask himself what's different, and bingo!'

Realisation hit Yvonne like a blow, her brain processing what she was hearing: they were stealing. Stealing from Danny Glass.

Jesus Christ Almighty!

A helluva lot of cash passed through the office – she'd seen it with her own eyes. Most people would be tempted to help themselves before remembering who the money belonged to and leaving it where it was. Eugene Vale was a pen-pusher; on his own, he didn't have the balls for something like this. It had to have been the sister's idea. It had to have been Nina.

Yvonne wasn't clever. Her most important assets as a secretary were her tits and her tight little arse. But she was streetwise enough to recognise an opportunity when saw one. This wasn't the time to make her move; she needed a plan. She plastered on a smile and went through the door. Eugene was behind his desk, head cradled in his hands, shoulders silently shaking, and didn't acknowledge her even when she put her arms around him and pressed his face between her breasts. Vale fell back in his chair. Yvonne pulled down his zip, then his trousers, and spread his thighs, relishing her new-found power. She had him where she wanted him in more ways than one.

Her fingers found what she was after. 'Now,' she said, 'where were we?'

* * *

Danny was right about the neighbourhood: I hardly recognised it. Night after night, lying in the dark in Wandsworth, it was the ordinary stuff I'd missed: buying a paper from the newsagents on the corner,

Aldo's greasy-spoon fry-ups, and sweet and sour pork from the Red Dragon. Everyday experiences, which grew in my mind into towering landmarks of the life I'd left behind. It didn't occur to me they might not exist. The drive became a search for something to connect with and as the truth that I wasn't going to find it slowly dawned, a depression even the novelty of the Audi couldn't shake settled over me: I didn't belong here any more.

I let Felix off so he could get his own wheels – no way was he coming with me, not where I was going.

Mandy was waiting at the kerb wearing a black and yellow off-the-shoulder print dress, a matching sunhat and the tallest high heels I'd ever seen. Getting into the car, she let me have a good long look at her legs. She took off the hat, pushed the shades up into her hair and sat back in the seat.

'Big Boys' toys.'

I thought she was talking about the legs – it took a moment for the penny to drop: she meant the car.

'Oh, yeah. A present from Danny. Don't worry, I'll pay for it one way or the other – he'll make sure I do.'

Mandy started to say something and stopped herself.

I said, 'Where do you want to go?'

She shook her head slowly and smiled. 'You're a nice guy, Luke, you really are.'

The 'but' was unmistakable.

'What's that supposed to mean?'

Mandy shrugged. 'I'm just saying you're nice. What's wrong with that?'

'Nothing. Except I'm not sure what it means.'

Her reply was unconvincing. 'Why does it have to mean anything?'

'Because it does. When a woman tells a man he's "a nice guy", she's saying more than he realises. I'm asking what.'

We pulled up at traffic lights. Two or three of the men crossing in front of us glanced at the car, sparkling in the London sunshine, and the redhead in the passenger seat. One of them unconsciously mouthed his opinion: lucky bastard. He'd get no argument from me.

Mandy's perfume was in my head – not the cool midnight scent from before, this was sweeter, the smell of summer.

'I want to know, Mandy.'

'You already know.'

She put the sunglasses on again so her eyes were hidden. Maybe it made what she wanted to do easier. Before I could react, her lips were on mine and she was kissing me: none of that slow-motion malarkey they do in the movies; the real thing. We broke apart when the car behind us tooted his horn. I had my answer.

* * *

We raced hand-in-hand up the stairs to my flat and burst through the door, clinging to each other like castaways staggering from the sea onto a beach. Mandy said, 'Give me a minute,' and went into the room, leaving me standing in the hall like a fool. I counted from one to sixty under my breath and abandoned it at forty-two. Not bad, considering. The dress and hat lay on the floor beside her underwear. Only the shoes with the high heels had made it to the bed. Mandy raised a perfectly toned leg in the air and dangled one shoe on her crimson toes, then slowly, deliberately, let it fall, her eyes not leaving mine. Her naked body arched and spread like a feast for a starving man.

I tore off my clothes and let the banquet begin.

* * *

My need was great. Hers was greater. Being loved how she wanted to be loved wasn't something she was used to, and it showed. Time after time, I resisted being drawn into the depths of her. Her response was to quicken her rhythm. Finally, she broke over my body, and we kept going until she was moaning again in my ear and I felt the sting of her nails cutting bloody lines in my back. Eventually, she had all of me in a spasm of mutual joy, which went on and on.

We lay with each other's sweat drying on us, not talking because there was nothing to say. But in the shared silence, with her heart beating against mine, the knowledge it couldn't last crowded in, souring my mood.

I sat on the edge of the bed while she ran her fingers along the welts on either side of my spine.

'I'm sorry. I couldn't help myself.'

I shook my head. She noticed the change and I sensed her daring herself to speak.

'Did I disappoint you?'

'You could never do that. It isn't possible.'

She disagreed. 'Everything's possible, Luke.'

'No,' I said, 'not everything.'

* * *

It was late. We were stretched out on the couch where we'd made love again, our arms round each other, watching a rerun of *Raiders of the Lost Ark*. On the TV, Indy was in the cellar surrounded by vipers slithering over each other, their forked tongues darting in and out of their mouths.

It had been quite a night. Mandy had offered to rustle up something to eat, but my fridge was empty apart from what remained of the lager Danny had left. Turning a famine into a feast took a phone call to the local Indian restaurant. Twenty-five minutes later we were wolfing our way through vegetable samosas, chicken jalfrezi, pilau rice and the biggest naan bread I'd ever seen, washed down with a plonk the Fatherland couldn't get shot of fast enough, so cold it didn't taste of anything.

I glanced across at Mandy, happily tearing lumps off the bread. Her face was free of make-up and I caught the girl she'd been before her life got complicated and difficult; there was an innocence and a vulnerability I promised myself I wouldn't abuse.

We moved on to the lager – almost as tasteless as the wine – and watched back-to-back soaps.

'Why don't you like my brother?'

Stupid bloody question; the people who disliked Danny would fill the Albert Hall three times over.

'He doesn't like me.'

I let it go and the conversation moved on. But the night was ending on a low note. She gave me the ghost of a kiss on her way out. Her lips brushed my cheek and she was gone.

It was almost two o'clock in the morning. Going to bed would be a waste of time; I wasn't tired. Danny had bought books to decorate the flat. The cover of the one I picked was cracked, the edges dog-eared; the others would be the same – he'd got them from a charity shop. Reading wasn't something I'd done a lot of in my life, but in Wandsworth I'd got through two or three crime-fiction novels a week. Then and now, the irony didn't escape me.

Sixty pages in, the words started to blur on the page. I lay back and closed my eyes; the book had served its purpose. A sound came from somewhere over my shoulder. Instantly, I was on my feet, tiptoeing towards it clutching the wine bottle by the neck, feeling its reassuring weight in my fingers.

The door handle turned. I couldn't hear anything except my heart thumping in my chest. Was this Anderson having another go? The bottle wouldn't be much use against guns; I traded it for the cricket bat – still not good enough, but better.

Without knowing how many of them I was up against, I hesitated. Seconds passed while I steadied myself. Finally, I pulled the door wide open and dived to the floor.

There was nobody there.

The sound of footsteps on the stairs had me running. Outside, the street was deserted apart from parked cars. In one of them I saw the featureless silhouette of a man hunched behind the wheel. When he saw me coming, he started the engine. But he was too slow. I threw the door open and dragged him onto the pavement. The coffee he'd been drinking spilled down the front of his coat and he stared at me, surprise in his eyes and fear on his face.

My fist connected with his nose. In the stillness of the early hours, I heard it break. Like a twig snapping underfoot on the forest floor. He screamed and threw his hands up to protect himself. I hit him again and hauled him to his feet. He was breathing hard, blood bubbling at his nostrils and down into his open mouth.

'Who're you working for? Tell me!'

His reply stopped me in my tracks and I let go.

'Stanford. Stanford sent me.'

* * *

The police were on the case: good to know I was safe... my arse. The man wiped his mouth and glared resentment at me.

'Did you see them?'

'See who?'

'Whoever tried to break into my flat?'

He got a tissue from a box in the glove compartment and dabbed his face. 'You've broken my bloody nose.'

He was due an apology. Right at that moment I couldn't raise one. People didn't come in silently and uninvited in the middle of the night to say hello.

'How long have you been here?'

'Since nine o'clock.'

I was in trouble if this guy was the best Oliver Stanford had.

'Do you want me to check around the back?'

'Don't bother. Whoever it was, they're gone. Why did you start the engine when you saw me?'

'It was a reflex when you came charging at me with the bat.'

There wasn't much I could say. 'And you didn't notice anybody hanging around?'

He shook his head. In the streetlight his nose was a lump in the middle of his face.

'Your girlfriend left. Since then there hasn't even been a car.'

I gave him another tissue – he looked as if he needed it; the engine was still running and he got behind the wheel. When his boss told him to sit outside my house, he'd probably thought his biggest challenge was not emptying his bladder all over his trousers: a broken nose didn't come into it. It would be agony in the morning.

He rolled down the window and offered me a piece of advice.

'Do me a favour. The next time something spooks you in the middle of the night, remember we're on your side, will you?'

He didn't believe anybody had been there. For a moment, neither did I.

12

George Ritchie got into the car and stretched. It had been a long day and he wasn't twenty-five any more. The strain was beginning to show on everyone connected to the Anderson crew. Danny Glass hadn't come back at them. For sure, he would. It was just a matter of when, where and how hard.

An assault in the heart of his own territory was an affront: four people – three dead, the other wounded – no way Glass wouldn't retaliate. Ritchie knew Danny of old: a mad-arse psychopath capable of anything. Hour after hour spent in the office upstairs in the Picasso Club, watching Rollie come apart, hadn't been easy. Long spells of silence when Albert's son hadn't said a word had ended with him boiling over, shouting wild talk about what he was going to do to the Glass brothers. For a man like Ritchie it was difficult to be around, yet he understood: the boy was scared. As his father's old lieutenant, he didn't blame him for that. Rollie was a chip off the old block, an idiot, just like Albert, and whatever angry nonsense he spewed, the ball was with the brothers.

The driver looked in the rear-view mirror and asked George the same question he asked him every night. And every night he got a different answer. 'Where to?'

'Clapham Common.'

'Clapham Common, it is.'

Ritchie sat back in his seat and closed his eyes. When he opened them again, they were at the Tube station. He got out and the car rejoined the traffic. His route home was never planned. Each night he picked a location out of the air. No pattern or logic beyond mixing it up and protecting himself from anyone anxious to know more about him than he wanted them to. It was clumsy, overly elaborate, but it worked.

He spotted them almost at once – the same clowns from the day before giving it another go – and allowed himself a smile. Glass would have to start using better people.

From Clapham he rode five stops to Elephant & Castle and changed to the Bakerloo Line, now and then glancing over his shoulder to see if they were still with him. At Piccadilly Circus he waited until the last second before stepping off and letting the train pull away before making for the exit, the late-evening sunshine and fresh air. For a few minutes he stopped to listen to two young blond-haired guys with guitars on the steps under Eros, singing songs Ritchie didn't recognise.

He strolled along Green Park, past the Ritz hotel and on to Hyde Park Corner where he crossed the road and made his way back again. To a casual observer, Ritchie would've seemed like somebody with no particular place to go, a relaxed guy enjoying the beat of the street on a late-summer evening. In fact, he was anything but relaxed. Last night and again tonight, he'd had company: three men in a car at the club, two on the Tube, then just one.

He also knew they weren't there now.

* * *

The man spoke reluctantly into the mobile phone, knowing what he had to report wasn't going to be well received.

'Lost him at Piccadilly. We need more bodies on this.'

Danny Glass reacted to the news exactly as expected, snarling, ready to blame whoever was handy.

'Do I have to do everything myself?' He singled out Marcus. 'Well, do I?'

Marcus tried to reason with him. 'Ritchie isn't just any old tosser, Danny. He's a fox. Streetwise and cautious.'

His boss wasn't having any of it. 'Cautious! Jumping on and off Tube trains is more than cautious. He knows we're after him. Knew it from the beginning. And how does he know?'

'Danny—'

'Because we're not good enough at our job, that's how.'

'We can give it another go tomorrow, put different people on it.'

'"Another go tomorrow". We've already had two. How many more do we need?' Glass shook his head. 'Though you're right, Ritchie's a fox, which means we have to be smarter. Think we're smarter than he is, Marcus? I don't. Not on this showing. The second he sussed we were after him, was the second it all got hard. We may have blown it. We're lucky he decided to just give us the slip instead of taking a couple of our guys out.'

'That isn't his game, is it?'

'You're having a laugh, aren't you? He'd slit your throat as soon as look at you. He was Anderson's enforcer for years. How do you imagine he got that gig? He's as ruthless as they come and, as we've just been reminded, he's clever. Albert's Brain, remember?'

'Yeah but—'

'When I was stealing fags and bottles of vodka from corner shops it wasn't Albert I wanted to avoid, it was George. Christ knows how many bodies are holding this city up because of him. As soon as we started our nonsense, he would've seen us off, no problem.'

'Why didn't he?'

'I'm guessing Anderson never said the word. George would've taken us out of the picture. Me and Luke would be part of a motorway somewhere.'

'You think he talked to Anderson?'

'I'd bet money on it.'

'He wouldn't listen?'

'Albert had been king of the hill so long he thought it was his birthright. George doesn't look for trouble. If it finds him, he'll face it head-on, but confrontation isn't his way. If Ritchie had been calling the shots, we would've hashed a deal that kept everybody happy. For a while. And when he'd convinced us everything was fine, he'd have made his move.'

'Then the bomb doesn't sound like Ritchie.'

In seven years, nobody had been stupid enough to mention Cheryl and Rebecca around Danny. He seemed not to have noticed where the conversation had gone.

Marcus said: 'I'm guessing Albert panicked. Luke went down for killing him and Rollie took over. Why didn't Ritchie leave?'

'To go where? No, he made the right choice. Rollie was nineteen, too young and too inexperienced to run things. He needed somebody he could depend on. George was in a stronger position than ever. Hunky-dory, until the son made the same impulsive mistake as his father.'

'The attack on the King Pot?'

'Yeah. Started the whole thing up again. Only this time we'll do what we didn't do before. Finish the bastards.'

'Meanwhile Ritchie knows we're after him.'

'Change the faces and increase the numbers. Could be we'll get another shot, though maybe not, this guy is nobody's mug. Get that message across.'

The history lesson was over. Glass added a final instruction. 'Remember, Luke isn't on board with this. Keep what we're about away from him. Understand? And, Marcus, one other thing. Mention the bomb ever again and I'll kill you.'

13

Golden light poured from the windows of the mock-Tudor building known as The Old Coach House, over the Mercedes and the Range Rover parked in the drive. Trevor Mills drew to a stop beside the expensive machines. They were the first guests to arrive by the looks of it. Not good. Too many opportunities for his wife to clock their hosts' lifestyle and compare it unfavourably to their own. Trevor preferred the Stanfords to visit them. That way Barbara wouldn't be reminded of the Aga, the cinema room and – the most recent addition – a conservatory bigger than their lounge backing onto a quarter-acre of well-kept North London lawn. Usually after a night spent with the Stanfords, he could look forward to an earful about the shortcomings of the Islington flat that only eighteen short months ago she'd 'had to have', even though it cost silly money. Tens of thousands more than they could afford. Nowadays only very rich or very poor people actually lived in the city; property prices were tearing the heart out of London.

He killed the engine and unbuckled the safety belt. His wife hadn't said much on the way. Trevor wasn't complaining about that. When she spoke her tone was husky, the words taut with envy. 'Why don't we have this?'

It was always the same when they were invited here, except tonight

Barbara was starting early. Off and running, and they weren't even out of the car – a bad omen for the evening ahead. Her husband gave his stock reply to a question he'd answered a hundred times.

'Because he's a DCI and I'm not.'

'But Oliver Stanford isn't smarter than you.'

Fifteen years earlier, Trevor Mills had mistaken that kind of assertion for admiration, married his wife on a rainy Friday morning at Marylebone register office and flown to a cheap hotel in a Spanish tourist resort – all he could afford – on honeymoon. His error wasn't long in showing. Three days, four arguments and a couple of short and unsatisfying love-making sessions later, he'd discovered the woman he'd fallen in love with had raised resentment to an art form and tied it to a rare gift where, to the untrained ear, accusation sounded like support. It hadn't been a happy union for either party. From the beginning they'd grown apart, keeping up appearances without knowing why. A 'marriage of inconvenience', Barbara Mills called it when she'd had a few. Which, these days, was often.

'Tell me he isn't. At least give me that much hope.'

Her husband wouldn't be drawn into the familiar harangue, although he believed she was right: Oliver Stanford wasn't smarter than Trevor Mills. Something his superiors at New Scotland Yard had so far failed to notice.

'Can't we just enjoy ourselves for a change? After all, these people are our friends.'

His wife's derisive laugh filled the car. 'Your friends, you mean. They're no friends of mine. Can't stand them, if you must know. He's an arrogant bastard. And if you had half a brain you wouldn't be fooled by the hugs and the kisses and the "Oh, you really must come to our coffee morning, the girls are dying to meet you" and see what a bitch she is.'

Her voice was shrill and a little slurred and Mills realised she'd been drinking. He hadn't noticed, but it didn't matter if she made a scene; it wouldn't be the first. He had bigger things to worry about.

To most of the population – Barbara included – Danny Glass and

Rollie Anderson were just names. 'Bad guys' who occasionally featured on the inside pages of the *Evening Standard.* As a DI, Mills had a deeper understanding. To him and his colleagues the gang leaders represented a lot more – this lovely house, for starters. Not to mention where they lived; the place Barbara suddenly found so lacking.

Christ alone knew how she'd react if he told her where the cash for that particular folly had come from. She couldn't seriously think they could afford it on his salary.

Stanford hadn't exaggerated when he'd given his grave summary: the raid on the King of Mesopotamia pub had put the wind up everybody with the slightest connection to the gangs who seemed determined to destroy each other. Picking a winner was anybody's guess and, as his shrew of a wife was quick to point out, Trevor Mills wasn't famous for picking winners. He wondered if she included herself in her caustic assessment.

No, of course she didn't.

The front door opened and their hosts stood in the hallway ready to greet them, Stanford in a white shirt, sleeves rolled back showing off his tan, an arm round his wife's slender waist. Beside him was a smiling Elise, every inch the upwardly mobile middle-class woman. Elise Stanford was almost as tall as her husband and shared the same bronzed skin, her green eyes clear, her teeth white and even. She'd chosen to wear a black dress set off with a matching choker: it worked. They were a handsome couple, no doubt about it.

On top of all that, they seemed happy. Trevor felt a pang of jealousy.

Mills and Stanford had joined the Met the same week and for much of the time their careers progressed along similar lines, almost in parallel, until Stanford was promoted to Detective Chief Inspector and became his boss. Any bitterness Mills felt he kept to himself.

Barbara put on her happy face and stepped out of the car. The women embraced, the men shook hands and the four of them went inside.

'You're early.'

'Are we? Seven-thirty for eight?'

Elise corrected Barbara's mistake. 'Eight for eight-thirty. No problem, we'll have more time to chat before the others get here.' The women disappeared into the kitchen with Elise gushing. 'We've had French windows put in. Honestly, you wouldn't believe the mess. A word to the wise, Barbara, never trust a builder.'

Trevor heard and sympathised with his wife. Under his breath he whispered, 'Fucking great.' Stanford drew him into the room to the right of the stairs, which served as a study, and closed the door. Unlike his wife, he kept his voice low.

'Before anybody else arrives you should know I'm expecting a telephone call later tonight.'

He poured two glasses of whisky and handed one to his DI. Mills accepted it without a word, his attention on what he was being told.

'About?'

'The information our mutual friend is so keen to have.'

'Wow! That was fast. Well done.'

'Not the moment to be dragging our heels, Trevor. I meant what I said this morning. Danny Glass can and will do us in. Depend on it. We have to give him what he wants.'

'Even if it causes a war?'

'The war has already started. Our best interests are served by making sure Glass is still standing when the dust settles. Any other result will be a disaster for us.'

'What about his other demand, putting a shadow on the brother?'

'Already taken care of.' Stanford made a show of looking at his watch. 'Luke Glass has joined the blue whale and the white rhino. He's a protected species.'

'An endangered species.'

'Quite. If anything happens to him, it won't be down to us.'

Mills was impressed. The DCI hadn't wasted any time and it occurred to him Stanford deserved to be where he was. Perhaps he was smarter than him after all.

'What can I say? Except, well done again.'

Stanford smiled his superior little smile.

'Of course, the best result, the very best result, would be if they wiped each other out, wouldn't it?'

'I disagree, Trevor.'

'Really? London would be a safer place, at least until some new vermin took over.'

'Maybe so, maybe so.' Stanford waved his arms at the book-lined room. 'Meantime, who would foot the bill for all this?'

Mills grinned. His boss was pleased with himself, and indeed it was good work. Better to play the game and appeal to his ego.

'A fair point, governor. This is the reason they made you chief.'

They clinked glasses. Stanford considered the compliment and the smile reappeared.

'One of the reasons, Trevor. One of the reasons. Cheers!'

* * *

Trevor watched his wife across the table splashing wine into her half-filled glass. Barbara was going for it tonight. Normally she'd make it to the finish line with her mascara if not her reputation intact – the drinking had seen to that long ago – but already she was in a world of her own, dull-eyed and disconnected from the conversation. The other guests weren't far behind. Winston Dunlop-Marshall – high court judge by day, piss artist and tit-groper by night – was telling a story Mills remembered from the last time he was in His Honour's company. Deborah, Dunlop-Marshall's wife and twenty-five years his junior, was plainly bored out of her mind and had dropped any pretence at listening, preferring to stare into space.

Bob and Isobel Wallace were the least affected by alcohol. As newcomers to this scene, they hung on every drunken word falling from WDM's thick, sensuous lips. Wallace had heard about his boss's soirées and viewed the invitation as significant.

Mills was surprised to find Wallace here, especially since, Stanford had more or less agreed he was suspect.

The judge finished his anecdote to fake laughter that quickly died. Deborah patted his arm. 'Very funny, dear. Now for Christ's sake, put a sock in it.'

Elise made her grand entrance with a tray of baked Alaska to wild applause. Barbara Mills was the exception. The sparks startled her and she knocked a glass of red wine over the white table cover.

The hostess was unfazed. 'No harm done. No harm done.'

Isobel Wallace dug her spoon into the meringue. 'Ice cream inside. How clever, Elise.'

Elise purred. 'Oliver and I had this in France. We loved it, didn't we?'

Her husband was unable to reply because his mouth was full and nodded instead. Isobel, pleased to be invited to a dinner party at Bob's boss's house, couldn't help trying too hard.

'Would this be nouvelle cuisine?'

The evening had been one of the least enjoyable Trevor had ever had. He took it out on Mrs Wallace. 'Does it look like a tiny bit of nothing on a big white plate?'

'No.'

'Then it can't be, can it?'

Bob Wallace had hardly spoken. With Dunlop-Marshall and his fund of unfunny stories, it wasn't noticed. For his sins, he'd been parked next to Barbara Mills, who now and then said something he couldn't make out. Wallace edged away, hoping none of the others noticed.

Stanford stood. 'More wine, anybody?'

Winston Dunlop-Marshall and Barbara Mills held their glasses aloft. He topped-up the visitors and missed himself out – the third time he'd done that. Mills gave him credit. Oliver Stanford was an excellent host and a consummate actor. No one would guess the pressure he was under.

A telephone rang in the lounge. Stanford excused himself and went to answer it. He was gone for only a few minutes. Mills studied his face when he rejoined the conversation but Stanford's expression was as relaxed as it had been before the call.

Brandy at the end of the meal pushed Barbara Mills and the judge over the edge, to a point where even several cups of Jamaican Blue Mountain coffee couldn't save them. Trevor's wife rested her head on the table, eyes closed, to all intents asleep. Oliver Stanford presided over the scene like Pan, surveying the excess he'd encouraged. Trevor Mills caught his eye and his boss waved him closer. 'Meet me in the study. Bring Bob.'

'Bob? Is that wise? I mean, I'm not really sure why you invited him.'

The DCI wasn't accustomed to having to explain himself and didn't like it.

'Just do it, Trevor.'

Mills did as he was told and, in the study, the three policemen faced each other.

Stanford said, 'I'll make this quick. We're in business. Anderson's moving a shipment early tomorrow. Ecstasy. Fifty thousand tablets. A decent haul.'

Wallace was impressed. 'Decent? It's a small fortune.'

Mills was more interested in specifics. 'How's he shifting it?'

'White Transit on the A285 to the city.'

Wallace said, 'Do we know the country of origin? Do we know—?'

Mills cut him off. 'Holland probably. Who cares?'

'Think that'll be enough to get Glass off our backs?'

'It's what he asked for.'

'And your informant's sound?'

The DCI barely hid his irritation. 'As a pound, Bob. Sound as a pound. Otherwise it's sod all use to us.'

Elise knocked on the door and came in. 'Our guests are leaving, Oliver.'

'Bit early, isn't it?'

His wife didn't agree. 'No, I think it's time they went. Where did you put Barbara's coat?'

'Didn't have a coat.'

'She says she did.'

Trevor sighed. 'I'd better get her home.' He kissed Elise on both cheeks. 'Thanks for having us. Sorry about the pudding and... sorry.'

At the front door the men shook hands. Wallace put his arm round Isobel.

'See you tomorrow, sir.'

'Tomorrow it's sir, tonight it's Oliver. Drive carefully, Bob.'

Trevor Mills made sure he was the last one out the door. He wasn't happy and not just because his wife was a lush.

'Why did you tell him? We don't know what's going on with him.'

'True, Trevor. Very true. But we soon will.'

'Are you sure that's wise?'

Mills was questioning his judgement. *Again.* And he didn't like it.

'Wise... no, perhaps not... but it's necessary.'

14

The door of The Lord Stanley shut behind him as a friendly voice called, 'Goodnight.'

George Ritchie pulled his collar up against the chill night air and looked up and down the street, seeing only a few parked cars. Further along, a couple he'd noticed the night before were joined at the mouth, oblivious to everyone but themselves.

His neighbours knew him as Mr Butler and, though he'd worked for the Anderson family for almost a decade and a half, even Rollie didn't know where he lived. George Ritchie was beyond private, he was obsessive – in a brutal world it was how he'd survived.

Closing time was still an hour away. No matter. His limit was two drinks and he'd had them. The regulars were used to him leaving early because he always did. He hadn't lasted as long as he had in his business by being careless. It paid to keep your eyes open, especially since the cock-up at the King Pot. Danny Glass hadn't come at them yet, though it was inevitable he would.

Even now, seven years on, Ritchie couldn't understand the logic behind the bomb Albert Anderson had planted in Danny Glass's Merc, and not because the targets were civilians. So much nonsense was talked about a code that protected women and children.

Noble old bollocks; it didn't exist. What needed to be done got done and anybody would be offed if it suited. No, the question he'd asked himself many times was simple.

What was gained by killing Danny Glass's family?

The answer was nothing. So, why do it? And why keep it from him?

He walked to his flat, allowing himself a final glance round before going in. At the top of the stairs, Ritchie put the key in the lock and opened the door. In darkness he moved to the window and checked the street below. Everything was as it had been. No movement from the parked cars; the couple were still wrapped round each other.

The flat was modest. Most of the furniture had seen better days. Ritchie wasn't thinking of changing any of it. All he did was sleep here. His neighbours imagined he was a lonely widower and felt sorry for a man living alone. Their sympathy was misplaced. There was no heart-breaking story to tell. Ritchie hadn't married through choice. It wouldn't have been wise in the business he was in. Occasionally, when he needed a woman, it was nothing more than a transaction; they went to her place and George Ritchie paid.

* * *

Down in the street the couple stopped kissing. The man took money from his inside jacket pocket and gave it to the girl. She took the notes, didn't count them and walked away. He spoke quietly into a mobile phone, nodding at whatever the person on the other end of the line was saying, and headed towards his car.

* * *

Further north, Oliver Stanford's guests had gone and the house was quiet apart from rain drumming gently on the conservatory roof. He helped Elise clear the table and load the dishwasher, then watched her climb the stairs.

Halfway up, she turned. 'Aren't you coming?'

'Soon. Big day tomorrow. I have to be prepared.'

His wife sighed. 'Seems like every day's a big day, Oliver. I preferred when you were on the beat.'

'No, you didn't. You hated it and you loathed Bayswater. "Knee deep in Arabs and Indians." If you said that once you said it a thousand times.'

'Yes, but—'

'Couldn't swing a cat in that grubby little bedsit.'

'At least I had you.'

Lately they'd been having this conversation, or a variation on the theme, a lot. Stanford tried to sound patient. 'Elise, you worried yourself sick most of the time. We bought our first ever bottle of champagne to celebrate my promotion.'

She smiled. 'It wasn't champagne, it was Asti Spumanti. Wouldn't have it in the house now.'

'And it made you ill.'

'It made me a lot more than that as I recall.'

'We talked all night about what we'd do when the kids came along. Your dream was to get out of the city. And here we are.'

'I know.'

'It isn't for nothing. You're right, every day is a big day. First to arrive and last to leave. It's called staying ahead of the game.'

'I understand, it's just...'

'Look, the party was a success.'

'Was it?'

'Yes, of course.'

'Didn't last long.'

'Not our fault Dunlop-Marshall can't hold his liquor. We won't invite him again. Thinks he's on the bench every time he opens his mouth. The man's a bore, drunk or sober. And Barbara Mills was pissed from the off. Trevor has his work cut out there. They brought their problems with them. You're tired and no wonder. Go to bed, I'll be there as soon as I can.'

Elise knew Oliver's hard work and his ambition had taken them higher than she'd ever thought possible. She ought to be more grateful. Instead she found herself in the past, imagining it was better than the present. For all their upward mobility, Elise Stanford was lonely.

Her husband closed the study door and took out a mobile, a phone with only one purpose. He punched speed dial and listened to it ring.

Danny Glass didn't bother with hello. 'Spill it.'

Stanford repeated what he'd been told. Glass was a difficult bastard to deal with on a good day and, as usual, he was unimpressed.

The policeman didn't kid himself that the hard work – 'first to arrive and last to leave' nonsense he'd told his wife – had much to do with his reputation as one of the Met's rising stars. Thanks to the South London gangster, he'd made a series of arrests in important cases, the kind of collars that got people's attention. In return, Glass was to be left alone to get on with his business. As a detective at New Scotland Yard and now a chief inspector, Stanford was in a position to make that happen. On a number of occasions, he'd disarmed investigations before they got started, getting word to Glass when his affairs were attracting unwelcome interest.

Oliver Stanford was tipped to go all the way to the top and Danny Glass, his partner in crime, was fireproof. Win-win. Until the raid on the pub rocked the boat. Rollie Anderson's failed attempt at revenge for his father's murder threatened to derail an arrangement that had served both parties well. Glass was convinced Stanford had known and had chosen not to tell him. Untrue. Danny Glass wasn't somebody you wanted to cross.

He went upstairs, stopping on the landing to crack the door to his daughters' bedroom open. The glow of a nightlight washed the innocent faces of the twins: his girls.

Nobody was going to harm them. He wouldn't let them.

15

I closed my eyes and imagined mist floating in white clouds over the shifting water of the channel forty-five miles away, the image soothing the tension in me, though not enough to completely calm the adrenaline rushing through my body. Wandsworth had been an education. At dawn, waking to the noise of hundreds of inmates dragging themselves into yet another twenty-four hours behind bars, the feeling in my gut that something bad was about to happen always with me. Every day, the sense of non-specific dread hanging in the air: a helluva way to live.

This shouldn't feel the same. But it did.

It was 5.30 and still dark. We were parked at the mouth of a country lane in Kent. Me and Felix in the back, Danny and Marcus in the front seats, a second car with four men in position a mile away waiting for the signal. Behind the wheel, Marcus held binoculars in one steady hand and a mobile on speakerphone in the other, clearly at ease with what we were about to do. I couldn't see his face. All I had to go on was his voice, even and confident, every couple of minutes asking our spotter further along the road the same question, getting the same answer.

'Anything?'

'Nothing.'

Stanford's information had brought us to this place. We'd been eating fish and chips and drinking beer from the bottle when the call came through to the office above the King Pot. Danny was in remarkably good form, considering: feet up on the desk, his fingers tapping along with Mick and Keith, Charlie and Bill doing 'Honky Tonk Women'. Today's monologue was on one of my brother's favourite subjects – why sixties music was the best. I'd heard it before, many times, we all had, and knew it came down to the rise of English groups – the Stones, the Yardbirds, The Who; The Kinks were a particular favourite – and how they were better than American bands, especially 'that soul malarkey' as he called it.

'Darkie music. I mean, what the fuck is that about?'

Nobody had an answer for him. At least, not any they were foolish enough to voice.

The jukebox was stacked with his favourites. Strangely, something I'd never understood, the Beatles weren't mentioned. But anybody connected to Stax, Atlantic or Tamla Motown – anybody black – should've been drowned at birth, according to him. Danny found the synergy between colour and immigration impossible to resist and had moved on to explaining the finer points of his views between mouthfuls of crispy fried cod.

Not difficult to follow; there were no finer points, just flat-out ignorance.

'We don't want them, we don't need them, and we can't afford them. Send the bastards back to wherever they came from and stop any more coming in. End of.'

The phone interrupted his diatribe. He put the call on speaker so we could hear Stanford in a few sentences give us everything we needed: the day, the time and the contact.

'Tomorrow, early doors. White Transit, French reg, on the A285 heading towards London carrying fifty thousand tablets of methylenedioxymethamphetamine.'

Methylenedioxymethamphetamine. Better known as ecstasy or Molly.

I expected my brother to be pleased. He wasn't.

'What the fuck do French plates look like?'

'Two letters, three numbers, two letters.'

'Haven't given us much warning, have you?'

'Only just heard.'

'We're talking five or six hours.'

'Leave it if you don't fancy it.'

Danny barked into the phone. 'Do yourself a favour, copper, don't get cute. And don't tell me what to do.'

He slammed the receiver down, picked it up again, dialled a number and spoke to somebody. 'Forget it. Get back here. Change of plan.'

Then he remembered I was there. 'What did you make of that?'

'Mmmm. Not sure.'

'What does "Mmmm" mean? Spit it out.'

'Doesn't feel right.'

'"Doesn't feel right." Hit Anderson where it hurts, you said. Suddenly you don't fancy it. I'm lost. Explain it to me.'

I didn't have an answer, not one based on anything concrete. He was right, it was exactly the kind of score we'd hoped for and it had been my idea. Except now I'd gone cold on it.

But this is what I know: if it looks like shit and smells like shit, it's probably shit.

I said, 'Could be a set-up?'

Danny held his exasperation in check. 'Not a chance. I've got Stanford by the balls. He goes wrong on us it's ta-ta to the good life for him. Oliver likes things just the way they are. He won't do anything to jeopardise it. Every dirty copper's worst nightmare is winding up inside. Dozens of cons with nothing but time to square old scores.'

He let me picture it, forgetting I'd been there. 'Better off dead and he knows it.' Danny licked his fingers, wiped them on page eighteen of the *Daily Mail* and tossed the paper into the bin. 'Nah, it's fine. It's kosher.'

I let it go. Maybe it was just me. Since my release I'd been edgy; easily spooked.

'What's a cargo that size worth on the street these days?'

'Three hundred, three fifty. Depends.'

He snapped. 'What's wrong now?'

I shrugged. 'Can't put my finger on it. But I don't like it.'

He rested his elbows on the desk. Dissension from the ranks wasn't what he was used to. Anybody but me pouring cold water on the news he would've been across the desk and at their throat. He settled for giving me a look that could've drawn blood.

'You've changed, do you realise that?'

Spending the best part of a decade in prison will do that to you.

'You're morbid. Everything's dark. And you're depressing the shit out of me. I'll go over it one more time. Trust? Fuck trust. Trust isn't what this is about. It's about leverage. Stanford's in our pocket. Snug as a bug. Our very own tame filth and remember this is what we're paying him for. This is why Mrs Ollie's so happy in her new house.'

'Yeah, I get it.'

'Do you? That's good. Tell you what, when we snag this E, you pocket a couple or twenty and get them down your neck. See if they're as good as they should be. Call it product testing. Cheer up, for fuck's sake.'

That conversation had been running round my brain ever since though it helped nothing. We'd asked for intel so we could knock a wheel off Rollie Anderson. Stanford had delivered. This bit should be straightforward.

Famous last words.

In the front seat Marcus kept his dialogue going.

'Anything?'

'Nothing.'

The clock on the dash said six minutes to six. I tried again to visualise the mist on the water, the small boat carrying the drugs and the seagulls hovering and swooping in its wake as it sailed towards the horizon minus its cargo. Like all the best plans: simple.

Three vehicles went by one after another, none of them the Transit. In an hour, this road would be busy. In two, it would be buzzing. Any later than that, robbing the van would be a non-starter. Stanford's information was beginning to look suspect.

At four minutes to six the darkness melted, the sky lightened, and the new day arrived. In the front, Marcus said, 'Anything?' and got the familiar reply.

Felix voiced what everybody else was thinking. 'Maybe it's not coming.'

Danny pulled his coat around him and spat through gritted teeth.

'It'll be here. Now shut it.'

My brother had to believe: dodgy intel meant his pet detective wasn't in control, maybe even gone over to the other side, and that pebble would cause ripples beyond anything he could allow himself to consider. He'd invested too much time and money in Oliver Stanford for it to go sour on a B road in the home counties.

Marcus kept his concentration on the exchange with the spotter.

'Anything?'

'No.'

Then it got interesting. The spotter said, 'Wait a sec. White Transit... French registration... Yeah, it's ours.'

Danny thumped the dashboard. 'See! See! I knew it.'

Marcus spoke to the other car. 'Target sighted. Get ready to fall in behind.'

Minutes later the van appeared, keeping a steady speed well within the limit. Our second car made to overtake but instead of completing the manoeuvre ran alongside until its nose was in front, horn blasting, edging the vehicle we'd been waiting for over. The Transit had no option. It left the road and ran down the lane to where Marcus had reversed and slewed, blocking progress.

Danny pulled a gun and ran with the big man at his heels. Between them they dragged the driver from behind the wheel – a guy in his forties, bald and heavy, wearing a zip-up jacket, and obviously terrified.

Marcus screamed at him. 'Hands on the bonnet! Do it! How many with you?'

The driver stammered as he tried to understand the question.

'Wha... what? What do you mean?'

Marcus used the butt of his weapon on his skull: one blow. He collapsed and lay still. Danny walked to the rear of the van and banged his fist on a panel.

'All right in there! Don't be heroes! When the door opens throw out whatever you've got!'

No answer.

He didn't hesitate. 'They've had their chance, let them have it.'

He threw open the door and dived for cover. The silence was the anticlimax of the century – there was no one. Danny got to his feet and stared at the wooden crates piled high, thrusting his hand into the nearest box, tightening his fist. Juice and pulp oozed through his fingers. I caught the familiar sweet smell on the early morning air and realised what had happened. I'd never seen my brother cry but I thought he was going to now. In the end he got a hold on himself, turned and faced his crew.

'Strawberries. We've jacked a load of fucking strawberries. Stanford, you cunt!'

A simple job had ended in farce. Here, at the crack of dawn, we'd been mob-handed and ready to take down... a vanload of fruit. Somewhere in the city, Anderson would be laughing into his cornflakes. I didn't blame him. The King Pot had caught us sloppy and off guard. This was worse. We looked like incompetent amateurs.

Rollie: 2; Team Glass: 0.

PART II

16

In a side street cafe called Dino's off Battersea Park Road, the clock on the wall said seven forty-five. Whenever the door opened, London rushed in, already hectic and insistent. The clientele hardly noticed; it mingled with the cooking sounds from the kitchen. The Dino whose name was stencilled in large red letters on the window wasn't around to complain. He'd died on the 7th of September, 1940 when the house he lived in, not two hundred yards from his business, was flattened during a Luftwaffe air raid.

Behind the counter, his grandson and the staff were busy serving full English breakfasts to workers coming off nightshifts in the New Covent Garden Market half a mile away.

Fruit wasn't on the menu. Plates of sausages, bacon, tomato, fried eggs, fried bread and beans were, fired out at conveyer-belt speed. Nobody paid attention to the guy in the corner with the laptop.

Jonjo Hart rubbed the 'Toon Army' tattoo on the back of his hand, too excited to eat. Or sleep. He'd been up for twenty-one hours straight, yet wasn't tired. After what he'd witnessed, going to bed was the furthest thing from his mind. He'd come to London determined to make a mark on his uncle's world. This would take him where he wanted to go. He ran the video again – for the tenth time – it still made him laugh out loud. As soon as he'd got in the car heading back from Kent, he'd called his uncle. Ritchie had answered on the first ring: his nephew hadn't disturbed him; he'd already been awake.

On Tyneside, Ritchie was an almost mythical figure. His nephew had grown up surrounded by stories of his criminal exploits. George Ritchie had never been charged with a crime. He was too smart for that.

The younger man was anxious to impress his famous relative and the video captured on his camera ninety minutes earlier would do just that: he'd been in position on the hill above the lane an hour before the cars showed up and his joints were so stiff they cracked when he moved. But it had been worth it. What he'd filmed would make the most feared gangster in the city a laughing stock.

Danny Glass – Big Bad Danny – was about to become a national joke.

At one point he'd zoomed in and almost felt sorry for him. In the early morning light, Glass's eyes were black pinpoints set deep in a grey face. Jonjo whispered to himself in a cheesy American accent. 'Gonna make you a star, kid.'

Ritchie came through the cafe door at ten past eight, ordered tea from a harassed waitress and sat down. Jonjo almost offered to shake hands but thought better of it.

His uncle wasn't amused. 'This better be good. Otherwise we're going to fall out.'

Jonjo confidently pushed the laptop across the table's chipped Formica top and pressed the play button. 'You be the judge.'

On the screen, dawn broke behind a white van travelling a deserted road. From nowhere a car drew alongside, forcing it down a lane and for moments it was lost behind a hedgerow, then reappeared and stopped, blocked from going further by a second car. Four masked men ran towards it and hauled the terrified driver from behind the wheel. One of the gang – a big guy they both recognised – crashed the butt of his gun down on his head; he fell unconscious to the ground.

The unmistakable voice of Danny Glass barked orders to the back of the hijacked vehicle. 'All right in there! Don't be heroes! When the door opens throw out whatever you've got!

Seconds passed. Nothing happened.

Glass said, 'They've had their chance, let them have it.'

The doors flew open and he threw himself to the ground. The camera went to a close-up of boxes stacked on top of each other and back to Glass, sheepishly getting up off the ground. He thrust his hand into the nearest one and faced where Jonjo had been hiding, so perfect it might have been staged.

Hart checked the volume so his uncle didn't miss the punchline. Glass said, 'Strawberries. We've jacked a load of fucking strawberries. Stanford, you cunt!'

The video froze on the image of strawberry juice dripping from his fingers. Jonjo waited for Ritchie's reaction while the waitress topped up his tea. He would've bet his life on his uncle laughing but he'd have lost. Ritchie's eyes bored into him across the table.

'What the fuck is this?'

'It's this morning. I got there early and shot it. Great, isn't it?' He was pleased and missed the signs. 'Wasn't easy trying not to laugh out loud and give the game away.'

His uncle grabbed his arm so hard it hurt. Jonjo was shocked – this wasn't how it was supposed to go. 'I don't understand. We've got it on film. The great Danny Glass making a tit of himself. Thought you'd be pleased. Rollie will love it.'

Ritchie scanned the busy cafe for somebody with no business being there. 'No, he won't. He isn't going to see it. Ever.'

'Why the hell not?'

'Because he's a clown. He'd use it. Wouldn't be able to stop himself. Anderson isn't somebody you should trust – he's a child in a man's body.'

'If he can get me where I want to go, what does that matter?'

'I told you when you came down here. Don't try to run before you can walk. Who else knows about this?'

Jonjo faltered. 'Apart... apart... from me and you... nobody.'

'How many copies are there?'

'This is it. But surely, it's dynamite? If I put it on YouTube the whole world will see it. Danny Glass'll be finished.'

George Ritchie remembered this was his sister's boy and spoke with all the gentleness he could raise. 'You're ambitious. I get it. Except this isn't the way. Sure, catching the great Danny Glass making a dick of himself is fantastic. But it crosses an invisible line, a line that will get you and a lot of other people dead. The video makes you a target. One day this war will end. The trick is to still be standing when it does.'

Jonjo was too in love with his work to listen. 'Don't you want to watch it again? It's even funnier when you know what's coming. "Stanford, you cunt."'

Ritchie pitied him – the bloody fool was going to get himself killed.

He held out an upturned palm. 'Give it to me. Give me the video.'

Reluctantly, Jonjo dropped a memory stick into his hand.

'Now, delete it. I want to see you do it.'

'I don't fucking believe this. I thought you'd approve.'

'Sure, we've put one over on Glass, but we've had to give up our most important route to do it. Not worth it. But I had to do it to keep Anderson from doing something stupid. He'd lap this up. Handing it to him would be just about the stupidest thing I can think of.'

Ritchie softened the blow and used the stick to make his point. 'You think because this will noise-up Danny Glass it's a good thing. It isn't. This implicates a detective in serious corruption. If he goes down because of it, every copper in London will be out to get us. The whole fucking force. No surviving that.' He put the stick in his pocket. 'There won't be a hardman in this city who won't be tempted to try it on.'

'You're saying I've screwed up.'

'Finally, you're catching on. Glass will come back. Harder and stronger than anything you can imagine. Do you want to be the man who made a right mug out of a psycho? Believe me, you don't. Try not to think about it or you'll never get a night's sleep again.'

He threw coins down on the table and stood. He'd saved this boy's life.

* * *

Jonjo watched his uncle thread between the wooden tables on his way to the door. The man he'd idolised had settled for being No 2. For the first time in his life he felt sorry for him. Most of George's career had been spent working for Albert and now for Rollie, although he was smarter than both of them put together. Smart but flawed: he was too careful. Always had been. Otherwise he wouldn't have taken orders from idiots like the Andersons. On the surface, he was hard. Underneath he was afraid. Christ, he was even scared to let his own nephew know where he lived. Jonjo had no intention of letting that happen to him. He'd come south with one objective: to get to the top and stay there. Ritchie was being offered a cast-iron opportunity to give Glass a bloody nose and all he wanted to do was bury it.

'How many copies are there?'

'This is it.'

Not true. His uncle might be a legend in Newcastle, but he knew fuck-all about technology.

17

There was only one guy on the door of the Picasso Club when George Ritchie arrived. Immediately he ordered another two to join him and waited until it was done before going inside. At times, his caution bordered on pathological; this wasn't one of those times. They'd humiliated the most ruthless gangster in South London and, like the fools they were, behaved as if that was the end of it. The very real possibility Glass's troops might come through the door and blow all of them away hadn't occurred to Rollie.

Rollie was standing in the centre of the office, telling the audience of sycophants and losers a funny story. He never got to the punchline. He saw Ritchie and threw his arms around him. Ritchie smelled booze – the moron was pissed. Celebrating what he imagined was a great victory.

'George! George! What d'you want to drink?'

Ritchie gently removed the arm from his shoulder. 'I like to keep a clear head, you know me.'

''Deed I do. 'Deed I do. We stitched Glass right up. Don't you ever just want to let go?'

Ritchie kept his disdain to himself. 'Right now, I'm more interested in when and how they'll come at us. Glass won't let what happened go unanswered. We need to be ready.'

'Not today. It's too soon. The bastard will be scared to show his face.'

George Ritchie doubted it. He'd been around when stories of two delinquents thieving cigarettes had got back to Albert. Anderson was supposed to be protecting shopkeepers. Letting the teenagers take a liberty sent a message that the fat man was weak. Better to break the young rascals' legs and show the world that nobody – not even a couple of cheeky boys – would be allowed to question his authority south of the river. Ritchie had urged him to stand on them like the maggots they were. Albert had refused and allowed them to carry on.

And the rest, as they say...

Albert's son was making the same mistake by being blind to the obvious danger. He'd made his move and assumed for the moment that was enough. Rollie patted his cheek. 'Do whatever you think, George. After all, that's what I pay you for. No point having a dog and barking yourself, is there?'

Ritchie faked a half-smile, clapped his hands and shouted to the troops.

'We haven't beaten Danny Glass, we've wounded him! Now get the fuck out of here and do your jobs! We're not running a social club! And double the numbers everywhere! Go to it!'

One or two of the thugs grumbled, the rest did as they were told. He spoke to Rollie. 'Why don't you go home and get some sleep?'

'Yeah. Maybe I'll do that. And, George, that was genius. Pure genius.'

Ritchie accepted the slurred compliment 'Told you we'd get them. But now isn't the time to congratulate ourselves. Once it's over, you can party.'

Anderson grinned drunkenly, reliving the moment. 'Wish I could've seen Glass's face. Bet it was fucking priceless.'

Ritchie steered Rollie towards the door and signalled to a couple of men to go with him. When they'd gone, his hand slipped inside his jacket pocket and fingered the memory stick.

* * *

The day that began in a dark country lane in Kent had blossomed into cloudless skies and warm sunshine. South London went about its business with a smile. Inside the King Pot the atmosphere was subdued, very different from the hilarity in the Picasso Club. The pub wasn't open – it was too early – and the barman leaned on a crutch, polishing glasses with the enthusiasm of a schoolboy forced to do homework. The bullet had only grazed him but had hurt like hell. Felix Corrigan and a group of foot soldiers stood with half-finished beers in front of them, drinking in silence. Now and then they raised their eyes to the ceiling, imagining Danny Glass's brooding presence in the room above. Danny was alone. None of them considered climbing the stairs to offer him support.

They weren't completely stupid.

Their appreciation of what had gone down was, at best, superficial: the raid had bombed, they'd been made to look like fools, and Danny was furious. Nobody suspected the fiasco had been captured on film. If they had, they would've been even more worried, because the fallout from humiliating their boss further was beyond thinking about. Men who'd been bought and paid for sipped their beers and waited for somebody to tell them what to do, while the clock behind the bar ticked off the seconds.

* * *

On the drive back from Kent, Danny had pulled his coat collar up and slumped in the front seat, closed down and shut off from the rest of us. In fairness, I didn't blame him. The raid had been a disaster, no other word for it. Danny's mind would be racing over the deeper implications. The tip-off had come from a totally reliable source, his bent policeman, which threw up two possibilities – the detective had been duped into giving wrong information, or he'd switched sides and was playing for the other team. A third alternative occurred, one I didn't like any better: word of the attack had got out and the plan had been changed. Any way it cut we'd been mugged off.

I'd sat in the back next to Felix, strangely detached from the pantomime the morning had become. Part of me, the part my brother refused to accept, hadn't changed. I still wanted out.

When we got to the city, Marcus dropped me in the next street to the flat so I could sneak in the back, the way I'd left. The copper parked in the Golf outside would swear I'd been at home. I'd surprised him with a cup of coffee to see him through the night. He'd rolled the car window down and taken it. I'd leaned in to say, 'See you in the morning' and he'd backed away. My reputation had gone before me. His night would've been uneventful. Unlike me, he'd probably slept through most of it.

I called Mandy and caught her on her way to the gym. Her smile came down the line when she heard my voice. 'I was just thinking about you.'

'Good to know. What're you doing later?'

'Nothing much.'

'Fancy a drive in my new car?'

'Yeah. I'll be back in a couple of hours. When will you pick me up?'

'Now' was the answer I wanted to give, except Danny would be expecting me to put in an appearance, not something I was looking forward to.

'Twelve o'clock.'

'Where are we going?'

'It's a magical mystery tour.'

Mandy was wise to me. 'You mean you don't know?'

'I mean it'll be a surprise.'

'To both of us.'

'Maybe. Twelve at your place. Be ready.'

She gave me the address and rang off. I showered, staying under the hot water as long as I could, then made scrambled eggs and toast and read the paper Danny thoughtfully had arranged to be delivered. Unfortunately, it was the *Daily Mail*. I made a mental note to ask the shop on the corner to change it for something a grown-up might read. It was half past nine and too late to go to bed even if I wanted to. My brother would be morose, licking his wounds and trying to figure out what had gone wrong. The smartest thing to do would be to avoid him but not showing up wasn't an option. I grabbed the car keys and headed for the pub.

* * *

A group of men were standing in front of a row of half-finished pints. Harry the barman shrugged and made a 'what-you-want-me-to-do?' face. It wasn't unusual for the troops to start early, except today their timing was off. If they'd been thinking at all they would've figured that out for themselves. Marcus wasn't one of them. Either he was upstairs or he hadn't appeared yet. Felix ducked behind his drinking buddies and tried to hide.

They eyed me warily; they didn't know my strength. I helped them out.

'What the fuck do you think you're doing?'

Before any of them could answer, my arm swept the bar sending their drinks crashing to the floor in a shower of glass and beer. They stepped away, suddenly remembering I was the guy who'd shown Albert Anderson the quick way down. There was fear in their eyes, and there ought to be because I wasn't pretending. These were the same clowns who'd almost got us killed. I let them have it.

'Do any of you understand what's going on? Are you completely fucking stupid? Anderson could come at us right now. Get your act together before we retire the lot of you. Permanently. We aren't paying you to get pissed. We're paying you to do your job. If you can't, fuck off, we don't need you.'

Was this really the best we could find? If it was, we were in trouble.

The barman got it next. 'From now on nobody drinks while they're supposed to be working. I catch you serving them and you'll be sorry.'

'Danny doesn't mind.'

'You're not talking to Danny, you're talking to me and, yeah, he does mind. Now, clean that mess up. Felix, help him.'

* * *

Upstairs the door was closed. I opened it and went in. Danny was still wearing the coat he'd had on in Kent. Slowly, he raised his head, his eyes heavy from lack of sleep. Silent rage boiled off him, a sign of the impotence he was feeling. All my life, anger had been my brother's default reaction. But this was bad. His jaw moved and nothing came out. Five hours after the raid and he was literally too furious to speak. Eventually he did, his voice thick and slurred as if he'd had a stroke.

'What kept you?'

I didn't reply and sat down across from him. He needed to take his frustration out on somebody.

'Took your bloody time getting here, didn't you?'

Being around Danny meant constantly having to navigate his mood swings. Usually it was wiser to just let him blow off steam, but occasionally – very occasionally – pushing back got a better result than going along with his bullshit. This was one of those times.

'Consider yourself lucky I'm not at St Pancras stepping onto the Eurostar.'

My defiance worked. Some of the aggression disappeared.

'Those bastards made a right show of us.' He rubbed the corners of his cheeks and laughed bitterly.

'By now it'll be all over London. Every loser south of the river will be having a good old chuckle and word will spread: Danny Glass is on the way down.'

He fought to get himself under control. This was a Danny even I'd never seen, wounded and capable of anything, in its way more disturbing because I wasn't sure how to deal with it. I leaned over the desk and pressed his hand.

'Fuck other people. Danny Glass is worth ten of them. Team Glass, remember?'

The veins in his neck were thin blue wires, taut under the skin. Suddenly, he relaxed and the tension went out of him, replaced by a sly smile. He eased his fingers free of mine, laughing again, and I realised I was being mocked.

'You really believe I'd let this morning get to me? You actually think that could happen? Not a chance, little brother. Not a snowball's.'

The anger had been real. The despair had been a performance for my benefit, an act to get me to buy into his idea of us. And I'd fallen for it. He'd even got me to say it: Team Glass. Danny patted my cheek none too gently and put a hand on my shoulder as if I were the one who needed comforting.

'Got a lot to learn, Luke. Thought you of all people knew me better than that.'

Apparently not. He went over to the jukebox and pressed a key. Joe Cocker rasped his way into 'With a Little Help from My Friends' and it dawned on me how badly I'd underestimated my brother. What happened next confirmed it.

I said, 'Some of the guys are downstairs waiting for orders.'

Danny tossed his reply casually over his shoulder, almost like he'd forgotten to tell me and wouldn't have remembered if I hadn't brought it up.

'They're too late. Made my move an hour ago.'

Before I could ask what he meant, his phone rang. Oliver Stanford was angry. Danny listened, ended the call and turned to me. 'Ollie's not best pleased.'

'What's his problem?'

'Who cares? The day I start worrying about what might upset him is the day I'm ready for the knacker's yard.'

'Be careful, Danny. If he needs sorting, do it, but not now, not while this lot's going on.'

He reached down and pulled a Beretta 9000S and a packet of Xanax from a drawer.

'Don't know which one you need most. I'll tell you, bro, you haven't been right since you came out of Wandsworth.' He tossed the gun and the pills across to me. 'Whatever you do, don't get them mixed up and blow your bloody head off.'

18

Elise Stanford slowed down and pointed the Mercedes towards the drive of her mock-Tudor house. Behind the wheel a headscarf hid her blonde hair. She wore no make-up – with the tan from their holiday in the Caribbean, none was needed.

As she admitted to anyone who'd listen, she wasn't 'a morning person'. Oliver was usually gone by seven o'clock, often earlier, which meant dropping their two daughters at school was her responsibility. Elise didn't mind. Her time was her own until she picked them up again at four. During the week the most taxing thing she did was sit on the committee of a local charity or have coffee with a group of like-minded ladies. None of the women worked, not because they were lazy – although most of them were – they already had jobs making sure their successful husbands stayed that way.

Today, her 'schedule' was free apart from lunch with Alison Bentner, an old school friend who'd had the good sense to marry a banker. Elise had her mind on what to wear when she noticed something odd: the electric gates were open. Strange. She was certain she'd closed them on her way out. Half the time the bloody things didn't work. The Mercedes rolled silently into the drive, past a tall man in sunglasses, a stranger to her upmarket neighbourhood, waiting on the pavement.

Seeing him annoyed her. She almost asked what the hell he thought he was doing.

The first hour after Elise came home was always spent reading the newspapers, full of the usual stuff – the goings-on of movie stars she'd never heard of, and politicians promising things they'd no hope of delivering. As Oliver's wife, Elise had met more than her fair share and didn't trust any of them. One piece caught her attention. According to the latest statistics, violent crime was on the increase and she quietly thanked God they'd moved to Hendon – a long slow drive into the city for Oliver, but not far from Aerodrome Road and the college when he was lecturing.

Sunshine flooded the conservatory, her favourite part of The Old Coach House and something she'd always wanted. Oliver had come home one night and surprised her by announcing she could have it, waving away questions about how they were going to afford it.

Elise remembered him kissing her forehead and saying, 'All taken care of, darling. All taken care of.'

Oliver Stanford was a good man.

Her tea had gone cold and she went to the kitchen to make a fresh cup. The stranger was sitting on a swing tied to the branch of an oak tree the girls had played on at the bottom of the garden when they were younger, staring at her from behind his shades.

Elise was outraged. This was private property. What the hell did he think he was doing? Obviously, he didn't know who her husband was.

Her indignation was short-lived. A second stranger rose from underneath the window, his empty expression inches from the glass. Elise cried out, backed away and dropped the kettle. Water washed across the flagstone floor. The man got off the swing and strode purposefully across the neat lawn. When he was close enough for her to see his eyes, he took off his sunglasses and smiled. Fear was a new experience for Elise Stanford. Being a policeman's wife, she gave no thought to her personal safety. What was happening terrified her. She fumbled for her mobile and the first number on her speed dial.

Oliver's irritation came down the line. 'Elise, we've spoken about this. I prefer you don't call me at work. I could be in a meeting with the commander and it doesn't play well. What is it? What do you want? If it's to confirm some dinner party or some other nonsense I promise you, I won't appreciate it.'

The impatient tirade hardly registered with his wife. She struggled to get the words out.

'Oliver... Oliver... there are two men at the window.'

* * *

I followed Danny downstairs and saw relief on the faces of the troops at the bar. These guys weren't employed for their brains. He was their leader and their meal-ticket. They depended on him to function. As part of Danny Glass's crew, they had a place in the world. Without him they were nothing and most of them got that.

Felix came forward with his hand outstretched. 'Glad you're okay, boss.'

Foolish.

Danny looked him up and down, pushed past and answered out of the corner of his mouth. 'What you on about? 'Course I'm okay.'

Said with a grin. Felix had to be tone deaf to miss the undercurrent of irritation in his voice. The others knew the score and stayed quiet while he bumbled on.

'I mean... after...'

A nod to the barman brought a large whisky. Danny threw it back in one go, wiped his mouth on his sleeve, and faced the setback head-on, his voice clear and strong.

'This morning was a balls-up. No use denying it. But it doesn't matter. Anderson's a dead man.'

Felix didn't learn – he interrupted. 'When're we going after the tossers?'

I pulled the idiot aside. 'Some advice for you, Felix. When you're with my brother, never miss an opportunity to shut up.'

'Have I done something wrong?'

It didn't deserve an answer and didn't get one. Felix worked at persuading me how loyal he was. 'I'm with Danny 100 per cent, 200 per cent. He knows that.'

'Then do yourself a favour and button it.'

Danny was standing in the centre of the group loudly telling a story as if he hadn't a care in the world – faking it. He delivered the joke, everybody laughed and he glanced to where I was with the same sly smile on his face. He'd conned me in the office. This was a variation on the theme, convincing his men everything was all okay.

Business as usual. Nothing to be concerned about.

I wasn't buying it.

He breezed past Felix and headed for the stairs. Back in the office he kept the charade going. 'Good guys. Rollie doesn't understand what he's started.'

Only days out of Wandsworth and already I was tired of his horseshit. Also, I disagreed. Anderson knew exactly what he'd started and, so far, he'd had it all his own way.

Danny sensed I wasn't happy. 'What's wrong? Not enough action for you? Didn't you say we should be unpredictable? No 'Gunfight at the O.K. Corral'?'

'There's unpredictable and there's stupid.'

He dropped the laid-back crap and waved a finger to make his point.

'Watch it, little brother. Just watch it. You haven't a clue. The business survived without you for seven years, or had you forgotten? This is Danny Glass you're talking to.'

'Then stop playing games. I told you something wasn't right.'

A vein throbbed at his temple and I realised that – brother or not – I was pushing too hard. The words were said quietly, almost conversationally. All the more chilling for that.

'Think you're ready to take over, do you?'

'That's not what I said. You have to admit they're taking the piss.'

'Wrong, little brother, I don't have to admit anything.'

Footsteps running up the stairs broke in before the confrontation exploded. The door flew open and Oliver Stanford burst into the room. At our first meeting he'd been smug, even when Danny was laying into him. The superiority was missing now and he was white with anger.

'You're out of order, Glass. What the fuck do you think you're doing, threatening my family?'

Danny's reply took both of us by surprise.

'Right reaction, copper.'

19

Stanford spoke through gritted teeth. 'My wife knows nothing about our arrangements and that's how it stays.'

'Then she's living in cloud cuckoo land. Where does she think the money comes from? She can't believe they pay you that well. You've married an idiot, Oliver.'

'Elise doesn't get involved with money.'

Danny leaned back in his chair. 'What a sheltered life you've given her. Hope she's grateful.' He made a crude gesture intended to goad the chief inspector. The detective gripped the edge of the desk so hard his knuckles poked through the skin. I appreciated his dilemma. He was angry but he wasn't a fool. My brother was moody and impulsive and capable of things he couldn't imagine.

Stanford worked hard to hold onto himself and just about managed it.

'Whether she is or whether she isn't, leave her out of it. Sending your goons to my house isn't part of our deal.'

Danny reached across the desk and roared into the DCI's face.

'I'll tell you what's part of our deal, Ollie Boy. Anything I fucking want!'

I gave the policeman credit. Coming here had taken courage,

though there was a point where courage morphed into idiocy and he was running pretty close to it. He wasn't sure what was going on and glanced over at me for a clue. No chance. I hadn't forgotten his disdain for me the first time we'd met, when he'd behaved as if I wasn't there – he deserved nothing and he got nothing.

Danny loosened his tie and opened the top button of his shirt. 'Thanks to your information we ended up looking like a bunch of amateurs this morning.'

That shocked Stanford – clearly, he hadn't known. 'What happened? It wasn't reported.'

'Somebody at your end's playing away from home. Either your contact's useless or you've got a rat in your team, Detective Chief Inspector.'

The DCI hit back. 'I gave you word for word exactly what I was told.'

Danny wasn't impressed. 'Then you got told wrong. Otherwise we wouldn't have been caught with our trousers round our ankles in fucking Kent.'

Stanford remembered the conversation with Trevor Mills and Bob Wallace. Trevor hadn't been happy talking so openly in front of Wallace. He'd told Trevor Mills it was a test: a test their colleague had failed.

'I can't believe that's true but I'll find out.'

Danny's tone mocked him. 'Good man. Good man.' He turned to Luke. 'Didn't I just say we can count on Detective Chief Inspector Stanford?'

His expression changed, the fake humour turned off like a switch.

'You've got forty-eight hours to come back with a name before I pull the plug on your nice life. You knew sod all about the hit on this place. Now your information's tainted. Understand?'

The policeman was wise enough to say nothing until he was at the door.

'What if the leak didn't come from my side?'

It was a question Danny had to be asking. Team Glass was me, him and Nina. Beyond that, apart from Marcus, his men were career criminals; thugs for hire. Some had even been on Albert's payroll and swapped sides when they saw Danny was on the rise south of the river. Their loyalty was bought with money and held by fear. The moment the pendulum started to swing the other way, they'd reconsider their future.

'Trust me, Ollie, it did.'

Stanford pushed his luck. 'So you say. How do you know?'

'That's easy, copper. It's not worth it. Anybody who crosses me, and I mean anybody, will wish their mother had never had them.' Danny added a question that needed no answer. 'Ever seen a man die slowly? No? My advice: keep it like that.' He turned the screw. 'The screams stay with you the rest of your life. Sometimes in the middle of the night they're all you can hear. When they stop, the silence is beautiful, just beautiful.'

Stanford was being given a warning. He'd do well to pay attention.

'Sort it out at your end. If it happens again I'm holding you responsible. Now fuck off out of it.'

After he'd gone, I said, 'He has a point. We don't know.'

'Correction: we don't know, yet.'

'What now?'

'I'm taking your advice. Being unpredictable by doing sod all.'

My brother was still playing games.

'You need me for anything?'

'Not right now.'

'Sure?'

'Absolutely. And don't worry. How do you think I managed when you were inside? Rollie will be off his face for at least a couple of days. I bet he's celebrating as we speak. We would be. Let him enjoy his moment in the sun. It won't last.'

'Then I'm off. Call if things change.'

'Where're you heading?'

'Haven't given it much thought. Brighton, maybe.'

'Going by yourself?'

I didn't reply and he smiled. 'Thought as much. Taking that tart with you, aren't you?' He wagged a cautionary finger. 'Just don't forget what she is. Being inside makes us go soft in the head about women. Ex-cons marry the first one who smiles at them. Happens all the time. Don't be a mug and fall into the trap, okay?'

'I hear you.'

'Make sure you do, little brother. And be careful. Take that waster Felix with you.'

'No, not today. I need some space.'

Something dark passed behind his eyes: I was disobeying him.

He blinked and was Danny again.

'Wherever you fetch up, call me so I know you're all right.'

* * *

The car drove like a dream, gliding through the slow-moving traffic towards the Kennington address Mandy had given me. In the rear-view mirror, the Golf had been replaced by a Fiesta and a Corsa; one courtesy of the Metropolitan Police, the other from my brother, Felix no doubt. I ignored them and tried to enjoy the trip.

On a whim I decided to visit Nina and fished out the card she'd given me. The business park was at the start of Brixton Road and easy to find, as it happened. She came to Reception, gave me a hug and led the way to her office, a thirty-square-metre box on the second floor, sparsely furnished and painted in neutral colours. Nina seemed relaxed, pleased to see me, and I was glad I'd come. There was an energy to her that was missing when she was around Danny.

'To what do I owe this surprise?'

'Do I need a reason to see my little sister? You look like you're in your element. Thought you didn't like working for our brother.'

'I'm okay so long as I don't dwell on it. Besides, it's a means to an end.'

'Is it?'

'Absolutely. My long-term plans don't include Danny Glass.'

'Do they include me?'

A light came on in her eyes. For a moment I had the feeling she was judging me. Nina knew I wasn't serious, but she answered my question anyway. 'Depends.'

'On what?'

'How you feel about having a woman as your boss.'

I laughed. 'If you mean you, I suppose I'll get used to it.'

She said, 'Where are you off to?'

'I haven't decided.'

'By yourself?'

The same question Danny had asked – it must be in the genes.

'No, not by myself.'

'C'mon, brother. Spill the tea.'

'It's a nice day for a drive to the coast.'

'And you're taking Mandy? The Mandy Danny had so much to say about.'

'The very same.'

'Will she be around long enough for me to meet her?'

'Maybe. Probably.'

'Good for you, Luke.'

'Why don't you come with us?'

Nina leaned on her elbows on the desk, pretending to think about it, and didn't reply. Finally, she said, 'I'm meeting somebody.'

'Secretive? Not like you. When you were a teenager, you'd flaunt the boyfriends Danny didn't like under his nose.'

* * *

Driving to Mandy's, I was struck again by how much had changed; the buildings were the same but the shops and businesses – even the people walking down the street – seemed different. Finally, I recognised a newsagent on a corner and a memory jumped out at me: it was smaller than I remembered, the plaster on the outside walls cracked and faded to a dull grey, the door and part of the window covered with

For Sale notices written on postcard-size cards Sellotaped to the glass. I'd raced through that same door with the owner, Mr Varma, after me, shouting and swearing in whatever language they spoke where he came from.

This was where it had all begun.

We were young and it was a laugh, at least it was for us. Until it stopped being funny. My job was to act suspicious and draw the bearded Indian away from the counter so Danny could reach over and grab as many packets of cigarettes as he could. Small stuff. Just what you'd expect from a couple of apprentice wide boys, and for a while it worked.

Until Mr Varma got wise and was ready for us. One hot summer's afternoon Danny was waiting for me at the school gates, his hands deep in his pockets, distractedly kicking at stones. I asked why he was there. He shook his head and started walking. I followed the way I always did back then. We got to the shop and went into our usual routine. Mr Varma pretended not to notice us but suddenly, he was standing in the doorway. Danny got past him. I wasn't quick enough. He caught me out on the pavement and had me by the collar, screaming about calling the police. Then, he let go and fell to the ground. When I turned, my brother was standing over him, eyes glazed like a sleepwalker, an expression of pure hatred on his face. He bared his teeth like an animal and really laid in, kicking him and calling him a Paki bastard – although he knew he wasn't from Pakistan. Blood poured from the Indian's head, matting his hair and his shirt, staining the dull grey concrete.

It ended when somebody shouted from across the street for him to stop and we legged it. Later, Danny sold the cigarettes to another shop and bought us fish suppers. We ate them on the way home and stayed up talking about the future, while our father slept off yet another bender next door. In six months, he'd be dead and I'd be my brother's responsibility.

That night Danny invented Team Glass and told me about the Lucky Bastards Club and how we were going to be in it. I believed him and went to bed in the early hours, tired but happy. What we'd done to Mr Varma never got mentioned again.

Sometimes the future was shaped by what *didn't* happen. In our case, we didn't get caught and the rest went the way it went: from watching an unarmed man being beaten over a few packets of fags to throwing Albert Anderson off the forty-third floor of a half-built office block.

Quite a journey. And it wasn't finished.

* * *

A dark-skinned girl in a pink and blue sari, probably Mr Varma's granddaughter, stood in his place. I bought a *Daily Express* to justify being there. She gave me my change and I saw her hands and arms were covered in henna.

'Nice.'

She answered without a trace of accent. 'Thank you.'

'I used to come here when I was a boy. There was a man. He had a beard. Think his name was Mr Varma.'

The girl smiled. 'That would be my grandfather.'

'Don't suppose he's still around.'

'No. I never knew him. He died trying to stop a robbery before I was born.'

I said, 'Sorry to hear that,' and left.

Outside, the newspaper went in a rubbish bin. All Mr Varma was doing was trying to pay his way in the world, more than could be said for us. His bad luck had been in running into Team fucking Glass. Now, the teenage thief who'd murdered him was in the middle of a gang war and I was on my way to see a prostitute who wrote lipstick messages on bathroom mirrors.

* * *

As soon as Mandy opened the door of her flat, I realised we wouldn't be heading to Brighton or anywhere else just yet. She was naked except for high heels and the ankle bracelet.

What happened next was entirely predictable. We didn't make it to the bedroom, or even the couch.

* * *

In the car she closed her eyes and let the wind blow her hair away from her face, a beautiful face. I tried to concentrate on the road. With her beside me, not a chance. A few days and already I was in deep. Deeper than was wise.

She turned her head and smiled. 'I feel like I'm in a dream and don't want to wake up.'

'Dream on.'

Her fingers ran up and down my arm. 'This was a good idea. I thought you might've changed your mind.'

Her fear was talking though we both understood what she meant. Silly girl. She wasn't the only one who was dreaming. I knew who she was and what she was and it couldn't have mattered less.

20

Oliver Stanford stood in the middle of the room surrounded by detectives, some on the phone, others with their eyes fixed on PC screens. The irony of trying to sound casual was clear to him. In the very heart of the Met he was playing a part, choosing his words carefully because somebody might be paying more attention than they should have been.

He called over to DI Mills. 'Going for an early lunch, fancy joining me, Trevor?'

Mills looked up, understanding immediately. His DCI rarely had a break. Eating and drinking took time when there were criminals to catch.

'Give me a minute to finish this.'

Mills typed a final few sentences, reached for his jacket and hurried to catch up with his boss. Neither man spoke until they were beyond the iconic revolving New Scotland Yard sign, which had followed them from 10 Broadway, the address of London's police force for forty-nine years. The new building was smaller and reactions to the move were mixed. Oliver Stanford had no opinion. He couldn't have cared less. The job didn't change.

Trevor Mills said, 'Where're we going, the Clarence?'

The Clarence on Whitehall was the nearest pub, usually filled with tourists and off-duty policemen. Mills was already a regular customer, often preferring to have cod and chips or beef and ale pie and a couple of pints in the Tin Belly dining room upstairs rather than go home to Barbara. The food was good; the booze was overpriced. Then again, the centre of every big city was a rip-off. In the end you got used to it.

'No. We need to talk. That isn't the place for it.'

'Where is?'

'Somewhere we're not known, Trevor.' He stuck out his arm and a taxi pulled in. Stanford gave the driver instructions. 'The Masons Arms, Hallam Street.'

They headed towards Regent Street crowded with visitors and shoppers enjoying the sunshine. Stanford loosened his tie and rolled his shirt sleeves up, but he still looked like a policeman. Trevor Mills had no idea what was going on and started to ask; his boss cut him off and put a finger to his lips. The taxi took them two miles across the city and stopped outside the pub. Stanford paid the cab and the men went inside. It was still only a little after noon – too early for the lunchtime crowd. Harley Street and a slew of medical businesses were close by. In another hour the place would be mobbed. Mills took a seat and let the senior detective do the honours – it was his show, after all. Besides, he made more money. That thought reminded him of his bitch of a wife's undisguised disappointment every time she saw where his boss lived. Stanford was at the bar with his back to him, taking notes from his wallet. Mills heard Barbara's withering words and felt a flash of resentment pass through him.

Oliver Stanford isn't smarter than you.

Tell me he isn't.

At least give me that much hope...

Stanford set the beers down and tossed two packets of crisps on the table.

'All we've time for, I'm afraid. Got a meeting with the commander at three.'

Mills lifted his drink – wet and clear and cold – and put the thoughts in his head aside for another day. 'Must be five thousand pubs in Central London, why here?'

'I've arranged for somebody to meet us. Better nobody knows who we are.'

'Who?'

His boss sipped his drink and appraised him over the rim of the glass. 'The snitch who told us about Anderson's drug shipment. We need to ask him face to face where he got the information.'

'What's his name?'

'You know better than that, Trevor.'

Mills inwardly sneered. Stanford was an arrogant bastard – Barbara wasn't wrong about that – it was 'we' and 'us' when things went badly and 'me' when they went well. In this case, it had gone off the rails and he was spreading the responsibility for the failure. A fresh wave of resentment rose in Mills. He said, 'How long has this guy been spilling for you?'

The reply was guarded. 'Long enough.'

'And the info's always good?'

Stanford gripping his pint was displeased at having his judgement questioned.

The pub gradually filled with office workers in groups of twos and threes, eagerly crowding the bar, determined to enjoy their hour of freedom in the middle of the day. Mills caught Stanford checking the clock above the gantry and sensed his anxiety.

He rubbed it in. 'Maybe he's changed his mind?'

'He'd better not have or I'll... wait... It's him. He's here.'

A thin man in a black suit jacket, white collarless shirt and blue jeans stood in the open door. He came over and sat down, immediately suspicious.

'You didn't say anything about bringing somebody else in. Who the fuck is this, Oliver?'

'Nobody to worry about. Relax.'

In his business, relaxing didn't end well. The latest call from the detective hadn't come as a surprise. He'd heard about the hit on the van and been expecting it.

'Before we start, my information was rock solid, 100 per cent.'

Stanford reassured him. 'All in good time, all in good time.' He turned to Mills. 'Get this man whatever he wants, Trevor.'

This guy stupidly assumed he was off the hook and reverted to type.

'Since you're buying, I'll have a lager and a large vodka.'

Stanford's expression hardened. 'Like hell you will. Think yourself lucky I haven't blown the whistle on you. And for your cheek, you're getting sod all.'

The informer faked offence. 'You told your boy to get me whatever I want, which happens to be a lager and a large vodka. What's wrong with that?'

'Don't push it. Tell me what happened in Kent.'

'Far as I'm concerned, nothing. The word was fifty thousand tablets were coming from the coast. Anderson uses that route a lot. Never has any problems. Should've been fine.'

'Except there were and it wasn't. Danny Glass's ready to string up whoever made a fool of him. Shall I drop your name in his ear?'

Mills wondered if his boss realised he was actually talking about himself. The decision to set Wallace up was Stanford's. *He* was the one who'd jeopardised Glass's hit by letting Wallace in on the call.

The informant with no name blanched at the threat, his weasel face got thinner and the wide boy bravado disappeared. 'Christ's sake, don't do that, Oliver. The information was on the money. Honest.'

Stanford let him sweat. 'Where did you get it?'

'You know how it is, people tell me things.'

'Which people?'

'Just people.'

'Not good enough.'

'If I tell you or anybody else, I might as well shut up shop. I'll say it again: the info was good. When I passed it to you, it was gold.'

'And you're prepared to stake your life on this guy? Because that's what you'll be doing.'

The man drew a hand through the stubble on his jaw, two days' worth at least.

'Wouldn't go as far as that, but he's straight, I'd swear to it.'

The informant got up. 'Weren't serious about telling Glass, were you? I mean, might as well shoot me yourself.'

Stanford smiled. 'Not a bad idea. Why didn't we think of that, Trevor?'

'It's never too late.'

When he'd left the detectives eyed each other, grimly. Mills said. 'A wasted journey.'

'Not exactly. We know more than we did. I believe him. In a dozen years, he's never been wrong.'

The DI threw his own line back at him. 'And you'd stake your life on this guy?'

'No, I wouldn't but he's straight, I'd swear to it.'

Both policemen laughed.

'That leaves three possibilities.' The DCI counted them on his fingers. 'One: you were right and Wallace is playing for the other side. Two: Anderson got wind of something and went off-plan.'

Trevor Mills swirled the dregs of his pint around the glass. 'And the third?'

'That maybe the leak isn't on our end.'

'Is that good?'

Stanford was well aware of his DI's opinion. The way their careers had gone, it would be a surprise if he'd felt any differently, especially with his lush of a wife whispering lies, telling him that he could be the more successful man. Understandable maybe to think that, but not true: detective inspector was as far as Trevor Mills would ever go. To rise higher you needed to be capable of appreciating the bigger picture. That let him out. Otherwise he wouldn't be asking such a stupid question.

'No, that isn't good. It's the worst option imaginable. Glass believes he's strong when, in fact, that would mean he's vulnerable. And whoever knows about Danny Glass knows we're involved.'

'Where does that leave us?'

'Okay, in reverse order: Glass is convinced his team is sound, so let's believe him until proved otherwise. We know Anderson didn't get his information from the street. That leaves us with your suspicion – Wallace. How the stupid bugger thought he could pull it off is a mystery.'

'What are you going to do?'

'The only thing I can do. Give him up.'

'To Glass?'

'Who else?'

21

The basement flat in Moscow Road, Bayswater was the first place George Ritchie stayed when he came south. He'd bought it with cash, though not for its aesthetic or investment values. Small didn't do it justice. Accessed from the street at the bottom of concrete steps, cracked and worn with age and covered in part with moss he'd never bothered to dig out, it was tiny: a single room with a sink and cooker in one corner, a bed in the other, and a WC in what had probably been a cupboard once upon a time.

A loner by instinct, Ritchie developed the habits that would define his persona in that claustrophobic hole in the ground in West London. Those same instincts had brought him back there.

In the early days his local had been the Daniel Gooch, for no reason other than it was at the far end of Queensway, a good distance from the flat. And, like he'd do in Camden Town years later, he drank his two pints and left long before closing time. Occasionally, at half-time in a football match on the TV screen, somebody would talk to him and find him polite and quietly spoken with an accent very different from their own. Behind his back the regulars called him 'Mr Two Pints' and let him be.

Ritchie had realised Camden was a bust as soon as he saw the kissing couple who were obviously not lovers – their embrace was the embrace of strangers, awkward and forced, not nearly passionate enough to deceive an old dog. And he knew they were on to him. From behind the ragged curtain he'd watched the man take a call on his mobile and pass something to the woman – money for services rendered. Then, they'd gone their separate ways.

In the darkness, Ritchie reached under the single bed for the suitcase kept packed and ready. The key to the Bayswater flat, his two passports and three bank books were in a safety deposit box at Victoria Station. Ritchie had no regrets: this was the price of the life he'd chosen and he left without a backward glance.

At Mornington Crescent he hailed a cruising taxi, took it to Great Smith Street and walked to Victoria Station. Getting what he needed didn't take long. A second cab dropped him off at the top of Queensway.

Moscow Road was deserted when he went down the stairs, turned the key in the lock and opened the door. The case went under the single bed. He took off his jacket, sat in the chair near the window and closed his eyes. The police would find the white van burned out on waste ground across the river from the O2 Centre. There would be no licence plates to identify it or fingerprints on the charred shell.

The van driver's body would never be found.

And tonight, the Daniel Gooch would have an old customer back.

George Ritchie wondered if anybody would remember him.

22

The nearest we got to the coast was Mandy looking at bikinis in Harrods. Half of the three grand Danny had given me – three thousand four hundred, to be exact – got spent between Sloane Square and the bottom of the Kings Road: my treat. Afterwards, we had a couple of drinks and the best steak I'd ever eaten in The World's End Market. She was wearing sunglasses pushed high on her head, white shoes and a sky-blue print dress, which showcased her figure and the light tan on her slender arms.

When the waiter cleared the table I said, 'How old is your daughter?'

'She's nine.'

'What's her name?'

'Amy.'

'Shouldn't you be getting back to her?'

Mandy shook her head. 'She lives in Manchester with her father.'

'And you're okay about that?'

She shrugged. 'Okay isn't how I'd put it. It's the way it is.'

'I'd like to meet her.'

'Maybe you will.'

The words were positive; pragmatic, but behind them I heard

regret. As if she'd accepted what she did for a living barred her from being a mum. Yet, there was no self-pity. No hard-luck story. She'd made her decisions and was coping with them the best she could.

'She'll be here soon.'

I was no parenting expert, but I knew that allowing her little girl to go to another city with somebody else – even her father – would come at a cost, paid in the middle of the night.

She played with the stem of her wine glass.

'I can guess what you're thinking.'

'Clever you.'

'You're wondering how such bad shit could happen to a nice girl like me.'

'No, that's not what I'm wondering at all. Bad shit happens to everybody.'

Mandy laughed. 'I'll tell you anyway. Amy was two when we divorced. My ex-husband's job took him back up north – he got promoted. He has family there, mine are dead – it made sense for her to be with him. He had more to offer. When he suggested it, I agreed.'

'More to offer a child than her mother? It must be hard for you.'

'Only if I let myself think about it.'

I didn't believe her.

'As for the job – nobody forced me. It's the road I decided to take, simple as that.'

She lifted her face, her eyes deep and clear, daring me to question her choices. This was the tale Mandy had settled for telling herself – the version of her life she could live with, the one where her daughter's best interests were served. How much of it was true was unimportant. I was the last person to judge.

She pointed to the bags at her feet and the designer labels unfamiliar to me. 'You've put out a lot of money on me today.'

'It wasn't mine. I didn't earn it.'

'Then I shouldn't feel bad about spending it, should I?'

'Absolutely not. I enjoyed myself.'

Mandy said, 'You sure you're Danny's brother? You're not like him.'

'Is that a compliment?'

She seemed surprised. 'If being told you're different from Danny Glass isn't a compliment, what is?'

'You haven't said why you don't like my brother.'

She backed away from answering and softened. 'He's a voice on the other end of the phone now and again, asking me to bring girls to a party. I spoke out of turn. Sorry.'

'No need to apologise. Everybody's entitled to their opinion. Besides, I've hardly seen him in seven years. We're strangers.'

'Yeah, but he's still your brother. Nothing changes that. And he's still Danny Glass.'

She looked away, leaving me with her cryptic verdict ringing in my ears –*'And he's still Danny Glass.'*

Before I could ask her to explain, my mobile rang. It was Danny.

'Oliver fucking Stanford's coming to the King Pot. Reckons he's got a name for us. Get back here. And before we go any further, forget boxing clever. It's not happening, so don't suggest it or we'll be falling out, you and me.'

The phone went dead. Mandy said, 'That was him, wasn't it?'

'Yes. We'll have to cut it short. He wants me at the pub.'

She touched my arm. 'Be careful, Luke. I meant what I said. You're not like him.'

Danny's caustic assessment of ex-cons who fell in love with the first female who smiled at them hadn't been forgotten. There was truth in there – sexual attraction was a rocky foundation to build a lasting relationship on. Mandy must've been thinking the same. She said, 'Can I ask something?'

'Of course.'

'Am I your girlfriend? I mean, is that how you see me? Or am I being silly? I'm being silly, aren't I?' She blushed and turned away. 'Forget I said that.'

Off-guard, my answer was flippant and vague and inadequate.

'You're a girl and you're a friend so, yeah.'

A shadow passed behind her eyes; it was exactly what she'd

expected. Was it a test? If it had been, I'd failed.

* * *

I dropped her at her flat just as it started to pour. It matched the mood. Our day was ending on a subdued note.

'I'll call you as soon as we sort this out.'

The trust I'd seen in her eyes in Chelsea was gone. Getting out of the car, she almost forgot to take the shopping from the back seat. I reminded her and she thanked me again. Instead of kissing me, she offered her cheek. Before she spoke, I guessed what she was going to say.

'Maybe we shouldn't see each other again.'

'I don't agree. As for what we are, it's early days. Let's be happy with what we've got and see how it goes, eh?'

Mandy wasn't convinced and it showed.

My reply to her question hadn't made me feel good. I wasn't thick. I knew what she'd been asking. Without meaning to, I'd hurt her. Tomorrow, I'd find a better response.

'I'm serious. I will call.'

She smiled a half-smile that didn't touch her eyes. 'I'll be waiting.'

On the drive to the King Pot, with the windscreen wipers slapping rain away, I replayed our conversation in the restaurant from its confessional beginning to how it had ended. Three things jumped out: Mandy's frankness in speaking about her life, her tentative hopes for a future for us, and the change when Danny's name came up. There was plenty to admire about her – honesty, for one – except she hadn't been totally honest.

She was afraid of my brother. And afraid for me.

* * *

Mandy watched Luke steer through the city traffic. He was a handsome man. And he was nothing like his brother – they were different in every way imaginable. Luke was uncomplicated where Danny was twisted; kind where he was cruel. She'd lied to him and he deserved better. But when the truth was shameful and ugly, what did that leave?

It had taken just two years after Amy was born for her mother's life to fall apart: depression followed her like a black dog she couldn't shake off. Discovering her husband's adultery had sent her over the edge and she'd become addicted to Xanax – a neighbour had found her unconscious on the floor with Amy crawling on top of her.

But the nightmare was only just beginning.

Her ex was offered a job in Manchester, nearer his family, and he accepted. Next came the bombshell: his plans didn't include her, though they did include *his* daughter. He called her an unfit mother, delusional and out of control, and had the proof already lined up; a friend of his was prepared to lie and say he'd slept with her with their daughter in the room; the neighbour who'd found her unconscious agreed to give evidence – in the interests of the child. Even the doctor who had originally prescribed the drug for her depression was against her.

The day Amy's father took her away, Mandy cried herself to sleep and slipped nearer the abyss. She was in bad shape when her path crossed Danny Glass. He'd weaned her off everything she was on and shown her a way to get her daughter back some day.

She'd taken it.

Then she'd discovered what being in Danny's debt really meant.

* * *

Yvonne rolled the stocking over her ankle, and slowly up her thigh, conscious of Eugene's eyes devouring her. She watched him lying naked and still hard on the office floor and didn't hurry to cover herself. He really couldn't get enough, thank God. As usual, the sex had been amazing; she'd shuddered and moaned through three massive climaxes and lost count of the minor ones during foreplay. It would be a pity if what she was about to say ended it.

'Enjoying the view?'

Eugene grinned. 'Loving it.'

He got up and stood behind her. She felt his warm breath on her neck, his fingers toying with her nipples; she didn't stop him.

'Haven't you had enough?'

'Nothing like enough. Want to go again?'

'You said you were meeting somebody.'

'Well, they'll have to wait, won't they?'

Yvonne laughed and let him pull her to the carpet. 'You really are a hound, aren't you?'

Eugene howled. 'You weren't complaining ten minutes ago.'

The laughter stopped, their lips met and their bodies melded again. When it was over, they got dressed. Eugene patted his pockets, checking for his car keys and wallet, frowning: he was late and regretting it. This was the moment she'd waited for.

Her tone was casual, throwaway, like she was making end-of-the-day inconsequential chit-chat. 'Will she be angry?'

He was tying his tie, only half listening. 'What?'

'I'm asking if she'll be angry with you.'

'Will who be angry with me?'

'Nina Glass. That's who you're meeting, isn't it?'

'As a matter of fact, no, I'm—'

Yvonne cut him off. 'Don't bother denying it, Eugene. I've known for a while. You're a great fuck but you're a terrible liar.'

'It's nothing... nothing serious.'

'It never is.'

'Not true.'

'Of course, it's true. Women are only good for one thing as far as you're concerned.'

Eugene hit back. 'We never said we wouldn't see other people. Where's the gripe coming from? I don't get it.'

She walked round the desk and sat in his chair. 'You're right, we owe each other nothing. So you won't mind if Danny Glass hears about what you're doing with his sister.'

Vale's lips curled in a sour smile. 'He already knows. Sorry to spoil your fun.'

She shook her head, unfazed. 'Not what I'm going to tell him.'

Eugene Vale's eyes hardened – he should've quit while he was ahead; the session had taken an unwelcome turn. He tried to bluff his way back to safer ground. 'You surprise me, Yvonne. I didn't think you were the jealous type.'

'Don't flatter yourself. I've been using you as much as you've been using me.' She got out of the chair and came towards him. When their faces were close enough to smell sex on him, she said, 'I couldn't care less who you're shagging. That's who you are. And you're good at it, otherwise I wouldn't let you near me. I'm talking about something else, something Danny Glass hasn't caught on to. Yet.'

The threat was unmistakeable.

'What the hell are you on about?'

'I mean the money you and his sister are stealing.'

'Stealing?'

Vale stared at the woman he'd had three times in the last hour. She said, 'At twelve o'clock today you went to the bank. The safe should be practically empty. I'm betting there's cash in there. Plenty of cash. Go on, I dare you. Open it.'

Vale stayed where he was.

'Glass is a violent guy. Being his sister might save Nina but what about you?'

The veins in Eugene Vale's neck stood out in angry lines; his voice was low and cracked.

'Don't... do this, Yvonne, I'm warning you. It won't end well.'

'For you, absolutely it won't. For me it'll end very well. Expect I'll get a nice little bonus.'

'What do you want?'

'Speak to your girlfriend. Tell her I want in. And when I say in, I mean 50 per cent, half of whatever the take is. Point out she doesn't have much choice. Danny Glass would love to hear what I'd have to tell him.'

23

I was getting used to seeing Danny's guys outside the King Pot. Until Rollie Anderson started his nonsense, it hadn't been necessary. Now, it was essential if we didn't want to get caught cold again. Once was bad luck, twice...

Harry nodded to me from behind the bar and limped to serve somebody at the far end. I climbed the stairs. Since I'd come out of Wandsworth, Danny's mood had been hard to anticipate; sullen and quick to take offence one minute, the next playing childish jokes at my expense. Thinking about it, he'd been a queer fish before I'd even got close to seeing the inside of prison, cutting me out of decisions and disappearing for days without telling anybody where he'd gone. Further back, when we were on the dodge, at times the vibe coming off him scared me.

He was sitting, as usual, under the photograph of the Queen, toying with a pile of paper clips. The laptop on his desk was closed and the jukebox was silent. I tapped the edge of the PC. 'Do you ever actually use this, or is it just for show?'

Danny looked up. 'It gets used, don't worry about that.'

Not exactly brotherly love but an improvement on some of his recent short-tempered greetings. He brought me up to date. 'Stanford's on his way. Wanted you to hear what he has to say for himself, and I'll tell you one thing: it better be good. None of his CID waffle. Otherwise, I'll pull the plug on him and his nice life. Might do it anyway just to screw him over.'

He pointed an accusing finger in my direction. 'And before you say anything, somebody's getting it. End of.'

We weren't sure what Stanford would say but Danny's mind was already made up. He couldn't control himself and had to lash out.

At somebody. At anybody.

He got up, strolled to the jukebox and let his fingers glide teasingly over the selection keys without pressing any. His back was to me. I couldn't see his face. The tone was casual. 'How d'you get on with that tart?'

I recognised the signs. The next words out of his mouth would be intended to provoke a reaction. If I gave him what he wanted he'd tell me to relax, calm down, and not take things so seriously, when, in fact, it was him who needed to chill.

'Fine.'

'Fine?'

'Yeah, it was fine.'

'You've spent the day with a prostitute and that's the best you can say? Doesn't sound like you're getting your money's worth. How much are you paying her?'

'None of your bloody business.'

His lips drew back in a mocking half-smile, mischief in his eyes.

'No need to get arsey, little brother. I only asked how you got on.'

'And I told you. Fine. Now let it go.'

He sat down again and went back to what he'd been doing. With anybody else the conversation would've been over. Except this was Danny.

'Wouldn't want you getting charged more than the rest of the boys. That wouldn't do at all.'

The urge to drag him across the desk was almost overwhelming. If he sensed the anger in me or saw my hands clenched at my sides, it didn't show. Understanding what he was doing didn't help. Of course, he knew my every move: he'd had me followed.

'Buy her something nice, did you?'

He coughed a throaty chuckle, added another clip to the chain and held it up like a child pleased with what it had created.

'Can read you like a book, always could. You dropped a bundle on a pro this afternoon because she spread her legs for you. You've forgotten that's her job. Next thing you'll be falling in love with the slag.'

'Let it go.'

Danny threw back his head. 'She's got a nice face, I'll give you that. Probably got a sweet nature. Don't they all at the beginning? Feed you a sob story, did she? And you believed her. No shame in having a good heart, brother. But she's a prostitute. At one time or another most of the boys have been through her. For fuck's sake, get a grip.'

It poured out too easily, like a script he'd rehearsed to goad me.

Once upon a time Danny had been my hero. Time's had changed.

'Danny, this isn't working.'

'What're you on about? It's working great.'

'I mean it isn't working for me.'

'Don't talk stupid. You've come out after seven years to a fistful of money and plenty more where that came from. 'Course it's working.'

'I'm sticking with my original plan. I'll be gone by the end of the week.'

'And miss my birthday?'

I didn't get a chance to tell him what he could do with his birthday. We hadn't heard Stanford on the stairs and didn't realise he was there until he was in the room. The row about to kick off didn't happen. I had a feeling it would keep.

* * *

Stanford had the same full-of-himself look I'd seen before. He glanced at me and nodded. Recognition. I'd come up in the world. Danny threw his arms in the air.

'Oliver! Good of you to come. Take a pew.'

The detective did as he was told. I stayed in the background and let them get on with it. Anderson, my brother and this bent copper deserved each other.

'On the phone you said you had a name. Glad to hear it. Very glad to hear it.'

Stanford drew himself straight in the chair and took a deep breath. 'I have. Before I give it – though I'm sure I'm wasting my time – I want to remind you that killing a policeman is one of the most serious offences under the law. It galvanises the victim's fellow officers into bringing the murderer to justice. I advise you to consider carefully what to do.'

A sardonic smile tugged the corners of his mouth. 'Of course, you'll go your own way. Wouldn't expect anything else. But if you do, there's no going back.'

Danny let him say his piece. Then, it was his turn. He began with a compliment – always a bad omen. 'You're wasted on the force, Oliver, d'you know that? Should've been a priest. Or maybe one of them motivational speakers. Thanks for the sermon. Now spit it out!'

Stanford hesitated and Danny went after him. 'C'mon, don't fuck me about.'

'I'm not. I wouldn't. The information about the drug shipment was solid. Only one other person knew about it.'

Danny leaned across the table. 'Who? Tell me or I'll break your back. See how much Elise loves you when you smell of piss day and night.'

'Bob Wallace.'

The anticlimax was deafening.

'Bob Wallace? What the fuck? Never heard of him. Who is he?'

'A detective sergeant. I wasn't sure about him so I let him in on the details. Hours later...'

There was no need to finish the sentence.

It sounded unconvincing. As if Stanford had stuck some poor unsuspecting bastard in the frame to save his own arse. Danny hadn't got where he was by being stupid – he was thinking what I was thinking.

'How sure are you about this? Because if you're not, now's the time to 'fess.'

On the surface the detective appeared unruffled. Underneath the tan I guessed he was pale. 'As sure as I can be. Only three people on my side knew. I can vouch for me and Trevor Mills. The third was Wallace. Which means he told Rollie Anderson about the hit.'

'What made you suspect him?'

'It was a test. Something about him... was off.'

'So you used me to set a trap for him?'

'That's not how it was. I was protecting us, both of us. If he was bent, we needed to know.'

Danny leaned over and slapped the policeman hard across the face.

'Should do you just for that. Maybe I will. But let's assume you're right. Tell me about this Bob Wallace and don't miss anything out. You've fucked up twice now, Oliver. You were in the dark about the attack on this pub and because of you Kent was a farce. One more and I'm cashing you in, understand? Then we'll see how "galvanised" your pals are. 'Course they'll have to find your body first.'

He grinned at me. 'Don't fancy their chances, do you, little brother?'

24

Danny had the name. Knowing him as I did, I didn't have to think about what he'd do with it: Bob Wallace was a dead man. Stanford had signed his death warrant. The DCI followed his betrayal with more cautionary words, in reality, distancing himself from the murder of a police officer. 'I meant what I said. It has to be clean.' He paused, gauging whether his message was getting through. 'Make sure the body isn't found. The Met's tenacious when it comes to avenging one of our own. They'll never close the case.'

Danny looked like he'd discovered something nasty stuck to his shoe.

'Shut it. Just fucking shut it, copper.'

'I'm only saying it has to be done quietly, for all our sakes.'

'And I'm saying put a sock in it.'

He ignored the detective and spoke to me. 'Before you start, don't dare.'

'I haven't said anything.'

'Yeah, but you're going to. I'm done letting Anderson walk all over us.'

He paced the room, raving and waving his arms. '"Make sure the body isn't found." What the hell good is that? We're sending a message

– don't mess with the Glass family. Shouting from the rooftops so everybody gets it.'

Settling the score was overdue. Yet, I saw where Stanford was coming from, and he was right. The last thing we needed was every copper in London breathing down our necks.

I said, 'Sending a message is one thing. Killing Wallace is something else. It's stupid. Can't you see he's a gift?'

'A gift? How so?'

'With a man inside Rollie's camp we can screw him.'

Danny looked as if he'd swallowed a wasp. Then, he got it.

'Fair point, bro. Except every bastard in London thinks he can try it on. That can't stand. I won't let it stand.' He remembered the detective was still there and dismissed him with a snarl. 'Make yourself scarce, copper.'

The policeman was relieved and left without another word. When he'd gone, Danny said, 'If you've got a plan, let's hear it.'

My brother needed blood. It was time to let him have it.

'We hit them on Friday night. After that, Wallace won't have anybody to report to because Rollie will be dead. It'll finally be over between us and the Andersons and you'll be the Birthday Boy. Drunk as a skunk with a room full of witnesses to prove it.'

The idea of revenge relaxed him.

'Time for a splash, I'm thinking.'

He took a bottle of Chivas Regal and two tumblers from the bottom drawer of the desk, poured a large one for each of us and gave the toast I'd been hearing most of my life.

'To Team Glass.'

It never got old for him. A familiar light came into his eyes and I groaned inside; he was about to take us on another stroll down memory lane.

'Meant to tell you. Remember that girl you were keen on when you were seventeen?'

I didn't answer.

'Yeah, you do.' He snapped his fingers, trying to recall. 'Janice.

Jennifer. Joan.'

'Julia.'

'Yeah, Julia, that's the one.'

I hadn't thought about Julia Kingsley in a long time. We'd gone out together for a year and were talking about getting engaged when it ended. Or, more accurately, when Danny ended it.

'What about her?'

'Saw her at a bus stop the other day. Didn't realise she still lived round here. Hasn't changed. Always was a looker.'

'You stopped me from seeing her. Told me I'd thank you someday.'

'So I did. Why was that? What was wrong with her?'

He'd forgotten, that was how important it had been to him. I hadn't. We'd had a major bust-up over it and I'd threatened to leave home. In the end, he'd sat me down and explained why Julia wasn't for me. Inevitably, it became another us-against-the-world speech. He was rolling out the Team Glass bollocks even then.

I refreshed the gap in his recollection. 'Her brother.'

Danny put his feet on the desk. 'That's right. That's right. She had a brother, didn't she? What was his name?'

'Zach.'

He slapped the arm of his chair. 'Of course. More than enough reason to split you two young lovebirds. A Zachary? From South London? Fucking hell!'

His fierce objection hadn't been Julia's brother's name – it was what he did, or rather what Zach Kingsley had wanted to do. 'It's coming back to me. Joined the Met, didn't he?'

'Yeah, and you stopped me marrying his sister because of it.'

Even after all these years, he was unrepentant. 'Too humpty-tumpty. If you'd got hooked to that tart, he'd be your brother-in-law. How was that gonna work?'

'She wasn't a tart, Danny. I was in love with her.'

''Course she was. They're all tarts. Time you wised up to it.' He sipped his drink and gazed into the past. What he saw amused him.

'Thought your life was over. Wouldn't speak to me for a month. Having a copper in the family? No chance. Not then and not now.'

Suddenly, I didn't feel like drinking with him and got up. Danny saw I was annoyed.

'Don't tell me you're still mad? It was nearly twenty years ago. Lucky escape, if you ask me. Surely you can see that?'

A message arrived on his phone and cut his laughter short. He passed the mobile across to show me a YouTube link and a strawberry emoji.

'Better play it, Danny.'

He tapped the screen and held his breath. At first, it was muddy. After ninety seconds of nothing, a white Transit came out of the pre-dawn mist. Suddenly, I knew what we were seeing and why. Rollie Anderson had failed to find his mark with the raid on the King Pot – Team Glass had survived. It wouldn't survive this.

I wanted to look away. Christ knows, I wanted to. But I couldn't. Beside me, Danny moaned a low moan and shook uncontrollably. Hearing his tough-guy speech to the back of the van was beyond embarrassing, even more ludicrous than it had been at the time. When the doors opened, the camera zoomed in, catching his stupefied expression in a close-up. Then, the unmistakeable voice of my brother... 'Strawberries. We've jacked a load of fucking strawberries. Stanford, you cunt!'

The phone dropped from his trembling fingers. Danny's eyes bulged in his skull, his face so red I thought it might explode. Nobody did rage as he did: rising from his core, spewing like lava, scaring those around him to the bone. He upended the desk, scattering everything on it, and let out a roar they'd hear at King's Cross.

His next target was his pride and joy – the jukebox – flipping it over as if it were made of cardboard. It hit the floor in a cascade of broken glass and cracked vinyl. Danny spun like a blind man in the centre of the room, punching his face, beating his head off the wall, again and again. I grabbed him in a bear hug and we crashed to the carpet, locked together, while he thrashed and struggled against the humiliation Rollie Anderson had dealt him and the demons it had loosed.

My arms ached, but I held on. We lay there for a long time. Until he whispered, 'It's okay. I'm all right. Let me up.'

Down in the pub, the gang of grizzled old guys in the corner would be sheltering their dominoes in the palms of their wrinkled hands, counting the white dots laid out in a line on the table, debating with themselves whether to play the four-two or the five-one. Harry would be pulling pints and chatting to the customers, laughing at jokes he'd heard before. Nobody would guess the crazy scene that had gone on upstairs. I'd been there and still couldn't.

Even before he told me to let him go, I sensed a difference in him. Danny got to his feet and helped me off the floor; his hand was firm and dry as always. I felt like a bus had run over me and doubled back a couple of times. He ignored the overturned desk and the jukebox on its side. None of it registered or, if it did, at that moment they weren't important to him. Almost the only thing to survive unscathed was the photograph of the Queen on the wall.

He sat in his usual chair facing me, his face bruised from where he'd hit himself, not looking at me – I might as well not have been in the room. My brother was as strong as an ox and just as unpredictable. But the shock of seeing Anderson's video and knowing he was already a laughing stock had affected him: his arms hung at his sides, his shoulders drooped, and there was an emptiness in his eyes.

The silence was eerie and went on for minutes. After a while I couldn't stand it. 'Are you okay? I mean, is there anything I can do?'

His voice was cracked and tinny and disconnected, how it had sounded on the phone seven years earlier, telling me about Cheryl and Rebecca.

they're dead, Luke

that bastard Anderson

'We've got to hit him and hit him hard. Send a message they'll never forget.'

'Yes, we will. Of course, we will.'

He got off the chair and crawled on his hands and knees until he found what he was looking for: his mobile. His fingers tapped a number. Danny mumbled to himself – I'd become invisible again. 'I'm not the only one who's fucked, copper. Deal with this.'

It didn't take a genius to figure out what he'd just done. If Detective Chief Inspector Oliver Stanford hadn't seen the video before, he had now. And suddenly, Danny was back, his eyes full of life.

'You still here?'

'Where else should I be?'

'Don't you have places to go and people to see? Like that Julia we were talking about.'

'That was twenty years ago. She could be married with half a dozen kids. I've no idea where she lives.'

'Then you're not trying hard enough. Go on. Give me some space. Got calls to make.'

The change was too sudden. Bravado for my benefit. After what I'd just witnessed, I didn't trust it.

'Not while you need me.'

He laughed like I'd heard him do all my life – harsh and cruel – though rarely directed at me. 'Need you? What you on about? Never gonna happen. Fuck off out of it before I lose my rag with you.'

* * *

Vale parked his car well away from the flat and walked the rest of the way, in no hurry to get there. Eugene was a coward. Knowing he'd have to tell Nina about the mess he'd got them into made him feel sick. Around six o'clock, when he was on the floor having Yvonne for the last time, it had started to rain, hammering against the window – the perfect soundtrack to what he was doing. She'd writhed and moaned under him. He'd fucked her harder, savouring his dominance.

Who would've guessed the dynamic was about to change?

The rain had stopped but the pavements were still wet and a cold wind had picked up, ruffling his hair, making his eyes water. Vale gathered his coat around him and kept his head down, not close to being ready to confess. He passed a young couple, too busy eating the face off each other to notice he was even there. Their lives would be bland and uncomplicated; he envied them. The truth was clear, the evidence overwhelming – one way or another he'd ruined every relationship he'd ever been in, because it was never enough. A woman only had to look at him a moment longer than she needed to and he was after her. Once they'd had sex, he soon lost interest and ended it. Though not always: he'd married two of them, a mistake he wouldn't be making again. Both wives had divorced him for infidelity and avenged themselves through their lawyers.

Bitter experiences. Bitter and expensive. He'd learned nothing from them, which was why he was here, dragging his feet to avoid Nina's predictable rage.

At the end of the street, he remembered how late he was and reluctantly quickened his pace while his brain searched for the words to explain. He didn't find them. Yvonne was a greedy little tart, that much was true, but if he'd settled for what he had with Nina, none of it would be happening.

Vale forced his nerves under control and pressed the buzzer, not expecting to be welcomed with open arms. Nina was feisty, a woman who wanted what she wanted when she wanted it – keeping her waiting wouldn't go down well. She detested her older brother and prided herself on not being the same. Of course, she was wrong – they'd come from the same gene pool: biochemistry had had the final say. Like Danny, Nina was driven and unpredictable. Now, his trampy secretary had him by the balls and was getting ready to squeeze.

The door opened. Nina looked him up and down, her expression blank. She was wearing a black and orange silk robe with a Japanese design. Eugene guessed there would be nothing underneath and silently cursed himself.

Her voice matched her expression, emotionless, at the same time, hostile.

'We agreed seven o'clock. Or am I wrong?'

Vale stuttered an apology. 'Sorry... Sorry, I'm late.'

She stood aside to let him pass and he caught her perfume on the air. Nina was dressed for a session – she was going to be disappointed. When he said what he needed to say, they'd have more important things to think about. On the coffee table, two red wines were already poured. She picked them up and handed a glass to him.

He refused it. 'I'd take a whisky if you've got any. Make it a large one.'

'What's the matter? Getting cold feet? I told you – everything's cool. Danny's got no idea what we're doing.'

'Cold feet? No.'

'Then what the hell's wrong with you?'

'We've got a problem.'

Nina tensed. 'What kind of problem?'

Vale took a deep breath and stepped into the abyss. 'Yvonne knows.'

Nina took a moment to let what she was hearing sink in. 'Yvonne? The little trollop who files her nails all day?'

'Yes. She knows about us.'

'About you and me?'

He hesitated. 'And the money.'

'She can't.'

'I'm afraid she does. She overheard us on the phone.'

Nina processed what she was being told.

'I called your mobile. She couldn't have been listening in?'

Vale said, 'Can I have that whisky?'

'No, you bloody well can't. How much does she know?'

'She was there, in the office.'

'She was there. Why would...?'

The flesh around Nina's eyes tightened, the corners of her mouth twisted in a mixture of anger and revulsion, as realisation dawned. For what seemed like a long time she didn't move, didn't even blink. Fury built from within, rising slowly, her limbs trembling. Vale sensed what was coming and edged away just as Nina erupted and threw herself at him, snarling like a wild beast. He stumbled and fell; she followed him down. The robe parted, revealing a flash of pubic hair, dark against the creamy thighs, and Vale knew they'd never part for him again. She straddled his body, out of control, beating his chest with her fists. He turned his head to the side but there was no escape; her flailing nails found him and raked his cheek. Eugene felt the sting and knew she'd marked him.

Then, as suddenly as it began, it was over.

Nina collapsed onto the sofa, pale and panting and spent. He lay on the carpet, his body aching, too exhausted to move. Eventually, she spoke, her contempt for him undisguised. 'You fool. You stupid bloody idiot. What the hell have you done?'

'Nina... Nina, I—'

'You were fucking her. That's why she was there. How she overheard.'

Vale gingerly fingered the tramlines on his skin: he was used to this kind of confrontation and knew the best thing was to admit to it. That wasn't the problem.

'You phoned at the wrong time. I'm sorry.' He hauled himself into the chair; when he breathed it hurt. 'Yvonne came after me.'

Nina felt a fresh wave of anger rise in her and had to hold herself back from going for him again. 'And – don't tell me, let me guess – you couldn't stop yourself.'

'It was only a bit of fun. Just a shag.'

Considering he'd put their lives in danger, the excuse was pitiful. Nina thought about the brothers she'd grown up with: Luke was ten times the man Eugene Vale would ever be. Even Danny, who she detested, was better than him.

She strode across the room and spat in his face. It landed on his chin and stayed there.

Nina said, 'I couldn't care less who you fuck. My interest in you is zero. Always was. Thanks to you, your *shag* has us where she wants us.'

'I'm sorry, Nina.'

'Too late for sorry. We need to figure out what we're going to do about it. What exactly does she know?'

'Everything.'

'Everything?'

'All of it.'

'And she's demanding… what?'

'She wants half or she'll tell Danny.'

25

It was raining when George Ritchie left the flat in Moscow Road – thin rain, not hard enough for an umbrella. Ritchie stopped to look in the windows of shops on Queensway, checking in the glass to see if he was being followed. The Daniel Gooch had closed down. He set about re-establishing a new routine in a new pub. None of the boozers he came across appealed, too bloody noisy for a start. Eventually, he couldn't have cared less and decided to go into the next one, whatever it was like.

Things changed.

The first pint lasted the best part of an hour while he read a newspaper someone had left on the seat next to him. Then he ordered again and pretended to watch the TV screen. No one paid any attention to him, that would come later, and with it the nickname 'Two Pints' or something like it.

Halfway through his second drink, just as he was getting ready to leave, he got the call. Immediately, he realised it meant trouble. Rollie was excited, his voice thick with whatever he'd been smoking. 'You have to see this, George, you won't believe it.'

'See what?'

Rollie's answer was a giggle. 'Get yourself down here. We've got a game-changer.'

Ritchie was outside in seconds. The rain was heavier than it had been; he didn't notice. Getting wet wasn't important. Yet, even now, he kept to the elaborate system designed to protect him and walked to the top of Queensway before hailing a taxi. By the time he reached the Bayswater Road, he was soaked. The cab headed towards the city centre and took a right turn at Marble Arch to join the traffic on Park Lane. In the back seat, the cryptic conversation replayed in Ritchie's brain and with it a growing feeling of unease settled round him. He was acutely aware of rain on his scalp and on his skin and his heart beating beneath his coat. He was afraid.

The cab reached Hyde Park Corner and the Wellington Arch, passed the Hard Rock Cafe and kept going while he grimly contemplated how it had come to this.

In those far-off days, London had been a huge adventure. The capital awash with possibilities for a man with his reputation and skills.

Albert Anderson had been his first mistake. Back then Anderson controlled most of the city south of the river and not because he'd been smart. In fact, he had been anything but, though Ritchie didn't know that in those days. Albert had needed what the northerner had been selling and offered him a job. He'd accepted and had been with the firm ever since. The second mistake had been not crushing the Glass brothers when the chance had presented itself. When they were still boys and no more than a nuisance, he'd told Albert he'd take care of them but Albert wouldn't sanction it – their audacity had amused him. They were 'just kids', he'd said. What they were doing was 'petty'. George Ritchie had been with him the day those same 'kids' beat an Indian shopkeeper to death for a few packets of cigarettes.

Albert had laughed softly and shaken his head at the impetuousness of youth, admiration sparkling in his eyes, and Ritchie had realised he was working for an idiot.

The fat bastard wasn't laughing now.

Ritchie had come close to quitting and going home to Newcastle many times, especially after the bomb he'd known nothing about killed the woman and the child. By then, thanks to Glass's brother, suddenly Albert was dead and Ritchie had allowed his nineteen-year-old son to persuade him to stay: mistake number three.

For a clever guy, he hadn't been very clever.

* * *

The taxi dropped him four streets away. The rain had stopped and he walked from there. Running a club had been Rollie's idea – he hadn't had many – and, in fairness, it worked as a legitimate business to clean the money and a place to sell drugs. Seeing his guys propping up the bar on a Friday night bolstered Rollie's ego. Ritchie had a different view. Being predictable made them an easy target.

Outside, women were chatting up the bouncer. One girl, who might have been twenty-five but was probably fifteen, was practically naked and it occurred to Ritchie he was old enough to be her father. If he had been, she wouldn't be leaving the house the way she was dressed, tits hanging out and a skirt up to her arse. The burly steward had cropped hair and a scar on his cheek. He recognised George, nodded and opened the door. Immediately, a wall of noise hit him, so loud he thought his eardrums might burst. His eyes took a minute to adjust to the darkness. When they did, he saw shapes crowding the small dance floor. The club wouldn't open for another couple of hours. Christ Almighty – Rollie was having a party. What the hell was there to celebrate?

A brunette in a red dress, obviously drunk, fixed glazed eyes on him and smiled. Ritchie ignored her. Too young and too foolish. Not his type. Not his type at all. In the office, Rollie was behind his desk. Across from him, another man sat with his back to the door. He heard Ritchie come in and turned.

The guilty look on Jonjo's face was all it took for his uncle to know his nephew had fucked the lot of them.

Both men had a whisky and were passing a joint between them, getting on famously, grinning because they'd just pulled the joke of the year. Rollie was flushed with alcohol and excitement, banging his fist on the desk. 'We've got him. We've got the bastard.'

The fool was babbling. Ritchie understood and glared at Jonjo, who drew his eyes away.

'How many copies are there?'

'This is it.'

'Your idea of switching the cargo after we got tipped off Glass was going to hit us worked out better than I hoped. Wait 'til you see what Jonjo's got.'

Jonjo basked in his boss's pleasure. His uncle wanted to strangle him with his bare hands. Rollie waved Ritchie closer and pulled the PC round.

'This will blow Glass's credibility to hell, George. He's finished.'

On the screen, a white van came towards the camera and was forced off the road by a car. Masked men hauled the driver from behind the wheel and clubbed him to the ground while Rollie mumbled to himself. Danny Glass shouted at the closed rear doors.

'All right in there! Don't be heroes! When the door opens throw out whatever you've got!'

Rollie swallowed his drink in one go, eyes dancing in his head, anticipating what was about to happen. Beside him, Ritchie watched unsmiling, in silence. Glass spoke to the men with him. 'They've had their chance, let them have it.'

He threw himself to the ground and Rollie giggled.

Jonjo had acted against his uncle and didn't regret it. This was a young man's game and Jonjo and Rollie were young men. Time for his uncle to step aside.

The camera panned to Danny Glass clutching a fistful of fruit.

Anderson nudged Ritchie. 'This is the best bit.'

'Strawberries. We've jacked a load of fucking strawberries. Stanford, you cunt!'

Rollie put a hand to his mouth and pounded the table again, so hard the computer jumped.

'Sensational, or what? When this gets around there won't be a hole deep enough for Glass to hide in.'

Ritchie spoke softly, repeating the words. '"When this gets around." What do you mean? Tell me Glass hasn't seen this.'

Rollie smiled a knowing smile and leaned back in his chair, drawing on the joint until his lungs couldn't take any more, exhaling slowly as the dope did its work. Marijuana smoke drifted on the air. His voice was ragged. 'Oh, yeah. First on the list. As soon as Jonjo loaded the video on YouTube thirty minutes ago. Fifty thousand hits already. In twenty-four hours, half of London will have seen it.'

A feeling of dread washed through George Ritchie.

What the fuck had these two clowns done?

* * *

Rollie Anderson threw his arms around Ritchie, slurring his words in his ear and breathing whisky fumes over him. 'This is the best day of my life, and I've got Jonjo to thank for it. Not in my dreams, not in my wildest bloody fantasies, did I imagine Danny Glass humiliated like that.' He punched his lieutenant's arm playfully. 'Tomorrow Glass's men will be leaving in droves. Can't blame them, can you? Nobody wants to work for the village idiot. By the end of the week, might just be him and that bastard brother of his left. It's sweet.'

For years – first with Albert, then with Rollie – George Ritchie had been the adult in the room, steering the father and the son away from actions that would harm them. Now he'd had enough of the Anderson family. More than enough.

Rollie ran a drunken hand through Jonjo's hair, letting the fingers rest longer than they needed to.

'Should be proud of him, George. We've got Glass by the balls because of him. How many hits have we got now?'

Jonjo dragged the PC over and checked the left-hand corner of the screen.

'Seventy-one thousand.'

'In how long?'

'Forty-five minutes.'

'And that's good, right?'

'Very good.'

'How many do you think it'll get?'

'Hard to say. Five hundred. If it goes viral, a couple of million.'

Ritchie understood. His nephew had gone against him. Ignored what he'd told him in the cafe and Rollie, bent on revenge, was on fire at the thought of his enemy humbled and blind to the consequences of what Jonjo had done. He noticed Ritchie wasn't celebrating.

'What's wrong, George? You don't look happy.'

'Take it down.'

'What?'

'Take it down now and destroy every trace of it.'

Rollie's good humour disappeared.

'Are you mad?'

'Do it or you'll be dead in days. Both of you.'

Rollie sneered. 'Who would've thought it, eh? The great George Ritchie's scared.'

Ritchie lost it. He grabbed Anderson by the lapels and threw him against the table.

'Don't you get it, you fucking idiot? Don't you get what you've done? Glass will kick over every stone in the city until he finds you. Albert's stupidity got him killed. You're going out the same way. Take the video down.'

Jonjo hadn't moved – he couldn't. What his uncle had said in the cafe suddenly made sense. You couldn't disgrace a psycho like Danny Glass and expect to live.

Ritchie let go of Rollie and screamed at him.

'What're you waiting for? Do it!'

A voice that wasn't Jonjo's said, 'Ninety-five thousand,' as the number on the bottom of the screen flickered and changed. 'One hundred and one. One hundred and ten.'

'Reverse whatever you did! Make it stop!'

Rollie's hand dug into Jonjo's shoulder, pinching the skin, his glazed eyes locked on Ritchie. 'Leave it. Leave it exactly how it is. Danny Glass has got it coming.'

* * *

Admitting the truth was like hearing it for the first time.

she wants half or she'll tell Danny

Eugene Vale dropped into a chair and put his head in his hands, devastated. Nina thought he was going to cry but wasn't tempted to reassure him; the horny bastard had landed them in an impossible position. Eugene wasn't the only one who'd made a mistake: her partner, her lover – the thought made her want to vomit – was a gutless waste of space. When it came to doing what needed to be done, he'd break, and she'd be on her own.

He sat up, wiping his eyes. 'She'll see reason. We split it three ways. If we take a bit more, Danny won't even notice. That could work, couldn't it? All we have to...'

The look on Nina's face warned him another attack was coming.

She screamed. 'Nothing! N.O.T.H.I.N.G! Do you get it? Who the fuck is that bitch to be demanding anything? Doesn't she realise who she's dealing with?'

'But she'll tell.'

Nina waited for her breathing to steady before she answered, her voice cold and flat.

'She can't talk if she's dead, Eugene.'

Vale jumped to his feet. 'Murder her? Are you insane? Look, I got us into this. I can get us out of it. It's simple. She wants half, we give her half. We give her my share.'

The solution was something only a moron would suggest.

She turned the words over and came back with a question. 'Give her your share. You think that'll work?'

'Why not? It's what she wants, isn't it?'

Nina didn't reply. The gun Danny had given her was upstairs at the back of a wardrobe. If she'd had it in her hand, she would've put Eugene Vale out of his misery – she'd let this imbecile screw her for Danny's money. What did that make her? At best a whore, at worst an even bigger fool than he was.

'Listen to yourself. Do you actually believe the nonsense coming out of your mouth?'

'It isn't nonsense.'

'Yes, it is. Unadulterated, bloody garbage.'

'Why?'

Nina didn't know where to begin. 'Right now, she's asking for half. Yours or mine, Yvonne doesn't care. When we give it to her how long do you think it'll be before she's looking for more – 75, 80 per cent? And if she gets it, why stop there?'

'She wouldn't.'

'Want to bet? What's to stop her going for the lot? She's holding all the cards. One phone call to Danny and it's over for us.'

Fear parched Vale's lips. His voice became a husky whisper as the reality of their situation dawned. 'Then... what're we going to do? What you're suggesting is...'

Nina had known the answer to Yvonne's threat the moment he'd blurted out his confession. Vale's whore had them where she wanted them and wouldn't hesitate to give them up. They had to act and quickly. Yvonne was a stupid tart, nothing more. The fact that the bitch thought she could take on Nina Glass with any hope of winning enraged her. But it pointed up something she hadn't considered: she'd take care of Vale when the time was right. But it was Danny who was the real danger. Eliminate him from the equation and...

The sense of power made her smile. She reined her imagination in: Danny was weakened, but still too strong for her to go up against by herself. If Luke was on board, that would be a different proposition. And Nina knew exactly what she could use to make that happen.

Vale said, 'Tell me, Nina, tell me.'

She turned away so she wouldn't have to look at his face. 'Like I said. Kill her.'

26

Oliver Stanford stood at the window overlooking the Embankment. Below him, a tug towed a barge of sealed containers, churning the muddy water of the Thames in its wake. Stanford remembered reading a story about fishermen drawing a shark into their boat, alive, but dying. In its belly they'd found a silver watch. When the details were published, a jeweller in The Strand recalled selling the watch to a Mr Thompson as a present to his son going on his first voyage. Somewhere off Falmouth, during a squall, the boy had fallen overboard and was never seen again. Mystery solved. And the moral of the tale: there were times the truth refused to be denied. The memory made the detective shudder.

Stanford heard the scrape of chairs on the floor as Mills and Wallace took seats at the table. Usually, at the beginning of a meeting, the DCI exchanged a few casual remarks to set the tone before getting started – there would be none of that today.

Stanford had a reputation as a model policeman and was always immaculately dressed. Today, his tie was undone, his white shirt crushed and stained at the armpits. They sensed the tension rolling off their boss and waited for him to share it. He studied each of them in turn, no attempt at hiding his contempt.

'You won't be surprised to hear I've been invited upstairs – due there now, as a matter of fact. Given that pressing engagement, what I have to say won't take long.'

He held up his mobile without asking if they'd seen the video. Of course, they had – along with half the population of London. Danny Glass opened the doors of a white van on a side road. Stanford turned the volume up in time to hear his name before it ended.

The DCI repeated it to them in a monotone heavy with suppressed anger.

'"Stanford, you cunt." Just one of a number of things I'm expecting to have to explain. Any ideas how I might do that?'

Silence.

'Me neither. So, let me say this: I need you to bring me evidence that will put Anderson away. Not tomorrow. Now. And I don't give a fuck who you lean on, how hard, or what you've got to promise to get it. One other thing to help concentrate your minds. Make no mistake. If I go down, you're going down with me, understood?'

Bob Wallace held up his hand. Stanford bit back an insult. This bastard had screwed them and would get what he deserved.

'How many Stanfords do you think there are in the country, boss?'

Stanford sighed. 'I don't know, Bob, tell me.'

'I Googled it.'

'That was clever of you. And the answer is?'

'Hundreds.'

* * *

The last time Nina had been in my flat would have been eight or nine years earlier with Cheryl. I'd opened the door to find the two of them sniggering like children. They weren't big drinkers and the wine they'd had at lunch made them silly and giggly. A gallon of black coffee went a long way to sobering them up before I'd called a taxi to take them home. Even back then, Danny was causing problems. When Cheryl went to the bathroom, Nina told me my brother hadn't been home in days. Rebecca – just a toddler – kept asking where her daddy was. Lunchtime boozing wasn't Cheryl's scene, but she'd been unhappy, and Nina had volunteered for the job of cheering her up.

A long time ago.

My sister cast an amused eye around the lounge without passing comment. There was no need.

I didn't disagree; by any stretch of the imagination it was awful. Coming across as ungrateful wasn't easy. 'Danny had it ready for me coming out.'

Nina said, 'I offered to help. He wouldn't let me near it. Does the roof leak?'

'Not so far.'

'Then you're winning.'

The small talk was wearing thin – neither of us had any talent for it. I said, 'I'm guessing this isn't a social call.'

She made a face and came to the point. 'I want to speak to you about Danny. I take it you've seen the video.'

'I was there, Nina, and everybody in South London's seen it. So what?'

'I'm worried.'

'About him?'

'Christ, no, don't give a monkey's about him. About how he'll react. What he might do.'

'You're afraid he'll start a war with Anderson?'

'We're already in a war. I'm afraid he'll blow us all up. You must've seen the change in him since you went away.'

She gripped the arm of the couch and leaned nearer. 'He isn't sane, Luke. I'm serious. Our brother isn't sane. Tell the truth, he's never been right, has he? And yeah, I'm not forgetting what he did for us in that hellhole of a house. But even back then, don't you remember?'

I did remember.

'Nina, why are you here?'

She looked away, her fingers playing with the band of her watch, and didn't answer, wanting me to get there by myself, reluctant to say what she'd come to say.

'This video is the beginning of the end for him.'

'How do you mean?'

'He's a laughing stock, a joke.'

'And... let's hear it. C'mon, Nina, spit it out.'

She took a deep breath. 'We have to get rid of him. You can take over. I'll get involved. We'll run things together.'

27

The clock on the wall showed a minute past five. Apart from its relentless ticking, the only sound in the office was the quiet click as the safe door sprang open. Eugene Vale knelt on the floor with his back to Yvonne; over his shoulder she saw his hand reach inside and reappear with a bundle of notes, bound with an elastic band. He got to his feet and sat down behind the desk; she noticed sweat marks at the armpits of his shirt. Eugene was nervous. That made two of them. On the surface at least, Yvonne seemed calm. Underneath she was anything but. It had all been so easy. She'd left them no choice, had them exactly where she wanted them and the excitement was almost more than she could stand. Nina Glass bowing down to her.

Unbelievable!

Eugene Vale weighed the money in his palm, using it as a prop to make the point he'd made several times already, looking and sounding more serious than she'd ever seen him. 'You're up to your neck in it now.' He pushed the wad across the table. 'This is a lot of cash and there's more coming. For Christ's sake be smart with it or you'll get us all killed.'

Yvonne lifted the banknotes and ruffled them through her fingers. 'I'm not stupid, Eugene. Or hadn't you noticed?'

He shook his head. 'Okay, just don't say I didn't warn you. Nina isn't somebody you want to fuck with, believe me.'

'I won't be fucking with her so long as she sticks to her end of the deal.' Yvonne came around the desk and kissed him on the lips. 'Fucking with you, that's a different story. Our new arrangement better not put you off me. That wouldn't do. That wouldn't do at all.' She traced the inside of his thigh. 'What about right now? Call it a celebration.'

Vale eased her away from him; sex wasn't happening. 'I can't, Nina's expecting me.'

Yvonne whispered in his ear. 'You're forgetting something, darling.'

'Am I?'

'Yeah. Nobody's interested in what Nina Glass wants. From now on, all that matters is what I want.'

It had taken less than two minutes for the threat to arrive. It wouldn't be the last. Nina was right, there was no other way, though even thinking about what they had to do made him want to throw up. But however bad he felt, it wasn't as awful as what would be waiting for him at Fulton Street.

Vale chose his words carefully, aware of how important it was to avoid upsetting this woman. He eased his hand inside her blouse and played with her erect nipple. 'Maybe you're right. We should have a party.' His other hand slid up her skirt and teased her through the flimsy material. He whispered, 'Just you and me. But first, let's go get smashed.'

'You said you're meeting Nina.'

'She'll just have to wait, won't she? And you're buying.'

* * *

Vale pulled the car into the evening traffic and changed through the gears. In the passenger seat, Yvonne watched him out of the corner of her eye. The proverbial shoe was on the other foot but, so far, he was taking it well. Getting him to agree to split the skim had never been in doubt. Yvonne had had more than her share of men and knew they came in types. In her experience, few were as strong as they thought they were. Women were the ones with character. Fortunately, it wasn't moral fortitude she was after. The Eugenes of the world had their uses, fine for having fun and not much else – she didn't really like Vale, if she was telling herself the truth.

'How did Nina take it when you told her?'

'Not good, as you can imagine. She isn't used to people telling her what to do and doesn't handle it well. Even Danny's found that out.'

'What did she say?'

'Went crazy. Threw stuff. Spouted a lot of wild talk. I pointed out that we weren't in a position to argue. Better to accept it and make a deal.'

Yvonne didn't believe him. She couldn't picture Eugene having the balls to go up against Nina Glass.

'And she agreed, just like that?'

The car rolled to a stop at traffic lights. Not "just like that", no, of course not.' He pointed to the mark above his eye. 'It took hours to convince her. You don't know Nina, do you?'

'She's looked down her nose at me a couple of times in the office.'

'If you did, you'd understand who you are dealing with and think yourself lucky to still be walking around. She's a Glass. Which means she's unpredictable. Getting her to agree to what you wanted was anything but easy. You should be thanking me.'

Yvonne stroked the inside of his leg. 'I'll thank you later. You won't have much left for her tonight and that's a promise.'

* * *

Vale picked a corner of the pub that meant their backs were to the bar so they wouldn't be noticed. He hadn't been here before, didn't know anybody and nobody knew him. It was early and still pretty quiet. Yvonne was in fine form, relishing her new status. 'What're you having, partner?'

'A whisky, preferably a large one.'

She laughed. 'It's your money.'

'Not any more.'

She came back with four drinks on a tray. 'No use doing a double run, is there? A toast. To new beginnings.'

Vale said, 'You're going to get pissed.'

'What if I am? You'll look after me.'

'You're liking this, aren't you?'

'Loving it.'

'My advice would be to enjoy it while it lasts.'

'Why wouldn't it last?'

He threw the first whisky back in one go.

'Why wouldn't it last, Eugene?'

'This isn't a game. If Danny twigs, everybody involved will disappear. Me, you, even his sister.'

Yvonne's teeth were white against the flush of hard liquor on her cheeks. She leaned closer, amusement sparkling in her eyes. 'I won't tell if you won't.'

* * *

Yvonne wasn't falling-down drunk, but she was getting there. She slurred when she spoke – which she did non-stop – her voice booming against the racket from the jukebox. Most of Vale's whisky had soaked into the dark earth in the potted plant next to him and every few minutes he checked the time on his watch. His nerves were shot; he wasn't cut out for this. Sober, Yvonne was volatile and headstrong; with a bellyful of alcohol, she would be uncontrollable. Returning her wet, unwelcome kisses was the surest way of shutting her up. Vale felt her tongue probe his mouth and shuddered. There was lipstick on the shoulder of her blouse – how the hell had that got there? – and at one point she had her hand inside his shirt. Inebriated women were the opposite of invisible. He had to get her to the car before her clumsy advances attracted enough attention for someone to remember the hot little ticket pissed out of her head and the guy she'd been with.

He put his palm over the top of her half-empty glass – the fifth double in two hours – in the circumstances, a high-risk strategy. 'I think we should leave, Yvonne.'

His suggestion confused her. 'Leave? I don't want to leave. And go where?'

'To your flat. We'll stop at an off-licence and get a couple of bottles of wine.'

The cunning she'd proved herself capable of was there in the corner of her drink-dulled eyes.

'You're horny. You're horny for me, aren't you? Admit it.'

Vale lied, hating himself and her. 'I admit it.'

It wasn't enough; she toyed with him. 'How horny?'

'Very horny.'

She grinned. 'You're an old man. Why should a young thing like me bother with an old man?'

Vale smiled at the insult, for a second thinking it was going to go easy. Then the grin morphed into a petulant frown and she turned on him like a child recalling some half-remembered slight. 'You haven't been very nice to me.'

He sensed trouble building and moved to cut it short. 'Don't be silly. 'Course, I have.'

'No, you haven't.' She waved a flaccid arm at the room. 'I could have any man in this pub. Any of them. All I have to do is snap my fingers.'

He took her hand to quieten her, gently massaging the fingers, whispering. 'But they won't be as good as me. When we get to the flat, I'm all yours. You can have anything you like.'

A sly smile flickered over Yvonne's red lips.

'Anything?'

'As long as you ask for it. You have to ask.'

'And you'll stay all night?'

'And I'll stay the night.'

Doubt reordered her features. 'But you're meeting her.'

He took her face tenderly in his hands, her skin hot and unblemished: he detested her.

'The only woman I'm interested in is right here. Let's go.'

* * *

Yvonne fell asleep in the car. At her front door, she took forever to find the key and an age to fit it into the lock, while he looked anxiously over his shoulder. All it needed was a guy out walking his dog or some nosey neighbour to spot them and the plan would have to be aborted. Bad news, because Eugene wasn't sure he could go through this again.

The flat was small, dimly lit and poorly furnished with a jumble of mismatched second-hand stuff: a maroon armchair beside an old TV, close to an unlit gas fire. Across the threadbare carpet, a faded two-seater couch that had known better days sagged in the middle where Yvonne parked her greedy arse and watched soaps when she wasn't chasing men – that particular piece of furniture would've seen plenty of action on many a Friday night after the pubs closed. A drying horse hung with towels and bras and thongs and there was an ironing board squeezed behind it against the wall. In winter, the room would be draughty and hard to heat. Yvonne's home was barely functional, yet it wouldn't be cheap. Vale was witnessing the life of a single girl in South London and understood why blackmail would seem attractive.

She dropped her handbag on the floor, kicked off her shoes and fell into the armchair; it sighed under her weight.

'If you tell me you love what I've done with the place, I'll fucking scream.'

She had a sense of humour, he'd give her that, and for a moment he almost forgot how the evil bitch had forced her way into their business. Then he remembered her threat to expose them to Danny Glass and felt his resolve return. Nina was right: it would never be over. What they were doing had to be.

And it had to be now.

There were tumblers on the draining board. Eugene screwed the top off the wine, bought when he'd stopped the car at an off-licence, and three-quarter filled each glass.

He shouted through to her. 'How long have you lived here?'

She didn't reply – maybe she'd fallen asleep. Sleeping wasn't on, at least, not yet. He took the tablets Nina had given him from his jacket pocket, dropped three of them into one of the drinks and started counting. The magic number was ninety. Ninety seconds for the Xanax to dissolve.

That was a fact – they'd timed it. Twice.

After twenty seconds nothing had happened. Vale kept his voice steady and called over his shoulder. 'Bloody hell, Yvonne. When was the last time you washed these?'

The question got the response he expected but bought him some time.

'Fuck off!'

At forty: the pills sat in the bottom like stones in a muddy stream and a pang of anxiety rippled in his chest.

At sixty, a faint line of bubbles peeled away and he relaxed.

By ninety, the Xanax had disappeared.

He lifted the glasses, turned and bumped into Yvonne at his shoulder.

'Christ's sake. Don't creep up on people.'

'I wasn't creeping. What's taking so long?'

He handed her the drink. 'Should make washing-up liquid your first investment. Does it never occur to you to clean this place up?'

'Won't be here much longer.'

'True.'

She leaned her head against him and let him guide her back into the lounge: her hair smelled of strawberries. Knowing what they were going to do terrified him; he was trapped between two women with cold-blooded murder the only way out.

Yvonne gulped down a quarter of the wine and wiped her mouth with her hand. Vale talked to keep her distracted. 'What're you going to do with the cash?'

'Get out of this dump for a start. After that... it depends.'

'On what?'

She giggled. 'How much I screw out of you and your girlfriend.'

'Today's only a fraction of what's coming.'

Yvonne took another pull. 'Then I'll retire and be a lady of leisure.'

'You're too young to retire.'

She put the glass on the floor and unbuttoned her blouse. 'I'm sure I'll manage to amuse myself.'

The material fell away and Vale felt himself stir. What a waste.

'And if Danny finds out?'

'I'll be long gone before that happens.'

'You better be.'

Yvonne wasn't listening. She took a step towards him and kicked over the tumbler. Wine spread in a dark pool on the carpet. Vale jumped to his feet. 'I'll get you another.'

'Forget it.' She dragged his head between her breasts and moaned quietly while he sucked her nipples. Eugene broke away. 'You've got a long night ahead of you, have to keep your strength up.'

In the tiny kitchen, he went through the process again, pouring the wine and adding three more Xanax. The drug wouldn't have time to dissolve – all he could do was pray she was too drunk to notice.

He needn't have worried; the rush of lust had passed. Yvonne was on the couch, snoring loudly. Vale shook her. When he got no response, he raised the tumbler to her lips. Wine spilled down her chin and pooled at her throat. He dialled Nina's number.

* * *

She was in her car anticipating his call and answered on the first ring.

'We've got a problem.'

'What kind of problem?'

'One I can't handle. You need to be here.'

Nina cursed under her breath – dealing with him would have to wait. Unless the police didn't buy the set-up. In that case, she'd have no choice. She'd shop him to Danny. He'd believe her because she was his sister: Eugene would die a painful death.

In the flat, the half-empty tumbler of wine and the unconscious Yvonne told Nina all she needed to know. She barked at Vale. 'How much has she had to drink?'

'Between the pub and here, a lot.'

'How many pills?'

'No idea. Her glass got kicked over before she could finish it. Been trying to get her to take the rest.'

Nina peeled off her jacket and threw it away. 'Hold her nose. If she can't breathe, she'll have to open her mouth.'

Vale did as he was told. Nina pressed the tumbler hard against the line of white teeth and waited. Yvonne groaned, her lips parted and Nina poured the lethal cocktail into her, only stopping when she started to choke.

'Christ, you're going to drown her in wine. If—'

Nina cut Eugene off. 'You had your chance, so shut the fuck up.'

The second attempt was more successful; some of the wine missed the mark. Yvonne spluttered and moaned, but most of it went down her throat. Nina produced a box of Xanax wrapped in tissue from her pocket and set it down on the carpet. Plastic gloves followed. She snapped a pair over her hands and gave another pair to him.

'We've been over this plenty of times but I'm going to say it again. Everything depends on what we do in the next few minutes and how well we do it. When the body's discovered, this has to look like an accidental overdose.'

Vale's mouth opened and closed. No words came out.

Nina gave him his instructions. 'Wash and dry her glass and the bottle and bring them here. Clean the other glass and put it back exactly where you found it.'

He nodded. She heard the tap running in the kitchen and a terrifying thought came into her head: in his frightened state was this guy capable of not fucking up?

She was about to find out.

Nina pressed the unconscious woman's fingertips against the packet and the silver foil inside, so her prints were all over them, went to the bedroom and put them on the bedside table. Next, the bottle and glass got the fingerprint treatment. When it was done, she sighed. All right so far.

Since the phone call, Vale had contributed nothing. Nina turned to him. 'Time to get into the game, Eugene. Take the rest of her clothes off and carry her to the bathroom. Be careful, we don't want bruising. What did you touch?'

'Just the bottle and the glasses.'

'You're sure?'

Vale didn't sound sure. 'Yes...'

'Where's the cork?'

'Cheap wine. No cork.'

'Get the top.'

Nina cleaned the metal and pressed Yvonne's finger to it. 'Leave it in the kitchen.'

She ran the bath and he lowered Yvonne's naked body into the water.

'It's not deep enough. It won't come over her head. Christ!'

Nina shot him a contemptuous glance. 'You're bloody useless, you really are. Get hold of her legs and pull her towards you. Bend her knees. Use the towel so you don't mark her.' He hesitated and she hissed at him through her teeth. 'Do it.'

Yvonne's head disappeared under the surface. Immediately, the instinct to survive kicked in, her arms thrashing and splashing as she fought a losing battle for her life. Fear brought her strength in her final moments and Vale had to tighten his grip to hold onto her. The struggle didn't last: her hair floated like seaweed on a tide, bubbles trailed from her mouth and her dead eyes stared up at him.

Unable to look, he turned away.

Nina wiped the taps and every surface Vale might have handled, covering their tracks, then carefully poured more wine into Yvonne's tumbler, and placed it and the bottle on the floor beside the bath. She stood, hands on hips, studying her work. 'We've done what we came to do, let's go.'

Outside, the light from a street lamp shadowed Nina's face, etching the sensual mouth and the hard line of her jaw in charcoal and chalk. Vale caught something he hadn't noticed before, even as she'd ploughed deep red lines on his back with her nails: the resemblance to her brother. They'd just murdered a woman yet there was no pity or regret in her eyes. Nina was a Glass. Getting what she wanted was all she knew.

They paused on the step with rain falling in silent gossamer sheets. Eugene was closing the front door when she grabbed his wrist, her eyes feral and untamed.

'Stop. For Christ's sake, stop.'

'What's wrong?'

She leaned against the frame, breathing in the cool night air, steadying herself before she replied. 'The money. We forgot the fucking money.'

28

The redhead and the blonde walked confidently through the lunchtime crowds towards Norrie and Fergie waiting for them at the Costa Coffee stand. The girls were young and pretty – or they would've been if they'd smiled – and stylishly dressed. People stopped what they were doing to watch them pass. On closer inspection, their faces betrayed the road they'd been on since their early teens: a hard road. Until they met in Cornton Vale prison and decided to be partners.

Norrie's phone call had come in the early hours of the morning – the job required a particular kind of female to pull it off. Sharon and Lexie were his first and only choice. And the paymaster was generous – they wouldn't have to work again for the rest of the year, although they would because this wasn't a career, it was a lifestyle.

High above Central Station, the giant electronic board showed the London train would leave in minutes. Norrie had been awake half the night and it showed; he was tired and tetchy, unsure whether saying yes to this job had been the best idea he'd ever had. He dropped his empty cup on the concourse, looked at his watch and took his anxiety out on the women, rasping his displeasure. 'Cut it a bit tight, haven't you?'

The blonde wasn't intimidated. 'We'd the wigs to pick up but we're here, aren't we? Chill out, for fuck's sake.'

He unenthusiastically agreed. 'Oh, yeah, you're here all right. Now remember, heads down. Don't get caught on CCTV.'

Fergie recognised the tension and tried to defuse it. 'Okay, we're all pleased to see each other and the wigs look great.'

'Hope Norrie thinks so when he gets the bill.'

Fergie doubted Norrie would care. At the end of the day it was somebody else's money. Norrie said, 'Let's get on the fuckin' train before the bastard goes without us.'

At the gate to Platform Two a guard gave their tickets a cursory glance and let them through. The guys hurried ahead, the women followed, heels clacking on the concrete. When they were settled in First Class, Norrie stared out of the window at the old station's walls, blackened by a century of coal dust. Even the most hardened criminal who'd seen and done just about everything – and this city wasn't short of those – would've passed on this job. Getting caught was only part of it.

The Glasgow gangster saw it differently. Success would open the door to a league beyond the one he was playing in. He'd leave Scotland and move to London.

He turned to the girls. 'You understand what we're about?'

Lexie replied with a bored sigh. 'Yes.'

'And you're cool with it?'

'What do you think?'

'I think you'd better watch your fuckin' lip.' His eyes held her and she backed down. A wise move. 'Before we get there, we'll go over the details until we can do it in our sleep. No room for mistakes on this one.'

She yawned. 'Worry about your end, we'll be fine.'

'You better be. This isn't an ordinary job. This one's special.'

'That's what you said the last time. According to you, they're all special.'

Norrie made a mental note to sort this bitch.

He said, 'Forget everything except doing this right. We won't get a second chance. The client isn't somebody we'd want to disappoint.'

Sharon said, 'Who is it?'

The reply was dismissive. 'You know better than that.'

Lexie ran a finger down his cheek. 'Relax, will you? We won't let you down.'

Norrie caught her hand and squeezed it white. 'If you do, you can say goodbye to your pretty faces. Fuck it up and the next contract will be on you.'

Her lips pouted. She blew him a kiss. 'I'm shaking in my Jimmy Choo's.'

The train juddered and pulled away. He moved closer, so close she could smell cigarette smoke on his breath. 'Shall I tell you whose money hit your bank account two hours ago? Do you really want to know? It'll concentrate your mind. Guaranteed.' Fear flickered in Lexie's eyes. 'Jack the tough-girl routine. Nobody's impressed.'

The speech hit home. Norrie headed to the bar for more coffee and left it to Fergie to repair the situation.

Fergie said, 'We're all a bit uptight, and no wonder. We're on our way onto tomorrow's front pages. With luck, we'll be back in Glasgow to read them.'

The girls ignored him as if he'd never spoken and he got why Norrie was pissed off. They'd do well not to push it too far with him.

Blondie had given the assurance so easily.

relax, will you? We won't let you down

He hoped to Christ she was right.

* * *

The journey passed, mostly in silence, the women reading magazines and whispering to each other, giggling occasionally at a secret they didn't share. Norrie wanted to beat their arrogant faces to a pulp. The hit required a couple of glamorous women to pull it off – they were certainly that. Offering it to these two had made sense but he'd forgotten how just having them around got under his skin. Soon, it would be over and he wouldn't need them any more. Then he'd give them something to giggle about, the blonde especially.

North of Rugby, they came to a stop for twenty minutes. Norrie anxiously checked his watch, fearing the unforeseen – the freak circumstance it was impossible to legislate for. When the train started moving again, he breathed a sigh of relief. Tomorrow wouldn't do – it had to be tonight. He took four sheets of paper from his inside pocket and gave one to each of them. On the paper was the rough layout and a sketch of the plan he'd put together in the wee hours after the phone conversation with Danny Glass. The reverse side of each sheet had a timetable of the sequence of events.

Norrie kept his voice low, going over the roles each of them would play, checking to make sure no one was paying more attention to them than they should before he continued.

'Stick exactly to the plan and we're sound. The only weakness is right before you drop the match.' He looked at Fergie, then the girls. 'Can't stress this enough. If anybody outside sees you – and I mean anybody – no hesitation, take them out. Immediately. Lexie, you watch the street. Sharon, you cover inside the door. I'll be waiting at the end of the road. Move fast, but don't draw attention to yourself. All clear?'

For once, the females dropped the attitude and behaved like the professionals they were supposed to be, asking question after question, clarifying how it would go down. The redhead – Sharon – was as sharp as her reputation had led him to believe and the Glasgow gangster was impressed.

This was the first time the women had had the details explained to them, the first time the hellish consequences of their actions would be clear. Fergie kept his eyes on their faces, searching for a flicker of unease, a trace of disgust, as the reality dawned and saw none.

Slowly he realised that behind the lipstick and the girly laughter lay killers as callous as he'd ever come across. They'd need to be. His head filled with sickening images of the aftermath: there were better ways to die.

He'd done more than his fair share of terrible things and slept like a baby afterwards.

This was something else.

Thirty miles from Watford Junction they went over it again. When the last query had been answered, Norrie said, 'Everybody sound?'

The others nodded. He gave them five minutes to memorise the sheets, then returned them to his pocket just as the announcement came over the speaker system.

'We are now approaching London Euston!'

They were there.

* * *

Out on the street they went into their act. Norrie took Lexie's hand and Fergie put his arm around Sharon. The women leaned into them, for all the world just two couples enjoying Friday evening in the capital. What could be less conspicuous? Tomorrow, when the police launched a manhunt, nobody would remember two guys and two girls on Euston Road.

They strolled, chatting and smiling, to the Greene Man on Euston Road. Fergie went to the bar and came back with drinks and crisps. They sat close together, playing the games men and women play in public, the girls giving their partners a playful slap when their fingers strayed too far. Only the keenest observer would notice the off-note – they hardly touched the alcohol. What they were about demanded clear heads and cold hearts.

Norrie checked outside: the car was there. Back in the pub, a barely noticeable nod of his head told his partners-in-crime everything was going as planned.

Further down the street, Marcus saw them coming towards him and drew a hand over his brow. The strangers got into the car; he didn't look at their faces – his interest in them was nil. After tonight, they'd never meet again. His eyes went to the rear-view mirror. When the road was clear, he tapped the accelerator, edged out, and headed towards the river.

29

The King Pot was busier than usual, the crowd swollen by punters who barely knew Danny Glass but were keen to wish him a happy birthday anyway, especially if the drinks were on the house. All of them had seen the video. Most hadn't heard the rumour – put out by Glass himself – that Anderson intended to hit the King Pot again, otherwise they would've remembered a previous engagement and given the party a miss.

To make sure there would be no repeat of the bloodbath Luke Glass's homecoming had turned into, four men guarded the door, their jackets bulging from the shoulder holsters underneath. Felix was at a table drinking orange juice and lemonade, glancing at the clock, nervously fingering the gun in the waistband of his trousers.

Marcus leaned against the end of the bar with his back to the wall, sipping an espresso, eating nuts from a bowl and chatting to a woman with an afro hairdo and huge breasts. He'd connected with the Glasgow crew in Great Portland Street and driven past the Picasso Club so they could see the place for themselves. Where exactly they fitted in, he couldn't say.

Fair enough. Danny was the boss. If he'd wanted him to know, he'd know.

The day before he'd gathered the troops together and given them their orders: be at the pub by eight-thirty and be sober. Nobody asked why, because, unlike the witless liggers, they'd heard the rumour. They were supposed to hear it – it was meant for them.

Every fifteen minutes, Marcus went to the front door to check things were as they should be and made a tour on his way back to the girl waiting for him: she was an art student from South Africa, or so she said, who claimed she was a colourist and talked endlessly about Monet and Matisse and dropped other names he'd never heard. He didn't understand what a colourist was and couldn't have cared less, so he kept his smile in place and switched off. The female was self-obsessed and didn't notice, though she was obviously impressed with him, standing closer than was necessary, breathing Southern Comfort over him while unashamedly letting her fingers test the muscles at the tops of his arms. Marcus hadn't had a woman in a month. If everything went to plan, he confidently expected that was about to change.

His eyes swept the pub, reassuring himself for the umpteenth time his men were in position. When he came to Felix he stared longer, recalling the dereliction that should have earned him a bullet in the brain and would have if Danny's brother hadn't stepped in.

Another time. Definitely.

Felix caught the animosity and returned it, tapping his jacket and nodding imperceptibly. Satisfied for the moment, Marcus brought his attention back to the female, still chattering away. By now, the liquor had done its work. Her voice was slurred. Monet and Matisse had become Claude and Henri. That was too much. He didn't mind how plastered they got so long as they shut their mouths and opened their legs. If she wanted him, she was going the wrong way about it.

* * *

Mandy hadn't wanted to come. Bringing her had been my idea. One of the men at the door said, 'Good evening, Mr Glass' like he was outside Claridge's rather than a South London boozer. We squeezed through the crowd, heading for the stairs. No sign of Nina. Not smart. As we'd both discovered as kids, going against our brother was rarely a good idea.

Danny glared when he saw who was with me. He poured two whiskies from a bottle of Bell's and offered one to me. I felt anger rise and fought it down: this wasn't the time or place to have a falling-out with my brother.

'No, thanks. Not tonight.'

He held out his arms as if I was spoiling the fun. 'What's the matter with you? It's my birthday.'

'The House of the Rising Sun' was playing in the background, Eric Burdon crying for his lost innocence above an unforgettable organ. Danny waltzed an invisible partner across to me, mouthing the words, his drink spilling on the carpet. I wondered if he really was drunk, then realised he was rehearsing for his performance downstairs. He put his arm round my shoulder, drawing me to him. I wasn't in the mood for another of his pep talks and braced myself. I was wrong.

He whispered in my ear, his breath hot and sour. 'What the fuck's that slag doing here? Get rid of her.'

I took his arm away and did my own bit of acting, aching to punch him, smiling instead. Through gritted teeth I gave him his answer. 'Sorry, Danny, can't do that.'

His eyes were inches from my face. 'Yeah, you can. I'm telling you to do it. Get rid.'

He danced away as if nothing had happened and fell into the chair behind the desk.

Mandy looked uncomfortable. She wasn't a fool and sensed she wasn't welcome.

She said, 'Maybe I should go?'

I didn't want her to go. My brother was out of order.

'Stay where you are. It's fine.'

'No, really. Be better if I left.'

Danny's voice cut over the music, sober as a judge. 'You're right, darlin', it would.'

There was no stopping her; I didn't try. When she'd gone, I waited until the song finished before calling him out. 'Ever speak like that to Mandy again and I'll forget we're related. Understand? What the hell's got into you anyway? She was my alibi.'

He emptied his glass. 'No, she wasn't. Your alibi is the copper sitting on your tail. I don't want her here. And if you don't like it then you can fuck off too.'

He was on a roll. 'I mean it. You and your brain-dead sister. What's the matter with you two? She can't be arsed to come to my party and you turn up with a tart hanging on your coat-tails.'

I let it slide. It had been a mistake to come back here – but the day was coming when Danny and I would face off. He poured the whisky I'd refused earlier and thrust it at me.

'Told you already. I don't want it.'

He came close to losing it completely with me. 'For once in your life just do as you're told, will you? Drink the fucking thing.'

I took it from him, raised it to my lips and reluctantly took a sip. It was tea. The whole thing had been a show, another one of his petty little jokes. Then he did what he always did, turned defence into attack by laying the blame at somebody else's door.

'I worry about you.'

'Don't bother, Danny, I'm good.'

He leaned over to make his point. 'No, you're not, you're anything but. That you could question, even for a second, that I'd be pissed tonight of all nights, tells me all I need to know about you. Tomorrow everybody will be able to swear you carried me upstairs, well out of it, and we'll have hit Rollie Anderson's poxy club and ended this thing once and for all.'

He stood underneath the photograph of the Queen and laid into me. 'Sort your head out and be quick about it.' He'd lost me and saw it on my face. 'The man who went into Wandsworth never came out again. They sent some sodding imposter who looks like him. He isn't. He's a doubter. And he's a wimp.'

Danny was just getting going. 'That knight-in-shining-armour routine, defending a lady's honour, proves it. Mandy doesn't have any fucking honour to defend. Yet you're ready to go up against me – your own brother – for a split-arsed bird. For Christ's sake, get your priorities straight and find yourself a special woman, like I did with Cheryl.'

This was the first time in seven years I'd heard him even acknowledge she'd existed.

'It started out as us against the world. Well, I've got news for you, nothing's changed. And yeah, I see your lip curl when I mention Team Glass. Convinced yourself it's all a corny load of old rubbish, haven't you? Thing is, the guy who went away... for most of his life he hadn't needed convincing... He remembered where he'd come from and believed it.'

Danny took hold of my wrist and checked my watch, the one he'd given me in a pub in Shepherd Market on that summer's evening when I'd trusted every word out of his mouth. He picked the bottle off the desk, leaving me wondering what had suddenly made him mention his dead wife and inspired his angry little speech.

Breakthrough or breakdown?

And then he was Danny, gruff and tough, again.

He said, 'It's ten to ten. We're going to a party. Plaster on a smile and let's do it.'

At the door he stopped. 'I'm going to say it, and, swear to God, if you smirk, I'll drop you where you stand.' He took my hand in his and squeezed until it hurt, his eyes fixed on my face, searching for even a flicker of fakery. 'Team Glass. Team Glass, Luke. Everything else is just bollocks.'

I didn't doubt he was serious about dropping me. Or that he could. So, I told him what he wanted to hear. 'Team Glass, Danny.'

30

Mandy was close to tears in the back of the taxi taking her home. The driver, a guy who looked to be in his sixties wearing a cap to cover his bald head, had seen the killer heels and the low-cut dress under her coat, and little else.

'Bit early to be calling time. Expected a young thing like you to still be dancing when the sun comes up.' He glanced through the windscreen at the overcast sky threatening rain. 'If it comes up, that is. Never know it was summer. What's the matter? Fall out with your boyfriend?'

'No, I'm just not in the mood.'

He didn't believe her and carried on talking. 'Well, whoever he is, he's a bloody idiot to let you out of his sight. If I was twenty-five years younger...' He shook his head at what would never be. 'Don't worry, girl, he'll come to his senses. Most of us do in the end. I finished with my wife a week before the wedding. She took me back when I said I was sorry. To this day she claims it was the worst mistake she ever made.' He chuckled. 'Lucky for me, though.'

Well-meant, but off the mark.

In the back seat, Mandy chastised herself for being an idiot. Going to Danny's party had been a terrible idea. She'd known it from the beginning, so she'd only herself to blame. Danny hated her and Luke didn't understand why. Mandy hoped he never would.

She leaned forward and spoke to the driver. 'I've changed my mind. Take me to the Shark's Mouth.'

He watched her in the mirror, his eyes flickering with concern, wondering why beautiful women seemed so often to be unhappy. His wife could answer that. 'Men,' she'd say, without having to think about it.

'You sure? It's pretty rough in there at this time of night. Be careful what you're about.'

'I always am.'

* * *

Eugene Vale lay in the dark with his hands behind his head, listening to the rain tapping against the window. The couple upstairs had been going at it for over an hour and showed no sign of stopping. In other circumstances, a prurient eavesdrop into the lives of others would be welcome. Not tonight. Sex was why he was in this mess. Pulling Nina Glass had been punching above his weight; he'd known it at the time. If only he'd been satisfied with that. Directly above him, the woman climaxed for the umpteenth time. He pictured the lovers, naked and panting, and hoped they'd call it a draw.

Their exertions hadn't wakened him – he'd never been asleep. He should've been at the King Pot but couldn't face it and decided, instead, to go to bed. Bad decision. Every time he closed his eyes, he saw bubbles breaking the surface of the bath and Yvonne staring accusingly at him from under the water. Holding her legs while she drowned was beyond anything he could've imagined himself doing; a scene from a nightmare he'd live with for the rest of his days. Nina had made it all sound easy. No surprise she'd coped better than he had. Violence was in her blood.

Vale slipped out of bed, went to the window and gazed into the darkness. He shivered. The police hadn't been to see him. It was probably too early to expect them; the body might still not have been discovered. But it would be, and there would be questions. When was the last time he saw her? Had she been depressed? On the day she died, what was her state of mind?

Nina had gone over what his story would be more than once, drumming the answers into his numb brain: his secretary had been a vivacious girl, a good worker and seemed fine when she left the office at five o'clock. Her usual cheerful self, actually. As to Yvonne's state of mind – how could anybody really know?

Eugene's chest tightened. Lying to women was one thing, lying to the cops was something else. They'd see through it and arrest him. He needed Nina to reassure him it was going to be all right. Vale recognised his weakness and wasn't ashamed of it. He lifted his mobile from the bedside table and dialled just as the couple upstairs started fucking again.

* * *

Nina was in a red silk dressing gown she'd bought in Harvey Nic's, curled up with a half-empty bottle of Jameson Black Barrel wedged between her thighs and a box of chocolates on the couch beside her. The television was on but she wasn't watching. In the King Pot, the back-slappers and arse-lickers would be knocking back Danny's booze. So long as it kept flowing, they'd stick around. He'd growled his order that she be there, a reminder of how she'd heard him speak to Cheryl. Except, she wasn't Cheryl. And she wasn't afraid of him. Didn't he know her well enough to realise what threatening her would get him?

Well, if he hadn't, he did now.

Nina sipped the lush mix of fruit and vanilla and held it in her mouth. The woman in the bath didn't cross her mind; she'd been a fool who'd brought what happened on herself and was unworthy of a second thought. Vale, on the other hand, was worse than a fool. He was gutless, as he'd proved in the flat. Nina had enjoyed sex with him – if he'd been smart, even a little bit, they might've had something going. But, as Danny liked to say, 'if your uncle had tits, he'd be your auntie'.

She refilled her glass, tasting spices and caramel this time, and stretched languidly on the couch like a leopard on a rock enjoying the afternoon sun in the Serengeti. The dressing gown's silk ties fell away and her fingers drifted between her thighs. Nina hadn't realised she was horny; the Irish whiskey along with thinking about Vale had been enough to light the fire – her legs spread and she surrendered to herself.

The mobile rang like a gunshot in the silence. She stopped what she was doing, cursed loudly and rolled off the couch. Maybe it was Danny on to demand she get herself down to the pub and start acting like a sister, for once. There wasn't a snowball's chance in hell of that happening and she hadn't the energy to argue with him.

'Nina?'

The voice at the other end of the line was frantic and whiny.

Nina snapped at him. 'We said no contact outside work.'

'I know. I know but—'

'Have the police been?'

He stumbled over his reply. 'Sorry... sorry, Nina... no... no, they haven't.'

'Then what's the problem?'

'I'm not sure I can keep it together. They'll suspect, they have to suspect...'

Nina lifted the whisky and let him talk. This wasn't unexpected. Absolutely predictable, in fact. She'd seen how Vale reacted under pressure and despised him for it. But it wasn't good news. Already, with nothing happening, he was closing in on a meltdown.

She put her mouth as close to the phone as she was able and spoke slowly, as if she cajoling a child. 'Eugene. Eugene, listen to me. You're overreacting. There's bound to be a background check. It's standard procedure when somebody dies in unusual circumstances. Drowning in a bath fits the bill. But that's all it is.'

Vale lashed out. 'Yeah, well, that's easy for you to say. You're not in the frame, are you?'

The implication annoyed her; she felt her patience slip. 'You're wrong, we're in this together.'

Eugene went into full-scale victim mode. 'Except it won't be you who gets the inquisition, it'll be me.'

Anger flushed Nina's face. The temptation to tell him to get a fucking grip and be a man was almost overwhelming. She whispered the last thing she'd ever intended to say to this creature.

'Why don't you come over?'

He'd seen the disrespect in her eyes. This was unexpected.

'To your place?'

The dressing gown fell away and Nina's hand slipped back between her thighs. Men had their uses. Even men like Eugene Vale.

'Yes,' she said 'To my place. Come over right now.'

31

Marcus hadn't spoken a word the entire journey. He dropped them at the car, stolen in Dover earlier in the day, and drove off. With time to kill Norrie and Fergie walked hand-in-hand with Lexie and Sharon, sticking with the roles assumed on the train from Glasgow – lovers totally wrapped up in themselves and each other. Above them the sky hung low and dark. At the Picasso they joined the queue forming outside while the monotonous beat of dance music filtered through the walls. The women whispered to each other, posing for selfies with their new bags. Everything about them drove Norrie mad. He couldn't stand being with them and wanted the job over so he didn't have to look at their stupid painted faces.

Sharon was quieter than she'd been earlier. Maybe he should be worried? No, it was understandable. On the other hand, Lexie seemed to have discovered an extra gear – chatting with the people behind her, striking friendships that wouldn't last the night; sharing cigarettes and laughing at the lamest jokes, while Fergie grinned stupidly beside her. She was hiding in plain sight. And making a hell of a job of it. A pretty girl in a pink and white dress and too much make-up, who was barely old enough to drink, asked where they were from.

Sharon joined in the deception. 'Aberdeen,' she said, rightly guessing the girl couldn't tell one accent from another.

'What're you doing here?'

Sharon forgot the empty feeling in the pit of her stomach, pulled Fergie to her and threw her arms round him. 'We're celebrating.'

'Celebrating what?'

'This handsome man has asked me to marry him.'

The girl's eyes lit up. 'Really. That's wonderful. Did you tell him yes?'

Sharon smiled a coy smile. 'Told him I'd think about it.'

The girl approved. 'Good on you. Make him sweat.'

Fergie threw in his crude twopenceworth to the charade.

'She does that, all right.'

The girl's mate looked even younger, her blue dress the size of a handkerchief. She spoke from experience she'd never had. 'Keep them keen, I always say.'

Sharon introduced Norrie and Lexie. 'These two are auditioning for best man and principal bridesmaid. What d'you think? Should we give them the job?'

Before she could answer a black car pulled up and two men got out, one of them wearing a fedora. The girl nudged Sharon's arm. 'Bet you don't know who that is.'

'No, who is it?'

'The one in the hat's Rollie Anderson. He owns the place.'

'Maybe I should marry him instead.'

Fergie mimed a broken heart and they all laughed. Sharon kept the act going. 'This your regular haunt?'

'I'm Tina and this is Paula. And no, we've only been here once before. We weren't going to come except Paula needed cheering up.' She gave her friend a hug. 'Her mother died recently.'

'Then make sure you enjoy yourself. You deserve it.'

Norrie stepped away from the girly conversation and whispered into his mobile.

'Your friend just made an appearance.'

Danny Glass said, 'Good, then we're on. And one more thing.'

'What?'

'Nobody gets out. And no witnesses.'

Norrie looked back at his crew. 'When you say no witnesses...'

'I mean none. Especially anybody who can be linked to me.'

'That isn't what we agreed.'

'No, but it's what's happening, unless I've got the wrong man for the job.'

'That isn't what I said. I—'

'I know what you fucking said. Can you or can't you? Simple as that.'

Norrie hadn't expected this. What he was being ordered to do shocked even him, but he responded like the mercenary he was. 'The price just went up.'

Danny Glass stayed in control. 'No, it didn't. Now you get four shares instead of one.'

The Glasgow hardman took a deep breath.

Glass barked impatiently. 'Make up your mind. Yes or no?'

'All right. But in case you're planning the same for me, I've got insurance. Anything happens to me... well, you know how that ends, Danny.'

He heard the laugh come down the line. 'Smart fucker. I like your style. When this dies down, we'll talk. Always an opening for somebody with the right kind of talent.'

* * *

At the head of the queue, an Asian boy said something Norrie couldn't hear to the bouncer. His four friends laughed. It didn't go down well with the burly man patting him down. An angry finger stabbed the young guy's chest; a contemptuous hand slapped his cheek. Norrie had met the bouncer's type before, outside every club in Glasgow, where they called themselves 'stewards' and bullied anybody who'd let them, for fun. If they poked him like that, they'd be sorry: he'd broken arms for less. He wanted to get into the middle of it and sort all of them out – he didn't need this shit. Not now. Not tonight.

He rubbed his palms together, more nervous than he'd been at any time today – if they were refused admission, the whole thing was a bust. He didn't fancy explaining that to Glass.

More bouncers arrived, outnumbering the boys. They dragged them down the road and laid into them, even when they were on the ground and had stopped fighting back.

A girl held her mobile in the air, filming the beating, her dull eyes glazed with dope, enjoying the show. When it was over, the thugs in dinner jackets rubbed their bruised knuckles, grinning sweaty grins at each other: this was what they lived for. It certainly wasn't the money.

The girl followed their victims with her phone camera as they helped each other to their feet and limped away. She giggled. Norrie wanted to punch her stupid face.

The boys had been taught hard lessons. Only fight battles you can win, and not everybody thinks you're as funny as you do, so keep your mouth shut.

Tomorrow, they'd be sore.

But at least they'd be alive.

* * *

Eventually, the four from Glasgow were at the top of the queue. Fergie paid. Norrie held out his arms and spread his legs, letting himself be frisked, and Lexie made lewd comments about how much he was enjoying it.

Another bouncer searched the girls' bags.

'What've you got in here?'

Lexie fluttered her false eyelashes. 'Wouldn't you like to know?'

'I would like to know. That's why I'm asking.'

'Big, isn't it?'

The guy was used to women coming on to him and went with an old joke.

'You wouldn't believe how many females have said that to me.'

'Maybe they're easily impressed.'

'Only one way to find out.'

'Thanks, but no, thanks.' She pointed to Norrie, patting his pockets. 'Brought my own.'

'Another time, then?'

She smiled, teasing him. 'You never know your luck.'

Norrie said, 'I've lost my wallet. Must've left it in the pub.' He kissed Lexie quickly on the cheek and spoke to the bouncer. 'Lost my bloody wallet. Have to find it. All my money's in it. I'll come back later.'

The man couldn't have cared less. 'Suit yourself, mate.'

'Will I get in all right?'

'Yeah, won't be a problem. Always somebody here.'

'Good to know,' Norrie said. 'Be as quick as I can.'

He crossed the street and hurried away.

The bouncer moved on Lexie. 'Maybe I'll see you inside.'

She toyed with him. 'Maybe. You can buy me a drink.'

'I'll do that. What's your name?'

Sharon dragged her away before she could reply; both of them giggling like kids. The bouncer followed her with his eyes, appraised the lean body under the clothes, imagining her without them. Whatever they were on, he wouldn't mind trying some.

* * *

Around the corner, out of sight, Norrie dropped the pace to a stroll until he got to the car. The day before, Danny Glass had emailed the floorplans – at short notice: how much had that cost him? Now the team was in position and ready to go. Explaining his idea to Glass over the phone had been easy; his reputation for violence was well known and well earned. He hadn't hesitated about giving the green light.

Raindrops exploded on the windscreen like tiny water bombs. By now, the others would be inside. He pictured Lexie and Sharon on the dance floor, men trying to squire them and being casually rebuffed.

Humiliated, they'd retreat stone-faced to the bar to drown their embarrassment in alcohol, telling themselves lies to soothe their wounded pride.

The second time he'd gone over the plan, Glass had asked exactly what he'd need so Norrie didn't bother to check the boot. It would be there. He pushed the seat back to make more legroom, closed his eyes and settled down. For the next hour there was nothing to do but wait.

Maybe the rain would be off by then.

32

Rollie toyed with the silk headband of his fedora, for the hundredth time giving them his impression of Danny Glass discovering a vanload of strawberries. For him, it never got old and never would. The people in the room knew the score and played along, although it had stopped being funny a while ago. Laughing at the boss's jokes was an important part of the job, especially if the boss was Albert Anderson's son and heir.

Rollie was in fine form. His mobile hadn't stopped ringing with people keen to talk about the video and how great it was to see Glass exposed as a coward and a clown. They assured him Albert would approve.

'What time is it? I'm in the mood for a party.'

Jonjo said, 'Still a bit early. Better wait 'til after twelve, when the serious clubbers arrive.'

Rollie put a drunken arm round him, ruffled his hair and poured a drink for himself and his new best friend. Jonjo was enjoying his status. Only one thing bothered him – he hadn't spoken to his uncle George since Rollie had told him about the video. George had looked at him just once in that meeting, and he remembered the contempt on his face.

Rollie read his mind. 'Where's George? Anybody seen George?'

Charlie Thompson wasn't a fan of Ritchie. The two didn't get on. Most of the time Ritchie ignored him and Thompson resented it. 'Doing his usual "man of mystery" shit. He'll turn up.'

Thin-skinned and immature even when it was going his way, Rollie saw Ritchie's absence as a slight. 'He should be here. We've got things to discuss. Hasn't been a peep out of the Glass camp. What does that mean?'

'Danny'll be trying to keep his crew together. Bound to be worried about how long he can hold onto them. At least some will want out.'

'Exactly, he's weak. We should be capitalising on it.'

Charlie put the mix in. 'Forget about Ritchie. We don't need him. It's Glass's birthday. The whole family will be there. We should go over and help him blow his candles out.'

Jonjo realised they were about to put the advantage the video had given them in jeopardy. Glass's stock, even among his own men, had to be rock bottom. If Thompson was right, people would start peeling away, one or two might even come over to their side. That would be the time to hit him. What was being suggested was foolish because it was unnecessary, except Rollie was too stupid to see it.

He said, 'After his brother's coming-out party, he'll be expecting us.'

Charlie dismissed the objection. 'No, he won't. Lightning doesn't strike the same place twice and all that.'

Rollie turned the idea over. 'I like it. Finish the bastards off, once and for all.'

'Yeah. Go in blasting, only this time make sure we get all of them, including the sister.'

'What would it take?'

Thompson pointed to the men in the office. 'We're all here, ready to go. Say the word and it's done.'

This was a mistake. Jonjo took out his mobile. 'Let me try George again.'

Rollie Anderson hadn't forgotten his bitter disappointment at the failure of the raid on the King of Mesopotamia and the revenge he'd waited seven years to savour. He overruled Jonjo. 'Fuck your uncle. Charlie's right. We don't need him.'

33

The taxi driver had said the pub was no place for a woman on her own at this time on a Friday night. By the time Mandy realised he was right, she'd ordered a white wine and it was too late to leave.

She moved to the end of the bar, conscious of the looks she was getting and how she was dressed. What the hell was she doing in this place? Danny Glass had called her a slag and she was proving him right. Her cheeks flushed at the memory – the humiliation still with her. Even Luke standing up to his brother didn't help.

Mandy caught her reflection in the mirror behind the optics and was filled with self-loathing. The hair, the make-up, the breasts threatening to tumble out, screamed she was a tart.

Luke was a good guy who treated her with a respect she didn't deserve.

Mandy emptied the glass and ordered a Lemonade Vodka. A voice behind her said, 'I'll get that. Good-looking women shouldn't need to pay for their drinks. Your money's no good in here.'

A heavy-built guy smiled and held out his hand. 'My name's Keith, what's yours?'

'Mandy.'

'Do we know each other?'

'I don't think so.'

'Then, I'm pleased to meet you, Mandy.'

* * *

Oliver Stanford sighed into his mobile. In the past he'd often told himself he worked well under pressure – maybe he was getting old. The weariness he was feeling came down the line.

'Tell me something good, Trevor. I could use it.'

Mills smiled. 'You're in luck, governor. Got a guy here ready to swear he saw Rollie Anderson outside the King of Mesopotamia just before it got hit.'

'What does he want?'

Mills ran his fingers over the bruises on his knuckles.

'Didn't come up. We didn't discuss it.'

'Just a public-spirited citizen anxious to do the right thing?'

'Got it in one, sir.'

Stanford relaxed. 'Really good work, Trevor. I'll tell our friend on the other side of the river.'

But Glass wasn't answering. His phone went to voicemail. If he was wise, he'd get out of London for a while: let the heat go out of the situation. The DCI left a message, cryptic enough to mean nothing if it was ever produced in court, and hung up.

* * *

I was with Danny, about to go downstairs, when we heard his 'God Save the Queen' ringtone. He shrugged it away. 'Leave it. This is more important.'

A TV show nobody was watching played soundlessly. The packed pub cheered as if they were welcoming a conquering hero instead of somebody who'd been publicly humiliated. They were eager to clap his back and shake his hand, yet there wouldn't be a man or woman present who hadn't seen the video and sniggered. I didn't blame them. It was pretty funny – so long as it wasn't happening to you.

How many actually gave a toss about my brother was easy to judge. Apart from me and maybe a couple of guys who'd been with him for years, probably none.

Somebody broke into 'For He's a Jolly Good Fellow' and the rest joined in. Danny grinned stupidly, his eyes heavy and unfocused. The crowd lifted him off his feet and set him down, swaying unsteadily, on top of the bar. He unscrewed the top off the bottle he was carrying and put it to his mouth to more cheers. Some of the whisky ran down his chin.

I gave him points for acting. Danny was drinking cold tea and playing the idiot so scores of witnesses would swear they'd seen him too pissed to attack Rollie Anderson or anybody else. Creating a cast-iron alibi for himself. He leaned at an impossible angle, for a moment defying gravity, then toppled forward. The crowd caught him and helped him back up, still clutching the bottle of Bell's. Sweat glistened on his forehead, his free hand yanked his tie loose and he looked suspiciously at the King Pot punters like he'd just noticed them and didn't much fancy what he was seeing.

'What the fuck are you lot doing in my pub?'

Everybody laughed and Danny said, 'Seriously. Who let you in?'

He smiled a sly smile, basking in the applause, and put a finger to his lips. 'Shush. Want to propose a toast so shut it. To the Queen!'

The crowd lapped it up and roared their reply. 'The Queen!'

It wasn't loud enough and he admonished them. 'That the best you can do? If it is you can just fuck off. Again, and give it some welly. To the Queen!'

This time he got the response he wanted. 'That's more like it.'

I moved to the door. Danny saw me and tried to drag me into his charade. He pointed an unsteady hand. 'That good-looking geezer over there, that's my brother, Luke.' Heads turned in my direction. 'He's the best brother I've ever had. Come to think of it, he's the only brother I've ever had. Right now, he's worried I'll fall off this fucking bar. But I won't. Get up here and say something. C'mon.'

There was only room for one actor in the family and it wasn't me. I shook my head and stayed where I was. A shout of 'Give us a speech!' distracted him and he let it go. Suddenly, his expression crumpled as if he was going to cry. He took another pull from the bottle, longer this time. When it was empty it dropped from his fingers and rolled along the counter.

Danny seemed confused, repeating what he'd already said. 'Speech. No speech. Give you a toast. To the Queen!' He tried to salute and didn't get there. His legs gave out and he collapsed. On cue, I went towards him with Marcus behind me. Together we carried him unconscious through the cheering crowd. When we got to the office, he opened his eyes and winked.

'Convincing, wasn't I?'

'The Oscar's in the post.'

'Pleased to hear it. Tell Harry to give them the free drink they came for and get rid of the bastards. And for Christ's sake get me a real whisky. It's my birthday, in case you haven't heard.'

* * *

A procession of men tried their luck with Sharon and Lexie and came up dry. Fergie stood at the bar with an almost untouched soda water and lime in front of him, making an effort not to look at the faces around him – the guys with their corny chat-up lines, the girls in their glitter, determined to impress somebody, even if it was only each other. A couple danced hip-hop, caught in the changing lights like frames from a silent movie. He felt sorry for them.

This was their last day on earth.

Fergie checked his watch, wondering why the hands hadn't moved. Lexie saw him from the dance floor through a break in the crowd and waved. He ignored her. The song finished. Immediately another started. Lexie and Sharon were beside him, bags over their shoulders.

Lexie said, 'What time is it?'

'Too soon. I'll tell you when.'

Sharon said, 'Where do you think Norrie is now?'

Fergie heard the anxiety in her question and was pleased. He shared Norrie's opinion that over-confidence wasn't good. 'Still in the car. He won't move until the last moment.'

Sharon faced the crowd, voicing what Fergie had been thinking. 'If only they knew.'

Lexie teased her. 'Having second thoughts, are we?'

'No, it's just—'

'Don't. It's not worth it. Imagine yourself in the shops in Buchanan Street with money to burn.'

The phraseology was an ill-chosen reminder. Coming down south they'd been giggling idiots noising Norrie up. As the time for them to act edged closer and the enormity of what they were about to do hit home, it had become real.

Fergie grabbed Sharon's arm and pulled her aside.

'Get a grip of yourself, you hear?'

'I'm sorry, I can't... I can't help it.'

'You'd better help it or Norrie will put a bullet in your skull. And I won't stop him. Where did the fuck-everybody stuff go? Get it back. Pronto. I'm not kidding. He'll kill you in a heartbeat for the fun of watching you die.'

Fergie didn't add he might do that anyway. He let go of her and ordered a large gin.

'Drink this.'

'Don't like gin.'

'Doesn't matter what you like, it'll calm you down. Drink it.'

Lexie brought a packet of cigarettes from her bag. She had no intention of joining the conversation. It wasn't her trip. Except Sharon's reaction was noted and, if she froze at the last minute, Norrie wouldn't get a chance to put her out of her misery. She'd do it herself.

34

Rollie put the fedora on his head, adjusting it to what he imagined was a cool angle. The drugs were working. With a drink in one hand and a joint in the other, he felt powerful. More than powerful – invincible. 'Okay. Get the troops together and bring them here.'

Jonjo tried his uncle George's mobile again, praying he'd answer. Charlie Thompson hid his satisfaction at how easily Anderson could be manipulated. All it had taken was flattery and a gentle push. Letting him think everything was his idea put him over the edge. Without Ritchie to veto it, he'd succeeded beyond his wildest dreams. Rollie was giving the go-ahead for an assault on the King of Mesopotamia based on nothing more than his inflated sense of himself. No information. No recce. Completely unplanned. Charlie could hardly believe it.

Jonjo tried to dissuade him. 'This is a bad idea, Charlie. We haven't thought it through. We've no idea what's out there.'

Charlie shrugged his objections aside. 'What's to think about? Glass's on the ropes. Chances are his own men won't fight for him now they've seen what a bloody fool he is.'

Rollie said, 'All I want are the brothers. Everybody else gets a pass.'

Charlie tossed a quiet insult at Jonjo. 'You've had your fifteen minutes of fame. Stick to what you know and let other people get on with doing what you can't do.'

Jonjo's promotion to Rollie's pal on the strength of the video ebbed away. There was barely controlled panic in his voice. 'George wouldn't do it this way. I know he wouldn't. It's a mistake. A big mistake.'

Rollie snapped. 'Hold it. Five minutes in the door and already you're some kind of authority. Who the fuck do you think you are?'

'Nobody, but this isn't the right move. I can feel it.'

Rollie didn't want to listen to any more. 'Tell you what. Tomorrow, get the first train to Newcastle and don't come back. This is my crew. I decide what goes, not your fucking uncle.'

'But it's reckless. He's still Danny Glass. It could end up a disaster. He's having a party, okay. How many troops does he have? What's the security like? We aren't prepared. It could go really wrong on us.'

Rollie wouldn't be quizzed.

'Shut it. Just shut it!'

He put his hand in his pocket, peeled off a twenty-pound note and threw it at Jonjo.

'Enjoy your last night in the club, northern boy. Don't let me see you around here again.'

* * *

Norrie took his feet off the dashboard and checked his watch. Time to go time. He turned the key in the ignition and felt the car come to life beneath him. Putting the plan together had required knowledge of the outside of the Picasso Club as well as the inside. Even at short notice, money – in this case Glass's money – got you information about anything.

He took a deep breath to steady himself: this part needed luck. What Glass wanted was grotesque but they were too far in to get out. If he enjoyed living, and he did, he'd deliver exactly what Danny Glass was demanding.

The Glasgow gangster drove until he was yards from where he

needed to be and stopped in front of a row of terraced houses, behind a blue Mondeo. The red neon sign of an artist's palette blinked above a lone man on duty at the door. Norrie wondered if he'd got his leg over recently. If he hadn't, he'd left it too late.

The queue wasn't there now and the music seeping through the wall sounded no different and no better than before. Norrie got out and opened the boot. As expected, it was all there. From a pub on the corner a piano tinkled out of tune under the pounding it was getting from a tone-deaf gorilla wearing boxing gloves. Voices and snatches of a song from another era reached him. In a strange way the prosaic nature of it calmed the last of his nerves. He gripped the two petrol cans, feeling their weight, and set them down on the road.

This wasn't it all, there was more. Once the cans were where they needed to be, he'd come back. Rain picked that moment to start falling, driven by a wind that had sprung from nowhere. Norrie cursed. His reaction was premature. At the door of the Picasso the bouncer raised his eyes to the sky and moved inside. If Norrie kept to the shadows, he wouldn't be seen. He bent against the downpour and walked to the lane shoehorned between the wall of the club and a metal fence, twisted and torn and almost falling down. The unmistakeable smell of cat piss filled his nostrils, forcing him to breathe through his mouth. The tight space was made tighter by crates piled high on one side and a bottle bank on the other. Fragments of broken glass that hadn't made it to the bins snapped beneath his feet and were lost in the noise coming from inside.

Norrie left the cans at the back door and returned to the car. As he opened the boot, an old couple came out of the pub and staggered away in the other direction. He took a moment to watch, pitying them. If there came a time when a Friday night sing-song down the local was the highlight of the week, it would be time to put the bullet he'd spoken about so often in his own head.

Then again, maybe he was being harsh. Were the morons damaging their septums and Christ knew what else with cocaine in the shithole on the other side of the wall really any better? At

Glasgow Central Station he'd been angry with the women. They'd been high. For years he'd sold the stuff and recognised the signs. Inside the club there would be a guy at the bar, smoking a cigarette, making one drink last hours. His job was to take the money. Somebody else would be hanging around the toilets, dishing the drugs to the needy.

Been there, done that.

Not any more. This would put him on the map.

He leaned into the boot and gathered the cruellest and most important pieces of the plan, cradling them in his arms like a baby. Yet Danny Glass hadn't paused. Destroying your rivals was one thing. Wilfully killing innocent bystanders unlucky enough to get in the crossfire was another.

Beyond heartless.

Cold metal pressed against his chest, glinting dully in the night light. Norrie forgot the rain and gave an approving nod; Glass had done well. This was exactly what he'd had in mind. The chain was heavy. So was the padlock to go with it. He sprung the lock and put the key in his pocket. It had served its purpose. It would never be used again.

Norrie was sweating. Just as well the other three weren't here to see him. He was the boss. There to make sure everybody did their job. Fergie and Lexie wouldn't be a problem but Sharon was beginning to crack and they hadn't even started. Fear was a contagion. If she freaked out, Danny Glass would hold him responsible.

The fire door opened, flooding the alley with light. He breathed a sigh of relief, passed everything inside, wiped his hands on his jacket and headed back to the car.

So far so good.

* * *

George Ritchie was unhappy. He'd broken his rule and he was angry with himself. In the Bayswater pub, a third pint sat on the table in front of him, a futile protest nobody would ever know about. Except he knew and that was all that mattered. Ritchie hadn't wanted the beer – might not even drink it – but he was tired of pretending.

In fact, he was tired of a lot of things, especially the never-ending task of saving Anderson from himself. Rollie was a dick. Worse. An ungrateful dick, blind to the advice that had kept him in the game after Luke Glass ended his father's miserable existence.

Albert had taken stupidity to new heights. Arrogant like his idiot son, the old man had been unaware of his many limitations. That was dangerous. Although, he'd been smart enough to hire him. And smart enough, more often than not, to heed his advice. In the end, he'd travelled on his own opinion, murdered Danny Glass's wife and child and paid the price.

Dozens of people had turned out to see Albert off. More if you included the plainclothes detectives hovering between the headstones in the distance, photographing the faces of everyone there. Or, maybe they had just been making sure the fat bastard was really dead. Ritchie had been next to a sobbing Rollie as the casket was lowered into the ground.

It had been cold that morning. Beside him the teenager had shivered. He had been pale, ravaged with grief, struggling to come to terms with his father's sudden demise. How he'd survive without him had to have been on his mind. As Albert's spawn his genes were against him from the moment he came out of his mother's belly. Inevitably, he couldn't be anything other than a fucking fool.

Seeing Rollie and his nephew smirking, believing the video could be used against Glass without bringing on the mother of retaliations, had finally brought home the uselessness of what Ritchie had spent too much of his life trying to do.

Even Albert, balloon that he'd been, would've figured that out.

He sipped the froth on his pint, absently watching the television screen, considering whether to stay or go home to the flat in Moscow Road. Living like a hermit was something else he was done with. When the brothers made their move – and George Ritchie had no doubt they would – there wouldn't be much left.

Tonight, tomorrow night; next week or month. The timing wasn't important. Late or soon, a reckoning was coming.

Meanwhile, in a pub where nobody knew his name, Ritchie was confronting his own failures, too many to remember. He hadn't forgotten them. He was in limbo. The best he could say about himself was that he was a survivor.

A survivor waiting for the hammer to fall.

35

Harry the barman put his head round the door. 'Just chucking the last of them out, Danny. Most were all right about it. Got a few grumbles as you'd expect from freeloading buggers getting settled in for a session. On the house, of course. One cheeky bastard actually complained. Wanted to make something of it. Felix kicked his arse out into the street.'

'Well done, Harry. Are the boys behaving themselves?'

'Yeah. Bored stiff and asking where you are.'

'Tell them we'll be down soon.'

'Shall I set you up with a large one?'

'Nice offer. Not tonight. Have one yourself.'

'Thanks, boss, I will.'

Danny turned to me and Marcus. 'Give it another half-hour before we make our move.'

Marcus said, 'When are you going to let the troops in on it? They have to be wondering what's going on.'

Danny snapped at him. 'They're not paid to wonder. They're paid to do what I tell them.'

'Yeah, but—'

'Yeah but nothing. They'll know when I want them to know, right?'

Danny was on edge. Unfortunately, it had become par for the course with him. I sided with Marcus. 'It's a fair point. They've been hanging around all night drinking orange juice. Be good to put them in the picture. Give them time to psych themselves up.'

My brother stared as if he couldn't believe I'd spoken, the corner of his mouth turning down in a sneer. 'You want some too, do you? Okay, that can be arranged.'

'I'm only thinking about keeping everybody in the loop.'

'And that's the problem. Too many bastards thinking. Too many jumped-up fuckers...' He moved towards me, rage etched on his face.

'You're starting to believe the hype, little brother. Telling yourself you're more important than you really are. Correct me if I'm wrong, but weren't you missing for... what was it... seven years? We did all right, even if I say so myself.' He hammered his fist on the desk. 'And I do fucking say so!'

Marcus had a sharper understanding of how the game was played; he stayed quiet and let the storm blow on by. When Danny had cut him down to size, he'd accepted the rebuke and left it alone. Not me. Where Marcus saw the boss, I saw my brother and assumed that gave me an advantage. Wrong, again. True once upon a time, maybe, not now.

He wasn't done with me. 'You seem to have forgotten a few things.'

'I haven't forgotten anything, I—'

'You wouldn't be here if it wasn't for me.'

He was so close to me he blocked out the light in the room. From deep inside him a fury had been unleashed, which had nothing to do with suggesting he bring the crew up to speed.

Danny backed away and lowered his voice, readying to give his favourite sob story an airing.

'Christ knows, I haven't asked for much. A bit of loyalty. Not a lot, considering. You're forgetting how it was.' Danny tapped his chest to make his point. 'How hard it was for me.'

He was off on one.

'I could've walked away. Let the Social have the two of you. Maybe I should've, for all the good it's done. Not what I did, little bro. Not what I did.'

His voice cracked under the weight of my ingratitude; he blinked tears away. 'You needed me. End of.'

A moving performance. Except I'd heard the speech more times recently than I could count. Nina was right. Whenever it looked like I was pulling away from him, out it had come in all its gut-wrenching glory. Sad.

Pathetic, actually.

It didn't get easier to listen to, because it was true – he'd done everything he claimed and more. And I'd been repaying him ever since.

Danny pointed a trembling finger at me. 'You're an ingrate. Get out. Get out!'

I backed towards the door. 'Why're you so angry? All I did was make a suggestion.'

He came towards me again. Marcus reacted quickly and put himself between us.

'Boss, not now. Leave it.'

Saliva bubbled at the corners of Danny's mouth, underneath his shirt his chest rose and fell. He stared as if he didn't recognise me, his eyes black jade against his ashen face. Then, the fury faded and he got hold of himself.

'No, little brother, no. That isn't all. You fucking know it isn't.'

* * *

Mandy couldn't remember where she was or how she'd got there. She was dizzy; her vision was blurred. She tried to clear her head and couldn't. Images floated behind her eyes, hazy and distant, fragments from a bad dream she was trapped in and unable to escape: staggering, almost falling; grinning men standing aside to let her pass, their eyes bright with lust and contempt; the hand on her shoulder helping her outside into the cool night air. And all the time his voice whispering in her ear that everything was all right.

He took her to a dark place. She stumbled, one of her high heels broke off, and he dragged her to her feet. His breath was on her neck, his hands inside her blouse, squeezing her nipples. A button popped, then another, the material ripped and rough concrete dug into her back. Mandy turned her face away from the unwanted kisses.

'What's the matter? You like it, don't you? A woman like you? 'Course you do.'

She pleaded with him through her confusion. 'Stop. Please stop.'

He hit her hard, tore the rest of the blouse away and laughed. 'Stop? I haven't even started, girl.'

36

Paula spotted the Scots girls they'd chatted with moving quickly through the crowd towards the door. One of them stopped to take a last look. Paula wondered if something had gone wrong. In the queue she'd been happy, laughing and joking, winding up the men. Now, her expression was strained and unnatural in the strobe lighting. Paula nudged Tina and both girls waved. Sheila didn't notice and left.

'A pity for them to leave so early after coming all the way from Aberdeen.'

Tina said, 'Maybe she's had an argument with her fiancé. Maybe the wedding's off.'

'Could be. He didn't seem her type, did he? Sometimes being in a relationship isn't all it's cracked up to be. Worth remembering...'

Someone crashed into Paula, spilling her drink over her new dress. Damn! It had cost a whole week's wages. Now it was ruined. She spun round, ready to let the stupid drunk have it. The blood disappeared from her cheeks: a woman on all fours was howling like an animal, her screams the most chilling sound she'd ever heard, while yellow tendrils licked the clothes from her back. Her chiffon blouse seemed almost to melt, the heat searing the flesh beneath, blistering and blackening it in seconds. Her partner frantically tried to help and bent forward. His hair caught fire. He dropped to his knees in agony, beating his head with his hands, his cries drowned by the music. Another couple panicked, tried to run and tripped over the burning man.

The nightmare in the Picasso Club had begun.

* * *

Paula couldn't believe what was happening: flames rose through dense smoke like special effects from a disaster movie; people were yelling, fighting with each other to reach an exit while a section of the crowd danced on, unaware. Three glasses of wine and the techno and house music the DJ was playing were enough to slow Tina's reaction until she saw her friend's expression.

Paula's voice was hoarse with dread. 'We have to get out of here.'

Tina stared, unable to move, as the horror of what was happening sank in. Paula grabbed her hand. Tina moved to search for her bag.

'Forget it, there's no time.'

A man on fire from head to foot crawled towards them.

'Oh, Christ! Oh, Christ, no!'

'Don't look! Don't look at him!'

Too late. Her friend lost it, whimpering, 'I don't want to die! I don't want to die!'

Paula slapped her hard. 'Get a grip or we'll both die!'

The girls pushed towards the front door – Paula leading, Tina close behind – to where Sheila had been – could it really only be a minute ago? A guy ran by, his shirt torn and his neck bleeding; he was crying. He said something they couldn't hear.

Paula caught his arm. 'What're you saying?'

His mouth opened and closed – no words came. She took his shoulders and looked into his smooth face, the face of a boy, no older than fourteen or fifteen – too young to even be here. His eyes were wild and wet with tears. Whatever he'd witnessed, his fear was greater than her own.

'What the hell did you say? Tell me!'

He shook his head and pointed to the front door. 'Can't get through the fire. We're trapped.'

She loosened her grip and watched him race into the smoke. Tina started to follow him. Paula stopped her.

'But he knows where he's going.'

'He doesn't, Tina. He doesn't know anything. Where are the toilets in this place?'

'At the back.'

'Is there a window?'

'Yes.'

'How big is it?'

'I've never noticed.'

A guy staggered in front of them, hands clutching at his throat; he sank to the ground. Smoke had created almost zero visibility, adding to the pandemonium.

Paula shouted in Tina's ear. 'Pull your dress up over your face. The fumes might be toxic.'

They ducked down and ran until they reached the toilet and fell inside. Paula scrambled to her feet and locked them in. For the moment, they were safe. The small bathroom was only large enough for two or three people at a time. A line of narrow iron bars cemented into the window frame, designed to keep people from sneaking their friends in without paying, made escape impossible. Paula pulled off her dress and threw it in the sink. Ironically, somebody hadn't bothered to turn the tap off.

'Wet your dress and put it over your nose and mouth.'

Tina did as she was told.

Paula said, 'Is there another exit on the far side?'

'I can't remember. Maybe.'

'Think, Tina, think.'

'Yes... yes, you're right, there is.'

'We have to reach it.'

'Wouldn't it be safer to stay here 'til somebody rescues us?'

Dark whispers of smoke drifting under the door answered her

question. Soon, there would be no air – they'd suffocate. Paula saw false hope flicker in her friend's eyes. It broke her heart to kill it. This was no time for lies: the truth was all she had.

'If we do, we might as well give up.'

The girls hugged each other – water dripped on the floor. Tina said, 'I love you, Paula.'

'I love you, too. Now let's go.'

They came out into hell, holding onto each other like the frightened children they were, stumbling forward. The sodden garments were no match for the super-heated air. Under their clothes their skin shrivelled. Breathing was painful, almost impossible. Acrid smoke made their eyes weep uncontrollably and Tina remembered the tap wastefully spilling water into the sink. After only a few steps they lost their sense of direction, bumping and being bumped, knowing that if they didn't stay on their feet it was over. Bottles behind the bar exploded like gunshots, showering shards of glass everywhere. Tina ducked, lost her footing and fell. Paula thrust out a hand, pulled her up and they went on.

Through the smoke they could make out the DJ dropped over his decks. Flames licked his arms: he was dead. From behind his booth a gang of men kicked and punched their way forward. The man Tina had pointed out when they were in the queue was in the middle of them. The callous violence of his henchmen, brutal though it was, paled in comparison to the panic-stricken crowd at the front door clawing at each other, jumping on top of people desperately searching for an escape from the deathtrap the Picasso Club had become.

The men turned and went back. The two girls skirted the madness and followed. As they reached a door, it started to close. Tina got her hands on the frame but couldn't stop it. Inside, Anderson shouted, 'Get that fucking thing shut!'

The guy looked at them without regret, knowing he was condemning them to death.

Tina said, 'Please. Please.'

Rollie screamed, 'Now!'

The guy prised Tina's fingers loose and closed the door.

* * *

Paula pressed her dress against her mouth and pointed to an exit sign glowing through the smoke. They moved towards it. Others had seen it, too: a woman, her head and face horribly disfigured, dug into Tina's arm hard enough to break the skin in an effort to get in front of her. Tina struggled to free herself and was thrown to the floor, again. Someone landed on top of her, then another, and another, burying her: a boot broke her nose; a heel punctured her cheek and blood ran into her mouth. Under the weight, her ribs cracked, pierced her lungs and she suffocated. Paula had no choice, she had to save herself – the exit was her last chance. She dragged herself towards the mob of people hammering at the closed door. Someone was screaming, 'Go back! You must go back! It's padlocked!'

Paula was exhausted and overwhelmed by the noise and the heat; she couldn't go on much longer. A voice in her head told her to lie down and accept whatever came. She pressed herself against the wall and jumped back; it was red hot. She spoke to herself to keep her fear at bay. 'The fire people will be here any minute. They'll get the door open. It'll be okay.'

Empty words. Less believable with every passing second. There were no alarm bells, no sound of rescue, only the anguished cries of the dying. She sank to the floor, tears running down her face. Where there had been music, all she could hear was wailing.

Above her the ceiling groaned and buckled and cracked, throwing out sparks. Then it roared and collapsed. Paula saw it falling towards her and called out for her mum.

37

Danny's crew stood in the King Pot nursing soft drinks like they'd done all night, watching the drama on the TV screen high on the wall. No one spoke; they were too stunned. They'd been ready to give Anderson a Friday night surprise he wouldn't forget – payback for the humiliation of the YouTube video. If their boss hadn't got pissed, they'd probably have been in the middle of it.

The sound was down. Nobody asked for it to be turned up. Violence was an accepted part of living for these guys; they were comfortable with it and had all done terrible things. But some were also family men with teenagers – lying about their age to blag their way into places like the Picasso Club was the highlight of their week. A few fingered their mobiles, itching to call home, needing to satisfy themselves their son or daughter was safe.

Felix lowered his eyes and turned away, unable to stomach any more. In that moment, I liked him. At the end of the bar, Marcus gazed, unblinking, at the disaster being played out in colour on the television screen, now and then sipping his orange juice. His expression was emotionless.

And I knew.

I took the steps two at a time, my heart beating so hard I could hear it. Danny was behind his desk, leaning back with his eyes closed, listening to the Yardbirds' 'For Your Love' and tapping to the beat as if he hadn't a care in the world. When he saw it was me, he went into his act, slurring for my benefit.

I shouted, 'You bastard! You filthy low-life bastard!'

He didn't ask what I was talking about.

'Spectacular, is it? Plenty of smoke?'

My throat went dry. My brother – the one who'd protected me after our father drank himself to death – was insane.

'Innocent kids with their whole lives in front of them will die in agony because of you.'

I dragged him over the desk, wanting to kill him for what he'd done. He stared at me and I saw the same emptiness I'd seen in Marcus. He didn't try to defend himself and I pushed him away like the loathsome creature he was.

'You planned it and used me and everybody else to set yourself up with a cast-iron alibi in the process.' I slow-handclapped him. 'Well done. Well done, Danny. You've outdone my expectations of you and, Christ knows, they weren't high.'

His voice was low and even, no denial or justification in it.

'Rollie isn't laughing now, is he?'

Not a question. A statement of fact.

He saw my horrified expression and stabbed a stubby finger at me, his face twisted in a snarl. 'Hear me now, quote me later: nobody mugs off Danny Glass.'

'Yeah, I hear you. Now you hear me, you sick fuck. I'm out. Get it? You're on your own. Team fucking Glass has left the building. And call off Felix. I won't be needing anything from you any more.'

I didn't bother closing the door. His pet policeman met me at the bottom of the stairs, how he felt written all over his face. Behind him, Danny's men weren't sure what to do.

'Is your crazy brother up there?'

In his brilliant blue eyes, I saw anger and revulsion to match my own.

'Brother? I don't have a brother.'

* * *

George Ritchie was drinking Chivas Regal without tasting it, his eyes fixed on the TV screen on the wall, willing the gnawing in his guts to ease. Ritchie was at a crossroads. In his mind he went over the years in the city where he was still a stranger – from stepping off the Newcastle train at Euston, until his sister's boy went against him with that damned video.

Wasted years. Because again, stupidity had won.

He knew what he should do. Why hesitate?

He ignored the bell for last orders and drained his whisky. The pub was emptying: a strawberry-blonde gripped the arm of the man with her on their way to the door, both of them the worse for wear; three younger guys finished their drinks and carried on with a dispute about football without missing a beat while the barman cleared their glasses, calling to the stragglers the same question he asked at this time every night.

'Haven't you got homes to go to?'

To Ritchie, he spoke quietly, 'Let's be having you, sir,' and wiped the table with a cloth. Over his shoulder the television cut into the programme with a flashing headline.

BREAKING NEWS – SOUTH LONDON CLUB INFERNO

Images of firemen hosing water into a blaze filled the screen as clouds of smoke and tongues of flames reached for the starless sky. He'd warned them and here it was – worse than even he could've imagined. Innocent kids dying unspeakable deaths because his nephew wanted to impress a moron.

What was there to think about? The decision was made.

Out in the street, he walked to the flat in Moscow Road for the last time, sure he wasn't being followed. Bigger things were going off tonight. Monstrous things Ritchie wanted no part of. On Queensway, he took the SIM card from his phone and dropped it in a bin. Tomorrow he'd be on the Newcastle train. If he regretted leaving, it didn't show.

38

Fergie set a brisk pace ahead of the women towards Norrie and the car. The pretence at being together had served its usefulness and was no longer needed. He felt relieved. They'd done what they came to do and, since leaving the burning club, hadn't spoken, each lost in their own thoughts. Sharon visibly struggled to keep a hold on herself. Violence wasn't new to her – she'd been on both sides of it. This was different. This was murder. Mass murder. When she'd been approached about the job, Sharon had understood exactly what she was being asked to do and had said she was all right about it. Now the deed was done she was far from that.

On the journey down, to please Lexie, helped in part by the line of coke they'd snorted in her Shawlands flat, she'd played silly girly games guaranteed to irritate Norrie. Lexie didn't like Norrie. Even if they had some crack it wouldn't be happening again. Not while the screams of people trapped behind the doors she'd padlocked filled her head.

The names of the girls in the queue escaped her, but she'd liked them. Liked their confidence, their energy. Behind the clumsily applied make-up, they were fresh and feisty and ready to take on the world; children playing at being adults. In those eager faces she'd caught a glimpse of her younger self from a time before too many wrong turns brought her to this.

Wouldn't look so fresh now.

Sharon forced the images of their charred bodies away and worked to keep up with the others.

Lexie lit a cigarette and passed it to her. In Cornton Vale, Lexie'd had a reputation as a vicious bitch who didn't take shit from anybody. Sharon hadn't asked and the other woman hadn't told her why she'd befriended her. Even Lexie, cold and mean as she was supposed to be, needed someone to hold her when the lights went out and the walls closed in.

Their heels echoed on the wet pavement and if she was suffocating with guilt, it didn't show. Or maybe it did. Before the fag came her way, Sharon noticed a tremble in the fingers holding it. She coughed into her other hand and avoided eye contact.

Lexie considered herself lucky because, long before the roof collapsed to let the poisoned clouds escape, she was in the car heading north.

For Fergie, it was the taste of petrol in his mouth and on his tongue. Underneath the music, it had sloshed unnoticed from the bottom of their bags as the girls had circled the club, cutting through the dancers, leaving a trail of death behind them. He'd waited for them, sizing up the bouncer at the door dressed in a tuxedo, ridiculous in the tatty surroundings.

Fergie had said, 'Bloody warm in here. Aren't you roasted in that thing?'

The bouncer had replied with a question. 'Haven't seen you in here before. Have I?'

Fergie had cupped his hand to his ear and spoken over the music; up close he could smell the guy's aftershave. 'First time I've been.'

'Where're you from?'

It wouldn't hurt to tell him.

'Scotland.'

The bouncer had nodded as if this information were significant 'Yeah? My old mum was Scottish. Where?'

'Glasgow.'

'Tough city.'

Fergie had smiled and shaken his head.

'That's what they say...'

The man would hardly have felt the blade which would end his life: an easier death than most tonight. He'd fallen against Fergie, his fingers impotently clawing at him. Fergie had cradled his head and lowered him gently to the ground. Blood had spread across the white shirt and he'd stepped away, careful not to get any of it on his jacket.

Sharon had checked behind her and nodded to Fergie. She hadn't waited for him to fire up the lighter: it was better not to see. Fergie had held it in his hand, studying the blue flame, imagining the mayhem it would create.

Lexie had shouted, 'The street's clear. For fuck's sake, do it!'

He'd dropped it into the liquid shimmering in the lights and closed the door behind him.

PART III

39

I was alone in the flat, still unable to believe the horror of what Danny had done. My first thought when my mobile rang was that it was him, on to try to sweet-talk me into making peace. A non-starter. His Glass-boys-against-the-world chat was played out. I let it ring a couple of times before answering. Pretending to be drunk wouldn't be necessary – he'd be well away – and I expected the kind of maudlin apology that was his stock-in-trade with me. It wasn't going to work.

'Got nothing to say to you. Not now. Not ever. As far as I'm concerned, I haven't got a brother.'

On the other end of the line I heard him breathe.

'Do you understand? You, me, and all that "Team Glass" shit. It's over.'

Nothing.

'Come on. Haven't you done enough damage? Stop fucking about.'

Only two people had my number: Danny and Mandy. I didn't recognise the caller ID.

The breathing was a gentle breeze in my ear, unhurried and even.

I lost it completely. 'You're sick, do you know that? You need help.'

Silence.

'Who the fuck is this? Who the fu—? Anderson, is this you?'

I threw the phone away, rattled and angry. It landed on the couch in front of the fire. I went after it and pressed redial to hear a recorded voice tell me the number I was calling was unobtainable. Fear crawled in my belly. My fingers searched for the reassurance of the gun. I checked the door was locked, turned out the lights, and listened. From the window, the road outside was quiet apart from my police shadow parked fifty yards away. Light from the streetlamps splashed the pavement and a black cat picked its way carefully along the wall on the other side, hunting for whatever it could find.

Someone was playing mind games with me.

Normally, I'd have assumed it was kids having a laugh or some drunk with a wrong number and not given the call a second thought. But, added to the door handle turning and the feeling someone had been watching me since I came out of prison, it was impossible not to be spooked. Xanax was an option. Instead, I poured a whisky, considered waking up my policeman pal and decided against it – they already had me down as a nutter.

I searched for a scrap of reality to cling to. Something to convince me I wasn't losing it. The reasoning part of my brain reminded me that coming out of prison is a freaky experience: everything is different; the world has moved on.

All very good. Only my gut didn't agree.

Since I'd come out of prison, it had been madness. Making sense of it wasn't easy and tonight Danny's gloating admission about the fire hit me harder than anything since Cheryl and Rebecca died. With them, there had been a way to give the rage a voice – and Albert had gone off a high-rise. But there was no angry response to dull this, no action with the power to redress the thing he'd done in our name.

I'd known him better and longer than anybody on the planet. What he was capable of wasn't news to me, or, at least, it shouldn't have been, because I'd seen it: when he was no more than a teenage thug, beating the defenceless Indian to death outside his shop. Over the years, I'd somehow managed to convince myself the inhumanity in his eyes that afternoon had been a one-off and gone along with his 'Team Glass' myth.

The awful scene in his office when the text and video had come through filled my brain: Danny's face, bloated with rage; the dulled sound of his skull hitting the wall, oblivious to the pain; and me wrestling him to the floor, holding on 'til the fever was spent and he was lying quietly in my arms. The strong older brother was more fragile than I'd known, a step away – maybe less – from total mental collapse. Witnessing a human being disintegrate emotionally was the worst thing I'd ever seen.

Not an excuse for what he'd done tonight. Not even close.

Before the YouTube video he'd been a cruel man; after it, he became a monster.

The fire would be all over the TV News.

I wouldn't be watching.

* * *

Not sticking to what I'd agreed with myself during those nights in Wandsworth prison when all I could think about was Cheryl and Rebecca was the biggest error I could've made. Once again, I'd let Danny talk me into doing what I didn't want to do with his Team Glass bollocks.

The cash he'd casually tossed on the table in the pub, the bank account, the car – all of it, even Mandy – were no more than shiny objects designed to distract and make me forget why I'd decided I was out. I'd always loved him. He was my brother. But I didn't kid myself he was any better than Albert or Rollie. The business they were in was a dirty business, and anyone foolish enough to get involved ended up with blood on their hands.

His tame policeman had found that out the hard way. And what I'd seen on his face as he'd passed me on the office stairs tonight had mirrored what I felt. He'd sworn he'd been in the dark about Anderson's attack on the King Pot. Then, I wasn't sure I believed him. I believed him now, all right. Danny had taken all of us – me, him and Anderson – by surprise. Nobody could've predicted my brother would do what he'd done. It was too awful to even consider.

Everything I'd wanted for myself had turned to shit. If Anderson had only waited 'til I'd quit Team Glass before making his move, life would be very different.

I resisted the option to fill a tumbler with whisky and drink until the bottle was empty or I passed out – whichever came first. Too easy. I deserved to suffer. Maybe it was some sense the night wasn't over. So instead, I made coffee and sat in the lounge, trying not to picture the hellish scene inside the Picasso Club, cursing myself for the idiot I'd always been where my brother was concerned. The minute the video had gone out on YouTube I should've realised there would be a push-back from Danny unlike anything I was able to imagine.

A knock on the door startled me, jangling my already frayed nerves. The sound came again, louder, demanding. My first thought was that Rollie Anderson had come to finish his vendetta. I picked up my old cricket bat, feeling the heaviness of its spine in my palm, and flung open the door.

It wasn't Rollie.

* * *

He saw the bat in the air above my head and blurted out his explanation before I brained him.

'This address was all I could get out of her. She said a name, over and over. Luke. That you?'

'That's me. Who the hell're you?'

'The taxi driver who took her to the pub.' He shook his head. 'I warned her it was no place for a woman on her own. Wouldn't let my wife go near it during the day, never mind at night.'

His arm was round Mandy's waist, holding her upright. Her head lolled to one side and her mouth was open: the cream blouse she'd been wearing hung in tatters, exposing her breasts, and there was a red welt on her cheek and bruises at her eyes where somebody had hit her. She was unconscious.

I lowered the bat and went to her.

'Found her lying on the pavement fifty yards from where I'd dropped her off earlier. She'd dragged herself out of an alley. Swear to God I thought she was dead. Reckon she's been given a Mickey.'

Drugging women to have sex with them was beyond my understanding. Pervs who did it deserved to have their balls cut off, dipped in chocolate, and fed to them on a spoon.

'Which pub was she in?'

'The Shark's Mouth. D'you know it?'

'Not yet, but I will.'

We got Mandy inside and onto the bed. The driver had done his Good Samaritan bit and was anxious to get away. I thanked him and held out one of Danny's fifty-pound notes. 'For your trouble.'

He turned it away. 'No, thanks, mate. I've got daughters – three of them – young enough to do what they're told, thank God. Still, you can't help worrying, can you? Maybe I should've taken her to hospital.'

'You did the right thing. By the way, did you call me ten minutes ago?'

He didn't know what I was talking about.

'Not me, mate.'

At the door he handed me his card. 'If you need help sorting the bastard out, give me a call.'

The driver was an ordinary guy who probably worked eighty hours a week to get by. I appreciated his offer though I wouldn't be taking him up on it. What had to be done was a pleasure I wouldn't be sharing with anybody.

When he'd gone, I sat on the edge of the bed and held Mandy's hand. Her pulse was slow, her breathing deep and even like a child's. Red hair fell across her pale face and I allowed myself to imagine she was sleeping. Then my finger drew the strands aside and uncovered the welts underneath, already changing colour, darkening to purple, yellowing at the edges, and the anger in me raged.

My knowledge of Rohypnol, or whatever he'd slipped into her drink, was limited to what I'd heard in Wandsworth. Cons called them 'roofies' and told stories they considered funny about how effective they were mixed with alcohol. Men with sisters and wives and daughters on the outside didn't laugh.

Thanks to me, Danny had another victim to add to his despicable night's work – the second he threw Mandy out I should've decked him and left him to it. If I had, Mandy wouldn't have gone to the Shark's Mouth and crossed paths with whoever had done this to her. But I hadn't. I'd let her go, humiliated and alone: the fault was mine.

Beside the bed the chair was hard and far too small for somebody my size. Getting comfortable wasn't going to happen. I turned out the light and settled for listening to the rise and fall of her breathing in the darkness. When she woke up, I'd be there.

40

South London was easing into the weekend under a clear sky. All over the city people would be making plans to have lunch, go shopping, or meet up with their mates for a few beers before the football. Stanford envied them. This morning, the five-bedroom house in Hendon, the cars, the holidays and all the over-priced extravagant rest of it he'd lied and cheated to acquire didn't seem important. The senior officer had been at the scene for close to eight hours and what he'd witnessed made him wish he'd never heard of Danny Glass.

He'd been asleep when the mobile had rung on his bedside cabinet and had stretched to answer it without opening his eyes – a reflex from years in the job. Beside him, Elise had stirred and turned over. Trevor Mills had spoken quickly and quietly. What he'd said had had his gaffer on his feet and racing for his car.

The memories of the night he'd just lived through would never leave him and he couldn't help re-living it again. Arcs of water poured from four fire engines into the burning building without making a difference – flames leapt in the air and the heat was intense. Mills was waiting for him. Stanford asked, 'When did it start?'

'As far as we can tell, sometime around eleven-thirty.'

'Who called it in?'

Mills pointed to three girls huddled together, comforting each other.

'They didn't see anyone and there are no cameras. Just what you'd expect from Anderson.'

'And I'll bet he's seen to it that there aren't any working within a mile of here. We'll get no help in that direction. How many people were in the club?'

Mills offered a guess. 'Friday night.'

'What does that mean?'

'Still early, so maybe a hundred, a hundred and fifty.'

Stanford took in the number and swore quietly. 'Has Anderson been told?'

'Haven't been able to contact him.'

'So, that's a no.'

'That's a no, sir.'

Stanford introduced himself to the fire chief, a sandy-haired Scot called Quinn, with twenty years' experience of thermodynamics, hazardous materials and the dozen other elements likely to have played a part in the disaster.

'How long before you get it under control?'

'Joking, aren't you? The best we can do is stop it spreading. A blaze like this only stops when it runs out of flammable material or oxygen. Best guess, we'll be here for a while.' The fireman shook his head. He pointed to an officer at the top of a ladder. 'There are bodies everywhere – piled at each door. Most of them already dead from suffocation and smoke inhalation before the roof came down.' He took off his helmet, drew a weary hand through thinning hair, and put it back on. 'This is the worst one I've seen and I've seen a few, believe me. Identification will be impossible. Be hours before we can get the victims out.'

The DCI said, 'Can't you just smash the doors in? People might still be alive in there.'

Quinn kept the irritation he felt out of his voice. 'The rush of air would feed the flames, otherwise we would've already done it.'

Stanford drew Mills away from the fire chief; both detectives were sweating.

'It doesn't look good, Trevor, and I don't mean the fire.'

'Danny Glass?'

'Who else?'

'Could be an electrical fault, a cigarette, anything.'

'It could, but it isn't.'

The DI chose his words. 'If you're right, he's gone up a couple of divisions. We're talking mass murder.'

Mills was naïve – another reason why his career wouldn't go much further. 'You don't think he's capable? This is a reprisal for that fucking video. This is his answer.'

'But we were going to take Anderson down, surely—'

'Surely fuck all. Glass wanted to send a message nobody will forget.'

Behind them, something collapsed and the fire roared. A new column of sparks and smoke rose into the air – Danny Glass's signature for all of South London to see.

Stanford sipped the coffee someone had handed him. It was cold and looked like mud with about as much taste. His gaze went to the blue and white cordon well away from the blaze and the crowd continuing its vigil, ghouls for the most part, addicted to other people's tragedy. When they started bringing the bodies out, some would be glad they weren't any closer. Later today, the flowers and teddy bears and scribbled messages of sympathy from strangers would arrive – a modern phenomenon the DCI didn't understand. But he understood the pain on the faces of parents whose sons and daughters had left home, dressed to the nines, and hadn't returned. Tear tracks on their cheeks and the despair in their eyes singled them out. Most stood sullen and silent, hoping against hope for good news that wouldn't be coming.

Threads of grey smoke rose from what had been the Picasso Club. Exhausted fire crews remained at the scene, helmets off, quietly talking to ambulancemen and paramedics. At this stage, the police had little part to play other than keeping the crowd and the media at a distance and maintaining access for essential vehicles – a major challenge on its own. Christ knew how many TV crews were here, apart from anything else. Quinn, like Stanford, had been called from his bed and immediately began rounding up his team.

The investigator shared what he'd seen with the detective. 'Pretty sure what we'll find before we even start.'

'Deliberate?'

Quinn scratched the stubble on his chin.

'That's asking too much at this stage, but they couldn't get out.'

'Yeah, I heard.'

Quinn said, 'We're going in. They'll search for survivors then start getting the dead out. Christ knows how long that'll take.' He patted the detective's shoulder. 'Better not to think about it.'

Stanford would've liked to take his advice. That wasn't possible. The DCI was tired. Tired of dealing with an evil bastard like Danny Glass. Tired of the whole fucking game.

Gangland feuds – thugs settling old scores or wrestling for control of territory – was a fact of life much like natural selection. Whenever they could, the police let them get on with it. So long as public safety wasn't endangered, nobody cared if they killed each other.

This was different. Revenge had reached a new level and, no matter how many witnesses were prepared to swear he was somewhere else, Danny Glass was responsible.

Unfortunately, there was a mile of difference between knowing it and proving it. And even if he could get the evidence needed for a conviction, he'd be signing, not only his own, but Elise's death warrant. And it wouldn't be pretty. For the time being, he was tied to the psycho bastard whether he liked it or not.

* * *

Driving across the sleeping city in the wee hours, listening to the reports on the police radio, revulsion at himself as well as Glass spurred a need to face this monster down and he'd pointed the car towards the King of Mesopotamia. Danny Glass hadn't been surprised to see him when he'd burst through the door into his office. Glass had sounded drunk. 'Was wondering when you'd show up, Ollie. What kept you?'

Stanford had let it all out. 'You mad fucker! Do you have any idea what you've done?'

The gangster's face had darkened. 'Careful, Ollie. Careful. It's my birthday.' He'd glanced at his watch. 'Or, it was. Don't spoil it, there's a good lad.'

The detective hadn't been intimidated. 'I left you a message. I told you... I told you we had him. That he was finished and you'd won.' Stanford's voice had cracked. 'I can't protect you even if I wanted to. Nobody can. You'd do better to get out of London. Now. Tonight. Everybody's seen the video. They know the fire at the Picasso Club's down to you.'

'Do they?'

'Yes. Anderson made a clown of you – or, rather, you made a clown of yourself – and this is your response.'

Glass had stood up. 'You're over the line, copper. Another word—'

'And you'll what? Kill me? Is that what you were going to say?'

Danny Glass had relaxed. 'Anyway, Oliver, I don't know what the hell you're on about.'

Stanford had gasped. 'Are you seriously trying to tell me you didn't order the hit on Anderson's place?'

Glass had sat down again, his fingers toying with the empty whisky glass. 'I'm not telling you anything, Detective Chief Inspector. You're the one throwing accusations around.'

'Come off it.'

'No, Ollie, you come off it. As I said, it's my birthday. Been here all night. Had a right old skinful, as you'll have noticed.'

'You're as sober as I am.'

Glass had laughed. 'Yeah? Gave a speech on top of the bar not long ago. Nearly fell off and broke my bloody neck in front of fifty-odd witnesses. Ask the barman for names, and sharpen your pencil, there's a fair few of them. Or ask the plods trailing my brother. They'll swear no one left here all night.'

'You're unbelievable, you really are.'

'Won't argue with you there. As for Anderson, hope he's dead, he won't be missed. Pleased to hear I can cross him off my 'To Do' list. Your dirty mate – what's his name again? – Wallace, isn't it? Haven't forgotten about him. He's still on there.'

* * *

The fire had smouldered for hours. In the rubble, one of Quinn's team was on their knees sniffing the ground. Others dressed in white suits gathered samples. Trevor Mills appeared again at his elbow. 'BBC News are predicting a hundred dead. Where the hell do they get their information?'

The DCI poured the coffee on the ground and threw away the carton.

'They make it up. Thought you knew that, Trevor?'

'Tossers.'

His boss touched his arm. The first victims were being loaded into a black van. In the distance, a hush settled over the crowd, broken by the sound of crying. This was reality. In a tatty club south of the Thames, young lives had ended.

Mills watched the macabre procession. 'Be our turn soon.'

Stanford wearily rubbed his eyes. 'Thanks for that, Trevor. Just what I need this morning.'

'I meant to go in, sir.'

'I know what you meant.'

He changed the subject. 'Our only way out of this is to take the spotlight off Glass.'

'With respect, sir, how is that possible?'

Stanford thought out loud. 'Torching a club isn't a gangland signature. So many civilian casualties could make terrorists the likely suspects. Feed that to the media – they'll lap it up. I'll go with the normal script... too early to be certain... not ruling out it being the work of a dissident organisation... as yet, nobody has claimed responsibility... you know, the usual bullshit.' He drew the corners of his mouth into a humourless grin. 'Where are the bloody Provisional IRA when you need them, eh? After I've written my report and passed it upstairs, we'll hand the whole fucking mess over to Counter Terrorism Command.'

'Will that fly?'

It was a good question. Stanford was asking himself the same thing.

'I'll guarantee you, Trevor. They won't find evidence that says otherwise.'

41

Nina rose through levels of ragged consciousness and broke the surface like a drowning woman coming up for air. Bile seared her throat, taking her to the edge of vomiting. It passed, and she lay breathless and clammy and trembling. Reluctantly, she opened her eyes. Harsh light flooded the room. Nina groaned and closed them again, unable to escape the nausea in her stomach or the damning flashes of memory behind them: tearing each other's clothes off; him carrying her naked to the room; his tongue and his fingers relentlessly exploring her.

She staggered through to the lounge. A bottle lay on its side under the table. Nobody had to tell her it was empty.

Nina pressed her hand against her throbbing temple. Danny had given her her first drink when she was thirteen and laughed when she'd retched and spat it into the sink. But, living with her hard-drinking brothers, she'd quickly acquired the taste.

Outside, the sky was blue. She lifted her mobile: five missed calls, all from Luke. Whatever he wanted would have to wait. Today wasn't the day. Tomorrow might not be, either. As soon as Vale woke up, she'd get rid of him – she'd had her fun; there would be no repeat. Nina slumped on the couch and switched the TV on.

* * *

Jonjo wasn't sure he had the energy or even the will to get out of bed. Yesterday, the future looked bright. Today he had no future, at least not south of the Thames. Going to Kent in the middle of the night had been his own idea and he'd struck the motherload with Danny Glass's hapless performance. Humiliating and hysterically funny. Rollie had loved every second of it and, for a couple of days, Jonjo had basked in glory as Anderson told the story to anybody who'd listen. At the club, he'd been waved through like a film star. Then Charlie Thompson had suggested hitting the King Pot and it had fallen apart. Instinctively, Jonjo had recognised it was a reckless move George Ritchie would never sanction. When he'd tried to stop them, Rollie had turned on him and dumped him. In minutes, Anderson's gratitude for capturing his arch enemy on camera had ebbed away and Jonjo was out.

Remembering made him sick. His uncle's reaction in the cafe had been unexpected. George wasn't afraid of much, but when Jonjo had shown him the video he'd been afraid – and not for himself. Back in Newcastle, if Ritchie had told him to throw himself in the Tyne, he'd have done it without asking why. Down here, things were different. Jonjo had seen an opportunity and gone his own way.

He sat on the edge of the bed with his head in his hands, fighting down the bile rising in his throat. An almost-empty whisky bottle lying against the skirting board, where it had rolled, reminded him why he felt so rough. Unlikely possibilities ran through his head: his uncle would speak to Rollie and get him his job back. Failing that, he'd approach another crew. The only result he couldn't live with was going home. That would mean he'd failed to make his mark in the capital.

Jonjo crawled towards the bottle, held it to his lips and drained it, which revived him enough to search his jeans for his mobile. Ritchie would still be angry with him – he expected a lecture. In his head he went over how to handle it.

A voice on the other end of the phone told him the number was currently unavailable.

Not having to face his uncle's wrath was actually a relief. As it subsided, he realised he'd no idea whether Rollie had gone through with the attack on Danny Glass's pub. For all he knew, Glass might be in the mortuary with a name tag on his toe and his brother with him. Anderson could be the undisputed king of the South Side. But without George Ritchie to speak on his behalf, he'd stay clear. Rollie was a mad bastard, as unpredictable as the weather. There was no telling how he'd react.

Jonjo poured himself a glass of water and checked his watch: ten past eight. For the time being he'd keep trying to reach his uncle and keep his head down. Money wouldn't be a problem for a while. By then, he'd have figured out what to do. More accurately, his uncle would tell him what to do and, this time, he'd do it.

He washed his face in the sink, then called again and got the same message. In an hour he'd go to the supermarket for whisky and beer. Better get something to eat, as well. There was no telling how long he'd be stuck here.

His fingers closed round the TV remote control.

* * *

I was wakened by my mobile ringing. It was dark and I was disoriented. Then the mist cleared and it came back to me. Against the odds, I'd somehow managed to sleep in the cramped chair – a bad-dream sleep, the kind that sucked your energy and emptied you emotionally.

The phone was still going. It was tempting to ignore it. Whoever was there wasn't giving up. At the other end of the line, the sound of breathing was like waves breaking on a beach. I lost it. 'Who the fuck is this? Anderson, is that you?'

The line died in my hand. If Anderson was trying to unnerve me, it was working.

* * *

Mandy was still out of it and I worried I should've taken her to hospital. It was ten to seven: The Picasso Club would be a blackened shell. I stopped myself thinking about how many had died in the inferno, and what kind of death that would have been.

My mobile rang again, shattering the early-morning silence. Something snapped inside me and I made a grab for the phone, only succeeding in knocking it to the floor. It lay on that god-awful carpet while an invisible vice squeezed my chest. If Anderson had been in the room with me, I'd have strangled him with my bare hands.

Years of resentment I hadn't been aware I was carrying poured out of me. 'You're going down just like your old man. Albert begged me not to throw him off that building. Cried like a baby because his miserable existence was coming to an end. He even offered me money. I told him to fuck off. Now, I'm telling you.'

She cut through my rant like a lance, her tone as cold as yesterday's rain. 'Tell me you didn't know about the Picasso Club.'

Nina.

'Are you serious? Of course, I didn't know.'

'Is that the truth?'

Trust was in short supply in the Glass family.

'I promise you. I'd have stopped him.'

That my own sister could consider, even for a moment, I was capable of such a crime rocked me to my core. She backed off, but only a little, doubt still whispering in her ear.

'I... I want to believe you, I really do, but...'

On top of the awful thing Danny had done, and the ordeal Mandy had gone through because of me, my sister's suspicion was more than I could handle: my eyes closed in a vain effort to shut out the world. Nina's lack of faith was the lowest point since I'd picked up the phone that morning and heard Danny say the words destined to keep me awake every night for seven years and still did now.

they're dead, Luke

that bastard Anderson

'Believe me or don't believe me, Nina. I've had it.'

She softened. 'You're right, I'm sorry, that was stupid. It's just... I can't get my head round it. Of course, you weren't involved – it's too big, too terrible – but he can't get away with it. We have to turn him in.'

It was easy to understand where she was coming from and I felt the same, except it wasn't so simple.

'And tell the police what, exactly?'

'The truth. Our brother's an arsonist and a psychopath.'

'Okay, I'm with you. Where's the proof?'

'Innocent people are dead, Luke.'

'They are, but what've we got that says Danny's responsible?'

'What do we need? It's obvious. Anderson humiliated him with that video, the fire's his revenge.'

'You're right, only he's got an alibi – me, a pub full of people and a copper on overtime outside. Danny was nowhere near the Picasso. Nor were any of his guys. And just to put a cherry to the cake, a detective chief inspector shows up and finds Danny three sheets to the wind, celebrating his birthday.'

She hesitated before she spoke again. 'What we talked about...'

'What *you* talked about, Nina.'

'Okay, what I talked about. Christ's sake, Luke, just how bad does it have to get?'

I had an answer for her, not one she'd like.

'Whatever happens from here on in has nothing to do with me. I'm out. If you're wise, you'll do the same.'

I ended the call aware I hadn't been able to give her what she wanted. The fact that she believed I could be even remotely involved with the hellish act my brother had committed in South London angered me, and I had to stop myself from driving to Heathrow Airport and booking a flight on the first plane to anywhere that would take me.

* * *

Mandy stirred and moaned and pushed the bedclothes away. In the morning light, I saw the damage to her face: her lip was cut; mascara smudged her cheek. Where the blow had landed was swollen, her eye closed. She moaned again and came awake. For a while she lay staring into space.

I squeezed her hand and whispered, 'Hi there.'

She didn't reply. After a minute she asked, 'Where am I?'

'With me.'

'How did I get here?'

'A taxi driver brought you.'

'I don't remember.'

Then she did and cried silently into her hands. I held her until she stopped and became quiet, my mind full of questions. This wasn't the time. Whoever had done this to her better be packing a suitcase.

She said, 'I'm sorry. I'm sorry. It's my own fault. I'm stupid.'

'You aren't to blame. How do you feel? Maybe we should get you to a doctor.'

'No, no doctor. I'm all right.'

She didn't look all right. I held a glass of water to her mouth and watched her drink it, wincing as it touched her lips.

'What happened after you left the King Pot?'

Mandy turned away. 'I'm not sure.'

I didn't believe her.

'Tell me as much as you can.'

She shook her head. 'It's better you don't know.'

'Why?'

'Because you're a Glass. You'll only make it worse.'

The pictures on the TV screen and Danny's admission in the office made it impossible to disagree. But I wasn't like him.

'What was his name?'

'I don't—'

'What's his name, Mandy?'

She looked up, startled by the force in my voice. 'I'm sorry, I really am.'

I was frightening her.

'Please, just tell me.'

'He said it was Keith.'

* * *

Jonjo rocked silently back and forth on the bed. What he'd seen on the television had blown his world apart. He switched channels hoping to escape the horror he was responsible for. No luck. The fire was on everywhere. In the studio, experts discussed the likely causes of the disaster ahead of a statement from the police.

Jonjo knew. If he stopped vomiting long enough, he could've told them.

Ritchie still wasn't answering his phone. He'd cut him out. Without his uncle he was on his own. Glass would discover who had uploaded the video and come after him. That was what he'd been trying to tell him.

want to be the man who made a right mug out of a psycho? Believe me, you don't

Pleasing Anderson had caused the deaths of who knew how many people, and put his own at risk. Rollie would be hunting him, too. The city was no longer safe – he needed to get out of it. But not yet. They'd be watching. The smartest thing he could do was lie low.

* * *

Oliver Stanford studied Bob Wallace and Trevor Mills. The DCI was wearing full-dress uniform. When the commissioner made a statement at one o'clock, he'd be standing behind him, impassive. Beyond the usual guff about hearts going out to the families and leaving no stone unturned, there would be nothing new. The commissioner liked to quote stats, though only if they painted the Met – and him, of course – in a good light.

Stanford opened the folder he'd been given. Inside, there were just two sheets of paper stapled together. He sighed. 'Is this becoming a habit, or is it just me?'

The question was rhetorical.

The senior officer spoke slowly, measuring his words, holding his emotions in check.

'I'll begin with what's known. As of eleven-fifteen this morning, one hundred and twenty-eight bodies have been recovered. Thirty-five people are in Intensive Care in St George's Hospital in Tooting and the Royal London Hospital on Whitechapel Road. Overspill is being handled by Croydon.'

He looked expectantly at Mills.

The DI said, 'We've got officers at each hospital ready to take statements.'

Stanford moved on.

'Thank Christ it wasn't later or the numbers could've tripled.'

Stanford read from the summary. 'Forensics aren't willing to commit to the cause without undertaking a thorough investigation. In their shoes, neither would I. However, they are prepared to reveal some interesting...' he searched for a more apt word '... make that suspicious, details. They judge the fire started at the front door, causing instant panic and a stampede towards the rear exit, which had been padlocked. Many of the deaths were due to smoke inhalation, suffocation from other people falling on top of them, or from toxins in the air.' He flicked to the second page and continued. 'There were bodies piled at the doors. The surviving few were among them. As you can imagine they're in bad shape physically, mentally, every way.'

Stanford closed the folder. Wallace sat like a fugitive from Easter Island. Good. He wanted him to hear the details. He'd played his part in this bloodbath. And there would be more to come.

'Imagine it. Imagine the fear, the heat, the choking fumes. You'd come in with your girlfriend or your mates. But you can't see them. You can't see anything. What would you do?' The DCI drew a finger along his jaw – he'd forgotten to shave: the commissioner would notice and be displeased. Fuck him! 'And, as if that wasn't enough, you look up just as the roof collapses on top of you, breathing new life into the flames everywhere around you.'

Wallace swallowed and cleared his throat.

His boss said, 'Makes you uncomfortable, does it, Bob? Should hope so, too. Makes me bloody livid. Unfortunately, we know who's responsible. We also know why that can never get out.'

Mills said, 'Will the brass go for the terrorist angle?'

Stanford leaned back in his chair. 'Of course, they will, when they consider the alternative. Think they'd admit they've lost control of the streets? The PM campaigned on law and order: where would that leave him? As for our lot... they may sound like policemen but, underneath, they're politicians. Putting it down to an unknown terrorist group lets them off the hook. In fact, it's what they want to hear. Means they can turn the screw on the public, reduce civil rights even further, all in the name of protecting the people.'

'Has Rollie Anderson been identified?'

'No.'

'Think he will be?'

'I fucking hope so.'

'If he isn't, where does that leave us?'

'Sir.'

'Where does that leave us, sir?'

Stanford steepled his fingers and considered his reply. 'Anderson and some of his men were regulars at the club on Friday nights. Nobody knows if he was there last night. So, to answer your question, Trevor, I've no idea.'

The door opened; a young policewoman handed a printout to the senior officer.

'Sorry to interrupt, sir, we just got this.'

'What is it?'

'From one of the victims' phones. A Twitter video of a disturbance at the Picasso Club before the fire. A fight between the bouncers and five young Asian men. Looks like they were refused entry.'

The photograph was grainy and blurred, impossible to identify anybody.

'Is the video clearer than this?'

'No.'

Stanford studied the picture. 'See anything, Trevor?'

'Not really.'

Stanford smiled – he couldn't help himself.

'Get this circulated. I think we've just found our motive.'

42

Norrie parked in the St Enoch car park and crossed Jamaica Street. The sound of a live band rocking through a blues number spilled from MacSorley's. He stopped to listen – he'd prefer to be going there. Across the Clyde, the sky had darkened and behind him a bus with its lights on headed for the Broomielaw Bridge and the South Side.

London was his destiny. But Glasgow was his town. He was going to miss it.

In The Crystal Palace pub, he pushed his way to the front and ordered a fresh orange and lemonade, dropping a ten-pound note on the counter when it arrived. The bearded barman took his money and didn't give him a second look. Norrie smiled to himself – twenty-four hours earlier he'd been in the Greene Man on Euston Road, pretending to be in love with Lexie.

He lifted the juice to his lips, wishing it were lager.

London had gone well and he was pleased with himself. In and out and back to Scotland before an investigation into the cause of the fire had even begun. He'd gone to bed and slept most of the day, the deep, untroubled sleep of a man without a worry in the world. It wasn't personal. It was a job. If he hadn't taken it on, somebody else would've.

Fergie had given up on sleep and was in the kitchen making toasted cheese. The call surprised him. 'You said we shouldn't meet until it was safe.'

Norrie had his answer ready. 'Change of plan. I need your advice.'

'No can do. Got something on.'

A lie. Fergie had no plans; he wanted to forget about Norrie for a while.

'Cancel it, this is important.'

'Where?'

'Nine o'clock in The Crystal Palace.'

Norrie considered himself a student of human nature. People were predictable. Fergie would come – he'd bet on it. That 'I need your advice' line was irresistible.

He took a seat near the door and noticed a couple of females standing in the middle of the floor where everybody could see them. The ash-blonde eyed him up and down. A pity to disappoint her. But business – especially the business he was in – came first.

Fergie arrived and sat down. 'Didn't think this was your kind of place.'

'It isn't.'

'Then, why here?'

Norrie toyed with telling him the truth.

Fergie said, 'I turned down a hot lady. Hope you appreciate it.'

Norrie remembered the two women – still there and still watching him.

'Know how that feels.'

'So, what's up?'

Norrie patted his shoulder. 'All in good time, mate. We're here, might as well enjoy ourselves. What're you drinking?'

* * *

They left the pub after an hour. At the bottom of Jamaica Street, they crossed the Broomielaw and started towards Anderston Quay and the Kingston Bridge. A yellow crescent moon shone its light on Glasgow;

Norrie was in good form, laughing and cracking jokes. Fergie sensed he was building up to the reason they were here. The walkway was almost deserted, too early for the junkies, the alkies and the weekend warriors – amateur-tough guys who'd scar an unarmed man for fun and boast about it the next day to their friends like they'd done something big. A couple passed them hand-in-hand, fresh-faced and happy. Ordinary folk living ordinary lives. Fergie watched them go and voiced what he guessed Norrie was thinking.

'Don't you ever wish you were normal?'

A strange question, considering what he'd done the night before was top of the news.

'You mean busting your arse for pennies so somebody else can get rich? That kind of normal?'

Fergie was defensive. 'Yeah, if you like. I didn't sleep, did you?'

'Like a baby.'

'That isn't normal.'

'Says you. We are who we are and we do what we do.'

'Did you see the news?'

'No.'

'We were the top story on Sky, the BBC and Channel Four.'

'What're the police saying to it?'

'They're hinting an unnamed terrorist group might be responsible. Which means they haven't a clue.'

Norrie snorted. 'Anybody buying it?'

'Why wouldn't they?'

'I wouldn't. What's the motive?'

'Terrorists don't need a motive. Everything they do's a statement. Bystanders are written off as acceptable collateral damage.'

Norrie leaned on the barrier. The Clyde whispered its way to the Atlantic and across the river the lights of the cinema on Springfield Quay twinkled like a Christmas tree.

He said, 'Thanks for coming tonight. Appreciate it.'

Fergie drew a breath; at last they were getting to it.

'So, what's up?'

Norrie stared down into the moonlight reflected on the water, as if he was wrestling with a difficult decision and couldn't bring himself to confront it.

'Danny Glass doesn't trust the girls to keep their mouths shut.'

Fergie wasn't surprised. 'Not hard to see where he's coming from.'

'I tried to talk him round. Told him if it got out nobody would work for him again. Glass isn't having it.' Norrie dropped the bomb. 'He wants us to get rid of them.'

'Get rid of them? As in?'

'That's right.'

'What did you tell him?'

'Said I wasn't sure. That I'd talk to you and get back to him. I don't fancy it. Those fucking two wind me up. Can't stand them, if the truth be told.' Norrie cleared his throat and spat. 'But killing them…' He shook his head in disbelief.

'Do we have a choice? What happens if we say no? I mean, is that the end of it? 'Course it fucking isn't. He'll send a team to do what we wouldn't. Except, our names will be on the list.'

'You're saying… what?'

Fergie had no reservations. 'Glass is not a guy you say no to. At least, not twice. Look at it from his perspective. Who you brought in to do the job was your call. This is his. No isn't an option. We have to protect ourselves.'

Norrie put his hand in his pocket. 'You're okay about it?'

Fergie shrugged. 'Okay isn't how I'd put it, but yeah.'

Norrie studied his shoes. 'Thanks, you've been a big help.'

'It's a no-brainer.'

Norrie laughed at a joke he wasn't willing to share. 'You're right, it is.'

The knife thudded against Fergie's belly, bending him like a scarecrow in the wind as he soundlessly mouthed his shock. Norrie dragged the blade up towards his ribcage, eased him against the barrier and whispered in his ear.

'I mean it. You really helped make my mind up.'

The body disappeared under the surface, then reappeared and floated, face down, into the night. Norrie walked back the way he'd come, keeping his head down. CCTV cameras were everywhere – too many to avoid. In the city centre, they'd spot you for sure – the trick was not to look up. He wondered if the women would still be in the pub. They'd remember him, no problem. Fergie was a different story; he'd had his back to them.

It was tempting to pick up where he'd left. Sex would round out the evening nicely.

Forget it; he'd work to do.

One down, two to go.

43

When I left the flat, Mandy was sitting up in bed wearing one of my shirts, on the phone with her daughter. A little girl's excited voice came down the line. Mandy smiled, pretending for my benefit, wanting me to believe she'd put the attack behind her because she was afraid of what I'd do.

The drug – whatever it had been – was out of her system, though the violence done to her was visible: one eye was completely closed, her lip had thickened and there were purple and yellow marks on her throat. I couldn't imagine the emotional trauma for a woman from something like that.

As I was leaving, she broke from the call to blow me a kiss. I joined in the charade, blew it back and smiled. Inside, I wasn't smiling.

Men had been using and abusing women since the dawn of time. Mandy and the millions like her learned to deal with whatever life threw at them and get on with it. I admired the approach, though it wasn't mine. Some cowardly bastard had raped her, and beaten her when she'd tried to fight him off. All day I'd watched the clock above the fireplace drag through the hours, waiting for night so I could go after him.

He wouldn't escape. I'd find him, if it was the last thing I did.

It was seven in the evening, with shadows lengthening in the room, before she was able, reluctantly, to describe what she remembered. At the end she said, 'Going to that pub was a mistake. My mistake. The driver warned me. I was hurt and angry and wasn't thinking straight.'

'Danny was out of order. He's to blame. And I should've done more. A lot more. I'll never forgive him or myself.'

She reached for my hand and shook her head sadly, as if I was a child with a child's understanding of the world. 'No, Luke, he's your brother. You had to be there. That's just who he is. But when you do what I do, why should Danny Glass or anyone else respect me? I don't deserve it.'

'Nonsense. This is one 100 per cent down to him. When I catch up with this "Keith", he'll regret he ever saw you. It wasn't about sex, it's about power and inadequacy.'

'I'd rather you didn't, Luke. What's done is done.'

What was it like to have such low self-esteem? To think of yourself as unworthy? I hoped I'd never find out.

The television had been off all day. I knew what I'd see if I turned it on. I didn't need that; there was already enough rage in me – I needed a clear head. Retribution would be measured, every blow from the heart. This low life couldn't have come at a better time. I needed to vent – for Mandy, the tragedy at the Picasso Club, and the senseless vendetta Albert Anderson's son was waging against me.

I was thinking like Danny. Maybe we weren't so different after all.

The thought made me want to be sick.

* * *

Mandy examined her face in the bathroom mirror, relieved to drop the pretence that she had recovered. The attack, the way the man had treated her, talked to her, reinforced her low opinion of herself and made her want to cry. She gingerly touched her eye. It hurt. Given time it would heal; the pain she felt went deeper than the black and blue marks. She'd made a mess of her life and knew it. Luke was a good guy though there was no future down that road. She hadn't worked since they'd got together and he hadn't asked. No work meant no money – the reason she was doing what she did in the first place. There was always her old job, hairdressing; paying the rent and no more. Her bank account had a healthy balance. Night after night she studied the figures, taking strength from them. But it wasn't enough. Still twenty thousand pounds short of what she needed to reclaim her daughter and run.

Time wasn't her friend. Her little girl wasn't so little any more. The questions had already started. In a year, two at the most, she'd be grown up enough to realise who her mummy was and what she did.

When that happened, Amy would hate her.

The alley where Mandy had been assaulted was a dark, forbidding place that might have been designed for men who wanted to take advantage. Just yards from the road but worlds away in terms of safety. Any woman who went down the unlit cobbles had to be sure she knew what she was doing. Mandy hadn't been fit to make a decision.

The pub was Saturday-night busy and I had to push my way to the bar. The barman saw me coming and looked away. I was a strange face. Strange faces weren't welcome in this boozer – unless, of course, they were female. He ignored me as long as he could, serving everybody who caught his attention, until he couldn't avoid it any longer. He was pale and weedy, somewhere in his thirties, no taller than five-six, bony shoulders rounded inside the shirt carelessly tucked half in and half out of his trousers. Style wasn't his thing. Apparently, neither was hospitality. He threw a curt nod in my direction then turned his back to drain whisky from an optic on the gantry, watching me in the mirror. An awful lot of hostility considering all I'd done was walk into his pub.

Before I spoke, I guessed what his response would be.

'What time does Keith usually get here?'

He picked up a dirty cloth and started wiping the counter. 'Don't know anybody called Keith.'

'Yeah, you do. Big guy. Was in last night.'

His eyes went to everything but me, suspicion falling like dandruff from his unwashed hair.

'Who's asking?'

'What time?'

He shrugged and moved away – I'd had my chance and come up short.

'Can't help you, mate.'

I grabbed his arm. Surprise forced him to finally look at me. 'I'm asking the questions. Seeing it's you, I'll make an exception and tell you. Glass. Luke Glass.'

I was a lot less famous than Danny. That didn't matter. It would be impossible to find somebody south of the river who hadn't heard the name and what it stood for. His eyes darted along the bar, searching for help. He could forget it. Nobody here would be up for taking on Danny Glass's brother.

I tightened my grip; his eyes narrowed in fear as he tried unsuccessfully to shake me off. A couple of minutes ago he was just a surly fucker giving a stranger a hard time and there was no problem. Now, he'd got himself into something he hadn't bargained for and wanted a road out.

Easy. I wasn't difficult to please. All he'd had to do was be civil and answer a simple question. This guy had done neither. Scaring him would be fun.

'Ever heard the saying "the customer's always right"? Last chance. What time does Keith usually come in?'

'Ten. He comes in at ten.'

People made things harder than they needed to be.

I smiled and let go of him. 'Point him out to me.'

There was only one door into the pub. For twenty minutes I kept my eyes on it.

When the man who'd drugged Mandy arrived, I didn't need the weasel behind the bar to finger him: Keith was a weekend Lothario, overdressed for a pub, even on a Saturday night. Most of the regulars were casual; he was wearing a suit and tie, as if he were stopping in for a quick gargle on his way up West. His aftershave would be overpowering, and in his pocket, he'd have the neighbour of whatever he'd slipped into Mandy's drink. A couple of regulars grinned and clapped his shoulder, pleased to see him. Good old Keith was a popular guy. I pegged him at forty-five, a big hit for himself; a sleaze who was going home without his teeth.

The barman saw him and shot a nervous glance in my direction. Behind his pasty face he was considering his options.

I called him over. Everything about his body language said he didn't want to go anywhere near me. 'Tell Keith Luke Glass wants a word.'

'Joking, aren't you? Leave me out of it.'

That ship had sailed.

I turned the empty whisky glass in my hand as if I'd only just realised it was there and was thinking about breaking it and shoving it in his eye.

'I'll meet him in the alley.'

'And if he says fuck off?'

I smiled slowly for effect. 'Then we'll do it here in front of everybody.'

From somewhere he found a scrap of defiance. Not much, though more than I expected from him. 'Start anything in here and I'm calling the police.'

I fought an urge to drag him over the bar and break his legs. He hadn't been so quick to take the moral high ground when a woman was being drugged in his pub.

'Do that and you'll be out of business in a week, believe me.'

He did.

I watched him call Keith over and whisper in his ear. This was the bastard's local. He was in with the bricks and probably thought he was going to hear some gossip. The smile froze on his lips. He tensed, realising his past had caught up with him. Mandy was the latest, not the first. Predators like him started early and kept on until somebody ended their streak.

Tonight, that was my job and I was well up for it.

Keith threw back whatever was in his glass, said something to the bartender, and left. I waved a warning finger and mouthed, 'Forget it.'

The alley might end up crowded if Keith's request for reinforcements was answered. Plan B was tucked into the waistband of my trousers, under my jacket. Danny's present would be enough to tilt the odds back in my favour. I didn't intend to actually use it, but then, a lot of stuff happened that wasn't intended.

Outside the air was cool. Keith was waiting for me, shuffling from one foot to the other as if he needed to go to the bathroom. In the street light, his skin was lined and unnaturally white; he was scared. He should be.

His opening line had nothing to do with anything.

'Who are you?'

It didn't deserve an answer. I gave one anyway. 'A friend of Mandy's.'

The name should've meant something to him – it had only been a day. The fact it didn't told me everything I'd guessed about this guy was right. He was scum. Further along the road the door of the pub opened and two men came out, drunk as lords. I backed into the alley, feeling the darkness fall around me. Keith didn't move. He hadn't recognised Mandy's name. He did recognise walking into the alley was the last walking he'd be doing in a while.

Keith took his eyes off me and looked up the street. No doubt wondering when the cavalry was going to arrive and beginning to worry: they were cutting it tight.

Keith came to the conclusion he was on his own and balanced on the balls of his feet, setting himself up to make a run for it. He could certainly try it. Nobody would blame him if he did. Wandsworth was good for me in some ways. I'd spent every hour I could in the gym and was fitter than I'd ever been. Keith pictured himself as a lover not a fighter. Me, I didn't have a label, unless you counted being THE GUY WHO WAS GOING TO PUT HIM IN A FUCKING WHEELCHAIR.

Try fitting that on a hat.

I moved towards him. He edged away. The door of the pub opened again; false hope lit his face and died. The barman stood in the frame, conversation tumbling from inside onto the pavement. Curiosity had brought him out to check what was happening. That was as far as he was prepared to go. He'd made the right decision, after all. A part of me regretted it – the part that ached to hurt him too.

I said, 'Ten point eight seconds.'

I'd lost him.

'Ten point eight. For the hundred yards. I'll catch you before you get as far as the pub. And you can have an audience hear you beg for mercy while I beat your fucking brains in. Up to you. My advice: Get it over with here. Take your medicine like a big boy. We both know you deserve it.'

It had been a night of choices.

For me. For the barman.

I was giving Keith a choice. More than he'd done with Mandy.

44

An orange light glowed from an upstairs bedroom. Not knowing if Lexie was alone didn't bother Norrie unduly – if it got complicated, he'd deal with it. He had a talent – the ability to separate himself from his emotions and do what had to be done without getting bogged down in sentiment – the perfect temperament for the business he was in.

Norrie had liked Fergie. In the end, that counted for nothing. When he'd driven the knife into his gut and tipped him over the barrier, it hadn't even been a consideration.

Lexie, on the other hand, he very definitely disliked. From the moment she'd turned up with Sharon at Central Station until they'd come out of the Greene Man on Euston Road, she'd been a giggly pain in the arse. A day in her company had been a day too long and before they'd got near the capital, Norrie had decided this would be her last job with him. Having said that, once it had kicked off in earnest, he'd had no complaints about her work. She'd carried out his instructions to a T: detached, professional and unaffected by the carnage they'd caused in the club. It wouldn't be exaggerating to say she'd enjoyed it.

Sharon was the weakest link – there was always one. Fine on the train going down, and in the pub, taking her cue from Lexie, treating it like a day out, joining in the stupid girls-versus-the-boys crap. Driving home through the night, she'd hardly spoken. In the rear-view mirror Norrie had caught the look on her face and recognised that, with or without Danny Glass's brutal instruction, they had a problem. Meeting the people in the queue put faces to the thing. Now Sharon was imagining the flames popping their eyeballs, licking the flesh from their blackened skulls, and remembering how young and trusting they'd been.

He waited until the moon went behind a cloud and crossed the road, walking quickly and quietly down the path to the back of the house. The conservatory was a surprise. An upwardly mobile cokehead; he'd never have guessed.

His elbow tapped the glass hard, once. It cracked, then broke, and he held his breath. This was the moment: if she'd heard, she'd be ready and Norrie would rather avoid a struggle. He reached in, turned the key in the lock and stepped inside. A wine bottle and two glasses sat on a cane table. All empty. She hadn't seemed the boyfriend type. Maybe the crazy fuck-you persona was an act and underneath was a one-man woman, whose biggest ambition was to have a handful of babies.

Yeah, like hell.

This was Lexie.

The moon flooded the conservatory with light. Norrie moved further into the house, instinctively edging down the hall until he stopped at the bottom of the stairs. Unfamiliar music drifted towards him and he understood why she hadn't heard the glass breaking. He tested his weight on the first step and started to climb, listening for voices, which would guarantee it would be messy.

At the top, he paused in front of three doors: two bedrooms and a bathroom. One of them, the one with music and an orange rectangle spilling from it, was ajar. Norrie's plans were always straightforward. Complicated was a formula for failure. Thus far, he'd been right. In London, the biggest hurdle had been getting the petrol into the club without being seen. Guys could've handled that, no problem. But how much attention would four out-of-town guys attract in the queue? What if they didn't get in? The whole thing would've been a bust before it even got started. Try telling that to Danny Glass. The solution was simple: pubs and clubs rolled out the red carpet for fine-looking women.

And it had worked. Yeah, plans were good.

So how come he didn't have a plan for Lexie, beyond breaking in and doing her?

Norrie pulled the blade from his pocket, peeked round the edge of the door and swallowed: Lexie was naked on the bed, her head turned towards the window. A woman knelt with her face between Lexie's spread legs. She was naked, too. Lexie arched, stretching like a cat and held her lover's shoulders. Norrie felt himself grow hard. He folded the blade and put it in his pocket. All in good time.

The females then lay side by side, kissing and fondling each other's breasts, their bone-white bodies grinding gently. Her partner moved down and took Lexie's erect nipple in her mouth, sucking on it greedily. A black dildo appeared, the size of a baby's arm. She strapped it on and lowered herself between Lexie's creamy thighs. Lexie gasped and climaxed almost immediately. Then they went at it, both of them moaning and crying out, their shadows trembling as one on the wall in the half-light. Twenty-four hours earlier, she'd been a cold-eyed assassin, unmoved by the suffering she'd caused. Driving through an almost deserted Brent Cross on their way north, Norrie had seen her in the mirror, mouth open, eyes closed, asleep before they'd even left the city, and wondered what ran in her veins.

This was a different Lexie, compliant, obedient, eager to be dominated.

Watching them, Norrie reckoned this wasn't their first time together. Later, there would be pillow talk. It might include what had happened in South London. Lexie came again, loud enough to wake the neighbours.

Danny Glass had been on the money.

Downstairs in the kitchen, Norrie hid behind the door. One of them would be here soon – it didn't matter which. If it was Lexie, her lover wouldn't die tonight. He heard footsteps on the stairs, his fingers closed round the knife and he held his breath. Lexie took out two mugs and filled the coffee machine with water. Her back was to him; he couldn't see her face, but she had a good body: slim legs, tight arse. Not difficult to understand the attraction – for a man or a woman.

When he'd asked how Fergie felt about killing the girls, he hadn't needed to think about his answer. Lexie would be the same. Feelings, loyalty, all that guff, didn't come into it. Up close the smell of sex was on her skin. At the last moment she sensed him behind her and tried to turn but he dragged her backwards with one hand and sliced her windpipe with the knife. Blood cascaded over her chest and breasts like the opening credits of a James Bond movie. Norrie cradled her to the floor. In moments, she'd be dead.

Lexie's eyes were empty, the life force already leaving them. Would she hear if he told her he was sorry it had ended this way? Maybe. Maybe not. Except, he wasn't sorry. He wasn't sorry at all.

He left through the conservatory, crossed the road and walked to his car. The sky was clear, the cloud gone and the moon had been joined by stars. Back at the house, the orange light was still on in the bedroom. Norrie started the engine and pulled out into the street.

Onwards and upwards.

Two down, one to go.

45

The police car would still be outside so I came in the way I'd gone out. Tomorrow the copper would swear I hadn't left the flat. An alibi wasn't the point – plenty of people at the pub had seen me – but the policeman would've stopped me doing what I had to do. I'd hoped Mandy would be asleep when I got home. She wasn't. She was sitting on the couch in front of the fire waiting for me: she looked awful. Lying wasn't what I wanted to do. If there was a chance of getting away with it, I would.

'Are you all right?'

'I'm fine.'

'I was worried about you.'

'No need. I can look after myself.'

She didn't know how to say it and hesitated. 'Did... did... you find him?'

'Yes.'

Her eyes went to my fists and she cried out.

'My bloody stupidity caused all this.'

I put my arms around her and held her close. 'We've been over this. You're not responsible for what somebody else does. Danny's to blame. And me. For letting him treat you like that.'

Through tears she said, 'I hope you haven't got yourself into trouble. Don't you have to be careful?'

I kept it light. 'No. I served my time. "Repaid my debt to society" as they say. There are no conditions on my release.'

The swelling at her eye and the side of her face hadn't gone down. If anything, it looked worse. I got ice from the kitchen. She took it from me and stroked my knuckles with the tips of her fingers. 'I appreciate what you did, but I really wish you'd left it alone. It doesn't change anything.'

'Except, I feel a lot better.'

'Did he say anything about me?'

The anxiety on her face made me wish I'd hit him a few more times for luck.

'I didn't give him a chance.'

This wasn't going anywhere good.

'How did you get on with Amy?'

Hearing her daughter's name made her break down again. She buried her face in her hands. 'Luke, I'm a mess. I don't know where to turn. My ex is right. I'm not fit to be a mother.'

And it all came tumbling out, every demeaning day, every sadness and disappointment and scintilla of self-loathing. I did the only thing I could do and held her until she got it all out. Then tried to move her on to something better.

'When's Amy getting here?'

'She's coming down next week. She's excited about it.' Mandy touched her cheek. 'God, I can't look like this.'

'You won't. Amy will see her mother at her most glamorous.'

'You really think so?'

'I do. Especially if she gets her beauty sleep. It's late. Time you were asleep.'

She kissed me and did as she was told, secretly pleased somebody cared enough to listen.

When she'd gone to bed, I took off my jacket and poured a whisky, drank most of it in two gulps and topped it up again. It tasted harsh and burned the back of my throat on the way down. Mandy was beating herself up about things in the past. Things I could sort. What happened in the alley wasn't pretty; the details from tonight's little adventure wouldn't help her state of mind.

Keith had been one of those guys who was in his element with people who weren't able to defend themselves. He'd no chance against me and knew it from the beginning. His heart wasn't in it. The barman telling him my name was Glass had understandably affected his confidence. Albert Anderson's legendary swan dive would be in his mind. Somewhere between the pub and the alley, he'd planned to give up and depended on me giving him a break. As plans went, it was a dog. This was personal. My first punch doubled him over. He went down on one knee, signalling with his hand he was throwing the towel in. No chance. I wasn't letting him off so lightly.

'Get up. Get up or I'll come after you anyway.'

He lifted himself to his feet and I noticed we were about the same height and weight. The difference was, I had an incentive. Then, he made a big mistake – he opened his mouth.

'Whatever she told you isn't true.'

I'd used my incarceration wisely. I'd been the boxing champion of D Wing in Wandsworth. This wasn't the time to tell him.

'She didn't have to say anything, I could see.'

Two punches landed in quick succession on his nose; he staggered further into the darkness, blood dripping onto his nice shirt. A third punch to his jaw convinced him he was getting the shit kicked out of him so he'd better start defending himself. He threw a couple of fresh-air shots, which probably made him feel better.

I circled, more to drag out the inevitable and make him suffer than any tactical advantage. I didn't need one.

'Please,' he said, 'I've got a heart problem.'

I hit him some more for being a wimp. He fell to the ground and crawled towards a line of bins overflowing with rubbish and lay in the filth until he got his breath back. The bottle was in his hand before I knew it – his heart problem had miraculously disappeared, along with his loser's attitude, and he grinned like the predatory beast he was.

I tried to warn him. 'That isn't your best idea.'

He didn't believe me and spoke through his teeth, sending a spray of bloodied spittle into the night. The bottle crashed against the edge of the bin. Something glinted dully in his hand. The change in him was remarkable.

'Fuck you. Want some of this? Come and get it.'

He deserved an extra slap just for his hokey chat.

That could be arranged.

He wiped blood and snot from his lip and took a step towards me. 'She was asking for it from the minute she waltzed in the door. Any of the boys will tell you. All I did was take her up on her offer.'

The first thing I broke was the arm with the ragged bottle on the end, then I mashed his nose into his face and heard his jaw crack. Before he passed out, I slammed him on the mouth and kept hitting. His teeth dropped onto the cobbles like pearls from a broken necklace.

I brought the whisky over to the couch and treated myself to a refill, not tired enough to go to bed. My knuckles were bruised and raw; I hardly noticed. Mandy was asleep. In the morning, she'd have questions. Questions better not answered, at least, not with the truth. When they came, I'd lie.

did he say anything about me?

Yeah, baby. He said he was sorry.

46

The lesbians were in Norrie's head. He could still see Lexie taking the dildo, her naked body writhing in pleasure. What a waste. But on balance, it had turned out okay. He yawned. It had been a long night and it wasn't over.

Danny Glass's instruction was clear and non-negotiable: no witnesses.

The club in London was a turning point. After that, killing the others on the team wasn't a big deal. Even without the gangster's uncompromising order, Sharon was going to be a problem. She was no stranger to violence. She'd been around it all her life, though nothing as bad as the club, and her reaction made her a danger.

Glass could've decided to pull the plug on all of them and would have if Norrie hadn't outsmarted him. From his first job he'd left a sealed envelope with a lawyer he knew. Insurance. If anything happened to him, the envelope would find its way to the police. So far, he'd never needed it. But there was always a first time. That was how insurance worked.

He parked in a side street near Battlefield Road and walked to where he'd dropped her off less than twenty-four hours ago. Sharon, drawn and white from lack of sleep, hadn't asked when she could expect her share of the money. She hadn't asked anything. Norrie watched her enter a tenement flat. A light had come on in a ground-floor window. They'd worked together once before though he hadn't known where she lived. Now, he did.

Handy.

Breaking in was a piece of piss. Norrie pulled on latex gloves and used the same trick again on Sharon's front door. Inside, the flat was quiet. He stood still until his eyes got used to the darkness, just as he'd done in Lexie's house. The lounge was typical of tenements: a large room with a high ceiling and a cornice running all the way round. The bedrooms would be almost as big. The place was tidy. No empty wine glasses lying around. and Sharon had straightened the cushions on the couch.

It was possible she wasn't home. The last time he'd seen her, she'd looked like a girl with a lot more than her social life on her mind. More likely, she was in bed, asleep along with most of the city. He looked at his watch: two-seventeen.

He stepped into the bedroom. Empty. The bed hadn't been slept in. Next door was the same. Maybe she'd freaked and gone to the police. He put the thought to the back of his mind. And if she wasn't here, he'd wait until she returned, then do what had to be done.

Norrie gently pushed the bathroom door open. Sharon was in the bath.

She was naked, her head half in half out of the water, eyes closed as if she'd fallen asleep. A razor blade lay on the floor where she'd dropped it once it had served its purpose. He felt her wrist for a pulse. It was there, faint and fading. There was still time to save her if she got help now.

Sorry, Sharon. Not happening.

Norrie dipped a finger in the bathwater – pink and lukewarm – and studied her unlined face and her breasts, floating under the surface. Moonlight from the window lent the skin a golden hue. Near death she looked younger than she'd been in life. Shame, really. He wouldn't have minded seeing her do a double act with Lexie.

Sharon had been a serious mistake. His mistake.

Next problem: was there a suicide note that would bring all of them down? When he didn't find one, he removed her mobile from her bag, lifted her PC from the dining table, and left.

Back in the car he thought for a while about how close they'd all come to disaster.

Norrie pulled down the empty street, surfing through the static on the radio with one hand until he caught the tail-end of the Rolling Stones, 'Paint It Black'. His favourite Stones' track. He tapped the steering wheel and sang along. He felt good.

Three down.

Job done.

47

Stubble covered Danny Glass's jaw and his eyes were bloodshot from lack of sleep. Marcus stood in front of him, rocking silently on the balls of his feet, waiting for his boss to speak. When Danny was in a mood, the best thing was to be somewhere else. Anywhere else. From the wall, the Queen looked down on the half-dozen newspapers spread on the desk. Discarded sheets had fallen to the floor, others rolled into balls and angrily fired across the office. Two days on, the fire in the Picasso Club dominated the headlines as the media speculated on who was responsible and where they might strike next. So far, nobody had claimed responsibility and public statements by the prime minister and the lord mayor hadn't convinced the city they had the situation under control.

Glass ignored his lieutenant and studied the front page of the *Mail on Sunday*. A member of the royal family was scheduled to visit the scene of the fire – the lord mayor had been the previous day, flanked by senior police officers, picking a path through what was left of the club.

'The royals always do the right thing. This country's lucky to have them.'

He turned the pages, mumbling to himself about the suspicion terrorists were responsible for the tragedy.

'Bastards want to destroy our way of life.'

Marcus did a double take. Danny was behaving as if the reports were real.

There were no terrorists.

They were the fucking terrorists.

Every paper carried a version of the story they'd run with the previous day, wildly speculating in lieu of fresh information. *The Times*, the *Telegraph* and *The Independent* – traditionally more responsible – kept the horror of the attack to a minimum. The less squeamish tabloid press breathlessly reported that bodies had been 'reduced to piles of black bones, as if the flesh had melted away'.

The question was asked casually but Marcus heard the edge in Danny's voice and tensed.

'Have they identified Rollie's body?'

'Not yet.'

'Any of his crew?'

Marcus shook his head.

'What're they doing over there?'

The big man hesitated. 'It's going to take time, Danny.'

Glass lifted his head, his eyes boring into Marcus. 'What do I pay you for? Remind me, I forget. Is it to drop clichés like "It's going to take time, Danny" into the conversation? Because, if it is, can't complain about not getting my fucking money's worth, can I?'

'What do you want me to tell you, boss?'

'Something I don't already know would be nice.'

Marcus didn't have anything.

'What's the word on the street?'

'Nobody's talking.'

'Yeah? Somebody telling them not to?'

Marcus shrugged. 'Could be.'

'Are you saying Anderson's alive?'

'All I know is, usually there's a lot of noise after a big happening. So far, it's like the whole of the South Side's in shock.'

Glass leaned closer, his finger pointing. 'Get out and shake the trees. If Anderson got out, he'll come after us. He's a mad-arse. Ritchie's the cool head. He'll be the one organising it. George Ritchie's the key.'

Marcus turned to go. Danny wasn't done. 'And, Marcus. Don't come back with ghost stories to spook the troops. They don't need them. Neither do I. It's simple: Rollie's alive or he's dead. Either way we have to know.'

* * *

Oliver Stanford read the caller ID and considered letting it go unanswered. Glass wouldn't stop. Today, tomorrow, the next day – the bastard would keep on trying, until finally he couldn't avoid him. Better to get it over with.

Glass's voice was hard; he sounded rattled. 'Is he dead?'

The question required no explanation. Stanford knew who he meant but acted as if he didn't. 'A lot of people are dead, Danny. Which one of them are you referring to?'

The gangster hissed his anger down the line, on a shorter fuse than usual.

'A word to the wise, Detective Chief Inspector, don't fuck me about. I'm not in the mood. Can you confirm he's among the dead? Yes or no?'

Less than thirty-six hours after the fire started, it was a stupid question. Maybe because the detective was at a low ebb, depressed and dog-tired, he treated it with the scorn it deserved and didn't attempt to answer it.

'Your guess is as good as mine.'

'What's that supposed to mean?'

'There are over a hundred bodies still to be identified. A lot of them don't even look human. If you've any suggestions that might speed up the process, we'd be happy to hear them.'

Stanford knew he was baiting the bear. Getting into bed with the gangster had always been problematic. On balance, he'd decided the risks were worth the reward. Friday night had changed that.

There would be months, maybe years of investigation: a public enquiry was a certainty.

Knowing his greed and ambition had put Elise and their daughters in danger ate at the policeman. The house in Hendon and all the rest of it weren't important any more. He'd no idea how the horror show at the Picasso Club was going to end. Anderson might very well have perished in the blaze and be a pile of bones in a black bag, waiting his turn. Stanford couldn't have cared less. He'd a lot more than that to think about. One thing he was sure of: when the dust settled Glass had to be dealt with.

The alternative was having a madman running every organised crime operation in South London; an insane fucker who might decide, for fun, to drop him in it at any minute. The arrangement they'd had was over. Danny Glass just didn't know it yet.

Stanford covered the mobile with his hand so he couldn't be overheard and spoke quietly. 'It's crazy here. Nobody knows what the hell's happening. As soon as I get confirmation on Anderson, the first call I make will be to you. Depend on it.'

Glass wasn't mollified. 'He has to be dead. He has to be.'

The detective smiled a thin smile, enjoying what he was hearing from the man who inspired so much fear in others. He offered the gangster a crumb. 'I was there, Danny. I saw it. I'm guessing Rollie's in worse shape than his old man.'

'What if he isn't?'

Stanford was about to hang up when Glass caught him off guard.

'By the by, soldier. Time's up on your boy.'

'Who?'

'The rat. Bring him in. Think I'd forgotten?'

'Bob Wallace?' The policeman could hardly speak. 'You... want me to do... what?'

'Bring him to me.'

'Me?'

'Your very own self, Oliver.'

The detective blanched. 'I... I can't... That's asking too much.'

He imagined Glass's mouth drawing back in a feral grin, the uneven teeth.

'Do what you're told, copper. Unless you'd rather I sent Marcus round to see Elise again.'

48

Shadows fell across the office above the King of Mesopotamia, surrounding him like enemies. Downstairs, the survivors of the weekend would be propping up the bar, pretending to believe each other's lies, putting off the inevitable reality of tomorrow and the return to work. Danny Glass envied them.

The day was ending. A hard day anxiously pacing the floor, waiting for news. Until he was certain Anderson had paid for humiliating him, there would be no music. Anderson could be out there with George Ritchie, plotting revenge for the fire, for his father, and every other slight, real or imagined, in his miserable life. At any minute, they could burst through the door and drag him away.

Danny couldn't remember when he'd last eaten. His eyes were gritty and raw from lack of sleep. He rested his head on his arms, overwhelmed by the fever in him.

Luke should be here. And there was no sign of Nina – that would be asking too much. Neither appreciated how difficult it had been for him. He was the one who'd put money in their pockets: the one who'd had to make the tough decisions.

A picture of the kids he'd protected after their old man began the long process of drowning himself in booze, rose in front of him. He'd never been close to Nina, a strange girl, always a pain in the arse. No change there. But Luke was the real disappointment; hearing him tell the detective he didn't have a brother had hurt more than Danny could bear. The past and the future melded in the present and he cried like a child alone in the dark, howling against the injustice of it. His hand went to the desk's bottom drawer and the gun he kept there, ready and loaded. The barrel pressed against his temple, cool and heavy, marking the skin, digging into the bone, inches from his brain. Sweat broke on his brow, his breath came in shuddering gasps and he felt the smooth downward sweep of the trigger against his clammy finger.

If only he had the courage, it could all be over.

The sound of footsteps stopped him. The door opened and Marcus stood in the frame, his muscular body backlit from the landing. He came towards him and slowly prised the gun from his hand, whispering, 'Easy, boss. Easy. That isn't the way.'

The big man emptied the bullets from the chamber and put them in his jacket pocket. He leaned on the desk, towering over Glass, quietly reassuring 'til the insanity faded from the other man's eyes and he returned from whichever circle of hell he'd been in. Danny had aged ten years since this morning.

'Want a drink, boss?'

Danny slurred. 'Yeah.'

'What?'

'Anything, doesn't matter.'

Marcus filled a tumbler almost to the brim with Johnnie Walker Black Label, then gently fitted Glass's fingers round the glass and covered them with his own much larger fingers. When he was satisfied Danny had a hold on it, he took them away.

Glass sipped it like a sleepwalker, unaware what he was doing. He gulped the whisky, took a second swallow and turned his head to look at the office, rubbing the numbness from his arms.

The question was childlike, whispered and innocent. 'I did it again, didn't I?'

'You did it again, Danny.'

'How long have I been like this?'

'Not long. You're all right now.'

Marcus paused before he spoke again. 'You wanted information. I've got it.'

'And?'

Marcus took air into his lungs and slowly let it out.

'Anderson was definitely at the club early on Friday. Since then, neither him, Ritchie, nor any of the major players in his crew have been spotted.'

'Which means... he *is* dead?'

'No. Nobody's seen them, that's all.' Marcus played with the gold strap of his watch. 'But we've found one of them.'

'Who?'

'A Geordie, name of Jonjo.'

'Never heard of him.'

'He's George Ritchie's nephew.'

'Then he'll know where his uncle is.'

Marcus allowed himself a slow smile; he'd been looking forward to this. 'That isn't the best bit.'

'Tell me.'

'This Jonjo's been boasting about a video he put on YouTube.'

Danny sat forward in his chair – back from the dead.

Marcus said, 'We've got him, boss. We've got the bastard.'

'Where is he?'

'A bedsit in Islington. Got somebody watching the place. He won't get away. Want me to lift him?'

'Give him one more day. We'll make it a double celebration.'

* * *

Danny Glass wasn't the only one who hadn't slept. In Hendon, Oliver Stanford tossed and turned most of the night. Tiredness had nothing to do with it. His time as a policeman hadn't prepared him for what he'd seen in the aftermath of the fire, and he lay in the dark, unable to forget the stench or the endless procession of bodies removed from the scene on stretchers.

At ten minutes to five, afraid his restlessness would wake Elise, he slipped out of bed and went downstairs to the kitchen. His wife never questioned where the money came from to finance their expensive lifestyle, but she wasn't a fool, she must have known. Nobody could be that naïve – unless it suited them.

Stanford made coffee and gazed round the state-of-the-art kitchen: a complete wall housed a multi-unit combination of gas burners, a griddle and a deep-fat fryer, all finished in gleaming stainless steel. Overhead, a full-length hood provided maximum ventilation and a rail for gadgets and utensils. He added sugar to his cup, asking himself if they really needed this stuff. Stanford didn't understand how most of it worked, and some, like the fryer, hadn't been used and wasn't likely to be. This was what he'd sold his soul for.

He put leads on the dogs and opened the back door as quietly as he could. Before Danny Glass's heavies had appeared at her house, being the wife of a detective chief inspector had been all the security Elise needed. Since then, she anxiously checked everything was locked up and he'd catch her glancing towards the bottom of the garden, to the tree where the big man had been.

The pre-dawn sky above a deserted Sunny Hill Park was streaked with blue-grey light and the air was cool and fresh. He let the dogs run free and watched them chase each other over the grass and along the hedgerows from former field boundaries; they loved it here, and so did he. But it would take more than a peaceful hour or two to ease his mind.

Danny Glass could be up to his arse in alibis; it made no difference. He was responsible for the atrocity at the club. Now, he was demanding Stanford personally bring Bob Wallace to him. The prospect chilled the detective. Luring Wallace into a trap, lying to his face right until the moment Glass's thugs seized him, was too much: he hadn't the stomach for it.

After the mess in Kent, he'd been certain the overeager Scot had ratted them out – there had been three men in the room when the information came through: Wallace, Trevor Mills and himself. Inviting him into the study had been a test.

A test he'd failed.

Stanford followed the dogs to the south-east corner of the park, near the Anglo-Saxon archaeological site. He pulled up the collar of his coat. Where was the evidence against Bob Wallace? The actual evidence? The beyond-a-doubt proof? There wasn't any. Word of the raid could've been leaked to Anderson by any number of links in the chain. Wallace might be innocent.

All too late. Glass was expecting him.

49

The bedsit was scarcely more than a box with a toilet. The window – the only window – was in the lavatory. Through the flimsy net curtain and the glass heavy with grime, the grey dome of St Paul's Cathedral on Ludgate Hill dominated the skyline as it had for more than three hundred years. Without the iconic landmark to remind him, Jonjo could've been anywhere. In Newcastle, he'd dreamed of living in London, imagining fantastical scenarios with flash cars and flashier women. The flat was as bleak as anywhere in the north-east: three storeys up, sharing a cooker blackened by smoke and grease and a sink on a bare-board landing with a Greek who hadn't spoken a word. The guy had a surly dark-haired woman in tow, who'd dismissed Jonjo with an uninterested glance. Listening to them going at it, two nights out of the three he'd spent here, while he drew the thin sheet around him and tried to sleep on a lumpy mattress, was a stark reminder of how far and how fast he'd fallen.

He thought about the last time he'd seen George Ritchie. The memory brought no comfort; his uncle's cold expression in the club had said all there was to say.

Since then, nothing. Ritchie was done with him. And no wonder. Everything he'd warned him about had come true. Jonjo needed to get out of this place, find somewhere decent to stay – well away from horny Greeks and their sultry girlfriends – and figure out what to do. He picked up his jacket, patted the pockets to make sure he had the cash with him, and went out into the world.

The first bus that came along was going to Victoria. As good a destination as any. Plenty of accommodation in that part of town. He paid the conductor and went upstairs, the only passenger on the top deck, his fingers tight around the wad of money, all that stood between him and sleeping on the street. At the terminus, he bought coffee and a sandwich from Caffè Nero in Buckingham Palace Road and went into the station to find a seat. The station was like an anthill under attack; people rushed past, manic intensity on their faces. Nobody noticed him and Jonjo basked in the anonymity only a big city could deliver. He studied the electronic arrivals and departures board across the concourse stretching out above Burger King, wondering if he should get a ticket. Better still, why not take the Gatwick Express and leave the country? That required a passport and he didn't have one.

In the end, he bought a second coffee – from Costa this time – and an early edition of the London *Evening Standard*.

The fire was still the main headline and Jonjo didn't want to read about it. He flicked through the pages from front to back without seeing anything about a gangland attack at the weekend. That didn't mean it hadn't happened. This was Tuesday. Both Anderson and Glass could be dead.

Wouldn't that be nice?

* * *

Bob Wallace manoeuvred a path through the traffic in the direction of Lambeth Bridge. It was a sunny day in late-June, hot and muggy, and at four o'clock in the afternoon progress was slow. London was rammed with tourists in shirt-sleeves and sunglasses, taking pictures of the Palace of Westminster and anyone who came out of the building, imagining they had to be 'somebody'. Wallace accelerated past a slow-moving Fiat and raced ahead. He was feeling good.

The whispered exchange with his boss in the corridor at New Scotland Yard had confirmed what the detective sergeant had already suspected. The Wallaces hadn't fitted in with the company at the party. Obviously, they'd been invited for a reason. There had been much more to the dinner than the drunken banter of a run-of-the-mill social event. He'd said as much to his wife. She hadn't seen it. Wallace had and the realisation had filled him with pride. Stanford had been sussing him out, running the rule over him, including him and gauging his reaction to the news about the raid on Rollie Anderson's drug shipment.

But then word had got out and the Transit had ended up all over the Internet. Wallace knew it wasn't him – he hadn't spoken to anybody – and now, apparently, his boss knew it, too.

'You're the only one I can trust, Bob. The only one. We need to talk.'

He'd asked where and Stanford had told him, his lips dry, struggling to get the words out. 'Across the river. An abandoned factory in Fulton Street. Say you've got a meet with an informant. Don't mention a location. And make sure Trevor Mills hears you.'

'Will do.'

'One last thing. If you get there before me, go inside.'

* * *

He drove until he came to the derelict factory at the end of a cobbled road, a relic from the Victorians, ripe for redevelopment, boarded and barricaded against trespassers. The car shuddered over the broken road and threatened to stall. A name on a crumbling brick wall scarred with white crystalline salt stains from a bygone age told him he'd arrived.

Wallace stopped yards from a cluster of buckled sheets of rusted corrugated iron, blown from the roof and left where they'd fallen. No sign of his boss or his car. The policeman stepped onto the uneven pavement littered with weeds and glass, wondering why this place had been chosen. Clearly, secrecy was everything. Nobody would discover them here.

Like the good soldier he was, Wallace followed the instructions. He drew the door open and went in.

* * *

George Ritchie stood on the Gateshead side of the river and gazed up at the steel arch of the Tyne Bridge in the evening light. The symbol of the city stirred nothing in him. This wasn't his home any more and he wasn't happy to be back. The place he'd grown up in had changed, and so had he. It wasn't possible to live twenty years in the south and be the same man who'd kissed his mother and sister goodbye on the platform of Newcastle Central Station, waving until they were out of sight.

The old lady hadn't lasted long. He'd come north for the funeral – arriving one day, leaving the next. He couldn't get away fast enough.

His only living relative was his sister, Hannah, Jonjo's mother. She'd have heard he was back, no doubt about that. He hadn't visited her yet and wasn't looking forward to it. Hannah had trusted him to take care of her boy. When they finally met, she'd ask why Jonjo wasn't with him. Would he say her son was probably dead? And even if he wasn't, with the way he was going, he wouldn't see thirty? Or should he soothe her anxiety with a lie? Tell her he was doing well, that everything was fine, and, yes, he'd make sure he called more often. Ritchie wasn't certain he could pull it off.

So far, he'd avoided his former haunts, although there wouldn't be many who'd recognise him after all this time. But there would be a few, keen to buy him drinks in exchange for war stories. But George was weary of war.

On his first day back in the north-east, he'd walked the once-familiar streets until it was dark before returning to his room at the Malmaison. London had been the adventure of a lifetime. From the beginning he'd planned what to do the second he sensed it ending.

And when it had – thanks to the stupidity of his nephew, Anderson and the insanity of Danny Glass – he'd acted as he'd promised himself he would.

So why did it feel so wrong?

* * *

Jonjo lay on the bed with his hands behind his head. His skin tingled from a day sprawled on the grass in Regent's Park, eyeing up the girls with four cans of Newcastle Brown Ale at his elbow and the sun shining down on him. He was hopeful now, thinking more clearly. Rollie was an unpredictable mess, that was the truth. Nothing he said, good or bad, should be taken seriously. Loyalty wasn't a concept his brain could process. His uncle George had had his own experience and tried to warn him. Next time, Jonjo would pay attention. According to urban mythology, George Ritchie had saved Anderson's teenage arse, taking the reins of the organisation and holding it together after his father died at the hands of Luke Glass. A wiser man would've been grateful to Ritchie and learned to listen. Rollie Anderson would never be that, not if he lived to be a hundred. He'd cut George out of the decision to hit Glass's pub both times because he knew Ritchie would see past the attack, understand the risk they'd be running, and nix the plan. Yet, even though the first attack had failed, the crazy fool was ready to do the same again only days after Jonjo had uploaded the video of Danny's humiliation to YouTube.

From hero to zero.

There was a lesson in there. Anderson blew with the breeze. Yesterday, you could be his friend. Today, his enemy. Tomorrow – who knew?

It would come out all right on the night. The trick was to stay with it and not run away.

* * *

The Greek wasn't around, thank God. Jonjo had the kitchen – such as it was – to himself. He peeled potatoes and opened a can of beans; not exactly five-star cooking but enough to guarantee he wouldn't starve.

A noise like wood cracking got his attention. Jonjo heard footsteps racing up the stairs and realised, too late, what was happening. Three men threw him to the floor and started punching. One blow winded him, another connected squarely with his chin. They took hold of his arms and dragged him head first. Outside a big guy stood beside an SUV. Jonjo was bundled into the back. Somebody tried to put a hood over his head.

The big guy said, 'Doesn't matter if he knows where he's going – he won't be telling anybody.'

* * *

Nina hadn't heard from Vale since the morning in her flat and assumed he'd managed to get a hold on himself. There would be no more sex with him, no matter how much whiskey she drank or how horny it made her. Calling him was the last thing she wanted to do but she had to know he hadn't put them in danger.

Vale answered on the second ring, his voice low and hoarse, awash with self-pity.

Nina said, 'How are you?'

'What do you care?'

'You're right, I don't. But I care about not ending up in Fulton Street and so should you.' She continued, 'Have the police contacted you?'

'Not yet. What do you think that means?

'It means the ball is back with us. We need to act normal.'

'I am. I'm at work, as usual, going through the motions.'

'Except the woman who works for you hasn't turned up for days and you've done nothing about it. That isn't normal.'

Mention of Fulton Street was enough to bring him back in line. When he spoke, his tone was devoid of whatever bitter emotions had lived there.

'What should I do?'

Nina rolled her eyes; at some point, Eugene would go the same way as Yvonne. She accepted it as inevitable and waited for him to repeat his question. 'What should I do, Nina?'

'Call her mobile. When you get no answer, go to her flat. Talk to the neighbours. It's important they remember you. Explain you're her boss and you're worried she might be ill. Then, back to the office and call the police.'

'Me?'

'Yes, you.'

'Will they believe me?'

'You're a conscientious employer – no reason not to. And for Christ's sake, calm down. The only person who can put us in the frame is you. Got that?'

Vale faltered. 'Yes... yes, I've got it.'

'Call me when it's done.'

50

I hadn't seen or heard from Danny since the night of the fire. Three days and twenty-one hours. But who was counting? The weight I'd carried around all my life had suddenly been lifted. I felt free. No more Team Glass. Except, old habits died hard. Whenever my mobile rang, I half expected it to be him, on with sentimental stories from the past and bullshit apologies to bring me back into the fold. It seemed he'd got the message his routine wasn't going to work and cut ties with me. I wasn't sorry.

Physically, Mandy was well. The marks on her face and neck were still visible but make-up would disguise them. Emotionally, the assault had affected her confidence. Her daughter was due to visit and she'd arranged to meet Amy the next day off the Manchester train.

She'd brought Eric Clapton's '461 Ocean Boulevard' – arguably his best album – and we were on the couch, drinking wine and listening, when she said, 'Do you think she really wants to visit me?'

'Of course, you're her mother.'

'I mean, what has her father told her?'

'Doesn't matter what he's told her. Nothing bad or she wouldn't be coming.'

Mandy's insecurity was threatening to break her.

'You can't be sure of that. And if she knew the truth, what would she think?'

I moved closer and drew her to me. 'Listen, your little girl is coming to see you. She'll want what all kids want – her mum to tell her she loves her. All you have to do is have a great time together and forget everything else.'

'You think I'm worrying about nothing?'

'Absolutely.'

She relaxed in my arms and was quiet. After a while she said, 'I'd like you two to be friends. It would mean a lot to me. Are you all right with that?'

I smiled down at the fading yellow around her eye. 'If she's half as nice as her mum, I'd love to.'

Later, I dropped Mandy at her place. Before she got out of the car, she kissed me.

'Thanks, Luke.'

'For what?'

'If you don't know, I can't tell you.'

I wasn't in a hurry and drove slowly, turning over what I'd agreed to in my head. The last child in my life had been Rebecca, Cheryl's daughter. From nowhere, sadness washed through me. I gripped the steering wheel until it passed.

* * *

As soon as I opened the door, I sensed something wasn't right. The lounge was like a picture puzzle where tiny things had changed and the challenge was to spot the differences. In the first twenty seconds I scanned the lounge and saw nothing. In the next twenty, I noticed four: the cushions on the couch had been rearranged – not much, just straightened a bit; the Clapton CD cover had gone from the floor to beside the television; the empty wine bottle was in the bin under the sink and the glasses had been rinsed and were on the draining board. Just small things Mandy might have done, but I didn't think she had.

The next change wasn't open to doubt. My passport was on the mantelpiece above the fire. I was certain I hadn't put it there.

Someone had been here, rummaged through my personal stuff and left it where I was certain to see it.

some people have long memories

The 'some people' in this case was Rollie Anderson. Had to be. He'd survived and was hiding, regrouping and waiting for a chance to strike back.

I checked the rest of the flat. The message wasn't subtle. He was showing me he could come into my life at any time and there was nothing I could do about it. From behind the curtain I watched the street and across to the windows at the other side. They'd made their move when I'd left to run Mandy home. It was possible they were still there. But not likely.

The point had been made.

I put the Clapton CD on again, poured a much-needed glass of whisky and stuck the gun my brother had insisted on giving me down the side of the couch. The phone went off like a cannon in the quiet. I let it ring, enjoying a feeling of control doomed not to last.

I held it to my ear.

No disguised voice threatening terrible things this time. Only steady breathing like before and a silence that went on forever. Every fibre of me wanted to shout meaningless threats and demand answers I wasn't going to get. Instead, I fought back with psychology of my own and kept quiet. My hands were clammy, my heart beating fast in my chest. After a while, the mystery caller rang off.

I drank the whisky without tasting it, recharged the glass and forced myself to sip.

I turned the lights out and sat in the dark, with the glass, the bottle and the Beretta next to me. After a while the alcohol worked its magic and I was able to think. Anderson was toying with me. Fucking with my head: Danny had been right – some people had long memories. I'd been right, too. It was happening. I wasn't suffering from jailhouse paranoia after all. Not the consolation it might have been.

They wouldn't be content with phone calls and uninvited visits for long.

51

The Spaniards Inn, 'perched on the edge of Hampstead Heath and oozing history' according to its website, was famous, although I'd never been there. The city north of Marylebone Road, and Hampstead especially, didn't attract me. Too many posh accents and posers. In the early days, Danny had taken me up West to remind us how the other half lived – the paid-up members of the Lucky Bastards Club he was so fond of pouring scorn on. If it had been anyone other than Oliver Stanford I wouldn't have come. But the tone in his voice had been miles away from the superior attitude and the smug look I'd disliked immediately above the King Pot.

On the phone, the detective chief inspector's words were as dry as fallen leaves. Not unusual for him; he couldn't help himself. Being the boss, barking out orders his minions weren't in a position to question, was the role he was born to play. His idea of a team game would be everybody doing what he told them. In another life, him and Danny might've been mates.

Arseholes in arms.

'We need to talk.'

No introductions. No small talk. Assuming what was important to him was important to everybody else. Vintage self-important bastard. I was wrong; he hadn't changed.

'Do we?'

His tongue clicked against his teeth and he let the sarcasm pass him by.

'Listen, Glass. I don't like making this call any more than you like getting it. But we really need to talk.'

I borrowed Danny's approach and treated him like a precocious child who deserved a good slap and was going to get one.

'Heard you the first time.'

'Then you agree?'

'Agree with what?'

'You're not blind, you see what's going on.'

'Why would I discuss any of it with you?'

He swept my obdurate response aside. 'I'm serious. We've both got a stake in this. Seven o'clock, The Spaniards Inn. Will you be there?'

Asking not telling. I wondered how it made him feel.

'No, I won't.'

He tried and failed to keep his disappointment out of his voice and stay in control.

'Why not? Why not, for Christ's sake?'

'Because you work for us, not the other way around. Or have I got that wrong, Oliver?'

Straight out of the Danny Glass instruction manual on how to deal with jumped-up coppers. Stanford exhaled deeply into the phone. I was trying his patience and enjoying it, and, for some reason, he was putting up with it. 'You're spending too much time with your brother. You're starting to sound like him.'

'If that's supposed to be a compliment, try again.'

He returned to his point. 'Will you be there or not? It's important.'

'Yeah, you said. Tell me more.'

The detective allowed his frustration to show.

'Not making it easy for me, are you?'

'Was I supposed to? Sorry, Oliver. Give me more or fuck off out of it, how's that?'

Stanford remembered he was a senior officer in the Metropolitan Police and asserted himself. 'Not until we're face to face. Seven o'clock in the beer garden.'

The line died in my hand.

I'd left Mandy sprawled on the floor with a pen in her hand and her red curls tucked behind her ears, surrounded by leaflets with London Tourist Board on them, agonising over an itinerary for Amy.

'Madame Tussauds would be good, wouldn't it?'

I didn't answer. She didn't notice. Her preoccupation was easy to understand – her daughter was the most precious thing in the world. Twice recently, I'd found Mandy by the window in the small hours, hugging herself, staring into the night. At first, I'd assumed it was the experience with the thug from the pub. That wasn't it. Giving up her little girl had been a life-altering moment she'd do anything to change.

While Mandy struggled to shoehorn the Planetarium or a Harry Potter tour into her plans, I looked up the pub up on the Internet. At one time, The Spaniards was the go-to boozer for robbers and highwayman: I'd fit right in.

Instead of driving across the city I took the Northern Line to Hampstead and walked the rest of the way. I was early and killed time on Parliament Hill. An end-of-day golden haze had settled over the city skyline. Behind the jagged silhouettes of the Shard and the Gherkin, St Paul's Cathedral and the Palace of Westminster, the horizon was on fire.

Spectacular. But Stanford hadn't dragged me up here for the view.

* * *

The beer garden was busy. In the shade, a crowd gathered round a TV showing the tennis. Stanford was sitting by himself under a red umbrella with Pimm's No 1 on the canopy, holding what looked like a whisky and ice in his manicured fingers. At the next table, a group of five young men with Australian accents laughed loudly at something one of them said and Stanford glanced brief disapproval in their direction before bringing his attention to me. His expression didn't alter apart from an almost imperceptible upturn at the corners of his mouth – his inner-smug-fucker staging a comeback.

He raised his hand in the air, sipped his drink, made a stab at being pleased to see me and failed. But the anxiety I'd heard on the phone was missing; Stanford made me wait. Finally, he said, 'Your brother has become a problem. I expect you've noticed.'

'Told you in the King Pot, I don't have a brother.'

On the TV, the fourth set was going into a tiebreak; the people watching leaned forward, playing every shot with their favourite. The Aussies spoiled it by picking that moment to leave. Still noisy. Still laughing. Big-boned suntanned guys who'd never done anything quietly and couldn't if their lives depended on it. Stanford waited until they'd gone.

'Then, I was right. We have something to discuss.'

'What do you want?'

The policeman took another sip of the whisky, his brilliant-blue eyes unblinking, more than likely a technique he used to frighten his subordinates. It wouldn't work on me.

'To find a way forward. Common ground.'

'Common ground? You and me? You're talking to the wrong Glass. It's Danny you should speak to.'

Mentioning his name brought a reaction: the edges of his mouth turned down as if somebody had swapped the Scotch for pond water. 'That wouldn't be...' he searched for the appropriate word '... productive.'

His mannered approach irked me. 'Say what you've got to say or I'm off. You don't like Danny Glass. Not exactly an exclusive club.'

He corrected me. 'You misunderstand. The relationship I have – *had* – with your brother was never dependent on approving of what he did. Liking him never came into it. It's simply a question of being able to do business. And I can't. Not any more. I'd assumed you'd have reached the same conclusion.'

My response was as uncooperative as I could make it.

'So, don't.'

Stanford smiled a small patient smile, realised how the conversation was going to go and launched into a history lesson for my benefit. 'In life we don't always get to choose our bedfellows. In the beginning, working with Danny made sense. Thanks to you, Albert Anderson was off the board and south of the river was up for grabs. It could've been one gang war after another with people trying to make a claim. Chaos, in other words. No winners and a lot of losers, on the front page of every newspaper in the country. Danny stepped into the breach. Actively enabling him was in the public interest. I'd probably do it again.'

A waitress arrived at our table and he stopped talking. When I'd ordered, he went on.

'That was my first mistake.'

Said almost wistfully.

'Anderson's organisation had lost its leader and was in disarray. I'd expected a short sharp exchange. The outcome should never have been in doubt. For reasons I still can't fathom, your brother—'

'Told you before. I don't have a brother.'

'Quite... decided not to move then. And that's why we find ourselves where we are.'

'I'd be lying if I said this was interesting. Get to the fucking point, if there is one.'

52

Applause broke out from the people watching the TV. Shouts of 'Bravo!' and 'Well done!' Stanford held onto his temper. More important issues were at stake.

'The "fucking point", as you so inelegantly put it, is this: the fire put Danny over the line. Not because it was an atrocity – although it was certainly that – but because it proved he's lost it. Sooner or later he's going down. But the end of Danny Glass won't mean the end. Business will go on. It always does. The question is: who'll be running it?'

Whatever he expected from his mini speech, he didn't get.

My voice was a monotone. 'I stopped listening five minutes ago. You carry on, since you're enjoying yourself so much.'

The detective didn't rise to it. 'The brother you claim not to have has had his day. He's reckless and unstable and won't last. The deeper consequence of the Picasso Club is I can't cover for him. Neither can anybody else. It isn't possible. There has to be a level of trust. Do you understand?'

I understood only too well – he was pitching.

To me.

Time to put him straight.

'I see where you're going. You're imagining I'll take over and we can have a nice civilised relationship, where you keep getting paid without the risk you're running now.'

His reply was frank. 'Something like that, yes.'

'Sorry to burst your bubble but I've no ambitions to step into Danny's shoes. I want out and have done for years. He talked me into staying after Anderson hit the King Pot. Otherwise, I'd have been on a beach pouring a bottle of San Miguel down my neck. You're both welcome to it.'

Stanford took the news better than I thought he would.

'Perhaps I misunderstood. I saw the mark on Danny's face—'

'And thought I'd kill him and set up shop with you? No chance. Told you already. I'm out and I'm staying out.'

He wasn't convinced. 'It's easy to say that now. Until the opportunity's in front of you, you can't be sure how you'll react. Believe it or not, you're more like him than you think. No offence.'

'None taken.'

'We'd make a great team.'

This copper didn't know my views on 'teams' or he'd have rephrased the statement. I said, 'Unless Anderson's dead, you're getting ahead of yourself. Has he been identified?'

'Not yet.'

'There you go.'

Down in SW19 the umpire called, 'Forty fifteen.'

The tortured patience thing was back on Stanford's face. 'Obviously, you weren't there or you'd appreciate we'll be lucky to identify half the bodies that came out.'

'Then he could still be alive?'

Stanford didn't hurry to answer. I looked for the girl who'd taken my order: no sign. The question Danny had asked in the pub on the Broadway jumped into my head.

who do I have to fuck to get a drink around here?

The DCI finished his whisky and set the empty glass on the table.

'Anderson alive? I very much doubt it. I wouldn't be here if I thought he was.'

No, he'd be making a deal with him instead.

'Nobody in his crew's been seen.'

'Yeah, that means nothing. George Ritchie's a smart guy. He'd persuade his boss to keep a low profile. They could come back and blow what you're suggesting to hell.'

The possibility made him uncomfortable, his tanned brow furrowed and he looked away. A roar went up: if the light lasted, the match on the centre court was heading to five sets. Stanford regained his composure and sniffed. 'Naturally, this chat needs to stay between ourselves.'

He was a bit late thinking about that.

My pint arrived. I was tempted to ask the waitress where she'd been. Instead, I drank a third of it down in one go, enjoying the coldness of the lager and the copper's new edginess.

'Goes without saying. Besides, who would I tell?'

The policeman stood. 'Oh, one more thing, which may or may not be of interest to you. Eugene Vale. Name mean anything?'

I was about to say no when I remembered he was Nina's guy and my brother's accountant.

'Not much. I know who he is.'

'Yes, I thought you would.' Stanford shoehorned suspicion into his response. 'Seems his secretary drowned in her bath.'

'And?'

'And nothing, it's just that when people die around Danny Glass, my antenna goes up. It's the copper in me. I'm told Vale's having a fling with Nina.'

Now how did he know that?

'One of his employees shagging his sister – don't imagine Danny's too pleased.'

He was fishing. I shrugged and looked towards the excited crowd in front of the TV.

'Sorry, Detective Chief Inspector, never met them.'

Stanford sniffed again. He was expecting Danny to fall and he wanted me to fill the void. But if this was his idea of persuading me, he was going the wrong way about it.

The ghost of a smile appeared on his lips, then vanished. 'Can't have too many friends, Luke. A fact of life, and the sooner you accept it, the better.'

'I'll bear it in mind. Meantime, there's something you can do for me.' I handed him the piece of paper with the numbers of my mystery callers scribbled on it.

'Find out who these are.'

It sounded like an order. The realisation that a new arrangement with a Glass would be an awful lot like his last arrangement with my family registered in his eyes. He glanced at the writing without reading it, put it in his pocket and made a final attempt to woo me.

'The world's changing, even as we speak. You're the kind of man I could do business with.'

I turned my attention to Wimbledon and ignored him.

53

The building was old. Originally, it had been stables, then a laundry in one era, a fireworks factory in another. For a while it was a brewery, the malt kept in bins as large as a three-storey house, while a standing army of cats kept the rats in check. Under its roof, children as young as eight had dipped matches into a dangerous chemical called phosphorous and contracted 'phossy jaw'. Sickened and deformed and unable to work, they were turned away to die in the street, their place taken immediately by a motherless waif from the many orphanages in the city of London. Danny Glass had owned it for years and had no interest in its bleak history. For him, it was an investment – one day it would be demolished and the land sold for a shedload of money. Until that happened, he had another use for it.

He bumped the car onto the pavement and killed the engine. It had been a beautiful day in London; the air was still warm. Glass sat behind the wheel, his fists like a boxer loosening up before a fight, conscious of the energy coursing through him. He could have come here earlier – everything had been in place for hours.

Waiting was better.

Better than booze. Better than sex. Better than anything.

Glass took a brown leather bag and a ghetto blaster from the backseat and got out; the CDs, carefully selected before he'd left the King of Mesopotamia, were in his pocket. Marcus was at the door, his hulking figure blocking the dim light from inside. He let his boss pass and followed. Beyond the grey stone floor and the thick wooden pillars running all the way to the roof it was empty; the machinery that had crushed young bodies and left them bleeding and broken, the vats of white phosphorous and the cavernous bins of malt were long gone. Only the rats remained. Out of the corner of his eye, Glass saw one scurry along the foot of the brick wall and tightened his grip on the bag.

Buffeted and weakened by decades of storms, most of the roof had blown away. Through ragged holes, stars twinkled in the night sky. Glass was too preoccupied to notice.

He swallowed and tried to sound normal.

'Any problems?'

Marcus heard the excitement in his voice and understood.

'None.'

'You're sure nobody saw you?'

'Nobody saw us.'

Exactly what Danny wanted to hear. This wasn't about his crew or Jocks from Glasgow or anybody else. This was personal and he'd deal with it in his own way. His fingers tapped the handle of the ghetto blaster.

'Where are they?'

'In the back.'

'Have they said anything?'

Marcus laughed. 'Oh, yeah. Plenty. Both singing the same song. "There must be some mistake. We haven't done anything."' He sniggered. 'You know, the usual.'

Glass didn't find it funny. 'Who else is here apart from you?'

'It's just me. That's how you wanted it, wasn't it?'

His boss didn't answer, but the big man was right. That was how he wanted it.

'Show me where they are.'

Marcus led him through a series of doors in whitewashed walls covered by graffiti with their footsteps echoing around them. The smell of disuse hung in the air. In the rafters a startled bird took flight, swooping and soaring in the confined space, its beating wings a match for Danny Glass's heart.

There was nothing in the room except a chair, an extension cable and the prisoners, gagged and tied with duct tape to wooden columns running from the floor to the roof. During the day, light would come through a window high on the wall; the other one at ground level was boarded and probably hadn't been opened in decades.

Bob Wallace was unmarked. Jonjo Hart had fared less well; one eye was cut and starting to close. Both men were naked. When they saw Glass, they struggled against their restraints and cried out. Danny Glass set the leather bag and the ghetto blaster on the floor, wild eyes following his every move.

Marcus said, 'I'll be outside. Shout if you need me.'

Glass assumed he was joking.

'If you hear shouting, ignore it. It won't be me.'

The extension cable had a double-socket – it was an old friend. He dragged it from the corner into the middle of the floor and took two CDs from his pocket. Over his shoulder Marcus read the titles: 'The Very Best of Cream' and 'Who's Next'.

Danny liked his music.

'Right.' Glass clapped his hands. 'You've done well. Now, fuck off.'

On his way to the door, Marcus glanced at Wallace and Hart, white-skinned and petrified. Next time he saw them they'd look very different. Danny was up for a session.

Poor bastards.

* * *

When they were alone, Glass took off his jacket and hung it over the chair. He unbuttoned his cuffs and carefully rolled the white shirt sleeves back while he examined his captives with cold clear eyes. They fell silent until he bent down, opened the bag and, slowly, deliberately, one by one, brought the contents out. Then they wailed and fought desperately against their fastenings, so terrified that when the skin chafed and broke and bled at their wrists and ankles, they didn't feel it.

The reason for their panic was easy to understand. Glass weighed the hammer in his hand – short and heavy. He nodded his approval, looking at his prisoners for theirs. Next came the nails – old and long and with a light rust stain.

Glass caressed them with his fingers and laid them in a line on the floor.

'Antiques, these. Beautiful. Been saving them for a special occasion. Think yourself lucky.'

Behind his gag, Jonjo Hart was sick. Vomit filled his mouth, burning and bitter; some of it came down his nose. Danny Glass realised what was happening and kept on about the nails.

'Saw them years ago in a builder's yard in Peckham. Knew straight away they'd come in useful. Pennies they cost me.' He shook his head. 'Not enough respect for the past, nowadays. New this, new that. Everything's got to be the latest model or it's no bloody good. Shame, really. Country's gone to the fucking dogs.

'Don't get me wrong. I'm not against progress. Far from it.'

He pulled an electric drill from the depths of the bag, plugged it in and turned it on. The silver bit whirred into life; he patted the handle proudly.

'British craftmanship. None of that Chinese rubbish.'

Glass connected the ghetto blaster to the extension cable and tapped it with his foot.

'Can't say the same for this. Junk. Made in Taiwan. Fucking Taiwan. Wouldn't have bought it if I'd realised.'

The terrified men listened to his monologue with tears in their eyes.

He hunkered down and emptied the bag.

'I mean, why don't we make this stuff? How hard can it be?'

Wallace hadn't been responsible for the video – that was Jonjo

Hart's work – but he'd seen it, and when the last item came out, he understood everything.

Glass placed the punnet of strawberries between them on the ground, incongruent in the dusty room. He lifted a ripe red berry and held it under Jonjo's nose. 'Smell that. Wonderful, isn't it? Kent's finest. Yesterday they were in the field. Sent somebody down to pick them.'

Bile churned in Jonjo's stomach; he shuddered and lost control of his bladder.

Glass acted as if he hadn't noticed, plugged in the ghetto blaster and held a CD up in each hand. 'What do you fancy listening to? Great bands. Up to you.'

Fear had exhausted the prisoners; they stopped struggling. They were in the presence of a madman.

Glass said, 'All right, I'll choose.'

He slipped 'The Very Best of Cream' into the player and took out a coin, shiny like the drill bit. 'Who wants to go first?'

The men moaned. Glass ripped the tape from their mouths and spoke to Wallace.

'Heads or tails, Bob? What's your pleasure?'

The policeman didn't answer. He couldn't.

Glass made a face. 'Not bothered. Okay. We'll save The Who 'til last and go with Cream. I'll skip the first track, if you don't mind. Not one of my favourites.'

He pressed PLAY.

Bob Wallace had done well; he'd been brave – braver than Jonjo, who'd been a whimpering mess from the start. It couldn't last and it didn't. His screams echoed in the room as Eric Clapton, Jack Bruce and Ginger Baker rocked into 'I Feel Free'.

Glass picked up the hammer and nails and came towards them.

'If you'd wanted The Who you should've said.'

* * *

Outside, Marcus waited in the car. His job had been easy. Taking Jonjo was a piece of piss. The other one, even easier. Stanford had betrayed his unsuspecting colleague. Served him on a plate. Soulless bastard. Wallace had been naked and tied before he'd known what was happening. Danny's instructions weren't new; they'd done this before – more than once. If you were forced into that building you never came out again. That was the rule. So far, nobody had broken it. Fulton Street was Danny Glass's private abattoir.

Sometimes he came and sat for a while, drinking in the energy or whatever it was he did. Weird, but when things got too much, it calmed him down. Marcus remembered bringing him to the abandoned building the day his wife and daughter were killed in the car bomb. Danny hadn't come out for thirty-six hours. When he'd finally emerged, clothes crumpled, hair all over the place, he'd said three words and got in the car.

'The King Pot.'

Behind the wheel, Marcus had seen his face in the rear-view mirror. His boss's skin had been the colour of putty, his eyes sunk into his head, an emptiness in them Marcus hadn't seen before. From then on, he'd come regularly, always alone, and stayed until his mind and emotions quieted – however long that might take. He kept his thoughts to himself, though he had to be plotting revenge.

And there was plenty to go round.

George Ritchie had protected Anderson and done a good job, otherwise – like the two sad bastards inside – he would've died an agonising death before his twenty-first birthday.

For Albert Anderson's son and heir, perishing in the fire was an easy way out.

* * *

Marcus looked at the night sky, yawned, and lazily checked his watch: ten past two. Danny was taking his time. The big man got out and stretched the tiredness from his legs. Further up the street a black cat arched its back and continued its nocturnal hunt. Marcus pushed the metal door open and went inside. It was dark. Familiar notes drifted towards him and he quickened his step. The room at the end was unlike anything he'd seen: there was blood on the floor, on the walls; everywhere. Wallace and Hart were pinned to the columns, their forearms and feet nailed to the wood. Holes had been drilled at different points in their bodies: both of Hart's eyes were gone. Strawberries had been forced between his lips; red juice mingled with his blood and dripped from his chin to the floor. In the crimson pool on the slabs, Marcus saw lumps of fruit and small stones. It took seconds for him to realise they were teeth and toes.

Danny's white shirt wasn't white any more. He sensed Marcus there and turned, his face streaked with red, the drill vibrating in his hand. Underneath the blood, Glass smiled like a kid in a toy shop the week before Christmas.

He said something Marcus couldn't hear; the music was too loud – The Who classic, 'Won't Get Fooled Again'. Pete Townsend's windmill cords crashing against the bricks.

When it finished, Glass threw his arms around the big man.

'Great to see you. Nearly done.'

'You okay, boss?'

'Never better.' He wiped sweat from his forehead with his arm. 'Jonjo didn't know where Rollie is. He didn't know where any of them are.'

'How did he get out of the club?'

'Rollie told him to fuck off.'

'Why?'

'They were leaving to hit the King Pot. He told them it was a crazy idea.'

'You mean the cheeky bastards were coming after us again?'

'Yeah, they were. If it wasn't for me, we'd all be laying on slabs. Luke's a dud – always was.'

'What's with him, boss? He hasn't been around. Is he out?'

'He's out when I say he's out.'

'What about the copper? What about him?'

'Nothing. Cut bits off him and he still didn't talk. Not even to save his life. Because he'd nothing to tell. That bastard Stanford's having us at it.'

Hart was obviously dead. Wallace was barely breathing. Glass grabbed Wallace by the hair and gently slapped his face – the only gentle thing he'd done all night. The eyes, dulled by unimaginable pain, flickered open, closed and opened again. Glass centred the drill in the middle of his brow.

'Think I owe you an apology, Bob. Sorry, mate.'

He sounded sincere.

PART IV

54

Euston Station was the usual madhouse; people coming and going to their destinations like robots programmed to ignore everything and everyone around them. We stood at the gate staring at the platform where the train from Manchester would arrive. Mandy hadn't said much all day. Her face had healed well – make-up, skilfully applied, had done the rest. She was nervous, chewing the inside of her mouth, tapping her foot and glancing every few minutes at the Arrivals notifications on the board above her head. Seeing her daughter again was a big deal and she was worried about how it would go. My role was largely passive. I was there and, for the moment at least, that was enough. Mandy was beyond reassuring pep talks.

She'd insisted on leaving in plenty of time and we were early. With nothing better to do I wandered over to WHSmith, bought an *Evening Standard* and leafed through it. Near the bottom of page four, a headline reminded me why I'd cut my brother out of my life: LATEST FIRE VICTIM DIES. There was no need to read on but I did: a twenty-five-year-old woman from Tooting had succumbed to her injuries bringing the death toll to one hundred and thirty-eight. No arrests had been made in connection with the blaze and the police had only been able to positively identify fifty-one of the deceased. The last line summed the horror up for anyone who didn't get what those people had suffered: 'a senior officer admitted they weren't expecting the figure to go higher'.

The newspaper went in the nearest bin.

Danny had got away with it.

My mobile buzzed in my pocket: Stanford. I wonder how he got my number.

'I have the information you asked for.'

'Good.'

'The first phone's a burner. The second belongs to a guy called Finnegan. Vincent Finnegan.'

Vincent must've changed his mind about me putting a word in for him with Danny. He'd missed the boat on that one.

The DCI got what he needed to say in before I could close him down.

'What we were discussing, made your mind up yet?'

'Still thinking about it.'

Not the answer he was looking for.

'Face it, Luke. It isn't going to get better.'

He wasn't wrong, though he wouldn't be hearing it from me.

Mandy was waving at me from across the station.

'As I said, I'm thinking about it.'

'Don't take too long. If you don't do it, somebody else will.'

Over by WHSmith, I saw a face I recognised – a smartly dressed geezer with a sallow complexion and long hair swept behind his ears, pretending to read the front pages of the newspapers on the stand at the front of the shop.

'Your man could do with a refresher course on surveillance.'

'Our man?'

'The one following me. I've seen him before. Right now, he's bringing his knowledge of world events up to speed. Tell him to hide behind something next time.'

There was a long silence before the detective spoke.

'I've absolutely no idea what you're talking about. We don't have anybody on you.'

'Since when?'

'Since Danny called it off.'

won't be needing anything from you any more

'What about Anderson – he's still out there?'

'Nobody could've survived. It burned fast. The building was old. The fire chief estimated it somewhere between 2,500 and 3,000 degrees: incredible temperatures.'

My voice was low and steady; he wasn't going to see my fear.

'You're wrong. Dead wrong.'

I didn't hear his reply. I was running.

* * *

The guy realised I was coming for him and dropped his act, headed for the Underground, changed direction and raced towards Eversholt Street. On the concourse, a party of disabled people were between him and me. By the time I got past them, he was gone. Traffic was heavy on Euston Road, the air thick, smelling of diesel. I stood on the pavement impotently balling my fists.

I'd lost him.

Back at the gate, Mandy wasn't pleased. Anxiety was getting the better of her. She barked at me, close to tears from the emotional overload.

'Where the hell did you go? I need you here.'

The lie came easily. 'Had to make a call. Sorry.'

'The Manchester train's late.' She pointed to the noticeboard. 'Won't arrive for another twenty minutes.'

I did my best to calm both our minds. 'It'll be fine. Honestly, it will.'

She exhaled and relaxed. Her whisper disappeared into my shoulder.

'You really think so, Luke?'

'I really think so. Children notice things. We can't let Amy see her mum's been crying, can we?'

'I'm freaked out with nerves.'

'Of course. This is your daughter we're talking about. She doesn't know it, but she's a lucky little girl to have you as her mother. Stop worrying. Everything's good. Everything's fine.'

She smiled and pulled herself together. 'Thanks. I needed to hear that.'

Mandy believed me. Thank Christ one of us did.

* * *

The train pulled into the station exactly twenty minutes late, which made me wonder why it hadn't been on time in the first place. A line of carriages stretching as far as I could see rolled slowly to a stop. All the doors opened at once and people poured onto the platform. Mandy stood on tiptoe trying to see over the heads of the crowd. When she saw Amy, she waved. The child started to run, threading a path through the passengers. That was my cue. I stepped back and let them have their moment. My stalker wouldn't be back – not today, anyway. If somebody else was in on it, they were better at it than he'd been, because I didn't see them.

Mandy hunkered down and threw her arms round a mini version of herself: red hair, corn-blue eyes, freckles and perfectly white teeth. The next minute was one long hug. A man stopped beside them: Amy's father was in his late thirties, tall and good-looking, wearing a tan jacket and a dark-brown scarf artfully draped round him the way Italian men had been doing for decades. I imagined him as every female student's idea of a university professor – well-read and handsome, prepared to put the age difference aside for the lucky nineteen-year-old in the front row who let him see up her skirt.

He smiled a cool smile and waited patiently for the hugging to stop. I'd listened to Mandy's side of why the marriage broke down. No doubt, he'd have a different tale to tell. Right and wrong didn't necessarily come into it. All too obviously, he'd rather the reunion wasn't happening and was struggling to keep it to himself. He glanced past his daughter and his ex-wife to me. I acknowledged him with a nod and got nothing in return – the guy didn't want to be here and it showed. The adults had a brief exchange I wasn't able to catch with him doing most of the talking. He kissed the little girl and walked away. Maybe I was misjudging him. Maybe this was hard. But he didn't look back.

Mandy introduced me to Amy. 'I want you to meet Luke. Say hello.'

Amy's question gave us a taste of what we could expect in the next seven days, cutting through whatever fiction we'd planned to tell her.

'Are you my mummy's boyfriend?'

Her mother laughed uncomfortably and tossed her hair over her shoulder.

I didn't hesitate. I'd made that mistake before. 'Yes, I'm her boyfriend. Is that all right with you?'

The answer confirmed her suspicions. She held out her hand. I took it in mine.

'Pleased to meet you, Luke.'

On the way to the Northern Line I bought three ice creams, my opening bid for Amy's affections. Behind her back, her mother blew me a kiss.

The holiday had officially begun.

* * *

Amy was great: bright, funny and – as I'd found out – alarmingly frank. It was going to be an interesting week. Buying the ice cream was a genius move. Sleeping with her mother in the room next door wouldn't be. I left at nine-thirty and got a taxi to my flat. It was early and there were lights in most of the windows.

I still couldn't place the guy at Euston Station. The only thing to do was sleep on it and hope it would come to me.

I kicked my shoes off and poured a large whisky – the first of the day. Setting good examples came at a cost. Before the week was over, I'd be a secret drinker.

I put my head back on the couch and was almost asleep when the mobile vibrated in my pocket. My mystery caller checking in. Except he wasn't such a mystery any more. I'd seen him. Three hours later I woke up again, cold and irritable. The phone lay silently on the floor at my feet; it had become my enemy. I was gripped by the certainty it was going to ring.

And I wasn't wrong.

My voice was hoarse and angry. 'Tell your boss I'm ready any time he likes.'

As usual, I was talking to myself. Where I'd seen the guy at Euston suddenly came to me – the smooth operator from the pub on the Broadway. Anderson had had eyes on me from Day One.

'Listen, you bastard. I know what you look like. Soon, I'll know where you live.'

I was tired though there was no point in trying to sleep. Adrenaline pumping through my veins had me on my feet. The street was very different from how it had been; every house was closed down for the night. But behind one of the windows, Anderson could be watching, weighing up whether he'd turned the psychological screw as far as it would go, or was there something to be gained by turning it a little bit more. In his eyes, seven years was light for what I'd done to his old man. I was his reason to live. Part of a plan a long time in the making. Between me and my brother, he'd lost everything.

All that remained was the reckoning.

Number one on his shit-list was me.

I brought the gun from the bedroom and sat in darkness, listening to my heart beat in sync with the clock above the fire. This couldn't go on. One way or another it would be over, and soon. Team Glass didn't exist. My brother didn't have my back this time – the advantage was with Rollie Anderson and we both knew it.

I was on my own.

55

Trevor Mills came into Stanford's office and closed the door behind him. He had something to say and his boss wasn't going to like it. His DCI was bent over a report on the desk. If he'd heard the sergeant enter the room, he didn't show it. The DI coughed to get his attention. Stanford looked up from what he was doing, clearly irritated at the interruption. Mills said, 'Isobel Wallace is here to see you.'

Unwelcome but not unexpected. The twenty-four-hour waiting period before a person could be reported missing was a Hollywood myth. Isobel had acted the morning after Bob Wallace didn't come home. Officers had already been to the house and taken her statement. Questions about the state of the marriage and her husband's drinking were rejected as ridiculous and offensive. Bob and Isobel Wallace were dull, individually and collectively, and perfectly happy.

Stanford put down his pen. 'Well, let's get it over with.'

Mills turned and stopped. 'Oh, and something else, sir.'

His boss held onto his patience, just. 'What?'

'You didn't come back to me about the report on Eugene Vale's secretary.'

Stanford's expression wouldn't have been out of place on Easter Island. 'The woman who drowned in the bath?'

'The very same. Should we take a closer look?'

'Christ, no. The last thing we need is another murder statistic. Life really is too short without raking around in whatever shit Danny Glass is knee-deep in now. Let it go, Trevor. Bring Isobel in.'

* * *

Without make-up, Wallace's wife was more nondescript than he remembered from the dinner party – her hair hadn't been properly combed and she wore black shoes with a brown coat. The DCI sniffed his disapproval. Elise wouldn't let herself go no matter how distraught she was.

'Trevor, get Isobel a cup of tea.'

She turned the offer away. 'No, nothing for me, thanks. I just had to get out of the house and didn't know where else to go, so I came here. I hope you don't mind.'

'Not a bit of it. You did the right thing.'

'Any word?'

'Not yet. Try not to upset yourself unnecessarily. It's only been a day. Bob might walk through that door at any minute.'

Isobel put her hand over her eyes and started to sob. Behind her, Mills coughed awkwardly into his hand. 'Perhaps you'd prefer I wasn't here?'

'No, stay. Please stay. You're his colleagues. He's so proud to be working with you, you've no idea.'

She missed the look that passed between the policemen. Stanford was on cue. 'And we're proud to be working with him, aren't we, Trevor?'

DI Mills concurred. 'Absolutely, sir. One of the finest officers in the building.'

Stanford's tone was measured. 'Your husband never stops being a policeman. Before he left here yesterday, he told someone he was meeting an informant. That could've led him to something.'

Isobel lifted her head. 'What informant? Bob never mentioned an informant.'

Stanford embellished the invention. 'He played his cards close to his chest.'

'Not with me.'

'Of course, though you must appreciate there are aspects to the job none of us share. The Bob we see is very different from the one who comes home to you. In the short time he'd been on the team, he's made a big contribution. Tenacious. Haven't met a better copper. No offence, Trevor.'

'None taken, sir.'

This wasn't the man Isobel Wallace knew.

'Why hasn't he called? Bob always calls. I've tried his mobile. He isn't answering.'

Stanford could've told her why.

Instead, he leaned forward and took her hands – damp and clammy – biting back his distaste.

'Go home. We'll do everything we can to find him.' He looked her in the eye. 'We're good at what we do, Isobel. I'll be surprised if he doesn't show up soon.'

When she'd gone, Mills said, 'What're we going to do about Wallace?'

Stanford shuffled papers on his desk and didn't look up. 'We've got a missing copper. We investigate it. Top priority. Get the ball rolling. I'll speak to the men.'

'Shouldn't we wait?'

'That wouldn't be appropriate. One of our own is missing.'

Mills smiled. 'I'll say this for you. You're a cool bastard, Oliver.'

Stanford accepted the compliment, adding a small important modification.

'A cool bastard, *sir*. We're not in the pub now, Trevor.'

* * *

Irritation flashed in Stanford's eyes when he saw Mills was back. The DI caught it and forced himself not to react. He'd had enough of his boss's superior attitude. Being promoted ahead of him didn't seem to be enough for him. He was determined to rub his nose in it. They were up to their elbows in stuff that would put them in prison for years, yet the puffed-up dickhead wanted to be called sir.

Stanford's tone was clipped. 'This better be good, Trevor.'

Good wasn't how the detective inspector would've described it.

'A jogger spotted a body bumping up against Vauxhall Bridge and called it in. They fished it out of the river an hour ago.'

'Anybody we know?'

'You're not going to believe it.'

'Cut the dramatics, we've got more than we can use. Just tell me who the hell it is.'

'Jonjo Hart.'

Stanford was underwhelmed.

'Never heard of him.'

'No reason you should've. He's nobody. Hasn't been in town long.'

'How did we identify him so quickly?'

'One of the uniforms at the scene is from Tyneside. Hart's connected up there. He recognised him. That and "Toon Army" tattooed on the back of his hand makes it pretty conclusive.'

'What happened to him?'

Mills crossed to the window. In the distance, a heat haze covered the south; outside the air would be sticky and foul. One hundred and seventy years earlier, the smell coming off the river was strong enough to affect the business of parliament. London was still a bastard of a place in summer: a shithole. Too hot and too many people. He gazed down at the traffic and the pedestrians on the Embankment; nonentities unaware of what was going on around them.

'Quicker to tell you what didn't.'

Stanford drummed his fingers on the desk. He already had a missing officer to deal with, by itself enough to bring nine kinds of crap down on his head from all directions. He wasn't in the mood to fuck about.

'Whenever you're ready, Trevor, I've got plenty of time.'

The sarcasm was undisguised.

'I talked to the DI down there. He says the guy was naked and he'd been tortured. Bits cut off. Holes in him everywhere. Before he died his eyes had been put out.'

Stanford made a face. 'Nasty. How long has the body been in the water?'

'Not his call. They're expecting Forensics to arrive any minute.'

'Then, apart from the city becoming less safe by the day – which isn't news to anybody in law enforcement – what's the significance?'

Mills kept him waiting, sensing the stress rise in the other man. Stanford was freaking out and doing a fair job of hiding it.

'He's small-time.'

'So why tell me about him?'

'Two reasons: he's one of Anderson's men. A peripheral player – not much more than a gofer – part of the crew, nevertheless. Could be Anderson's guys are fighting amongst themselves.'

'Why torture him? Why not stick a knife in him and be done with it?'

'Good question... sir.'

Insubordination needed proof, hesitating on a word wasn't enough. But it was there; the DCI had heard it. Stanford moved on – he'd get his chance.

'What's the second reason?'

'He's George Ritchie's nephew.'

Stanford lost his temper. 'Why the fuck didn't you say that in the first place? Can you really not understand just how deep in the shit we are? If Anderson and his men are alive, I guarantee they're not fighting each other – they're preparing for war. And if somebody's done this to Ritchie's family, we can expect a bloodbath.'

56

Nina had said she believed me when I told her I'd known nothing about the Picasso Club fire. Maybe she did, but since her phone call, she'd stayed away from me. I was already a brother down, losing my only sister wasn't the result I was after. She sounded different at the other end of the phone – edgy, wired, or just not in the mood for conversation, I couldn't be sure, so I kept it as light as I knew how, although it was late in the day to expect her to welcome me as the protective big brother I'd never been. Thanks to Lord Justice Peyton Richardson and the twelve good men and women on the jury, that ship had sailed, too much water had gone under the bridge.

'Just checking in. How's things?'

Her reply was jaded. 'Much like you'd expect when your brother's a mass murderer. Fucking grim. How's Mandy?'

'Improving and nervous. Her daughter is visiting. It's a big deal for both of them.'

'I wish her luck.'

'Thanks, she'll appreciate that. By the way, had an interesting conversation with Oliver Stanford, or, rather, he had one with me.'

'Wouldn't have believed that was possible. Is he any closer to putting Danny away?'

'For what? Where's the proof?'

'Is that a no?'

I didn't answer.

'What did he say?'

'Eugene Vale?'

'What about him?'

'His secretary's been found dead. He suspects Danny had something to do with it.'

Silence on her end of the line.

'Nina?'

'What makes him think that?'

'He knows Danny, isn't that enough? And the circumstances are odd – she drowned in her bath.'

She processed the information. 'Doubt he even knew Eugene had a secretary.'

She was right; the policeman was reaching. So was I.

'Though, it would be poetic justice if he went down for something he didn't do.'

'Is Stanford investigating it?'

'No idea.'

'Let me know if you hear anything.'

'Didn't Vale tell you about it?'

'I haven't seen him. We aren't together.'

'Sorry to hear that.'

'Don't be.'

'But you're okay, yeah?'

'As I said, when your brother's a mass murderer...'

I ended the call – it wasn't going anywhere. The fire had affected Nina more than I'd realised, and with her romance ending as well... clearly, she wasn't in a good place. Danny would be pleased Vale was out of the picture, though he wouldn't be hearing it from me.

* * *

In the bank, the girl who'd served me when I'd asked for a printout was there again, behind a Perspex screen. I'd given the notice they'd asked for with a request to withdraw the money two days later. She counted out the notes – crisp clean twenties that snapped between her thumb and forefinger – and edged them across to me. I waited for a variation of her sales pitch but she let me go. She was subdued, her dark-brown eyes lacking the enthusiasm for other peoples' cash that had shone so brightly before.

Towards the end of the transaction she raised her game and tried a smile on for size.

'Hope you're planning something fun.'

'It's not for me and it's not for fun.'

The truth. I'd withdrawn the amount Mandy was short and put a bit more on top for luck. She could bail today if she wanted with her little girl or hang on for a better opportunity. Her choice. Out on the street, I didn't spot anybody following me. That didn't mean they weren't there.

Giving was more satisfying than receiving, no doubt about it, and I walked to my car feeling good. Being around Amy had given me an insight into what childhood should be.

I hadn't had one. None of us had.

And I'd had no idea the city was such a great place for kids. In the last three days we'd been to the zoo, the Sea Life London Aquarium and taken a sightseeing trip on the Thames. But the star of the visit was Harry Potter. I'd walked in the boy wizard's footsteps and sat through a two-and-a-half-hour film of the locations and inspirations behind the books. Today we were taking it easy. Just mooching around getting our breath back. Tomorrow we were booked to go to Warner Bros. studios for more of the same. A driver would pick us up at the corner of Baker Street and Porter Street, in front of Starbucks coffee. I told myself I was doing it for the kid though really, I was having as good a time as she was.

* * *

Family wasn't something I was used to; I hadn't known the woman who'd given birth to me and, growing up, my father was too often in a whisky stupor to realise I was even there.

Little girls are cute – this one was no exception. She liked me and wasn't afraid to show it. The feeling was mutual and when they went home, a sense of loss beyond anything I could explain settled over me.

But it was her mother I was drawn to most. The more time I spent in her company, the more I appreciated qualities her husband had missed. She was smart, kind, funny and well able to call bullshit on me. It was easy to forget the relationship was doomed and had been from the beginning.

And that was the problem. I had forgotten.

* * *

The money was a no-brainer. I didn't need it and Mandy did. To me it meant nothing, to her it was a second chance with her daughter and I was looking forward to seeing the look on her face when I handed it to her. She'd ask me to go with them. That wouldn't be right. What we'd had was good, but it wasn't love. I knew the difference.

It had been a whirlwind few days, everyone was exhausted, so I wasn't surprised when I phoned to tell them I was on my way home and got no answer – they'd both still be in bed; they'd moved into my place when Amy decided she liked it better. They shared a room. I had the other one.

At the end of the second day, Amy had decided I was cool and held my hand wherever we went. Mandy saw her and smiled. 'She likes you.'

'Seems she does.'

'That makes two of us.'

The money for Mandy lay in two neat bundles on the passenger seat. I ought to be feeling pleased. Instead, I was uneasy. A check in the rear-view mirror showed nothing, but the hairs on the back of my neck said different. Back at the flat I took the stairs two at a time, my heart thumping in my chest, cursing myself for leaving them alone.

The door was open. Sweat broke on my brow and I inched forward, afraid of what was waiting for me. It only took a moment to know my worst fears had been realised.

Mandy and Amy weren't there.

I was punching her number on Quick Dial when my head exploded and the lights went out.

* * *

How long I lay unconscious was anybody's guess – probably only minutes – more than enough time for whoever had been there to get away. Understanding what had happened wasn't easy. If this was Anderson's work, I'd be dead. So maybe it wasn't about me. And if it wasn't, then it had to be about Mandy. The guy from the Shark's Mouth flashed across my mind. This might be payback for the mess I'd left him in.

I drove like a madman to the pub and burst through the door. Keith wasn't there but the memory of me was in the barman's eyes. He busied himself polishing pint measures, pretending he didn't know I was there. Until I grabbed the front of his shirt and dragged him across the counter.

'Where's Keith?'

The guy was scared and he should be.

'He doesn't come in during the day.'

'Where does he work?'

His teeth ground together, wanting to resist, accepting he was going to break.

'How would I know?'

I tightened my grip, put my other hand round his throat and repeated the question.

'Tell me where he works.'

He gasped the information out like he was always going to.

'Drives a forklift in a warehouse in Lewisham.'

I shook directions out of him and let him drop to the floor. Sorting him would keep. Getting Mandy and Amy back was all that mattered.

* * *

The barman's directions were sound and I found the warehouse straight away, a cavern of a place on an industrial estate, fronted by a series of roller doors. Trucks were loading and unloading in the docking bay. Nobody asked who I was, why I was there, or tried to stop me entering.

Inside, Keith was the first man I came across, behind the wheel of a yellow forklift truck, moving a pallet of boxes from one end of the shed to another. He was wearing brown overalls with the company logo written on the chest and his hair was swept back. His face was marked from our fight in the lane where he'd assaulted Mandy. When he saw me, he leapt down and tried to run – not easy in his condition. The forklift tipped and spilled its load. I didn't go after him. He was a low life, capable of a lot of things, and one day he'd really get what he deserved. But he wasn't responsible, not this time. Drugging women was his stretch. You don't abduct somebody and turn up for your shift.

It wasn't him.

Contacting Stanford crossed my mind. All I had to do was ask and he'd throw his resources into finding Mandy and her little girl. Except, then I'd owe him – at least, that was how he'd see it. And I'd learned enough to know owing the Stanfords of the world never ended well.

Better to make a deal with the devil.

The devil you know.

Against everything I believed, I did the only thing that made sense in the circumstances.

* * *

Danny answered on the first ring and I blurted out the terrible news.

'Anderson's got Mandy.'

He processed what he was hearing. When he spoke, it wasn't the out-of-control hothead on the other end of the phone – the man who'd sanctioned the death of innocent people – it was the brother who'd protected me and kept me safe.

'Slow down, Luke. Slow down and tell me again.'

I choked down my fear. 'He's got her. Anderson's alive. He's got Mandy and Amy.'

57

I'd intended never to set foot in the King of Mesopotamia again, yet here I was. To hell with principles. My brother's influence in the South London underworld couldn't be underestimated. Anderson had taken Mandy and Amy to get back at me. If anybody could find them, Danny could.

A few of his guys were hanging round the bar. When they saw me, they stopped talking, shuffled uncomfortably and stared at their shoes. Being Danny Glass's brother was still my only claim to fame. They answered to one man – the man I was here to see.

Felix was the exception. Danny still didn't like him. The smart thing for him would've been to take himself somewhere else but he'd stayed, and I admired that. And he'd been serious about watching my back. My choices weren't great but, given the alternatives, Felix was the only one of them I trusted.

Harry the barman greeted me with an indifferent nod and I climbed the stairs to the office, sick with worry, impotent and overwhelmed.

Danny wasn't alone. Marcus was there, along with a face I hadn't seen before: a guy with blond streaks in his hair and a strong chin that jutted out assertively. Studying his shoes wasn't for him; he met my gaze with undisguised confidence and didn't blink. Maybe it was my imagination but I got the impression he'd already decided he didn't like me.

Danny closed his PC and met me in the middle of the room. He wrapped his arms round me and clapped my back. 'I've missed you, bro. Coming here's the right thing. Anderson won't have taken them far. He doesn't know the city. Hardly been north of the river in his whole life. Sit down and tell me what happened.'

My eyes strayed to the newcomer. Danny reassured me.

'This is Scotch Norrie down from Glasgow to join us. He's a good man, even if he is a Jock. And he's been warned – no independence chat or he's back up the fucking motorway.'

The corners of Norrie's mouth rose and fell and settled in a thin line. He didn't laugh. Nobody laughed. Danny poured two whiskies and handed one of them to me.

'No, thanks.'

He cajoled me. 'Go on. Do yourself a favour. Just a splash.'

I didn't have the energy to argue.

'Right,' he said. 'From the beginning, and don't miss anything. No use chasing around like busy idiots until we're sure what we're up against.'

I left out visiting the bank and withdrawing the money – it didn't take a big brain to guess what my brother would make of that – and started with arriving at the flat and what I'd discovered. Danny let me speak without interrupting, stroking the stubble on his chin. When I finished, he said, 'How old is the little girl?'

'Nine.'

'Why was she staying at your place?'

'I've got room. It made sense to be together.'

The explanation fell short of convincing him.

'You fond of her?'

'I've only just met her.'

'Not what I asked. Cute, is she?'

'Yes, and yes, I am.'

'Rollie's the obvious choice. Any chance one of her mother's less satisfied customers might be behind it?'

On another day I'd have laid him out for that remark.

'No, it has to be Anderson,' and left it there. He realised he'd crossed the line with me and altered his approach.

'You didn't see who hit you?'

I shook my head.

'If the kid and her mother were already gone, why was there anybody there?'

'I've no idea, Danny.'

'They could've topped you. Why didn't they?' He answered his question himself. 'Because they didn't want to. That isn't the plan.'

'My thinking, exactly.'

'You still getting those calls?'

'Yeah, and somebody was following me at Euston Station.'

Danny nodded. 'Anderson's turning the screw. He's spotted you playing happy families and saw a way to hurt you. When he thinks you've suffered enough, he'll finish the job.'

Danny spoke over his shoulder to Marcus. 'You getting all this, Big Boy?'

'Yes, boss.'

'Then why're you still here? Move your arse. Put feelers out. Do whatever you have to. Somebody knows where they are. Get going. You too, Norrie. This isn't a rest home.'

* * *

The downsides to asking for my brother's help were many and I didn't need anybody to remind me. Having to listen to the abuse he casually dropped into almost every conversation was one of them. We'd come close to blows already about Mandy. He seemed to have forgotten.

'Warned you, little brother. Can't say I didn't. Falling for the first female who takes you on is the oldest mistake in the ex-cons' book.'

I was on edge as it was, I didn't need this.

'It isn't like that, Danny.'

''Course it is. You come out after years inside. You're vulnerable. Females can smell it on us. A wiser man fucks them, goes on to the next one and body-swerves the "I love you" bollocks.'

He lifted his hands in resignation at the ill-considered consequences of me being kind to a woman and her daughter. 'This could all have been avoided. Mandy and her kid wouldn't be where they are.'

If he was trying to make me feel better, he was doing a piss-poor job of it.

'Thanks for reminding me.'

Danny sighed. 'Sounds harsh. The wrong time to be giving you a lecture, I get that. But I'm telling you for your own good. Some women you just don't mess with.'

His diatribe was interrupted by footsteps on the stairs. The door opened and Oliver Stanford came in. I hadn't seen or heard from him since The Spaniards Inn and didn't expect to. If Danny got to hear about that little slice of betrayal, the detective's worries would be over.

The policeman had left his delusion of superior at New Scotland Yard, yet I recognised the steel and the ruthlessness in him. Self-preservation was a powerful motivator.

Danny covered his surprise and went into the act I'd witnessed so often – his jokey all-pals-together routine. 'Ollie, just the man I need to speak to. What you drinking?'

Stanford hooked a thumb in the direction of my brother, his jaw tightening as he forced the words into the world. 'Thought you were done with this bastard, Luke.'

He wasn't expecting an answer and didn't get one.

Danny sensed the shift in dynamics; his pet policeman wasn't in the room.

'I asked what you're drinking.'

Stanford's focus stayed with me. 'Your brother's finished. Tomorrow. Next week. Doesn't matter, it's happening.'

Danny said, 'Got out the wrong side of bed this morning, Detective.

Now, calm the fuck down or I'll break your legs. What's the problem? Spit it out.'

The detective had taken a lot. Those days were gone. This was a different man.

'I couldn't care less what you vermin do. You can slaughter each other until there's no one left. London won't miss you...'

'Steady on, copper.'

'...but when you start behaving like lunatics, then I care. In fact, I care very much.'

'What you on about?'

Stanford was warmed up and ready to go. 'I'll tell you what I'm on about, Glass. Dumping Jonjo Hart in the river was a move only a fucking simpleton would make.'

Danny didn't deny it. 'I had my reasons.'

Stanford stepped closer to him. 'I don't give a flying fuck for your reasons. The bottom line is this: a missing police officer is a major event in this town. If you've pulled the same stunt with Wallace's body, nothing can save us, we're all going down.'

'Nobody's going to find anything. Credit me with some intelligence. Now, like I said, calm down. We've got a new problem. You were wrong. Anderson didn't die in the fire. He's abducted two people. One of them's a nine-year-old girl. I'm doing what I can do. Need you to do the same.'

Suddenly Stanford understood. 'So, that's why you're here. Should've come to me instead of crawling back to your brother.'

I could've told him that, on balance, Danny was a better bet. I knew the worst of him. Nothing he did would surprise me.

the devil you know

The policeman got himself under control.

'Where were they taken from?'

'My flat.'

Stanford figured the possibilities. 'Can't send detectives here. Go back to the flat. Somebody will be waiting for you. Tell them what you know. We'll do our best. If they're still in London, we'll find them.'

He headed for the door and asked a final question.

'How can you be sure it's Anderson?'

* * *

He pretended DCI Stanford's outburst hadn't shaken him, but it had. Danny refilled his glass and forgot about mine, then stood at the window, getting himself together before he turned and let me see his face.

'I'm not missing something, am I, little brother?'

'Like what?'

'Like, when did you two become so pally?'

'I've no time for your shit, Danny. The guy's trying to help. Right now, I'll take it from anybody, even a bent copper.'

'Stanford's a bottler. I put George Ritchie's nephew in the Thames to make a point.'

nobody mugs off Danny Glass

'After what he did there was no other way.'

He pointed to me and I sensed another speech coming.

'Being the boss is about choices. Hard choices. Our enemies are everywhere and they're jealous about what we've achieved.' He faked a grin and dipped into the past like he often did. 'Don't forget, we're the kids who started out thieving packets of fags.'

I remembered.

'The first sign of weakness and they'll take what doesn't belong to them. I won't let that happen.'

58

Going to Danny for help had been the right thing – the lives of people I cared about were in danger. If they were still alive, he'd find them.

Amy had brought a vibrancy to the flat with her insatiable curiosity about everything, especially her mother and me. Without her energy, it would be a cold, empty place. Booking into a hotel crossed my mind. Instead, I decided to get it over with.

The policeman Stanford promised was waiting for me and introduced himself as DI Mills. He was polite and asked his questions though I got the impression he was going through the motions. Talking to him was the last thing I wanted. I suddenly felt exhausted and depressed and defeated. The tit-for-tat reprisals and the craziness I'd vowed in Wandsworth to not get caught up in were back in my life.

To emphasise the point, the flat had been trashed.

In my desperate rush to find Mandy and Amy, I hadn't noticed the extent of the damage. Whoever it was had enjoyed their work and suddenly a hotel seemed the better option: the coffee table had been tipped over, its glass top smashed and lying in shards on the carpet; most of the unread book collection was on the floor, pages ripped and shredded; the TV screen was cracked from top to bottom, and a knife had sliced through the back of the leather couch, revealing yellow stuffing, seeping like pus from an ugly wound. Every room had been given the same treatment, malicious and unnecessary.

The policeman saw what I saw and made no comment. He asked his questions and made notes. I answered, adding little to what he'd already got from his boss, and sent a picture to his phone of Mandy and Amy taken at the Aquarium two days earlier. Mandy was kneeling with Amy in front of her, both of them smiling at the camera. When he left, I sat on the burst sofa and forced myself to think. The furniture could be replaced. All it took was money. Thanks to my brother, I wasn't short of that. Mandy and Amy couldn't be replaced. They were innocents, dragged into a feud they had no part of. Detective Chief Inspector Stanford's interest was in ending the hold Danny had over him. Fair enough. But he'd get there by himself or not at all. Right now, my brother was the best hope I had.

And there was no escape from guilt. If I'd given Mandy the cash on the way to Euston Station, she and Amy could've disappeared there and then and none of this would be happening. I'd sensed I was being followed from the moment I'd come through the prison gates. Apart from mentioning it to Danny, what had I actually done about it? Like everybody else, I'd suspected Anderson died in the fire along with his obsession with me. The fact the calls hadn't stopped with his presumed death should've told me something: Danny was right. I had gone soft. Soft and lazy. Fuck's sake, I hadn't even noticed the police tail was gone.

Or, maybe I'd imagined being the great Danny Glass's brother was enough.

It wasn't. Not even close.

* * *

Slowly, I realised I was on the couch with the lights turned off; the shrill, insistent ringing of the mobile in my inside jacket pocket had woken me. I fumbled for it, already breathing hard, my mouth dry, my fingers thick and clumsy with nerves. It could be Danny. Maybe he'd found them.

The caller ID glowed like a new moon in my palm. And it was familiar – not Vincent Finnegan – the one Stanford couldn't trace. I answered and wished I hadn't. Her scream went on forever – the sound of agony. I recognised my name and babbled nonsense.

'Mandy! Where are you? Mandy!'

She couldn't hear me.

'Mandy! Talk to me!'

The screams got louder.

I screamed, too. 'Anderson! I'm going to tear the head off your fucking body!

In the background a frightened Amy cried for her mother. The call ended and I was standing in the middle of the floor, tears running down my face and a man's laughter echoing in my ears.

59

It was raining in Newcastle. Pissing down. George Ritchie's sister didn't care; he had to persuade her to let him in. Eventually, reluctantly, she did. The lights were on and a white sheet covered the window where, once upon a time, a boy had sat listening to his mother and his famous uncle talking. That boy was dead. That boy was Jonjo.

Hannah played with her fingers and stared at the raindrops drumming against the glass, racing to the bottom, while the clock on the sideboard ticked the seconds away in silence.

She wasn't able to look at her brother, knowing if she did the dam inside her would break and anger beyond her control would come gushing out. Ritchie could only guess the pain she was suffering. There were no words, yet he had to tell her something – Hannah was owed that much. All he had was excuses.

'I warned him, Hannah. Swear to God, I did. He went his own way.'

Hannah repeated each syllable slowly, searching for its meaning.

'You... warned... him.' She lifted her eyes, brimming with tears. 'Is that supposed to help? Because it doesn't. It doesn't help me at all.'

'I'm sorry.'

'Are you? I doubt it.'

Ritchie tried to explain. 'Jonjo was headstrong, you said so yourself often enough. Always in a hurry. He thought I'd lost it when I laid it out for him, and he crossed somebody he should've avoided. Once he'd done that, there was nothing I could've done. Nothing anybody could've done.'

His sister's reply stung. 'If you're looking for absolution, go to St Anthony of Padua in Church Street. You won't find it here.'

'That's not fair. He knew what he was doing was dangerous. I believed I'd stopped him.'

'Except you didn't, George. Your whole life's a list of what you didn't do.'

She was talking about the last years of their mother's life, when Hannah had cared for her. George had promised to visit and hadn't. Something had always got in the way. In the end, she'd passed without seeing her only son.

His contribution had lasted three whole days. He'd come north, paid the funeral director in cash, left an envelope stuffed with money on the sideboard and returned south.

Ritchie changed the subject. 'What're the arrangements?'

Hannah wiped her cheeks. 'I'm going to London to bring him home.'

'I'll come with you.'

Spoken too soon.

She rounded on him, her face stiff with contempt. 'No, no, you won't. You won't do anything. Don't come to the funeral, you're not welcome. Don't dare leave money. After today, I don't want to see you again. Go back where you belong and stay there.'

* * *

Ritchie let himself out; it was still raining. He dug his hands into his pockets and bent into the wind. At the first pub he came to he ordered a large whisky then another and threw both of them over in a couple of gulps. It didn't help.

His sister's words seared his brain. 'Go back where you belong.'

Where was that? George Ritchie didn't know any more.

60

Trevor Mills knocked on his boss's door and went in. The previous day he'd been off-duty and hadn't appreciated having to drive across London to take a statement – another gripe in a long list. He'd left his wife, Barbara, in bed today, claiming she wasn't well. He'd taken her a glass of water and a couple of paracetamol earlier and was still waiting for her to say thanks. On the coffee table in their lounge, the front page of the *Daily Mail* had carried the latest news on the hunt for the Asians who'd been in the queue at the Picasso Club and an op ed railing against the hordes of immigrants pouring into the UK. The detective had smiled grimly to himself. The good men and women of the National Crime Agency were going to be disappointed. He almost felt sorry for them. They were chasing the wrong people.

Not only that, they wouldn't find them. The video wasn't clear enough to allow identification. He'd bet his pension the communities the Asian boys were from wouldn't let them come forward to be fitted up for something they didn't do.

Mills had no direct contact with Glass – Stanford dealt with Danny – and that was how Trevor Mills liked it. Life was complicated enough without having to jump whenever the gangster felt like putting you through your paces. In any case, it had been a wasted journey. Luke

Glass hadn't had much to give in the way of information yesterday, though, from the state of his flat, he'd upset somebody.

DCI Stanford's white shirt might've just come out of the box.

Mills held up his mobile to show him the picture of the missing mother and daughter.

'Good-looking for a hooker. Tough on the kid having that for a mum.'

Stanford didn't comment – he'd given Luke Glass the chance to pick a side. Predictably, he'd gone with his brother.

Mills said, 'How do you want me to handle this?'

The response surprised him. 'I don't, Trevor. Yesterday was a show. It's gangland stuff, same as the body floating in the Thames. They're animals. This is how they live. Unless it spills onto the streets and upsets the commissioner, I don't give a flying fuck what they do to each other.'

'Didn't you say we'd handle it?'

Stanford's lips pressed together. 'I say a lot of things, Trevor. Doesn't mean they're true. Glass had a chance to be smart and turned it down.'

This was the first Mills had heard about it.

'What did you do?'

'I offered him an opportunity, a new deal.'

'And?'

'He didn't take it.'

'More fool him. What about the sister? She might be up for it.'

'Maybe, she's certainly got the balls, but no, I still think Luke's the man we want.'

'You said he turned you down.'

'It's a long game, Trevor, a long game. Now, how's the investigation into Bob Wallace going?'

'Got every available man on it. Christ knows what it'll do to the budget.'

'Let me worry about that. The important thing is that we leave no stone unturned. Bob was a good officer; he deserves our best work.'

Mills wondered if the conversation was being recorded. Stanford sounded plausible – almost as if he believed what he was saying. Except they'd just had an unguarded discussion about Danny Glass. Oliver Stanford was a bigger conman than Glass, able to move between reality and fantasy and remain completely convincing.

Mills said, 'It would've been easier if Luke had stepped into Danny's shoes.'

'Agreed. When his brother falls – and he will – he's going down with him.'

He changed the subject. 'The red herring about the Asians in the Picasso queue has caught on.'

'Seems so. Which means Danny Glass is going to get away with it?'

'This time, maybe. But not for much longer. He thinks we're inside the tent. His reign as King of the South is nearly over. One of these days, it'll be him they fish out of the drink.'

'The end of an era.'

Stanford wrote a headline in the air. 'Gang boss dies in shoot-out.'

'So long as he does die.'

'He will, Trevor, we'll make sure of it.'

* * *

Although it was eleven o'clock in the morning, Danny sounded tired, as if he'd been woken from a sleep. At first, he didn't realise it was me. When he did, he pulled himself together.

'Luke. Any news?'

I told him about the phone call, Mandy screaming and a man laughing in the background. He didn't interrupt. Even when I lost it and couldn't finish a sentence.

'The laugh, did you recognise it? Was it Anderson?'

'I couldn't be sure.'

'Did you hear anything that might give us a clue to where he's holding them? Think – traffic noise, trains, water.'

'Only Amy crying.'

'Nothing else?'

'No.'

He paused, choosing his words, softening his tone. 'You and I have had our differences over Mandy. Believe me when I tell you I'm sorry. Nobody deserves what Anderson's done to her and her little girl.' Danny hissed down the line, talking more to himself than to me. 'He's a soulless bastard. Just like his old man.'

He was thinking of Cheryl and Rebecca and wasn't going to like what I had to say.

'I appreciate it, but I've made a decision. If Anderson contacts me again, I'm going to offer to trade places: me for Mandy and Amy. I'll show up wherever he wants. Alone.'

Danny's reaction was predictable. 'Don't. For Christ's sake, don't. Whatever he promises, he won't deliver. You'll be walking into a trap. Rollie's a reptile, he can't be trusted. He'll kill all of you.'

It was the truth.

'I have to do something. I'm going insane.'

'Stupid doesn't help anybody except Anderson. We won't give up until we've found them.'

He meant well. It wasn't enough. The dread I'd lived with since discovering Mandy and her daughter weren't at the flat crushed my chest, choking me.

My voice was a whisper. 'They're dead, aren't they?'

He came back strong. 'Luke, listen to me, you don't know that.'

But I did know it, and so did he.

* * *

The call from Stanford was unexpected. He'd tried and failed to do a deal with me in Hampstead. Going to Danny for help rather than him must've rankled.

'My guess is they're still in the city.'

He was offering me hope.

The trouble was, I didn't believe him. Not about any of it.

He had no interest in Mandy or Amy or me. He was saving his own arse or trying to. Maybe he'd get lucky. Maybe Anderson would finish what he'd started with his failed attack on the pub. The game was still in play and when the dust settled, he'd do business with whoever was left standing.

Convincing me he cared was a non-starter. Deep down Stanford was just another twisted human being prepared to step on anyone and anything on his road to the top, confident he wouldn't be coming back down.

Not so different from Danny or Anderson.

His next comment caught me off guard.

'George Ritchie was caught this morning on CCTV at King's Cross Station coming off a train. We tailed him but he lost us.'

'Ritchie?'

'The very same. The only sign that Anderson's crew might've survived. So, we're redoubling our efforts to locate them. Wherever they are, the woman and her daughter won't be far away.'

'You better tell Danny.'

The detective then burned the last bridge between himself and my brother. I imagined him smiling. 'You tell him. Better still, let him find out for himself.'

61

The flat had become a cell and I was as much a prisoner as I'd ever been in Wandsworth, pacing up and down trying to keep my imagination in check. Sometimes drinking yourself into oblivion is the only thing that makes sense. I felt like it but didn't do it. At any minute my mobile could ring with news. Finally, I couldn't stand it any more and left.

I was in the car when Nina called. 'Why didn't you tell me? This is awful.'

'Sorry, I'm a mess. All over the place. This whole thing is my fault.'

'Don't say that. I'm coming over.'

'No, don't. I'll come to you when I've checked in with Danny.'

The drive to the King Pot passed in a blur, the thousands of decisions, big and small, needed to navigate the city traffic made without input from me. Harry was serving somebody at the other end of the bar and didn't notice me come in. Apart from Felix, none of my brother's guys were around. He acknowledged me with a nod and came over.

'Sorry about Mandy.'

'Thanks.'

'I haven't forgotten what you did when Danny wanted to put a bullet in my brain. If you need me, I'm here.'

The office was exactly as it had been. He lifted his head and saw the replacement jukebox, the computer on the desk and the photograph of the Queen on the wall. There was one important difference: it was empty.

Danny wasn't here.

I ran a finger up and down the neck of one of the whisky bottles. Tempting. If Danny had been here, he would've insisted and I'd have had a glass in my hand whether I wanted one or not. Nobody ever dared sit in Danny's chair. Without thinking I dropped into it. An application for a pub licence in a name I didn't recognise sat on top of the desk. One of Danny's many business fronts. On paper he'd own very little.

An amber light blinking in and out told me the PC hadn't been turned off properly. Typical Danny. Technology had never been his thing. I tapped the space bar and went into shock. My brain refused to accept the evidence of my own eyes. What I was seeing was beyond anything I'd expected. I backed away from the screen, a hundred thoughts piercing my mind like poison darts.

I had to get out of there.

* * *

The car was driving itself again. Behind the wheel confusion lay like a weight on me. I pulled into the kerb and switched off the ignition. The images on the screen had made me doubt my sanity. It hadn't felt right from Day One. Like a fool I'd refused to tackle it head-on. Now the scales were lifted, I felt numb and alone.

No one had warned me.

That wasn't true. Somebody had.

some people have long memories

* * *

From a distance, still wearing the same threadbare coat he'd had on when I'd met him the first time, Vincent Finnegan looked like an old tramp in out of the rain. Close up didn't improve things – he hadn't had a shave in days, his shirt was creased and frayed. He'd lost weight, making deep hollows of his cheeks. The former hardman was by himself at a table, leaning against the back wall of the bar giving him an early sight of everybody who came in. A lingering trace of the callous enforcer he'd been skulked in the flinty corners of his eyes and there was a humourless half-smile on his lips as he assessed me walking towards him. He swirled the almost-empty pint measure in his hand and the dregs at the bottom, like he'd been waiting for me to arrive and buy him a refill.

I came straight to the point. 'You know why I'm here.'

He didn't feign surprise. 'I can guess.'

Finnegan pushed his nearly empty glass across to me. His timing was off. There were gaps in what I knew only he could plug. He'd get a drink when he'd told me what I needed to know.

I pushed the glass back. 'Don't get ahead of yourself, Vincent. You said you and Danny had a falling out. A "misunderstanding". What about?'

The question wasn't one he was keen to answer – even for free booze. His attention wandered to the men at the next table playing cards, then around the bar, everywhere but me.

'Leave it alone, Luke. There's nothing good down that road.'

'Got the impression you were thirsty.'

'Not that thirsty.'

'You're afraid of Danny, aren't you?'

The suggestion brought a mirthless grunt but no denial.

I mocked him. 'Vincent Finnegan scared. If all those women you used to pull could see you now. I can't believe it. You and Sean Poland terrified people. Or maybe that was just Sean.'

The Irishman's circumstances had changed – he still had his pride. Stomping all over it forced the reaction I wanted. Finnegan drew his coat open to reveal the gun tucked into the waistband of his trousers. I wasn't impressed.

'All that tells me is you live in fear.'

'No, Luke, I live in expectation. I'm not going out like Poland.'

I'd no idea what he was talking about. He saw my ignorance and a light came into his eyes. He had the upper hand, once upon a time a common occurrence – not these days.

He pointed a nicotine-stained finger at me.

'Surprised it's taken a bright guy like you this long to figure it out.'

'I'm not so bright, Vincent.'

He raised his walking stick and tapped it on his leg.

'None of us are, mate.'

'And I haven't figured anything out.'

He nudged the pint glass at me again. 'Then, I'd order a double if I was you – you're going to need it.'

* * *

Finnegan watched me make the call. One pint had become three. His spirit was reborn and he sat straight, eager to hear the exchange. When Danny answered I said, 'Where are you?'

The abruptness fazed him and he faltered. 'You… all right, little brother?'

I ignored his question and repeated my own. 'Where are you?'

'At the house.'

'The house? Which house?

'Our old house. We own it, you and me. Own most of the fucking street as a matter of fact. Told you we were into property, didn't I?'

'Stay there. I'm coming.'

* * *

Bile rose from my gut, burning the lining of my throat, leaving a foul taste in my mouth, and I had to stop the car and be sick before I could drive on. I'd stared in disbelief at Danny's PC screen and the live camera showing my flat and the couch where Mandy and I had made love. My first reaction was confusion, then embarrassment as I tried to work out what it meant. Danny had anticipated Rollie Anderson would pursue his vendetta and had it put in to protect me. When? I checked the files. The camera footage dated back to a month before I'd been released.

And suddenly, I understood.

On that first day coming out of Wandsworth, I'd been right – I *was* being watched. It had taken all this time to figure out who was behind it. Now, I'd bet everything I had that if I called my anonymous 'breather', a burner would ring in Danny's pocket.

A picture of Mandy and Amy came to me. Mandy had been terrified of Danny.

With good reason.

Vincent Finnegan's extraordinary tale, added to what I'd discovered, rocked me to my core. A part of me wanted to dismiss the Irishman as a bitter guy, eaten with resentment, and doubt his story. But that was the old Luke. Me – I believed every word and was ready to kill.

I hadn't been near this part of South London in more than two decades – not since I was fifteen. Coming here should've been nostalgic, poignant even. Today, I was blind to everything except the fury boiling in me. The front door was ajar, a portal to another time, one where I was a kid, my brother could make me laugh, and the future would take care of itself.

The golden past: a place beyond reach. A place that didn't exist and never had.

62

He was standing with his hands crossed behind his back, younger-looking than the day he'd tracked me to the pub on the Broadway when I went AWOL from my homecoming party. Like a fool, I'd swallowed his big brother act whole without questioning his sudden interest in me after so long. I'd told myself my brother was going through a tough time, and he had been, just not for the reasons I'd imagined. Now I understood. The corny 'Team Glass' pitch was for a reason – he wanted me where he could keep an eye on me until he was ready to turn the screw.

I wanted to rip his heart out.

The room was exactly as I remembered, right down to the yellowed net curtains on the windows and the faded carpet on the floor. The furniture, even the wallpaper and the pictures, were the same.

A finger scolded me. 'Kinda spoiled the surprise, bro. Shame. Had a notion we'd come here someday – you and me – and kick-over old times together.' He paused as the irony hit home. 'Got that right, didn't I?'

Whatever response he expected he didn't get. Hearing him go on about a house neither of us had lived in for two decades while the horror story Vincent Finnegan had told me played in my head was more than I could handle.

A voice, husky with anger, stripped the nonsense he was talking away: it was mine.

'You killed them. You killed Cheryl and Rebecca.'

Danny blinked and didn't answer, like he didn't understand what I was saying.

The words came out cracked and broken.

'For Christ's sake... they were... beautiful people. Why?'

The question physically changed him: the flesh at his neck coloured, his eyes became hooded and puffy as blood and rage met on his face. 'Why? You're asking why?' He screamed at me, spraying flecks of spit in the air. 'You were fucking her! You were fucking my wife!'

My reaction shamed me. 'You knew?'

Danny's laugh at my naiveté was brittle and bitter.

'From the beginning, little brother, from the very beginning.'

'You didn't love Cheryl.'

'You're right. I couldn't have given a monkey's. I was done with her. But she was mine. She belonged to me.'

'She tried for you, you bastard, you pushed her away. Pushed her away for your whores.'

'And you were there to catch her. Sounds noble when you put it like that. Knight in shining armour saving a damsel in distress. Leave it out.'

'It's the truth.'

'Truth. I'll give you some truth: my wife betrayed me with my brother.'

He laughed that laugh again and I guessed what he was going to say next.

'Nobody mugs off Danny Glass. Thought you knew that.'

I felt as if I were drowning in quicksand. Every move I made sucked me in deeper. Vincent Finnegan's clipped Northern Ireland accent had offered no apology for who he was and for who he'd been. Listening to him quietly describe Danny's unspeakable crime had chilled me.

On the morning they died, I was waiting for Cheryl in my flat. She was late. I'd spent my whole life believing in Danny, and I'd believed him again when he'd given me the awful news.

they're dead, Luke

that bastard Anderson

Albert hadn't been innocent – far from it – but he hadn't murdered Cheryl and Rebecca.

I turned the syllables over in my mouth and spat them out like bad meat.

'You killed both of them.'

His rejection of the accusation was pathetically sad. 'Rebecca wasn't supposed to be there.'

'Except she was, and she died before her life had even begun. You murdered your little girl. How can you live with yourself? You're a monster. A fucking savage.'

Danny absolved himself; his daughter's blood wasn't on his hands.

'Rebecca died because of you. Because of you, brother. All because of you.'

'What about Mandy? What've you done to them?'

Before he could speak a noise from over my shoulder made me look round. Marcus was Danny's shadow – wherever my brother went, the big man wasn't far away.

He leant both hands against the frame of the door like Samson about to bring the temple down, casually observing the scene, his eyes as empty as a cadaver. Behind me, a shoe scuffed where the carpet didn't cover. Scotch Norrie emerged from the kitchen. Danny was taking no chances. I'd been outnumbered from the start. The Scottish guy was a stranger – I'd met him a grand total of once, in the office above the King Pot; there was no history, good or bad, between us. He ran a fingertip along the blade of the knife in his hand. Unlike Marcus, his eyes were alive.

Danny came back to my question. 'You'll find out what I've done to them. Forgot who you were messing with, bro. I always square the account. Assumed you'd know that. Did it often enough for you when you were a kid.'

The past, always the fucking past.

'This is between me and you. Nobody else is involved.'

Danny laughed; I'd said something funny. 'Tell that to Sean Poland.'

I'd asked Vincent Finnegan about his taciturn friend. He'd told me: after the bomb went wrong, Poland was found one Sunday morning hanging from a tree in Norwood Park, his death made to look like suicide. Of course, it wasn't. The unnamed people who'd strung him up from a branch late on Saturday night broke into Finnegan's flat and crippled him with baseball bats. Vincent had had no part in the explosion – in fact, he hadn't even known about it. Danny judged him guilty by association. Vincent reckoned he'd got off lightly considering who he was dealing with. But every good thing he'd ever known was behind him, and ever since he'd expected Danny's heavies to finish the job – explains why he carried a gun.

'Where are they?'

My brother chose his words, searching to do justice to what he had to tell me.

'Let's just say they're waiting for you. Will that do?'

I had my fingers round his throat before his thugs could reach me. Blows rained down on my head and shoulders – I hardly felt them. Eventually, they dragged me off and laid into me, kicking and punching. The last thing I remembered was Danny standing over me shaking his head and wagging his finger, as if I was a little boy who'd done something wrong and needed to be punished.

* * *

I opened my eyes and closed them again. I was naked, my hands behind my back, tied with rope to a wooden stanchion running all the way to the roof. When I struggled, the rope bit into my wrists. After futile attempts to free myself I gave up. My body ached and my head hurt but, for the moment at least, I was alive.

I guessed this was Fulton Street.

A shaft of sunlight, dust dancing like plankton in its beam, pierced the darkness, allowing me to see my prison. The room was large, smelling of damp and mould and stale air. Decades of rain seeping through the mottled plaster had cracked it like eggshell, exposing the black crumbling brick underneath. Stumps of wood – the supports for what had once been a loft – dotted the gable end in a high horizontal line. Above them, boards, rotted and broken, were nailed across a window large enough to be a door.

It was cool but I was sweating.

The flagstones in front of the pillar I was shackled to were stained a deep brown. Blood – dried and ingrained. If I didn't find a way out of here, mine would be added to it. Rollie Anderson waited seven years to avenge what I'd done to his father. Danny's had been longer in the making.

from the beginning, little brother, from the very beginning

He'd accused me of betraying him and he was right – I had. We hadn't set out to hurt anyone. 'It just happened' is a cliché – in our case, it was true.

Danny had become distant and remote, even with me, cutting me out of decisions, disappearing for days with no explanation. I was Rebecca's godfather and had always been close to Cheryl. The marriage was failing. Like a friend she confided in me. And like a friend, I listened. Until, inevitably, friendship changed into something more.

* * *

Cheryl had showed up unexpectedly at the flat. Danny wanted to talk and had sent her to tell me. Her eyes had been wild with unhappiness. When I'd asked what was wrong, she'd broken down and told me my brother hadn't come home again. I'd held her in my arms until the sobbing stopped. Then we were kissing, tearing each other's clothes off and I was having my brother's wife.

* * *

The first time is never the best time. Strangers meeting in the dark. Too many unknowns for the earth to move. It didn't move for us. But it was good. I knew it would be. When it was over, she lay with her head on the pillow, tracing my face with her eyes, her voice husky with something she was reluctant to admit.

Eventually she said, 'I lied to you. I promised myself whatever happened I wouldn't and I have.'

'About what?'

'About Danny.'

'What about him?'

'Danny didn't send me.'

* * *

After that we couldn't have stopped even if we'd wanted to. Occasionally, we'd go to a hotel. Mostly we met at my place. It went on for months. At first, Danny loomed large in our conversation. Gradually, we stopped talking about him. Sometimes, we didn't talk at all.

* * *

My need was great. Hers was greater. Being loved how she wanted to be loved wasn't something she was used to, and it showed. Time after time, I resisted being drawn into the depths of her. Her response was to quicken her rhythm. Finally, she broke over my body, and we kept going, until she was moaning again in my ear and I felt the sting of her nails cutting bloody lines in my back. Eventually, she had all of me in a spasm of mutual joy, which went on and on.

We lay with each other's sweat drying on us, not talking because there was nothing to say. But in the shared silence, with her heart beating against mine, the knowledge it couldn't last crowded in, souring my mood.

I sat on the edge of the bed while she ran her fingers along the welts on either side of my spine.

'I'm sorry. I couldn't help myself.'

I shook my head. She noticed the change and I sensed her daring herself to speak.

'Did I disappoint you?'

'You could never do that. It isn't possible.'

She disagreed. 'Everything's possible, Luke.'

'No,' I said, 'not everything.'

And I was right. Danny had eyes and ears everywhere; pretending he wouldn't find out about us was a lie we both bought into. Once, when he was away 'on business' we went to Margate for the day. The night before, the madness of what we were doing made me almost call it off. I didn't and was glad because it was the best day of my life.

In the car she closed her eyes and let the wind blow her hair away from her face, a beautiful face. I tried to concentrate on the road. With her beside me, not a chance. A few days and already I was in deep. Deeper than was wise.

She turned her head and smiled. 'I feel like I'm in a dream and don't want to wake up.'

'Dream on.'

Her fingers ran up and down my arm. 'This was a good idea. I thought you might've changed your mind.'

Her fear was talking though we both understood what she meant. Silly girl. She wasn't the only one who was dreaming. I knew who she was and what she was and it couldn't have mattered less.

* * *

The signs had been there for anyone with eyes. Albert Anderson was causing trouble, which meant Danny wasn't around much. When he was, he avoided me. That was a warning. Because I was lost and hopelessly in love, wanting – no, needing – to be part of them; I didn't see it and selfishly risked their lives.

Family wasn't something I was used to; I hadn't known the woman who'd given birth to me and, growing up, my father was too often in a whisky stupor to realise I was even there.

Little girls are cute – this one was no exception. She liked me and wasn't afraid to show it. The feeling was mutual and when they went home, a sense of loss beyond anything I could explain settled over me.

But it was her mother I was drawn to most. The more time I spent in her company, the more I appreciated qualities her husband had missed. She was smart, kind, funny and well able to call bullshit on me. It was easy to forget the relationship was doomed and had been from the beginning.

And that was the problem. I had forgotten.

The years in Wandsworth were deserved; I didn't grudge a day of them – not for what I'd done to Albert Anderson. Danny had ordered the bomb that went wrong. Sean Poland was the man who set it. They weren't responsible for Cheryl and Rebecca dying.

I was the one who'd killed them.

63

Distant voices broke into the memories. They were coming for me. I braced for the worst. Marcus ducked under the lintel and came into the room with Scotch Norrie behind him. They'd been arguing about football – Arsenal and Rangers were mentioned – casually going on with their lives, and stopped when they saw me. Norrie took his knife from his pocket and played with it, opening and closing the blade to intimidate me. Marcus plugged in an extension cable, dragged a rickety chair from the shadows and sat it a yard from where I was. My clothes were lying in the corner; the gun was on top.

I made a stab at defiance – ridiculous in the circumstances.

'Where's Danny?'

Marcus ignored me and carried on. He lifted a duffle bag, carried it into the centre of the room and slowly emptied the contents, one at a time in a performance for my benefit: a hammer, a handful of reclaimed and rusted six-inch nails; a pair of long-handled bolt cutters powerful enough to snap chain; an iron bar a foot long; and last, a blood-spattered hand-held electric drill. I thrashed against the rope, my wrists on fire, until I was exhausted. Danny's men watched me. They understood the psychology of terror: silence was their weapon.

When they finished, they left, and I was alone with the tools of torture at my feet.

Thinking was the enemy. Awash in fear, my brain refused to function. The beating I'd taken had sapped my energy; every bone in my body ached. Nothing compared to what was coming. I was more tired than I'd ever been in my life. My eyes wouldn't stay open, my head fell forward and, unbelievably, I slept.

* * *

Danny's rough laugh brought me awake. Sunglasses, jeans and a white shirt open at the neck gave him the look of a guy who'd watched England have a promising first day against Australia at the Oval and was pleased with what he'd seen. One hand held a ghetto blaster, the other a bunch of CDs. Bottles of Camden Pils nestled in the crook of his arm, beads of moisture gathering like tears on the outside of the dark-brown glass. He set the lager on the flagstones, popped the top off one of the bottles and raised it to his lips. Experience had taught him this was thirsty work; he'd come prepared.

'The old man hated lager. Said it looked like piss and tasted worse.' Danny sniggered and kicked at something on the floor. 'Rich coming from a man who'd drink anything so long as it was alcohol. 'Course, he hadn't tasted this.' He turned the label so I could read it. 'The best of British. Streets ahead of the junk they brew across the channel. Next time you're in the office, we'll crack a few.' He hesitated. 'Or, maybe not. But it's good stuff. Take my word for it.'

Danny straddled the chair the way movie stars did in films and rolled up his sleeves.

'Looked after yourself in prison, give you that. While other poor bastards like me are grafting, you're down the gym in Wandsworth. No wonder Joe Public thinks it's a fucking holiday camp.' He burped, loudly. 'Now, where were we?'

He was enjoying himself.

'Oh, yeah, that's right. You were about to tell me why I shouldn't cut your balls off and feed them to you. Am I right or am I right, bro?'

The bottle swung menacingly between his first and second fingers and there was a glint in his eye: he was on the edge. One word – any word – and he'd smash it and stick the jagged edge in my face. He fired the bottle over my shoulder, close enough to feel the air move. It crashed against the back wall and Danny leaned towards me.

'I said, am I right or am I right?'

'Tell me where Mandy is.'

He took his mobile from his back pocket, his lips a tight line.

'I can do better than that, little brother, I'll show you.'

* * *

The light from the camera cut through the darkness like a tiny moon, arcing over a narrow dirt path covered in leaves, while the audio recorded the soft pad of footsteps on the earth and the rustle of a branch, bending then falling back. A male voice quietly whistled the old Fleetwood Mac tune 'Man of the World', against the ghostly outline of the trees and the first shafts of dawn lancing the tops. Suddenly, the forest disappeared and a man leant on a spade beside a mound of brown soil, smoke drifting from the cigarette in the corner of his mouth. I recognised him.

Scotch Norrie.

The hole in the ground was deep. Mandy and Amy were lying side by side at the bottom like discarded mannequins. Mandy's face and naked body wore the marks of torture, her red hair, matted with blood, crudely cut – the final indignity. Amy had been treated with more respect; her neck was broken and her young head rested at an angle on her mother's breast.

Danny waited for my reaction and wasn't disappointed.

'Why? For God's sake, why?'

The question seemed to surprise him, as if the answer to it was obvious.

'Should've thought you wouldn't need it explained, little brother. Squaring the circle. Payback for what you did to Cheryl and Rebecca.'

His twisted logic stunned me.

'What I did?'

'Yeah, if it wasn't for you Rebecca would still be alive.'

'You're completely off it, Danny. See a doctor. You need help.'

The bravado would be short-lived and we both knew it.

'Am I? Refresh my memory: who chased Albert Anderson across London and threw him into space? That was you, wasn't it?' He chuckled. 'Old Albert, quietly eating his morning fry-up when along comes the fucking Lone Ranger and splatters him and his sausages all over the road.'

'You said he'd killed them.'

'Not my fault you're stupid enough to believe me. Though you aren't that stupid. Saw what's on the computer in the office and figured it out, didn't you?' He tugged at a white sleeve and spoke to himself. 'Should've worn red.'

'There's a camera in the clock. You've been spying on me from the beginning.'

'In the clock, in the bedroom, in the kitchen. All set up and ready for you to arrive. Been watching you twenty-four seven. Saw you playing happy families with Mandy and her kid.'

'They had nothing to do with any of it.'

He disagreed. 'Oh, but they did, little brother, they had everything to do with it. They evened the score.'

Danny filtered me out and focussed on the tools on the floor.

'Decisions, decisions.' He pointed gleefully like an excited child. 'Eeny, meeny, miney, moe.' Then leered, picked up the metal bar and tapped the palm of his hand.

'Got to laugh, haven't you, bro?'

He leaned on the chair, staring hate.

'Why didn't you have me killed in Wandsworth?'

He considered the question, but not for long.

'Too easy. Far too easy. You had to suffer, the same as I'd suffered.'

He pushed the chair away and came towards me until we were face to face, spit gathered in the corners of his mouth, his breath beery, sour from the evil living in him.

'You're a monster, Danny. A fucking aberration.'

He bared his teeth like a rabid dog – the look I'd seen the day he kicked the Indian shopkeeper to death. If he cracked, the pantomime would be over; he'd kill me, there and then.

Slowly, he got himself under control, walked to the bottles on the floor and opened a fresh one. A minute passed. Then another. He wiped his mouth on his sleeve and broke wind.

'In case you're wondering, your girlfriend didn't go quietly.'

'Am I your girlfriend?'

I didn't want to hear it.

'Didn't fancy it myself. Marcus and Norrie gave her a good seeing to. Meant to ask, Marcus, was she any good?'

Marcus joined in the fun. 'Nah, her heart wasn't in it. No worries, mine was.'

Danny laughed. 'Can't say that was a problem when I was with her. Sorry. Have I shocked you, little brother? Didn't she mention she was with me? Well, she was. A couple of years on and off. Mostly on. Should've let the bitch do herself in when she tried and saved us all a lot of bother, eh?'

He ran a hand over the smile on his lips; he was enjoying this.

And suddenly, it all made sense: the comments and jokes I wasn't in on, not visiting me in Wandsworth, and his insistence on having me around so he could take his revenge in his own way and in his own time. Mandy and her daughter were collateral damage in the war of attrition he was waging against the brother who'd betrayed him with his wife.

* * *

Nobody noticed Nina standing by the door until she burst forward holding the gun Danny had given her in both hands, feet spread and knees bent like a TV cop, her eyes crazy with anger.

She screamed, 'You bastard! You killed them! You murdered Cheryl and Rebecca.' Tears of rage welled and rolled down her cheeks. 'You'd lost her so nobody else could have her, was that it? Once you marry the great Danny Glass, you belong to him forever. And little Rebecca.' Nina's head moved slowly from side to side. 'That was low, even for scum like you.' She edged towards him and nodded towards me. 'No wonder Cheryl loved Luke. Let him go. Let him go, Danny, or I'll drop you.'

Danny's expression didn't alter; he wasn't fazed, not even a little bit. He said, 'Well, well, look who's here. Britain's next property tycoon. Using my money, of course. Another fucking loser who thinks she can put one over on me. Don't worry, sis, I haven't forgotten you, you're next on my list. Think I wouldn't catch on to what you were doing with Lover Boy?' He grinned. 'Soon as I found out you'd hooked up with him, I knew something was going on.'

Danny spat on the ground and turned to me. 'Our little sister's been thieving from us, brother. Yeah. Our own flesh and blood. Shakes your faith in the human race, doesn't it?'

Nina hit back. 'I forgot, you're a big believer in family.'

'You knew about them and did nothing.'

Nina's mouth twisted in a sneer. 'Cheryl and Luke? Why would I get in the way? She was my friend and, for the first time in a long time, she was happy. Apart from Rebecca, Luke was the only good thing in her life. You treated her like shit; humiliated her. Your trophy wife. She loved him – they both did. Do you understand, you bastard? Your wife *and* your daughter. Rebecca adored her uncle Luke. Asked me once why he couldn't be her daddy. How does that make you feel? Even a child knew what a worthless piece of trash you are.'

Her focus was absolute, all of it on Danny; it might've been just him and her in the room. She wasn't aware of Norrie edging closer until he grabbed her from behind. Nina struggled but the Glasgow hardman was too strong for her – the gun dropped to the floor and echoed in the derelict building.

I fought against the ties binding me, oblivious to the sear of pain as the rope burned the skin from my wrists. Seeing my sister mauled by this animal was more than I could stand. Danny acted as if it was just a day on the farm but his eyes said different; the light in them hardened. Even he couldn't bear to hear his child had wished another man to be her father.

'Put her in the boot. I'll deal with her later.' He clapped his hands and came back to me. 'Where was I before we were so rudely interrupted? Oh, yeah, I remember. The morning the bomb went off. Ask me where I was.'

'Fuck off.'

He pressed his forehead, damp with sweat, against mine. 'Ask me, you bastard.'

I didn't rise to it and he screamed, 'Fucking ask me where I was!'

I stayed silent – he had all the cards.

'Then, I'll tell you – between Mandy's creamy thighs, that's where. When I should've been with Rebecca, I was with that slag. Now you understand why I hated her.'

Insanity explaining itself – the scariest thing I'd ever heard.

Everyone involved had been paid out: me, tricked into going after Albert Anderson; Sean Poland, hung from a tree in Norwood Park; Vincent Finnegan, crippled for life. He'd even blamed the prostitute he'd been with for what he'd done.

Everyone culpable but himself.

Behind him, Norrie slipped a CD into the ghetto blaster. Danny listened to the opening chords and shook his head. 'Must've been ten or twelve when I bought this for you. Not long stopped wetting the bed. You've probably forgotten. The way you've forgotten all the stuff I did.'

He'd murdered his wife and child.

I hadn't forgotten that.

Danny's memory was different from mine. 'You played this bloody track so often I couldn't hear myself think. Wanted to smash it over your head.'

On cue, the intro of 'Roll With It' rocked the room. He grinned across the room; we were sharing something from a happy past instead of the soundtrack to a teenage wasteland.

'Takes you back, doesn't it? Oasis. Only know the name because of you.'

The blow caught me high on the side of the head. Pain like I'd never known cut through me. Danny hit me again, harder. Something snapped in my chest and I howled. He lifted the hammer and one of the nails, changed his mind and put them back down.

'There's no hurry. Got all day if we want. Why don't I put the video on a loop so you get a good look at it? Leave you alone to take it in properly. Yeah, that's an idea. Everybody appreciates a bit of time to themselves. We'll be outside if you need us.'

Danny balanced the mobile against the back of the chair, the screen facing me, and left with his thugs in tow. At the door, he turned. 'Need to make sure our bitch of a sister's comfortable. Don't understand where I went wrong bringing you two up, honest to Christ, I don't.' He winked. 'See you in a bit, bro.'

64

Every time I breathed, pain shot through me; my ribs were cracked – and this was just my brother's opening move. Worse was coming. Danny would get started in earnest: I could look forward to a slow death. The tools spread on the flagstones were capable of inflicting more hurt than I could imagine. He wasn't in a hurry; he'd said it himself. Before he was finished, I'd be pleading with him to put me out of my misery. Danny was at home in the role of jolly psychopath; there wasn't much acting involved.

Everybody who'd been connected to the bomb or the bomber was either dead or maimed. I was the icing on the cake.

I turned from the phone and the video on the screen, ashamed to have played even an unwitting part in what had happened to Mandy and Amy. Thinking about it was more than I could handle. I'd do anything to turn back time and do what I should've when I'd had the chance – give them the money and take them wherever they wanted to go, so long as it was far away from Danny Glass.

A hand on my shoulder startled me. Then the rope binding my wrists loosened and I was free. My first reaction wasn't gratitude, it was anger. 'Took your time.'

Felix said, 'You had to be sure what Danny had done with them.'

He pressed the off switch and the mobile closed down. 'Now, you know.'

He was right. Now, I knew.

Nina: I had to get to her. Right now, I needed to be patient and pray there was enough time.

Vincent Finnegan came out of the shadows, beads of sweat gathered on his brow, his skin the colour of old wax. The man I remembered would have punched a hole in the wall if he'd had to. Like most of that life, those days were over. Climbing through the window had taken more than he had, and I wondered just how badly my brother had damaged him.

'You okay, Vincent?'

He nodded.

I didn't believe him.

Felix handed me my gun.

I said, 'Turn the video on.'

He gave me a look. 'Sure?'

'They have to think nothing's changed. Put the boards back on the window. When I make my move, so do you. Take out Marcus. Leave the other two, they're mine.'

Finnegan was ready to argue; the Irishman had his own scores to settle. I wasn't having any.

'He's mine, Vincent. It's non-negotiable.'

'I need this, Luke. Swear to God. Sean was only carrying out orders. Danny's orders. He didn't deserve what they did to him. Leave me something.'

'Sorry.'

Finnegan wouldn't give up; his friend had been murdered and he'd been left a cripple – dragging himself through the window had taken courage. More than I could know. Like me, he was driven by revenge. And I was denying him.

His brittle accent softened. 'Any idea what it's like to wake up every morning with this?' He beat his fist off his gammy leg. 'To know you'll never be with a woman? Danny should've finished me when he had the chance. Would've been doing me a favour.'

It was a strong claim.

Mine was stronger.

* * *

Danny returned the same as he'd left, grinning like a crazy man. His eyes lit up when he saw me bent forward, tied to the wooden column.

'Apologies for keeping you waiting, bro. Norrie was telling a funny story. The stuff they get up to in that Glasgow, you wouldn't credit it.'

Another beer got opened. He took a swig and sighed. 'It's all right laughing. Let's get to it.'

Over by the door, Marcus and Norrie waited for the show to begin.

Danny said, 'Did you love her? I mean my whore of a wife, not the hooker. Nobody could love a hooker. Her kid got to you though, could see that. Sitting beside you on the couch, holding your hand, wanting to marry you when she grew up. Cute.'

He ran a finger along the marks on my chest and poked the skin.

I winced and he said, 'Oh, dear. Something not right there, little brother. Got a couple of cracked ribs, I'm thinking. Funny things, ribs. Doctors can't do nothing for them. Heal themselves, apparently. Yeah, and broken ribs are supposed to be fucking agony. Better hope you don't get any.'

Danny swung the iron bar above his head. I dived upwards and caught his wrist at the top of the arc. Surprise bought a vital second but he recovered quickly. We struggled, locked together, straining for an advantage, his eyes not leaving mine, years of pent-up hatred boring into me.

I returned his stare with ice – our lives, everything we'd been, everything thing we'd done, was in this moment.

Only one of us would survive.

Marcus went for the gun in his jacket and didn't get there –

Finnegan shot him in the heart. He dropped full-length, a pool of blood spreading around him on the flagged floor.

Scotch Norrie decided he was onto a loser and threw his hands in the air, preferring the live-to-fight-another-day option. Until then, my brother had been confident he could take me. Suddenly, he wasn't so sure. His fingernails dug into my skin and he hissed his festering regret in my face.

'Should've done for you soon as I found out. My little girl would be alive.'

'Except you didn't, Danny, and I'm going to kill you.'

He took in the electric drill on the floor, wondering if he could get to it in time, decided he could and made his move; the iron bar fell to the floor; the drill whirred into deadly life in his hand. I grabbed the Beretta. Danny looked pathetic – an electric drill against three guns.

Doubt fell like a veil over his eyes. Fair play to him, he blinked it away and brassed it out. 'Gonna shoot me? Gonna shoot me over some tart and her sprog? You're having a laugh.'

'That isn't why. Somebody needs to put you down.'

'And that's you, is it?'

'And that's me.'

'Don't believe you, little brother. Remember that time your first girlfriend—'

I'd heard enough of his bullshit to last me the rest of my life. Felix brought the butt of his gun down on Danny's head. Scotch Norrie's brain raced to come up with something that might save his life. Fear thickened his already thick Glasgow accent.

'C'mon, Luke. C'mon, man. This is between you and your brother.'

He'd killed Mandy and Amy. Nothing he could say would make me let him go. The next words out of his mouth sealed the decision. His tongue flicked nervously over his lips. 'The club. That was me. You can use somebody like that, can't you?'

The bullet entered his eye, came out the back of his head and ricocheted off the wall. Norrie's brain would've registered a millisecond of blinding light, then nothing. No flames roasting the flesh from his bones. No super-heated air destroying his lungs.

I'd given him an easy death. Few men deserved it less.

* * *

Danny was naked and bound to the same pillar that had held me, his body flabby from lack of exercise and too much booze, the skin off-white and wrinkled; the instruments of hideous torture he'd used on others lying before him.

His reaction wasn't what I'd hoped for. I'd wanted him to feel the humiliation and fear he'd inflicted on others – I was going to be disappointed.

He looked at the tools on the floor, stained with the blood of their victims, then at me.

'This isn't your game, little brother. You don't have the bottle for it... never had, never will. Better let Vincent take over.'

Finnegan shuffled and stayed where he was.

'He could do it, couldn't you, Vinnie? How's the leg, by the way? Not be pulling too many ladies though, eh!'

I picked up the drill Danny had intended to use on me and moved closer, so he could see the cold truth in my eyes and realise I could and would kill him – for the innocent victims at the Picasso Club, Cheryl and Rebecca, Mandy and Amy and an Indian shopkeeper who didn't deserve to die.

The vicious blade marked his forehead. My finger gently squeezed smooth the trigger.

'You're wrong. Nothing would be easier. Except that would make me like you and I'll never be that. But know this, Danny. Everything you've worked for, everything and everyone you own, belong to me now.'

That got to him. He screamed. 'Fuck you! Fuck you! My sweat built it. You did nothing. Nothing!'

He pressed his head to the drill, breaking the skin. A thin line of blood ran down the side of his nose into his mouth. 'Do it, you useless fucker! Do it!'

I threw the drill away, picked up the Beretta and taunted him.

'Promised you'd get me into The Lucky Bastards Club, and you have. Cheers, bro.'

Danny had always been unstable. From where he'd come from – where we'd both come from – maybe that wasn't the surprise it might've been. What he thought of as my betrayal with a wife he'd never loved had sent him over the edge. He breathed hard through gritted teeth, stamping the ground at his feet – the great Danny Glass reduced to a crazed beast.

I almost felt sorry for him.

Almost.

But this was what I knew: I hadn't looked for this – it came looking for me. Squaring the circle was one of his expressions – now it was my turn.

My brother. My responsibility.

England expects and all that bollocks.

The gunshot echoed in my brain.

I guessed it always would.

EPILOGUE

The jukebox and the photograph of the Queen were gone. So was the computer Danny had used to spy on me. Felix watched me ease into the chair behind the desk. He'd done a decent job of taping up my chest, though when I breathed, a noise like worn brake pads groaned inside me. I'd been lucky – compared to what my brother had planned for me, it was nothing.

That didn't stop it hurting like a bastard.

Felix said, 'Sure you're all right, boss?'

Boss!

I was the guy who'd wanted out. If it hadn't been so painful, I would've laughed.

* * *

Oliver Stanford was the first visitor of the day and was his usual insufferable self. The smile I'd come to hate drifted over his lips.

'The rumours are correct, it seems.'

'What rumours?'

'The ones that say you've taken over.'

Stanford wasn't as relaxed as he pretended to be. He'd come in person to the King Pot to gauge how much jeopardy he was in and make another stab at staying relevant. His next sentence revealed the casual attitude and amused indifference were an act.

'Be helpful to know if it's true.'

The detective wouldn't get what he was after from me.

He balanced on the balls of his feet and looked around. 'We met in this office. Not so long ago, either. Doesn't feel like it. You'd just come out of Wandsworth. Danny's famous brother – his silent partner.' The policeman reconsidered the phraseology. 'Not silent, junior. Danny's *junior* partner. How quickly the world turns, eh?'

I was bored with him already.

'What do you want, Stanford?'

He drew a languid finger along the desk. 'What I proposed in Hampstead still stands. I'd take it if I were you, now Danny's out of the picture.'

'Is he?'

'You're in the chair.'

A hand came up to stop me denying it. Light from the window flashed off his cufflinks. Gold. Paid for by the man he was so keen I replace. Like an animal sensing change on the wind, he was readying to seize whatever opportunity presented itself. Underneath the urbane, well-spoken policeman lurked a voracious appetite for power and money, and a ruthlessness destined to take him higher or take him down. There was more and he wanted it.

'Don't take too long to make up your mind. As I said before, you can never have too many friends, Luke. There are other players out there, anxious to take advantage. The two top dogs are off the board. Plenty of room for men with ambition. People who appreciate the value of what I'm offering. Better not to find that out the hard way.'

He talked a good game. Except by coming here he'd shown his hand. The implied threat was meaningless – we were prisoners of each other; whatever harm he could do me would be returned and we both knew it. The relationship he'd had with Danny would survive, but it would be on my terms.

I started as I meant to go on. 'I'll be in touch. Close the door on your road out.'

* * *

Felix said, 'George Ritchie just walked into the bar looking for Danny.'

My fingers closed round the gun in the third drawer down, weighing it in my hand; it was loaded.

'Who's with him?'

'He's on his own. What do you want me to do?'

'Put men on the front door. And for Christ's sake do it right this time. Any sign of Anderson?'

'No.'

'Make sure he isn't carrying and send him up.'

Ritchie was sharper than Albert and Rollie put together – him and eight million other Londoners. The last time I'd seen him was at a meeting in Peckham Rye Park on a chilly winter's morning, when Albert and Danny met to defuse the tension building between them because my brother was stealing Albert's territory. A bloody confrontation was on the cards and though talking produced nothing – Danny kept doing what he was doing – it staved it off. They'd sat on a bench, just the two of them, surrounded by grass and trees white with frost. Our instructions were to stay well back. Ritchie ignored them and walked his boss to where Danny was, eyes darting right and left, checking every bush, every tree. Then, he turned and went back to the car. He was dressed in a dark-blue overcoat, black leather gloves and a maroon scarf, more like a hedge-fund manager than a gangster. Lean and spare, even under the heavy coat. What struck me most about him was his determination to protect the fat bastard he worked for, and his lack of fear. I couldn't imagine someone less concerned with their own safety.

Ten years on, the hair was thinner, there was greying at the temples, and his face was lined. But the wariness was still there as he paused in the doorway, Felix at his back. I laid the gun on the desk where he could see it and waited for him to come forward.

He sat down and asked the question soon to be on many lips in bars and bookies and building sites south of the river. 'Where's Danny?'

'Where's Anderson?'

The meet in the park had been a bust; this one might be headed for the same fate. We stared at each other until I said, 'Taking a chance coming here, George. What do you want?'

His reply was unexpected. 'To be left alone. Whatever happens from here on in has nothing to do with me.'

If Rollie Anderson really had perished, a fortune was there for whoever had the balls to go for it. George Ritchie had balls – he'd shown that in Peckham Rye.

'Did you get away before the fire started?'

'Wasn't anywhere near the fire. I quit working for Rollie before it all kicked off.'

'Where've you been hiding?'

'What makes you think I've been hiding?'

'Okay. Where's Anderson?'

'Search me.'

'You haven't heard from him?'

'Why would I? I told you, we're finished. I came to speak to Danny.'

'Forget my brother. Is Anderson dead?'

Ritchie took a tired breath. 'Friday nights most of the crew hung around the club. Rollie encouraged it. Made him feel like a big man.'

'But not you?'

'Not me. I assume they were there as usual. No reason to believe anything else.'

Not quite what I wanted. 'Which means, they're dead?'

His eyes bored into me and I saw the steel in them, the fearlessness he'd shown on that frosty morning a decade earlier. 'Which means your guess is as good as mine. The difference is: you care and I don't.'

'Then what's the deal? What're you after?'

'To retire without having to look over my shoulder every day for the rest of my life. I've done enough of that.'

'Retire? You?'

My scepticism didn't amuse him. 'I came to speak to the organ grinder.'

'You're speaking to him. Things are straight between us, don't worry about it.'

He nodded and walked to the door. 'Since you've been so reasonable, here's something for nothing. You've got a problem.'

I shook my head. 'We *had* a problem, not now. Everything's squared away.'

Ritchie smiled. 'Not everything. Not the informer.'

'Dealt with.'

'No, he wasn't.'

He seemed sure.

'You're talking about the copper. It's sorted.'

'It isn't. You got the left hand. Should've been looking at the right hand. Mills has been feeding us stuff for years.'

The policeman's death would've been hard. Tortured and mutilated in Fulton Street for information he didn't have. Poor bastard. I tried not to imagine it.

'Somebody told me you can't have too many friends. What do you think?'

He stared across the floor. 'Depends on the friends, doesn't it?'

'My thoughts exactly.'

Ritchie was leaving. If he did, I'd never see him again. I said, 'Retiring isn't for you, George. You wouldn't like it – I've got a better idea.'

* * *

I hadn't seen Nina since Fulton Street when we'd watched Felix and Vincent Finnegan put Danny's body in the boot of the car and drive off. We didn't speak – what was there to say?

Her hair was shorter and she wore a brown leather jacket over a black T-shirt and jeans, the image of the rebellious teenager who'd given Danny a hard time. Standing in the doorway, she was my little sister again, pale and uncertain.

I'd considered the options and already made my decision: any bullshit and it was over – she could go her own way and that would be that. Otherwise... otherwise, we had things to discuss.

Her sharp eyes took in the differences around her and made a stab at an icebreaker. 'Got rid of the music. Good decision. But what's Her Majesty done wrong?'

She didn't expect an answer and didn't get one. The time for jokes might come – this wasn't it.

'Why, Nina?'

She looked straight at me, her voice free of apology or justification.

'I needed the money.'

No story. No explanations. No excuses.

'Simple as that?'

'Simple as that. He'd never have let me go. You weren't the only one who suffered the "Team Glass" speech.'

'You understand Vale won't be around much longer.'

A statement, not a question.

She shrugged. 'Do what you have to do.'

I leaned back in the chair: for better or worse what I was about to say would define the future. 'I'm drawing a line in the sand. Done is done, Nina. But this is the one and only time.'

Her expression didn't alter though something came alive behind her eyes. I said, 'Rollie Anderson's dead.'

'You sound sure.'

'I am. Everything's ours. But we need to move fast.'

'Thought you wanted out?'

'Out from under Danny.'

She nodded; she'd felt the same. 'Where do I fit in this new world order?'

'Once I have a firm grip on both territories, the businesses will be split. The street stuff won't be your concern. You'll handle real estate, more or less doing what you've been doing. With one big difference. It'll be completely legit and scaled up – hugely. In five years, between us, we'll be running the whole of the South Side and have one of the biggest property portfolios in the city.'

It was everything Nina wanted. Everything we both wanted. She studied my face, looked away, and came back with regret in her voice. 'You've changed, Luke, you know that, don't you?'

She was right. I had changed.

'It was time, Nina.'

POSTSCRIPT

Despite a nationwide media campaign carried out by the Metropolitan Police, the whereabouts of the five Asian men wanted in connection with the arson attack on the Picasso Club are still unknown.

Roland Anderson was eventually identified as a victim of the blaze along with several members of his organisation.

DS Bob Wallace's body has never been found. The case remains unsolved.

DI Trevor Mills was killed in a hit and run incident in York Way, Islington, in the early hours of Saturday the 18th of September. There were no witnesses.

Oliver Stanford has been promoted to superintendent.

Nina Glass manages one of the fastest growing property portfolios in London. Her brother, Luke, has a substantial shareholding in the business.

George Ritchie works for Luke Glass. Every night he goes home by a different route.

A man fitting Danny Glass's description was sighted in Marbella on the Costa del Sol. Spanish authorities have been unable to confirm he is in the country.

ACKNOWLEDGMENTS

A book is never just the work of one person; the talents and hard work of many are needed to bring it into the world. I would like to thank the team at Boldwood Books – Amanda, Caroline, Nia, Megan, Ellie, Sue and Mills who made me welcome from the first day. But especially, my editor Sarah. I love your energy.

Alasdair McMorrin who shared his long experience of the underworld and the police and is always generous with his time. Thanks, Alasdair.

And lastly, my wife Christine, who brings her limitless imagination to the pages of everything I write. Her contribution is immense. Without her, this book doesn't exist.

Owen Mullen

Crete, July, 2020

MORE FROM OWEN MULLEN

We hope you enjoyed reading *Owen Mullen*. If you did, please leave a review.

If you'd like to gift a copy, this book is also available as an ebook, digital audio download and audiobook CD.

Sign up to Owen Mullen's mailing list for news, competitions and updates on future books.

https://bit.ly/OwenMullenNewsletter

ABOUT THE AUTHOR

Owen Mullen is a highly regarded crime author who splits his time between Scotland and the island of Crete. In his earlier life he lived in London and worked as a musician and session singer. He has now written seven books and *Family* is his first gangland thriller for Boldwood.

Follow Owen on social media:

twitter.com/OwenMullen6

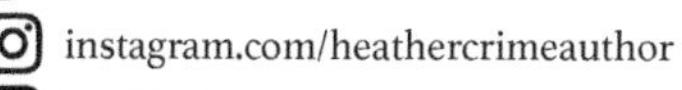
instagram.com/heathercrimeauthor

bookbub.com/authors/owen-mullen

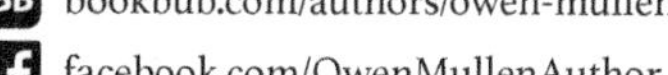
facebook.com/OwenMullenAuthor

ABOUT BOLDWOOD BOOKS

Boldwood Books is a fiction publishing company seeking out the best stories from around the world.

Find out more at www.boldwoodbooks.com

Sign up to the Book and Tonic newsletter for news, offers and competitions from Boldwood Books!

http://www.bit.ly/bookandtonic

We'd love to hear from you, follow us on social media:

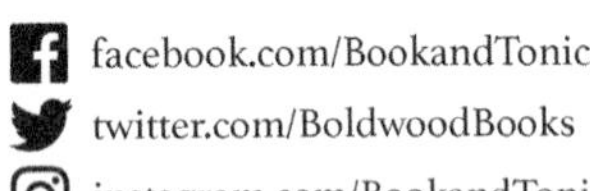

facebook.com/BookandTonic
twitter.com/BoldwoodBooks
instagram.com/BookandTonic

Printed in Great Britain
by Amazon

61928667R00234